I AM
JUSTICE

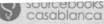

sourcebooks
casablanca

Published by Sourcebooks Casablanca, an imprint of Sourcebooks, Inc.
P.O. Box 4410, Naperville, Illinois 60567-4410
(630) 961-3900
Fax: (630) 961-2168
sourcebooks.com

Printed and bound in Canada.
MBP 10 9 8 7 6 5 4 3 2 1

N

This book is dedicated to my husband, for a lifetime of moments, blinding and brilliant moments, especially for those that were always and only ours.

Chapter 1

APPARENTLY, CAMO COULDN'T HIDE YOU FROM EVERYTHING. Justice yanked free of another thorn in the brush-choked woods. She squatted at the tree line and focused her night vision goggles on the rear of the bleak home turned bleaker business. The battered, white-shingled two-story sat on the poorest edge of a rural community in Pennsylvania.

Rural as hell. They didn't even have their own police force and had to rely on staties.

She snapped pictures of the gravel-and-stone backyard and the rusty propane tank propped on wooden legs like a miniature submarine dry-docked after fifty years at sea.

The whole "massage parlor" was dingy, dirty, and depressing.

Given the choice, most people steered well clear. Not Justice. She wanted inside. Planned and plotted on it. Call it a childhood dream, making good on her vow. Call it redemption, making it up to Hope. Call it revenge, making them pay for Hope's death.

It would help if Momma's oft-heard mantra—patience...reconnaissance always comes first—didn't keep popping up like a jack-in-the-box to wave a scolding, white-gloved finger at her.

Momma. What a fun sucker.

A single light, green through her goggles, shone over

the steel back door. She zoomed in on it as her breath fanned against the midnight air. Her camera *click, click, click*ed. No exterior handle. They'd have to pop it. And no security cameras. Figures. See no evil. Hear no evil. Or at least, record no evil.

She snapped photos of barred and blackened windows and a rusty fire escape that led up to a metal-gated door secured with thick, elephant-proof chains.

These guys weren't taking any chances. Which meant more surveillance and late nights for her. Unlike her other siblings, she always got saddled with recon for the family's underground railroad.

Not for long though. After two years of planning, the mission as dear to her as her own heartbeat—breaking up a human trafficking ring—was only a few weeks away. *Yeehaw!* She was going to bust heads.

Her earpiece clicked, and her brother's voice came through. "Justice, youse…uh, you in position yet?"

Tony. He worked so hard to weed out his South Philly. She liked his accent. But being adopted into her big, crazy family had taught her people could have some weird issues.

"Aw, Tone, can't spot me? Is it my expert camouflage or that stealth gene you're missing?"

Tony snorted. The sound tightroped between amused and annoyed. "Yeah, you know as much about being a Choctaw as I do about being a Chihuahua."

"It's in my blood. Only thing in your blood, paisano, is cement shoes and boosting cars."

Laughter feathered through her headphones, making her want to scratch through her face mask to dig the tickle from her ears. "Just get the pic—"

The massage parlor's back door crashed open. A dark-haired girl, maybe fifteen, sprinted out, wearing a too-loose bustier and a thong as inconsequential as her chest.

A man broke out after her, hauling back with a belt thick enough to double as a swing.

"Tony."

"No. Think larger mission here. Not one girl. All of 'em."

The heavy slap of leather on flesh ricocheted like a gunshot.

Soundless, the girl tucked her shoulder and veered to the side, toward the woods, toward Justice.

Justice's chest tightened and heated until it became as hard and fixated as the steel on her Sig. Adrenaline flooded into her body. The scene slowed and intensified.

The girl's eyes were wide and frantic. The desperate eyes of a hunted child.

She couldn't sit here—ass on haunches—and do nothing. As ineffective as government raids that took months to organize and ended with not one conviction of a principle. Not one.

This was what the League of Warrior Women was about: Stopping the shit that other people stood by and let happen. It's what her sister would have done. It's what Hope *had* done for her.

Every nerve in Justice's body begged to act. But she kept absolutely still. Movement attracted attention. Stillness went unnoticed.

The man grabbed the girl's hair and yanked her back. The girl struggled and flailed, twisted and fought. The man drove a belt-wrapped fist into her neck. She sagged, gasped.

Tony's voice came through the headset, smooth and controlled. "Stay put, Justice."

Too late. She'd already stood, raised her gun, and was in fact mid-motion of pressing the trigger when he'd spoken.

There was a sharp snap, like a broken twig, as the bullet fired from her suppressed Sig. The man's head flung back. He dropped to his ass, surrendered to the gravel.

The girl skittered away. Her eyes swung left and right before she darted for cover behind the derelict propane tank.

"Not for nothin', J, you don't listen to shit."

Justice flipped up her NVGs, pulled down her face mask, and ran across the gravel. She checked inside the doorway for movement. All quiet.

She spotted the girl crouching by the propane tank, squeezed between the building and the rusty cylinder. The kid looked like a terrified skeleton—all haunted eyes and jutting bones.

Tony ran up, checked the dead guy for weapons. "Glock. Figures," he said and slipped the weapon into the back of his belt.

Justice reached forward. "It's okay. It's okay. I'm on your side."

The girl's copper-brown eyes tracked Justice's gloved hand like it came equipped with teeth and venom. For a moment, she was sure the girl wouldn't take her hand. But she did.

Brave kid. Justice pulled her out. She'd shouldered heavier backpacks. Shrugging off her jacket, she helped the girl put it on. Keeping eye contact, she pointed at the dead man, then at the building. "How many more men inside?"

The girl held up her arm and poked two rabbit fingers from the long sleeve. Two more men inside. Justice shrugged at Tony. "No choice."

His dark eyebrows knitted tightly together, but he started for the house. He bumped Justice's shoulder as he passed. "Call it in."

She elbowed him hard in the ribs. He *oomphed* and kept walking.

Justice put a hand on the girl's shoulder. Even with the gloves, it felt like she'd grabbed a coat hanger.

Shielding Tony's view, she held out the G19. Tony could be pissed later. And not just because she'd so expertly pickpocketed him. "Can you use this?"

The girl hesitated. Then with a face as starved and empty as a runway model, she took the gun, capped her fingers across the top, and racked the slide.

Justice pointed toward the woods. The girl dashed away, and Justice pressed the button on her earpiece. Gracie answered on the first ring. "You're kidding me, right, Justice?"

Why were her siblings always giving her such shit? "Just get a van to site six, Gracie."

She hung up and went inside. A dangling, red lightbulb lit a narrow stairway and slim corridor.

On the stairs, Tony gave her a what-took-you-so-long look? She shrugged. He motioned he'd go up. She nodded and crept the other way, down the hall.

At the end of the dim hall, gun raised, she sighted around a doorway. Ugh. That smell. BO and whiskey.

Once a living room, the space had been turned into an office. A desk, a television turned to QVC, a potbellied man in boxers passed out on a saggy couch.

She reached for a zip tie, stepped inside, and...*crash and churn*. Shit. The bottle of Jim Beam sailed across the hardwood.

Drunky leapt up, saw her, and lurched forward like Frankenstein's monster. Biggest guy she'd ever seen, but slow and lethargic.

Justice skated around him, reached up, and slammed her gun into his head. One, two, three times. He dropped.

Still conscious? If anything, the hits had woken him up.

He grabbed her ankle. She fell in slow motion. Skull cracked against floor. Hand cracked against desk. Gun dropped.

Drunky reared up and slammed into her like a wrestler, pinning her neck with one beefy limb. He held her right hand. Her left arm was trapped and pressed between them.

Justice's heart pounded electric currents through thinning veins. Pinned. It felt like the dream, the nightmare that still haunted her. Her gaze bucked around the room. She couldn't move. Couldn't breathe.

She fought off panic. Off the memory. She wasn't a little kid. She wasn't helpless.

Hand trembling, she groped past his boxers, located one sweaty ball. Squeezed.

Drunky cursed and pressed harder.

Justice's eyes watered, black spots clouded her vision. She couldn't black out. She'd die if she did.

No. Not like this. Not like Hope.

She kicked blindly again and again. Her foot connected with his ankle. He jerked, lost balance.

Justice thrust up her right hip, swung her foot flat, got leverage, and pushed. Drunky toppled.

Snakebite fast, she rolled and belly-crawled away. Where was her… Gun. Justice grabbed it.

Drunky came for her. She rolled, aimed. "Stop."

Bam. The guy crashed back and down.

She looked up. Standing in the doorway, the girl lowered the Glock.

Holy Shit. The kid had killed the guy.

Wheezing through a throat still aching, Justice lurched to her feet. She sucked in hot, rank air as her legs Jell-Oed under her.

Ignoring the twist of nausea and the feeling of wrong, she picked up her night vision goggles and staggered away from the corpse. She went over to the girl. "You didn't have to."

Tiger-fierce red-brown eyes scanned away from her over to the body. The girl spit on the floor. "I wanted to."

Justice knew that anger, wasn't sure she disagreed with it, but still… "You wait here. Right here."

She went back down the corridor and up the narrow stairs. She swung her gun around as she checked the upstairs hall. Tony had taken out the other guard. He was passed out and hog-tied in the hallway.

Tony stepped from one of the corridor doorways. "Did I hear a problem?"

"Not anymore."

"Seriously, J? Stop killing people."

She glared at him. Definitely not the time to explain. "Guy had a hundred fifty pounds on me."

Literally.

Tony pointed to the man knocked out, hands bound behind his back and tied to his feet. "That guy's no featherweight. It's called training."

Dick. What did he know? Sometimes the only thing that made her equal to those she went up against was a gun. She gestured at the doors in the hall. "Where are the girls?"

He reached past her and pushed a door open. He nodded toward the occupants. "Salvadoran."

She walked into the room. The young women and girls who'd been stolen, tricked, or coerced from their lives and countries huddled together in a dark corner. The windows had been painted black. There was one dresser and a full-size bed. Probably the same setup as every room up here.

She automatically gave the instructions in Spanish. "Stay calm. No one will harm you. We are rescuing you. You will be cared for. You will not be harmed. Stay calm. Follow us."

The group began to panic. Cry out. Someone threw a shoe at her. *Ouch. Great.* She stepped back to Tony. "You got this?"

He nodded and lowered his gun. "Always a people pleaser, J."

At the pickup location designated as Site 6, they loaded the freed slaves into the white panel van. The girl who'd saved Justice refused to get inside.

Justice put her hand on the kid's bony shoulder. "What's your name?"

She looked away, then down. "They called me Cookie."

Cookie? That wasn't a name. That was a dessert. Well, if she'd learned anything from *Sesame Street* it was that *C* was for Cookie.

"Thank you for saving my life, Cee."

The girl's fiery-brown eyes, prematurely set to suspicious, appraised Justice. "Am I free?"

Justice pointed at the back of the fifteen-passenger vehicle. "Get in the van. Freedom is your next stop."

The girl shook her head. "I want to go where you go. I want to…" She hesitated as if looking for words in a language she didn't know that well. "I want to be what you are."

Kid had no idea what she was saying, what would be required of her, but rules were rules. If they asked and showed any kind of real promise, they got to try.

"Get in the van. A woman with red hair will be at your destination. Her name is Gracie. Tell her what you told me."

The girl nodded, turned, climbed into the van, and dragged the door shut.

Justice hit the door twice. The van pulled away, trailing a cloud of exhaust. When the taillights faded, she turned and slipped into the front seat of the black rental, next to the elephant in the room. Tony.

She cast her brother a sideways glance. Every inch of his five-foot-eleven frame looked ready to pound her to a soft, mushy pulp.

Tony ripped off his hat and gloves. He ran agitated fingers through black, wavy hair damp with sweat, causing it to stand on end.

Justice started the car and adjusted the heat to "off." She let out a breath, tightened gloved hands against the steering wheel. *Aw, hell*. "Stop pouting."

Tony hit the dash. "You gotta get over this cowgirl, *Kill Bill* bullshit. Why not send up a signal flare telling the Brothers Grim we're after them?"

The wheel spun through her fingers as she turned the corner. She flicked on the headlights and accelerated onto the highway.

Tony was so uptight. If only she'd known when she'd first seen him—a twelve-year-old runaway scrounging for scraps—what a pain in the ass he'd become. Never should've begged Momma to adopt him. The first boy in the family. "Get over it, Tony. An eye for an eye."

He flung himself back against the seat. "You know, an eye for an eye eventually leaves the whole world blind. It's stupid. Like your stunt tonight. We don't bust into a place like some eighties Schwarzenegger movie. You think this won't get back to them? Raise suspicions?"

He had her there. The League of Warrior Women wasn't just smash and grab or brute strength. It was the velvet hammer—negotiations, forums, and charities that supported women. And the chain saw of assassination, deceit, and violence.

Sometimes things just get messy. "Sorry, Tone. Really."

He made a sound of dismissal, stripped off his dark jacket and bulletproof vest. His tight muscle shirt showed off a navy-blue tattoo on his right arm. Half of the family motto: "One for all."

The other half, "All for one," was tattooed on his ribs, over his heart. Hey, let a bunch of kids choose the family motto and you were bound to get something plagiarized.

Justice swung up to the dark country road where Tony had parked. "Come on, let it go. We saved the lives of eleven people. Tomorrow they'll wake up in a warm place, with good food, and no one will treat them like that space between their legs is all that matters."

Tony's eyebrows rose. He flashed wide, pearly teeth

that looked like they belonged in an ad for braces. "Guess that's why you have so many boyfriends, because you talk so sexy. Oh, Justice, tell me more about that space between your legs. What do you call it? The vortex of doom?"

Boyfriends? Like after what her father had done she'd ever trust any man outside of the League.

She leaned across him and opened the door. "Get out."

He did. Still laughing.

Chapter 2

Dust and debris from the explosion laced the hot, oppressive Syrian air and clung to Sandesh almost as thickly as the village mud to his combat boots.

His eyes watered. His ears rang from the blast of the barrel bomb, but he held steady—or at least held his arms steady to protect the child. It didn't help. She let out small, injured sounds as more of her skin sloughed off against his Special Forces uniform.

The barrel bomb had been filled with chemicals and had inflicted burns reminiscent of napalm. Her once-healthy skin was red and raw.

One of his Rangers pointed his rifle toward the sky. "Heads up, Sandman."

Sandesh raised eyes toward the muffled—to his ears anyway—whir of an approaching Black Hawk. His foot caught in a muddy depression. His knee buckled.

The child in his arms cried out, her eyes springing open. He whispered soothing words. Hopeless. The small, delicate body stiffened. Her head tipped back.

His heart tightened in his chest, a fist of hard anger. The Syrian government had attacked its own citizens, injuring bodies, hoping to also injure minds. It would probably work. Violence usually did.

It was only a coincidence—at least he hoped it was—that he and his Rangers had been in the area. They weren't technically supposed to be here. Their mission was outside of Syria, supporting the Free Syrian Army with training and weapons. But someone higher up had wanted a better take on Assad's chemical profile, so they'd come into the country.

Guess they'd found out.

Behind him he could smell the chemical fire, even with the water someone had turned on to douse the victims. His stomach lurched. At least nineteen girls had been injured. Some shuffled forward like the walking dead, skin and clothes in tatters.

The helo landed. He got up carefully, but the child trembled. Fuck mission parameters. They needed to do something.

The girl in his arms stirred. "Please, Poppa." She knew English? "Don't be angry."

He looked into her face, expecting to see confusion and delirium. Her dark eyes stared directly at him, into him. Her raw hand rose to his chest, touched his heart. "There is more."

An awed gasp whooshed from her mouth. Her hand dropped. She stilled.

Sandesh had seen people die, seen how the body suddenly looked less real, less full. But this was different. It was as if he could feel the soul sink from the body, feel the tendrils of spirit wrap around his heart and whisper, "Poppa. Don't be angry. There is more."

Sandesh woke up sweating and hacking. He grabbed blindly for the lifeline. The phone that had woken him. He clicked Accept and brought the cell to his ear. "Yeah?"

"Sandesh Julian Ross, head of the IPT?"

"That's me." This guy sounded like he'd had too much tequila last night. And every night of his life.

What time was it? He checked the clock on his night-stand. Five a.m.? "Who's calling?"

"My name is Leland Day. I work for Parish Industries, specifically Mukta Parish. We've been told your charity, the IPT, works along the Jordan–Syrian border."

Sandesh blinked the sleep and fog from his eyes and mind. "No. I mean… Sort of." He'd given the speech so often to media and at luncheons the words came by rote. "The International Peace Team aligns with organizations around the world. But yes, we've aligned with Salma's Gems in the Middle East."

"Yes. I read about you online. *HuffPost* called you a complex combination of righteous anger, surfer-boy looks, and gritty naïveté."

Sandesh cringed. That didn't sound anywhere near a compliment. And sure wouldn't help him secure the funding he so desperately needed.

He sat up, flicked on the light in his bedroom. The essentials only—bed, nightstand, and lamp—snapped into focus. "Why are you calling?" To harass me about my pretty-boy media image?

"I'm calling to set up an appointment between you and Mukta Parish. She's starting an initiative to expand global philanthropy. You've no doubt heard of Parish Industries and the Mantua Academy for Girls?"

Of course he had. Mukta Parish, hell the entire Parish clan was mega-wealth. A global powerhouse, they also ran an exclusive boarding school for wealthy families. The elite campus was home to Mukta Parish's It's a Small World clan. She'd adopted girls from all over the world. "This isn't camp. We're run and staffed by former soldiers for a reason."

Leland cleared his throat. "I understand. But we'd mostly be a financial support system. Completely at your disposal."

Sandesh swung his legs out of bed. Guy had just offered him exactly what the IPT wanted, needed: funding, a tie to a big name, and complete autonomy. It sounded too good to be true. "What exactly would I have to do to warrant this kind of support?"

"We'd like to discuss that. Are you available to come to our Center City office?"

"Sure. When?"

"Is this morning at seven doable?"

Sandesh was already up and moving toward his shower. "Make it eight."

Chapter 3

Bucks County, Pennsylvania

DEEP INSIDE THE STONE-AND-SPIRE MAIN BUILDING OF THE 160-acre campus of the Mantua Academy for Girls, Justice's determined footsteps resounded across gleaming marble floors.

She knew the thing that sucked most about a family business. The family part.

She reached her sister's office...door? Great. Bridget had followed through on her promise to have the door removed.

She rapped on the wood framing the empty doorway. Inside, Bridget sat cross-legged on her mesh, Ergohuman office chair, eyes closed. Her frizzy, dark hair stabbed with a silver comb drooped lopsidedly, like a hairy modern art sculpture.

Justice smiled. This was so perfectly Bridget it almost deserved its own word, like *freaktacular* or *weirdiful*.

Justice knocked again. "Bridge?"

Bridget's eyes fluttered open and locked on her. Justice instantly felt seen. As in seen below the skin— all her small, broken secrets, fear of suffocating, and her dislike of the color blue. She fidgeted.

Shiva, *uhm*, Bridget quirked an eyebrow. "What can I do for you, Justice?"

"I need to talk to you about the yoga class. Is it true you have the girls chanting in Sanskrit?"

"Yes, but I'm not sure of your question. I submitted the yoga for approval through the director's office."

Justice walked into the office and plopped into a chair. She took off her right flat and rubbed her sweaty toes on the shag throw rug. "You got approval for yoga, She-pak Chopra. Not to have the girls chanting in Sanskrit. This isn't good PR. And that's bad for me. Means I have to do work."

Bridget rested her hands on the desk. "I will limit my teaching to poses and centering music."

Justice smiled. "Dammit, Bridge, you're so easy. Why can't I have more sisters like you?"

"Perhaps, because you are as abrasive as a starving boar," a voice said from the hall.

Justice turned. Sheared head, lips painted bright red, skin as satiny smooth and dark as a starless sky, and cocked against the doorway, the generous curve of boys-can't-help-but-wonder hips clad in a leopard-print skirt. Dada, six-foot-two in spiked heels.

And this was the problem with having no doors. Justice slipped her shoe back on, rose, and crossed the room. "You're home? Aren't you supposed to be contacting your Brothers Grim informant?"

Dada's forehead creased. She looked around the hall, but the school staff, a.k.a. no-idea-a-secret-society-of-vigilantes-existed-under-their-feet staff, weren't in yet. "Have you checked your secure email this morning?"

―∽∼∽―

After passing through security, Justice whisked through the headquarters of the Parish empire in Philadelphia. She marched down corridors lined with sharp corners, glass walls, attractive twentysomethings, fortysomethings, and fiftysomethings in power suits.

She was too pissed to pay attention to the repeated nods and hellos. Momma's morning email had sent her scrambling for her Jeep keys. The mission to take down the global trafficking ring had been put on hold.

Nope. Not happening.

She didn't care if the Brothers Grim had been alerted by her screwup with Tony last week. Or that they'd moved their meeting up by six weeks. Or that they'd moved the location to Jordan—the one place on the entire fucking globe where the League had no established cover. This was bullshit.

Loosening the scarf covering her mostly faded neck bruises, she headed toward the mahogany double doors at the mouth of two intersecting hallways.

Momma's executive assistant, straitlaced Lorena of the cotton button-downs and starched pantsuits, stood from her desk and crossed her arms. Huh. A human barricade.

Good thing Justice had been trained for just such an event.

Sprinting forward, she lifted her foot, planted the arch of her shoe against the edge of the desk, toed herself into the leap, and vaulted into the air.

Lorena ducked and cried out.

Instant classic.

Justice landed with a thud. Lorena was still sputtering vague threats when Justice closed Momma's office door. *Click*.

For a confused moment, she stood within the inner sanctum. A huge corner office with buttoned leather couches, two flat-screen TVs, a hulking Thor of a desk, and a well-stocked kitchen. The self-satisfied grin slipped from her face.

Shit.

The man—built like a hot night of unforgettable, wild blond hair like a sandstorm, eyes the color of the ocean after a lazy day in the sun—drove the air from her lungs.

She couldn't move. Struck deaf, dumb, and blind meet deer-in-headlights. Damn, the man was tall. Like a wall. A wall of man muscle. So hot.

"Justice." Leland, Momma's oldest friend and most trusted adviser, extended his hand with a warm smile, as if so very pleased she'd joined them. His silver hair gleamed under the canopy of recessed lights. The gray-checkered Armani suit draped over him as if upon the confident shoulders of dignity itself.

Justice took Leland's smooth hand. He pressed down firmly and tugged her farther into the room.

"Sandesh, I'd like you to meet Justice Parish." Only the stern grip of Leland's hand told her how annoyed he was. "She does PR for the Mantua Academy and will be working on the Greenville Initiative. She is familiar with all aspects of our newest philanthropy venture."

Dude was good. Calm. Graceful. And full of shit. *Greenville?* What was that project about? Giving away money, judging by what Leland had said.

Behind Leland, Momma's brown eyes showed as little as the rose-colored niqab that covered her hair and face and scars.

Justice turned and gave Leland a rictus grin meant to

be a smile. It would probably be the scariest thing he'd see all day.

She was usually more successful at hiding her feelings, but a high-pressure situation—you know the kind where you Jack-be-nimbled your momma's executive assistant, barged into a business meeting, and eye-appraised-seduced-and-fucked a total stranger—had her off her game.

"Actually, my role in all philanthropic projects is still advisory. I wouldn't want to mislead, uhm, what was your name?"

Blue-Eyes reached for her hand. "I'm Sandesh. Head of the International Peace Team. We're partnering with Greenville in Jordan."

He slid his long fingers along her palm in a hot brush that sent her skin tingling. He grasped her hand. Heat suffused her body, brought a flush to her stomach and a smile to her lips. Nice.

Who said philanthropy wasn't sexy?

Wait. Jordan?

Chapter 4

SANDESH TRIED TO REFOCUS ON THE CONVERSATION AND NOT the heat of the woman standing before him. Not happening.

From the moment his ears had picked up the administrative assistant's objection, the *thud* of something he couldn't puzzle out, and another heavier *thud* before the door opened, he'd gone from *corner office mode* to *time to take someone down*.

And then she'd burst into the room.

First thought: He hoped he did have to take her down, because that body underneath him would make his day. Second thought: Sucked to be wearing a damn monkey suit, because he recognized a woman of action. Third thought as she was introduced and her eyes swept his body: If she kept eye contact for more than two seconds, he wasn't leaving without her number.

She did keep contact. Her eyes were so direct, sensual, and interested that the world fell away. Her mischievous, dark eyes and the fan and flutter of those thick eyelashes swallowed every decent thought from his mind.

His eyes returned the exploration. She had the cheekbones of an American goddess, Cher-length, sleek black hair, round breasts pressed against a cream silk blouse, long legs in bold print pants, and the curve of rise-to-meet-you hips. All of that combined with her unmistakable interest was almost too much.

"Jordan? Sandesh, you've aroused my interest." She paused. "Tell me more about your organization. IPT?"

Dear God. If her eyes had been direct and aware, her voice was the promise of sex and the slipping of silk sheets against hot skin. His entire body caught fire.

Justice cleared her throat, her eyes slid over him in a lazy, feline way.

He gave her a smile he hoped wasn't laced with lechery as he fished the question from memory. "The IPT is run and staffed entirely by former soldiers. It's designed to aid victims of war and disaster globally. We're focused on creating self-sustaining businesses. Giving options to people in difficult regions other than starve, flee, or fight. Die or be subjugated."

She frowned. "Why soldiers?"

"Soldiers are skilled and adaptable. They're used to discomfort. Used to keeping calm and navigating through difficult situations. Used to assessing problems, implementing strategies. Not having to train civilians saves us money. But I also wanted to give those soldiers having a problem going from warrior to Walmart an option. A way to recover the compassion they might have had to shut down in order to get the job done."

Those fine, gemstone eyes—onyx black and hot as pitch—widened with curiosity. Or doubt. "But a man's natural instinct, his base emotions, are geared toward aggression and fighting, right? The military amplifies that. Aren't you afraid that your volunteers are going to create more problems than they solve?"

He cleared his throat. He couldn't help himself. Her point was too close to one he'd heard again and again. Soldiers, men specifically, were dogs of war, trained and good for one thing: killing. If he recruited them for his charity, he was asking for trouble. It pissed him off. "No. I'm not. Are you?"

She smiled again, that coy smile that made his mouth go dry. "I just find it bizarre to expect them to act like Boy Scouts."

"Bizarre?" His voice rose before he could help himself. Seriously? He ran a hand under his collar, massaged his tense neck. "Why is it so bizarre to believe most men, just like most women, are capable of a whole range of actions?"

And that most men aren't made to be mindless butchers as well as mindless fucks? That last part he had the good sense not to say.

"That's not exactly what I meant by—"

Mukta Parish began to laugh, taking the conversation down a degree. She moved closer. Her astute brown eyes were framed by her rose niqab. Her powder-pink business suit showed off a determined-shouldered, Hillary Clintonesque form. She clapped her hands, her heavy bracelets jangling. "Justice, I hope you'll be more supportive of Sandesh's charity when you're doing PR for him in Jordan."

Justice's eyes widened, as if she'd been caught with her hand in the cookie jar. "Of course. I'm just playing devil's advocate. I know how best to defend the charity. When do we leave for Jordan?"

She wanted to go to Jordan now? She'd just put down his entire mission. He had enough issues with organizing; he didn't need to add her to the list.

Mukta stepped forward. "We were just discussing the fact that Sandesh wouldn't need to worry about transporting weapons for his own security. He could use one of our private jets. And, of course, take off from our private airport."

Oh. That was right. These people were scary rich. And the IPT was in dire need of capital.

Leland grabbed Justice by the forearm. "That's our cue, Justice. Let's leave them to the details."

He guided Justice out of the room. Sandesh watched them go with growing concern. This was the woman who was supposed to do PR for him in the Middle East. Didn't that job require tact? Seriously. She was going to get him killed.

Chapter 5

SUNLIGHT STREAMED IN FROM THE LARGE WALL OF WINDOWS. The entire conference room gleamed with light and the hum of business. As if everyone who came through those glass doors, sat in these leather swivel chairs, and rested arms on this table shared a drive toward financial success.

Justice twisted her chair back and forth. Leland hadn't answered any of her questions. Just deposited her here and exited discreetly. Man did everything discreetly. He was probably a stealth pooper.

The door to the conference room swung open. Momma came into the room with a billow of veils, a jingle of jewelry, and a whiff of Une Rose—a heady Turkish-rose-meets-Tennessee-mountain-soil.

"I'm sure you've realized that I have provided a cover for your Jordan trip."

For a woman who hid her face, Momma was incredibly direct. "Yeah. I noticed the hot humanitarian in your office. Kind of big to miss."

"And I can imagine you are wondering why I'd send your team an email stating there would be a delay when I am providing the cover. A cover that will put you in Jordan within the week."

The week? "Yeah. Why?"

Momma let out a breath so heavy it seemed expelled from the nethermost regions of her soul. The rose niqab moved with her breath. "I need to tell you something, something painful."

Justice nodded. Her heart had already begun to fence with her ribs.

"I believe we have a traitor among us."

"Us? The League, us?" Justice's blood plummeted below cold, past chilled, down to Arctic. She shivered. "No. You're jumping at shadows."

Momma toyed with the ten or so colorful bracelets weighing down her forearm. "Am I, Justice? I've managed to keep this organization a secret for forty years. And my instinct tells me the fact that the Brothers Grim changed the location of their meeting, to a place where we have few resources, is not mere coincidence."

A jagged spike of unease punched through Justice's stomach. "Someone in internal security? Someone hired. Not family."

Momma looked through the glass toward Leland. Justice followed her gaze. Leland and Sandesh stood by the front desk, going over some papers.

As head of the League's tactical security and Momma's oldest friend, Leland knew more about Momma and her secrets than any person alive. Justice often wondered about their relationship. It was close, but it couldn't be intimate. Not Momma. Never that.

Momma shook her head. "Internal has been cleared. And besides, the information on your mission was given to a limited few."

A limited few? Besides Leland and a few in internal, it had been given to…her unit. Justice's hand shook. She rested it atop her knee. Momma suspected her unit?

In numbers, the Parish family could give the reality

TV Duggars a run for their money. Except, all twenty-eight of her siblings had been adopted. She was loyal to them all. But it was her unit, those four she'd trained with, played with, fought with, attended classes with at the Mantua Academy that she was closest to—Tony, Dada, Gracie, and Bridget.

"How can you even think that?" How could Momma? No. She'd escaped people like that. People like her father, who'd let the Brothers Grim, Walid and Aamir, hurt Hope. The League was good. Honest. Real. They knew how much this mission meant to her.

Her mother's eyes softened. "It was destined to happen, Justice. When dealing with the injured, the group dynamic won't always supersede the instinct for self-preservation."

That was bullshit. Not her unit. Not hers. "Why?" Not for money. They had plenty. "Why would someone do it?"

"Perhaps money. Not everyone is comfortable working within the League, being paid by Parish Industries."

She was talking about Gracie.

Her mother looked beyond her, outside the window to the city. "I can think of many other reasons. To stop the League, to cripple us, to protect you, to make a point known only to them."

"Protect me?" Her unit knew that this was her chance to make it up to Hope. For letting her die. For letting Hope die in Justice's place.

"Many of my children have tragic pasts. A broken mind is a mind in turmoil. You can't excise all those demons."

"No. No. So you think Tony? Never."

"He is angry, Justice. He accused the League of reverse sexism."

What? When? Justice shook her head. That was bullshit. And the others? "You can't think Bridget would? She's practically a saint."

Momma's patient, brown eyes evaluated her. She could almost see her survey the texture of her words. Momma was careful like that. "Being a Buddhist doesn't make you a saint. If anything, her recent foray into pacifism might lead her to try and thwart our more aggressive goals."

"Gracie? She runs the underground rail—"

"She's still angry about John—"

"And Dada's—"

"No one from your unit can be ruled out."

No one? What the hell? "So what, I have to replan this entire mission, in a few days, and keep it secret from my four closest siblings?"

"I have all the information you need. The false identities the Brothers are using. Where they are staying. The layout of their hotel suite. And a tentative plan waiting your approval. Including a PR convention in Houston your siblings will think you're attending."

Ice needles prickled under her skin. She wasn't kidding. "You're wrong. They wouldn't betray me. Us. The League. Isn't it more likely that my fuc—uh, mess-up last week alerted the Brothers? Made them cautious."

Momma shifted forward, met her eyes. "Maybe. But are you willing to stake your life and the freedom of thousands of women on that?"

No. She wasn't. This mission was too important to her. She needed to stop anyone else from being hurt. And the Brothers Grim needed to pay for what they'd done to Hope. And for what they'd done to Cee. Justice let out a breath. "And you're okay using Sandesh?"

"He needs money. We need a cover. It's win-win."

Sure except for the part where Momma usurped his peace-loving purpose by secretly bending it to support her covert group of global vigilantes.

"Send me the details."

Chapter 6

SANDESH STEPPED INSIDE THE ELEVATOR AND PRESSED THE Lobby button. The doors began to slide closed. A sultry voice called, "Hold the elevator."

That voice was unmistakable. He tapped the Hold button. Justice entered. Her body electrified the empty space between them. His heart decided he needed more blood flow and kicked into high gear.

God, she smelled good. Something soft and feminine, like a bath filled with milk and lavender.

He so didn't need this. He still smarted over their conversation in her mother's office. He tensed, waited for her to continue the jousting. She didn't. Her eyes brushed over him as if distracted. Was this a game? Or was she worried about something? Their upcoming trip to Jordan?

"Are you okay?" She stared blankly at him. He repeated himself. "Justice, are you okay?"

She startled, came back from wherever she'd been in her thoughts, and winked at him. "Better than okay. Care to find out? The Ritz isn't too far."

Her glossy, dark eyes skimmed over him like he was the meal, and damn if it didn't shoot him full of hormones. But that open invitation to fuck got right under his skin, and not in a good way.

Not all in a bad way either, but he was ignoring that part—the part of his body swelling with heat.

He wanted her. That was obvious. But what she'd said about the IPT, her derision of the work he'd been organizing for years. Work he found worthwhile, even redeeming, really got on his nerves.

Worse, she'd been so casual about it. She'd first made every nerve in his body light on fire and then put down his work and practically accused him, and all men, of having no more feelings than fight or fuck. And to drive home the point, now she invited him to the nearest hotel.

"Justice, I think we should work on the business aspects of this interaction. There are a lot of details we need to work out first."

Her eyebrows rose. Smooth, Sandesh. He'd sounded like he was only putting things on hold. That's what happened with lack of blood flow to the brain.

The elevator dinged again and the doors slid open. A woman in a sleek, dark suit holding a thick, buckled briefcase stepped inside. She pressed the elevator keypad. He stepped past her and out.

Justice's eyebrows rose. "We're not on the ground floor."

No kidding. But he couldn't be in that confined space, smelling the invitation on her skin, when he knew damn well that he couldn't sleep with her.

Not just because her mother was his biggest investor, but because he didn't want to be that guy. He'd seen men and women who put all their energy into giving up control to anger or lust or the emotion de jour, and he wasn't going to end up that way. Not again.

The elevator doors began to close. Justice stepped forward and held them open. "Are you sure you want to *get off* here?"

The double entendre in "get off" made his cock jump. And, sure, he wanted a lot of things, her included, but degrading himself for sex hadn't been part of his programming since high school.

He inclined his head toward her. "I'm sure we'll see each other soon."

She smiled a grin so seductively promising he nearly bolted back onto the elevator. She let the elevator doors slide closed with a, "Probably on the plane."

Chapter 7

Seated at his desk, Walid answered his cell with the first genuine smile he'd worn in days.

The white adobe walls in his Mexican villa caught the waning light from the afternoon sun as his brother's voice came through as a booming spectrum of energy. "Hello, dear one, we are once again embarking on a journey to secure our world. And all the forces in the universe, seen and unseen, bend to our will."

His heart thrashing with joy, Walid unhitched his shoulders and spun his desk chair from the cattle ranch's dark wood beams, moldings, and comfortable red-leather seating to the window beyond. His eyes skimmed over the dry fields and distant mountains. "You can never just say hello, Aamir."

"Because I have such a fine voice made for songs and speeches and winning hearts."

Walid absently ran a hand along the scar on his neck. The scar made his voice sound congested and raw. It should never have been a scar. It should've been his end.

Aamir had saved him. Saved him for years after. Until they had become strong and wise enough to understand that the only way to be truly safe is to destroy that which oppresses you.

Rest in peace, Father.

"Yes. You are the beautiful one with the beautiful voice. Tell me, how are the forces aligning to our will today?"

Aamir paused. The considered beat drew Walid up in his chair. He turned away from the window as one of his men walked past carrying an AK-47.

"It seems the attack on our distribution center and the plot to assassinate us originates from information gained in your territory."

The heat of accusation nipped Walid's cheeks. The mole was here, at his ranch in Mexico. Would he ever have the loyalty of his men, like Aamir did?

No. Few people found him attractive. But they adored his brother, Aamir, who was both attractive and charismatic. Walid's homely face, strangle-marked neck, volatile temper, and sexual proclivities earned him little respect. Let alone admiration.

There had already been a threat that he'd had to eliminate last year. Thankfully, his new head of security had proven himself both loyal and ruthless. Dusty had come into the organization with a fire in his belly. He'd doggedly replaced all of the men who'd guarded Walid, rotating them to see who could be trusted.

Still, the process of weeding out his part of the operation wasn't complete. If there was a weakness for this type of exposure, it was with him in the Americas. Not Aamir in Europe.

"Did the informant tell you this?"

The informant, even though he had warned them of the assassination, irked Walid. He was an unknown who'd contacted them only through email. He'd used multiple proxies and thus they had not been able to locate him. Yet.

"Yes. After the original warning advising us to change our meeting to Jordan, I was contacted again. I paid again, was told of the spy and that this group desires to take us out together. They will wait an additional two years for us to meet again. By this, we can surmise this group knows that killing both of us leaves no successive leadership."

Walid ground his teeth. Their tactic, never employing men under them for too long or who were too ambitious, had guaranteed no one tried to overthrow them. Or so they'd thought. "And this is the world turning in our favor?"

Aamir tsked. "We make fortune. The world responds to our will." His brother's tone had become slightly sterner. "If it had not been for our power, we would have walked into a trap. Now, we have time to find our enemies and make a great profit."

Walid eyed the portrait of the Indian slum in which they'd lived as boys. A dark and distasteful image that reminded him obstacles could not only be overcome but pulverized. "So you are settled? We will move our focus to the Middle East. Diminishing our channels in South America?"

"It makes the most sense. With the buildup of refugees and smugglers looking to profit, we can easily secure product and use our existing distribution chains in Europe and North America."

Product. He meant females, but Aamir would never say that. He was careful. Mostly. "But the Middle East suppliers are men with fevered minds. They have a morality as tied to the wind as the clouds. It is always shifting. Perhaps it will shift against us."

"Their focus is not on us, but in continuing their fight. They have boxed their ambitions along with their libidos into the smallest corner possible."

"Yes. I'm surprised they can take a shit without prais-ing God."

Aamir laughed. A sound so welcome it made Walid's heart leap.

"True. And like any trapped, wild animal, they will run through the first opening. Our money is a doorway. They need it to keep their war going. We are invaluable to them. And, even better, it will be some time before any agency of significance notices."

Walid nodded as he did the mental calculations in his head. Ten women, servicing fifteen men a day, even minus food and shelter, could net them a million dollars a year. And this agreement would get them a thousand times that amount. "Fine. We will move forward with the Middle East. And to weed out the spy, I will contact my head of security. The man is brilliant. Former FBI. He is just the type of wild dog we need for this hunt."

"Yes. I've seen the file. Set him loose."

Walid gripped the phone a little tighter. Watched the second hand sweep the sun-shaped clock that hung upon his wall. "We will be together soon?"

"Next week, Walid. In Jordan. Get your papers ready."

Walid exhaled a deep sigh of relief. Jordan would not be so bad.

Chapter 8

SWINGING HER BRIEFCASE STRAP OVER HER SHOULDER, Justice cut across the Mantua Academy's parking lot, her jaw tensing. Late again.

Sandesh was probably already at the airport. Thankfully, it wasn't far from the school.

She grabbed the door handle of her black Rubicon, a.k.a. Gypsy. Her cell vibrated. She pulled the phone out and looked at the text. Gracie had finally gotten around to answering her text asking about Cee.

Gracie: The kid is scary.

What did she mean scary? For someone who ran the underground railroad, the family's computer operations used to find and safely place abused women, Gracie could be so judgmental.

Justice: She's had a rough road. Just process her.

Gracie: She'll never pass a psych eval.

Justice: That makes two of us. Do your job. I'm off to a convention in Houston.

A.k.a. secretly going to kill the Brothers Grim. She

shoved her phone in her pocket, grabbed the car handle. Her phone rang.

She lifted her eyes to the blue sky. Really, God? I'm one of the good guys. She answered. "Yep."

"Ms. Parish. This is Guadalupe from external security. We need you at southie."

"No can do. I'm late."

He paused. "But your father's here."

Shit. Shit. Shit. "Don't call him that."

She hung up.

Justice exited the school's main gate and drove to southie—a side lot at the head of the long, winding road that led to the school.

People who didn't have clearance to get on campus waited here for approval or for someone inside the school to come out to them. Usually teen boys waiting on teen girls.

Justice parked in the open lot, got out of her car, nodded at Guadalupe, and walked past the flagpole, whose metal clip *clang*, *clang*ed against it.

"Cooper." Justice pushed up her sunglasses and examined the man wearing worn gray pants splattered with paint. He had shifty eyes, a shifty body, and a shifty smile.

His dull eyes blinked. His sleepy mouth rolled into a smile. "Hey, kiddo."

Cooper Ramsey. A drug addict, narcissist with a poor work history. Hard to believe he was related to her. He was. Proved by paternity test two years ago.

Time to press his buttons and scare him away. Again.

"Are you ever going to tell me who gave you the money to come here?"

He distributed his weight from side to side, rocking like a child. He shook his head. The line of his mouth tightened. Genuine fear blanketed his eyes.

Yep. It was always the same.

Two years ago, Cooper had been living in California. Out of the blue, he'd boarded a plane for Pennsylvania. He'd landed, gotten in a cab, and come straight here.

The day before he'd boarded that plane, he'd had fourteen dollars in his bank account. She'd checked. He had no credit cards. No credit.

Someone had bought him that ticket.

Momma swore that it hadn't been her. And though Justice had investigated, she'd turned up nothing.

She waved him off like shooing a fly. "Go home, Coop. I have no idea why you keep coming here."

He flinched as if her tone was as solid as a missile. His brown eyes carried their usual misty gleam. It reminded her of that old commercial with the American Indian sitting horseback over pollution.

Blinking his eyes, he pulled the Indian head nickel medallion from around his neck. He held it out to her.

She stared at it. No way was she touching that thing.

A runnel of confusion gathered the earthy skin of his broad brow. "Your birthday's coming up."

The hair on her neck stood on end. High alert sounded. Adrenaline flooded into her system. "My birthday isn't for weeks."

He frowned. "I wanted you to have it." His voice was low. His slacker shoulders slumped. He opened the medallion. A locket?

He urged her to take it. Swallowing her irritation, she leaned forward. Inside were two small and faded photos.

One of her mother at twenty-five or so, right before she'd died. God, she'd been beautiful. A blue-eyed, blond-haired woman who looked nothing like Justice but everything like…Hope. The other photo was of Hope and her, arms over each other's shoulders.

Justice reached out and took the locket.

She brought it closer, hunched over it. She fought the lump in her throat and the tears behind her eyes.

"Happy birthday, Justice. Love you."

The muscles in Justice's shoulder blades snapped to attention, unbending her posture. An image of her child self as she clung to Cooper's long legs, begged him, "Please take us. Please. Daddy! Don't leave us here. Please!" slammed through her.

He'd shaken her off the way you'd shake off dust.

Her heart stiffened to stone in her chest.

"Stop coming here." Awash in memories, she turned and walked away.

If Mukta hadn't saved her… A flash of that dark basement, being tied to the chair, the tape across her mouth, and the roiling hunger.

She held the locket to her chest, as if to defend her brittle heart from even the thought. Not everyone was lucky. Not everyone had such a savior.

No. Some got left behind. And that's why she was about to board that plane to Jordan. She had to remember that. Remember that the men who'd killed Hope still needed to pay.

Chapter 9

THE EMERGENCY TEXT HAD COME WHILE SANDESH HAD been making his way to the airport. His gut was still clenched with worry.

The driveway leading onto the Mason Center grounds wound through pristine lawns and aged oaks. It reminded Sandesh of driving onto the grounds of a cemetery. He shuddered. So much of his mother had been lost already. Five years ago, at fifty-three, she'd developed early-onset Alzheimer's. Sandesh had been stunned. Angered.

The woman had worked hard her entire life, never took a sick day, and rarely complained. She didn't deserve this fate.

He pulled up to the main building and parked in his designated spot. His father had paid extra for the spot, and though it galled, it had come in handy. More than once.

He jammed his F-150 into park, flung open the door, and shut it backhanded as his feet had already begun to stride forward.

He raced up the nursing home's front steps, and the security guard buzzed him through with a nod. No formalities. No checking of ID. It must be bad.

He heard her before he saw her. Her voice, shrill and bitter, echoed through the hall like smoke from a raging fire. "You bitch! You bitch!"

He pushed back the ache, the simultaneous loss and anger and fear. He rounded the corner. The woman who had soothed his cuts, taken him to football practice, and told him he had a "lovely" singing voice when he couldn't carry a tune stood trembling in front of the doorway to her suite. Her thin, blue shift showed a frail and wiry form. They had a hard time getting Ella to eat these days. Her hands shook as she brandished a worn teddy bear. She held the matted brown bear, which normally she'd coo and sing to as if a child, as a shield of sorts.

She screeched at two women and one man—the nurses alongside the twenty-four-hour personal caregiver his father had hired. Paying for her caregivers and for her to be in this premiere facility was his father's last-ditch effort to make up for his emotional abuse.

The staff spoke in soothing tones, tried to break through the fog of delusion by playing into the delusion.

Today, as with most freak-outs, his mother played dueling roles on the drama loop. Both the tormentor and the tormented. The screeching bitch comments were a memory of his father. His father had never been a violent man, just a cunning manipulator and an aggressive, demeaning prick.

A deadly combination.

If he'd always been loud and angry, she would've dismissed him, but his father would alternate between faint praise, openly criticizing, and carefully constructed manipulations meant to destroy her confidence and wheedle at her independence.

Even after his father had divorced his mother—claiming she was a drag on his success—she had never recovered her sense of self. Mostly because just as she'd begun to accurately assess what he'd done to her, what she'd continued to do to herself long after he'd divorced her, she'd gotten sick.

For a long time, Sandesh had hated his father. Not just for abandoning them and living in Hong Kong for twenty years, but for always seeking the aggressive way forward, even in conversation with those he should've cared for.

The only reason he had any contact with his father now was because he'd recognized the same angry tendencies in himself. It was hard to hate someone when you understood them.

Sandesh neared with his hands out. "Ella, that's a fine baby you have there."

The male nurse cleared his throat, almost apologetically. "We already tried that."

Sandesh ignored him. "He reminds me of you. Your son."

His mother jolted, as if she'd physically slammed from some other place back into her body, into awareness. She looked down, clearly realizing she held the teddy bear—her baby—as a shield.

She began to shake. Her eyes cleared, then misted with the slow buildup of tears as she clutched the bear to her chest. Her blue, watery eyes flew to his face. "Is it okay? Is it okay?"

His heart buckled under. "It's okay, dear. It's always okay between us."

Her face twitched as tremors, aftershocks of awareness, pinched the muscles beneath her too-pale skin. He understood.

She'd been trapped beneath the cold ground of her

disease, pressed beneath its weight, and now surfaced from that crushing depth to reacquaint herself with the bright world above. It must hurt.

He reached her, wrapped a protective and sturdy arm around her delicate and thin shoulders. He drew her to him, like a tiny bird in need of great care.

He looked back at the nurse. "Please get her something to drink. Apple juice."

The male nurse gave him an appreciative nod and left.

The first female attendant, the one personally paid to sit with his mother, looked abashed. "Would you like me to contact her private physician, Mr. Ross?"

He nodded. "Yes. And I believe the first visitor coming in my absence, my buddy Victor, will be stopping in tonight. Make sure the guards know."

"Oh. Yeah. I already have."

Good. That was something. Oh so gently, he led his mother's trembling and broken body back into her suite. She clung to him, pressed the ragged, stuffed bear between them. He led her past the last nurse—a twentysomething female who worked at the facility. The woman smiled at him, then checked out his ass with a wink.

What an idiot.

Chapter 10

EXCEPT FOR THE FLAT-SCREEN TV SHOWING WORLD NEWS, the only lights on in the private plane marked the galley, an outlet at the conference table, and along the cabin floor. But Justice knew well the sounds and sights of a nightmare.

She watched helplessly as Sandesh's body twitched and jerked in the prone seat next to hers.

Should she wake him? Would he be upset? He'd definitely be startled. But how many nights had she wished someone would pull her out of her damn nightmare?

To her, to people who had the same nightmare for decades, the notion that dreams weren't real was little consolation. Not when they felt like torture. She placed a hand on Sandesh's strong forearm arm, squeezed.

He jolted awake, gasping for breath. He sat forward, clicked his footrest down, jerked his arm away, and hacked into his hand.

With the light from the television glancing across his blond hair, he looked over at her. His eyes were still uncertain, still back there, in whatever place had held him.

Justice leaned forward, careful not to touch. He smelled of sweat and fear. "Are you okay?"

He didn't answer her. He rubbed a hand across his face.

"Do you want to talk about it? The dream?"

He dropped his hand. "No."

He said the word like a wall. A do-not-cross, guard-dog-on-duty, enter-at-your-own-risk wall. She got it. And she didn't need him to tell her his dream, but she wanted him to know she got it. Somehow, it mattered to her.

He pushed aside the blanket on his lap, looked as if he considered getting up, but settled for adjusting the vent. Cool air flowed out.

She fingered the headset in her lap. She worked a kink from her neck and spoke without lifting her head. "I have this bad dream all the time."

He let out a breath, as if he couldn't deal with her trying to compare her "bad dream" with his nightmare. She wanted to keep her mouth shut, wanted to let him think he was alone, so she wouldn't have to share. But he was like her. He knew about nightmares. And she couldn't let it go.

"I'm little. A child. A man is holding me down. He's so heavy. So heavy it hurts. He has his hand over my mouth. I guess to keep me from screaming. I can't breathe. I'm little, and he's cut off my nose as well as my mouth. It's a dream. But I can't wake up. I can't breathe. And I can't wake up."

The explosive power of her words suddenly felt wrong, rash, stupid, like a punch to her gut. She took in deep, heavy breaths.

Beside her, she could feel him go still. Rage-filled still. Deadly still. "Justice, did someone hurt you? Did something like that happen to you?"

"No." She lifted her head, let out a breath. She didn't want him to think that. "It was Hope. My biological sister. She died saving me from that. Our maternal grandmother, an utterly crazy woman, let some very sick men make kiddie bondage films in her basement. My father gave us to her for drug money."

He looked away. She could see the tension in his jaw, as if he fought for control.

Fuck. What had she been thinking? She'd tossed her pain out there like a live grenade. And it had exploded the peace of the cabin. Even as the quiet, smooth sound of the jet slicing through the sky continued to brush the plane's hull.

He waited a long moment, enough time for her to regret again her compulsive decision to share, before he softly asked, "How do you wake from the nightmare?"

She shuddered. "I pray. I mean, at first I fight and struggle and thrash. Bite. Nothing works. I'm not a religious person. At all. But when I give in and pray, something in that prayer lifts me."

She paused, fiddled with the tiny red light on one of the earphones of the headset in her lap. "The waking is the worst part. Because I know exactly how she must've felt. And that…"

Her voice was so low the wind against the plane almost carried it away. "My prayers didn't work for Hope."

Silence. She returned her eyes to him. It was an invitation for him to talk if he wanted. A way of her saying, *See. I do understand.*

He nodded. "Thanks, Justice. For sharing. For waking me. I'm gonna leave it there. Okay?"

He reached out as if to put his hand on top of hers. His hand hovered, as if waiting for her to reject him for not sharing his story. She didn't. Would never.

She flipped her hand over. He dropped his hand into

hers, threaded his fingers with hers. His hand was warm, covering, and strong. Her body heated from head to toe.

Her mind filled with bold images of their lips colliding, him dragging her into his seat, into his lap. Hands tearing at clothes. Mouths and tongues searching.

"Justice." One word, but that tone, the invitation was there.

Justice pushed back and closed her eyes. She wanted to answer him, wanted to engage in some hot, steamy sex. But she wanted to screw Sandesh, not his charity. And not her mission. Getting involved with him would complicate things. He might feel a greater need to keep tabs on her, diverting his time from his work, endangering himself in something he knew nothing about. She might worry more for his safety and feel even more guilt. No. She had to stay clear, focus on her job, and let him focus on his work.

Maybe when this was over they could sleep together. Definitely when this was over. But not before. Until they were safely back, she wouldn't, *couldn't* sleep with him.

She kept her eyes closed. She could feel him watching her, waiting for her as her body drifted into a sleep layered with long, slow dreams of him and her.

Chapter 11

MUKTA HAD BEEN GOOD TO HER WORD. AFTER THEY LANDED in Amman, the customs official had entered the private plane, smiled, spoke kindly to him and Justice, stamped their documents, and left. Unbelievable.

He stowed his passport and multi-entrance visa inside his backpack, hit Send on the response to a non-urgent email from his mother's care center, stowed his laptop, and slipped out from behind the round, wooden conference table.

From across the cabin, he caught Justice. Her midnight-dark eyes stared up at him. He smiled at her. She returned to checking her emails or text or whatever had her interest on her cell.

Instant agitation trod its muddy shitkickers down his spine. She'd been distant since waking this morning.

He didn't know what her problem was. They'd seemed to connect last night and shared, well, a moment. It shouldn't bother him, but it did. Worse, he was about to get himself in more trouble. He walked over to where she sat. "We need to go over some rules."

Her eyebrows and eyes rose. She lowered her phone and put it into her backpack. "Rules?"

He'd handled military knives with a less sharp edge than the one she'd put on that word. Maybe he could've chosen a better word. "Let's call them guidelines. And not even my guidelines. More like the country's guidelines."

"Like?"

"Jordan is normally safe, but these aren't normal times. Amman is flooded with refugees. Not all are innocent. Don't leave the hotel without me. When we're working at Zaatari, keep a low profile, let me know where you are. Don't wander around without me."

He waited for her to argue. He waited for her to tell him to shove his rules up his ass. Her face said that was exactly what she was thinking. And, honestly, he wouldn't blame her.

"So the Grand Hyatt in Amman is now like a Taliban hut in Afghanistan?"

"There are a lot of people here. Not just Jordanians. Not just people playing by the rules. This area is in flux. So if I'm eighty klicks away in Zaatari or even working with Salma within Amman, you're pretty much on your own. Try to have some situational awareness."

She let out a breath deep enough to knock over a tombstone. "I get it. In fact, I was thinking that after our initial inspection of the camp, I'd leave you to work with Salma. I know you'll be doing a lot of traveling, and I don't want to get in the way."

Okay. She was definitely mad. Well, she'd have to cope. He held out a hand. "You ready?"

Her eyes rose, pinned him with midnight pleas and hot sighs. He wanted to drop to his knees, kiss her lips, find her center, and pull free every soft and needy sound.

After a moment, she took his hand. A surge of electric lust shot up his arm and increased his urge to kiss her. Did she feel it? How could she not?

Justice stepped closer. Yep, she felt it. She lifted

onto her toes. The space between them heated to Death Valley temperatures. His breath came out hot and loud.

She pressed her front to his, grabbed his waist, pulled him flush against her. He grew instantly hard. He couldn't move. Couldn't think. She kissed his lips, opened her mouth against his.

He pushed his tongue inside her mouth, explored her wet warmth. She ground herself against him, moaned so deeply it cut off all other sound, but the driving yes, yes, yes in his chest.

Then she stepped back. Shrugged in apology. "Let's keep this PG while we're here. I don't want to get caught up in anything that could mess things up for you."

A slap of disappointment hit him in the gut. What had just happened? "That's fine with me."

Huge lie. Growing bigger by the minute.

Chapter 12

AFTER JUSTICE AND SANDESH HAD CHECKED INTO THEIR hotel, they made their way across Jordan to Zaatari. Their transportation, an old pickup truck, drove alongside the Zaatari refugee camp. Layered with sand and trash and plastered with Arabic graffiti, Zaatari sprawled across the desert in a seemingly endless expansion.

The city-camp was sloppy and beautiful in places. Well tended and ignored. Serene and damning. Crude and artistic. And inside, a hundred thousand minds worked and reworked the tragedies, pressures, boredom, and inequalities of mounting displacement. Metal trailers used to house people, homemade shacks, and rectangular buildings with sheeted windows pressed up against miles of fencing topped with barbwire.

Above all of it stood the trunks of electrical poles, brown, skeletal fingers draped in black wires, crisscrossing dry roads that connected districts housing refugees, fatigued fighters, aid workers, and camp organizers.

To Justice, it all looked like a threat. She'd been told they needed to pass through security to get into the camp, but on this long, dry road, she could see many open places to enter and leave. A thousand porous places to take advantage of people already victimized by circumstance.

Feeling too much like a war tourist, she turned her eyes away as the old pickup bounced along the road.

Warm air rushed through, pushed strands of hair from her ponytail and fluttered it across her face.

The cab of the old pickup smelled like figs and antiseptic. Stuffed into the back seat between Sandesh and a box of figs, Justice readjusted her legs with a swoosh from her cargo pants. Sandesh readjusted as well.

Good to see she wasn't the only hyperaware one. Because, really, could there be any man more suited to wearing sunglasses? Doubtful. The desert wasn't the only thing hot around here.

Add to that desert-sand sweatpants that rode low on his lean hips and accented his, uhm, very nice equipment. A dark-blue shirt tight against his chest, sleeves rolled up on biceps that didn't need to flex to be flexed. And sexy, almost-a-beard stubble. A girl couldn't help wanting to fan herself.

His sunglasses blocked the sun and her curious stares, but she could see his nerves. See the soldier coming out as they drove the road parting this bleak, impoverished desert. Their Jordanian contact, Salma, had already explained that there were gangs inside and very dangerous areas within the twelve districts.

And that explained Sandesh's weird rules thing on the plane.

She wasn't mad. She got it. He thought she did PR for a living. And badly at that. Besides, it worked for her. She didn't want to be tied to his mission. Ultimately, she needed to be at the hotel—not the hotel she and Sandesh had booked rooms at. No, the hotel where the Brothers Grim were staying. Sandesh's rules had given her the opportunity she'd needed to make an appearance at the camp and move on.

But he probably thought she was pissed. She might be if she wasn't planning on blatantly ignoring his warnings. And if she didn't feel so damn guilty.

Guilty for using him. Guilty for involving him. Guilty for kissing him when she knew she was using him, the IPT, and Salma. But he'd just been so damn cute. Wanting to take care of her. As if she needed him to. So funny. Well, he had good intentions.

And damn, what right did Sandesh have to smell so good in this heat? The musk of him made her want to lean closer. Lick.

That might get a bit awkward. Especially with Salma—the Jordanian woman who'd created Salma's Gems—and their driver, her teenage grandson, in the front seat.

Things were awkward enough. No one really spoke as the dry desert air whooshed through the windows. Sandesh was busy texting his partner at the IPT, a guy named Victor. There had been a flood in the Midwest of the United States and Victor was organizing volunteers and aid, already working with local centers to supply water and clothing.

The IPT seemed incredibly well organized. Which was the point Sandesh had first made when they'd met. It was easier to organize military personnel used to hitting the road at a moment's notice.

She put her hand on the seat to steady herself as the truck bounced to a halt at the inspection station outside of Zaatari Refugee Camp. About time. How would Sandesh make that drive every day? Although, really, it probably wouldn't be every day. The mission would have Sandesh traveling to different areas. Throw a stone in Jordan, and you were likely to hit a Syrian refugee.

Her heart tapped Morse code against her chest at the sight of the guards, even though she'd been told not to worry about getting herself and her gun inside.

Entering legally meant a lot of rules, but there were a lot of ways around those rules. Money, basically.

Many men paid to enter illegally to look for girls they'd "marry" and then discard when they were done. Or "marry" off into sexual slavery.

That was why scum like Aamir and Walid were here, to take advantage. It was so huge. No wonder so many women and orphaned girls fell through the cracks, despite the monumental effort of aid organizations, Syrian vigilante groups, and the Jordanians.

After Salma spoke with a guard, they were waved through. Justice relaxed. Let out a breath. Both she and Sandesh were armed. She watched Sandesh's hand, which had been fisted at his side, release.

They bounced into the camp and proceeded slowly down rangy streets and past flapping tents, trailers, and individually constructed buildings, nailed together with sheets of metal and topped with corrugated scraps.

The white-and-tan UN Refugee Agency tents, trailers, and buildings were dusted with sand, but her eyes caught the bright garments and splashes of colors along these duller patches.

Color was everywhere. It was in the laundry drying on lines. Splashes of red and blue in hanging painted wooden signs. The trailers themselves had been painted bright and bold. Different colors in the fruit at produce stands, in the awnings of market trailers, in pink rows of plastic sandals on display, and the elaborately colored women's veils.

They turned right and traveled down a wide dirt road with people slow to get out of their way. As he drove, Salma's grandson called out to a few people in greeting. You simply did not rush in a desert.

Now that the truck had slowed, allowing conversation, Salma turned toward Justice and Sandesh. She was a small woman, bent forward, as if fighting against an unseen wind. She had brown eyes and a white hijab tucked around her face, and a traditional dark-blue dress or abaya.

She pointed out where the French had set up a hospital on a bustling street filled with one-story buildings, trailers turned into stores, and open fruit stands. "The aid workers call this the Champs-Élysées, like the street in Paris, but most who live here call it simply Market Street."

Market Street. Big difference from the one in Philly. This one smelled like humans and cooked zucchini, not car exhaust and steel. People milled about on the long dirt road. Most paid no attention to the truck until it was nearly upon them. Then they moved out of the way with a casual, almost disinterested stride.

Wires hung in snarled knots and strands on electrical poles were awkwardly congested in places. Atop some of the trailer homes sat satellite dishes.

Besides the slam of hammers on metal from repairs and construction, the wind made the most noise as it blew through the open truck windows. "I thought it would be noisier."

Salma laughed. "You expected bombs? Gunshots and screams?"

Actually, she had. Salma shook her head. "You will hear those things. And laughter. And prayer. And songs of joy and wails of grief. You will see streaks of aircraft across the blue sky. And plumes of distant smoke. There are many good people here stuck in a very bad situation. People who not too long ago lived a much different life."

Justice nodded and looked out at the tents and trailers and briskly erected buildings that stretched for miles. Sandesh seemed to take it all in, asking relevant questions about the organization and the needs of the women in Salma's care.

A few streets over, through the rows of trailers, she glimpsed children playing soccer.

Others filled water jugs from a huge red tank, and still others played along the street. A girl, no older than nine, carried a baby on her hip. "There are so many kids here. Kids caring for kids."

Salma's almond-brown eyes flicked down, adjusted something in the front seat as the driver steered past people. "Yes. Many orphans. Which makes it easier for those who wish to take them."

A sick sort of anger fisted in Justice's stomach. Trying to save the women and girls was one thing, but stopping the hands—at least one of the biggest ones—that kept snatching them away was another. She wouldn't fail. She would not.

Which meant she had to snap some photos here, interview a couple of women, and make her excuses, because—as Momma would undoubtedly remind her—reconnaissance always comes first.

Chapter 13

INSIDE THE TRAILER THAT HOUSED SALMA'S OPERATION, Sandesh watched Justice interact with the dozen women being taught to do the screen printing for the T-shirts, while others were taught to sew pajama pants and robes. Although, being taught screen printing was a stretch. They had three sewing machines to teach on, but for now only a manual for the screen-printing equipment.

Still, all the women were eager and attentive. And full of a lightness and purpose that Justice had instantly found her way into the middle of. She sat crossed-legged among the women on the floor, asked questions about the simple pattern they would be using, and joked in Arabic.

How did she know Arabic? Strange. This woman continued to surprise him. One minute she seemed as tough as nails. Putting him and all men in the world down. The next moment, she was showing him she was both tender and understanding. Sharing secrets with him on the plane, even though he could tell how very much giving those secrets away cost her.

Here she was, again revealing herself among these women, interacting, engaging, and becoming part of them in the amount of time it would take children to make friends.

It was like some of the things Justice had shown him, the anger and distance, was all a front. But here was the real Justice. Unblocked by walls. She cared a hell of a lot more than she wanted anyone to know. It was touching.

And confusing.

Not because of that kiss, so scorching hot he got hard whenever he thought of it. But because, despite her obvious concern for these women, she'd already begun to distance herself from the operation. And it had started on the plane, even before that kiss, with her telling him she'd spend most of her time at the hotel organizing PR.

So why come to Jordan? Why not organize PR from the States? That would've made more sense, considering the attitude about the structure of the IPT she'd shown in her mother's office.

It shouldn't bother him, but it was almost like she was a war tourist. Here to look around. Or like she was patting him and Salma on the head, saying "Good job" while getting to what she thought was the real work. But that made no sense.

He watched Justice as she knelt on the floor in the trailer beside a young woman with one arm. The woman showed her designs that would be used for the shirts once they had the equipment. She'd drawn the designs herself. Justice praised her, genuinely praised her, because the woman drew stunning designs.

Justice cared. He could see that she cared.

"You have got to stop staring at me."

Sandesh's skin heated as Justice turned those join-me-in-the-dark eyes on him. A few of the English-speaking women laughed at her teasing.

Sandesh held Justice's gaze. Mostly because he could think of no way to force himself to stop looking. "Can I have your camera?"

She raised an eyebrow, then shrugged. She put one hand on her thigh, steadied herself, and took the camera from around her neck. She held the camera out to him. He took it.

"I mean, if I'm going to stare, I should at least do something a little useful."

She eyed him skeptically, but the woman who'd been showing her the designs took the initiative. She moved closer to Justice and put her arm around Justice's shoulders. And the two of them smiled. He snapped photos as the other women around them showed an interest and posed for the shots.

The moment seemed full of promise. These women, who'd been through so much, lost so much, even of themselves, had a deep strength. They were ready to take their pain and create a new future.

But Justice? He couldn't figure her out.

Chapter 14

THE FOUR SEASONS IN AMMAN REALLY PLAYED UP THE whole desert aspect. Desert-tan marble floors, walls, ceiling, chairs, and even the uniforms on some of the staff were tan. It made Justice, dressed in all black, stick out like a sore thumb.

Good thing only her eyes showed.

She wore the traditional niqab and abaya. A burka, with its mesh screen for the eyes, would've made her stand out more here. Most of the Jordanian women wore only the hijab head scarf, nothing over their faces, and had some style going on with jeans or fashionable clothes. She'd opted for an abaya, an all-black, bland, loose-fitting dress.

Nice thing about the regional customs was a woman assassin didn't have to work too hard to go undercover. Just pop in a couple of blue contacts and ghost around.

She sat in a lounge area off to the side of the check-in desk with an open book of Sufi poetry. She didn't feel even close to poetic. She felt fidgety.

The Brothers Grim were staying here in a two-bedroom suite for two weeks. Only two weeks. They usually met every two years for at least a month, but had changed plans. They were being awfully cautious. Which made Momma's paranoid delusions seem that much less paranoid.

Distress winged up and brushed frantic feathers

against Justice's breastbone. Her meeting with Momma before she'd come here had been damning.

Not one of her own. Please not that.

She couldn't imagine facing a day without one of her four closest siblings.

But right now, that wasn't something she could think about. She had other things to worry about. The patched-together plan wasn't foolproof.

Sure, Momma had placed a reliable connection at the hotel. A former rescue, who'd get Justice a key to the suite and ID, but not a weapon.

And Justice couldn't get a gun past hotel screening, and surely not past whatever security Walid and Aamir would have at the room.

So she'd be going with plan B. Poison.

Not too difficult to get a good poison when one of your twenty-eight siblings was a leading chemist at one of the top chemical manufacturers in the world, a.k.a. Parish Group Holdings.

But it also meant Justice would be vulnerable. She'd have to go in when the Brothers were scheduled to go out. She'd need to get a uniform. She'd have to sneak in for turndown service with nothing but some mints in her pocket. She'd appear harmless. She wouldn't even have cleaning solution on her.

Just a little pouch containing a substance that would first make the Brothers sick, like a bad case of food poisoning, and then kill them.

The poison had been developed from a cyanide derivative. She'd have to put it somewhere the Brothers alone were guaranteed to use. Toothbrush seemed the best option. Momma had said, "It works remarkably fast."

It better.

She just hoped the Brothers' security thugs wouldn't find the pouch on her. It wasn't huge, but large enough to create a bump that could be felt by the guards. And suspicious-looking enough that if she'd had to carry it onto a public plane, she would've been sweating bullets. Every assassin should have their own plane.

Having the pouch and knowing all that could go wrong with poison made her the most nervous. She wished she could've had something a little more direct. More deadly. Beggars can't be choosers. Hotel security was strict. Another reason she'd checked into this hotel under a false identity. That gave her a reason to sit here, scanning the hotel.

Her eyes perked up as she spotted her prey.

One of the Brothers. Not Aamir, the slick one who dressed like a *GQ* model, but the younger one, Walid. Early forties, lanky with the start of a belly; dark-black hair; sharp, brown eyes; and a scar that looked like a rope burn along his neck.

She watched him sweep across the lobby and near an elevator surrounded by a two-man security detail. His guards seemed casual. Almost too casual. That could work in her favor.

Walid changed course abruptly. His guards stayed at the elevator, holding it open. What the hell?

Walid marched directly past Justice's alcove to get to the concierge. He smelled like expensive cologne.

Fuckedy fuck. He was so close. She nearly dropped her book and attacked.

She held steady as Walid, with his raspy voice and oh-so-coy British accent, asked the concierge to change his dinner reservation for tomorrow night, moving it up one hour.

The concierge didn't miss a beat interpreting the language. He looked at his watch, as if seeing into the future. "I will do so right away."

Walid thanked him, turned on his shiny, black loafer, and went back to the elevator.

Luck of the Irish or luck of the draw; if there were a deity dedicated to saving women's lives, that deity had clocked in for Justice.

Yeah, it meant moving the timeline up on her assassination plan. Ignoring Momma's reconnaissance-first rule, but this was too good of an opportunity—both Brothers wouldn't be in their room. If all went according to plan, the Brothers would be dead within forty-eight hours.

Chapter 15

Inside his spacious hotel suite, one of Walid's guards handed a suit for dry cleaning to the hotel staff. It wasn't until the staffer moved off and the guard kept the door open that Walid noticed him.

Looking like a Bollywood film star in his buffalo-leather racing jacket over a white V-neck, with his black beard trimmed tight against his sharp jawline, his brown eyes alight with mischief, Aamir strolled into the suite. And brought with him the sun.

Walid stood without even knowing he'd stood. He waited, still and dumbstruck.

Aamir rushed forward, the way a child rushes toward their favorite toy. He embraced Walid with big, welcoming arms. Warm. Sincere. With the subtle scent of sandalwood.

Oh, he'd forgotten. He'd forgotten the smell of him, the look of him, the feel of him. Perfect Aamir.

Walid's heart, an organ he had not realized had been plodding along with a listing beat, fitted together, healed, and found its true pace. Ah. His brother's arms.

For a moment, he regretted his choices, hated with a bitterness that coated his tongue that they could not be together at all times. And he hated the assassin. The reason he would have only two weeks with his brother, and not their usual month. Just a precaution, but an annoying one.

Aamir stepped back, brought two bejeweled hands to his brother's biceps, and clapped them twice against his arms. "Look at you, Walid! A man of excellent taste who has taken the world for his own."

Walid smiled despite the bitter thorn that had lodged in his throat. He felt like such a man, full of excellent taste, only when Aamir used those words and smiled at him. He felt love only when his brother bestowed love on him.

Walid swallowed his emotions. "It is good to see you, Aamir. Now we are as we should be."

Aamir's dazzling smile, like pearls pulled right from the soft lining of an oyster, widened. "We are better. See here, I have brought you a guest."

He pointed back at someone who'd entered. Walid had not noticed the woman or Aamir's security guards standing behind her.

What was a woman doing here? He frowned. He'd thought to have time with his brother, time to catch up. Who was this creature? She was covered from head to toe in the traditional veil and abaya.

Walid instantly disliked her. "Who is this? Why is she here?"

Aamir tsked. "Is this any way to treat our business associate?"

Walid cleared his throat. Business associate? A woman? Here?

Annoyance flashed in his chest. He straightened. Aamir always kept him on his toes. He acknowledged the woman with a tilt of his chin but did not reach out to shake her hand. She was not western. Would not accept such a greeting. And, honestly, he was grateful. He had no desire to touch her even for a moment.

"Walid, this is Fidda."

Walid doubted her name was Fidda, but she obviously did not wish to share her real name. "Welcome, Fidda."

Though Walid had put the exact amount of disrespect and disbelief on her name as he felt, the woman nodded back as if honored.

"Fidda is from Syria, the wife of an ISIS commander. She will serve as our go-between."

Go-between. Why was there even a need for this meeting? This was a connection he had no desire or need to be involved with. A dirty woman with a dirtier mind. "From Syria? So you sell your own people? How typically female."

Aamir laughed. "True, dear Brother, but she is selling them to us."

The woman, Fidda, shook her head. "Not all are Syrian. And those who are, are infidels. At least this way their lives serve a higher cause. And these women will go to North America and Europe. Places where their sins will be as meaningless as a speck of mud in dirty bathwater. I am doing them a favor."

Walid didn't really care what her reasons were. He'd seen women like this his whole life. Piranha. "Why is she here?"

"She is here to discuss the transportation of a truck-load of product across the border. It is good for both of us to know all aspects of the operation. Even if you will not be involved at this end."

The last was meant to be an admonishment. Walid shook his head. He knew his brother better than that. The transport of the girls had always been the plan. Meeting Fidda, bringing her here to their hotel, had not.

Did he not see that this woman was trying to gain something? Did his brother not see how her eyes swept the room, assessed what they had, assessed them and their capabilities? To allow a befouled creature such as this into the sanctity of their suite made Walid's stomach turn. "Again, Brother, why is she really here?"

Aamir waved his hand as if he were a magician's assistant revealing the obvious. "She has brought us a sample product. See, they are not all dark haired. And she speaks English."

Walid took a step back, noticing the girl half-hiding by the woman's side. She had blond hair and almost comically wide, blue eyes. Aamir was out of his mind.

"What is this?"

Aamir smiled, wicked and clever. "This, dear Brother, is my wife."

Chapter 16

GIVING A BIG "FUCK YOU" TO THE FACT THAT SHE'D HAD TO hide in an abaya all day, Justice sat at the hotel bar in a short silk dress. Good thing Jordan was a lot less strict than other parts of the Middle East.

She tapped her fingers against the lip of her espresso cup as she imagined Walid dying. She felt her hand slicing the blade up and under his ribs. The sharp point puncturing his heart as that boom-boom beat slowed.

She pictured his large body—he had to be six feet tall—jerk back, fall to his knees. Pictured his hands reaching out a second too late.

Take that. You fuck. She was so fucking mad. He had looked so damn ordinary. He was in a fucking suit. Fuckedy fuck. How dare he prosper? It wasn't his hands that had denied the breath to Hope, even as Justice had screamed and begged him to let her breathe.

No. That had been his brother, Aamir. But Walid was the other half of the organization. He was just as guilty.

And the people working at that hotel had showed him deference. Did they know? Did they care? She cared. She fucking cared. It mattered to her. She had to do this. She could not screw up. Fuck. She needed a distraction. A way out of her head for two fucking minutes.

"Justice, are you going to drink that?"

Huh? Her eyes refocused on the dim bar's polished dark wood. She looked at her espresso. Her taps had caused the dark liquid to spill onto the white ceramic saucer. She put a finger on the edge of the small plate and pushed it toward Sandesh. "You're welcome to it. It's a little cool now."

He took the cup and the seat beside her. "Are you okay? You looked a little intense."

Gawd, she *would* happen to be traveling with a man who had been instructed how to pay attention—and not just regular attention, military-detail attention. She could feel the laser of his observation as if it were a shiny, red light pointed between her eyes. "I'm fine."

He snorted. God, he was hot when he was skeptical. She doubted he could get more skeptical. Hmmm, maybe he needed a distraction too.

Oh, she was not a good person.

She really shouldn't. Then again…

He was on break now, right? So it wouldn't distract him from his mission. And it wouldn't be taking time from her mission.

Oh, she really needed a few hours of not thinking. He probably did too. She pumped her eyebrows at him, swung her chair toward him. "Let's dance."

Chapter 17

STANDING IN THE ORNATE BAR, ONLY HALF-FULL OF PATRONS, with music playing softly, Sandesh felt Justice's sultry invitation to dance run down his body like a hot finger. He couldn't control the hungry leer that traveled the silky, blue dress that spanned her body, her hips, and the satisfying curve of a great ass like a warm hand.

Damn, he wanted to rest his own hand against that fine ass, pull her to him. The short, midnight-blue dress showed off sun-drenched legs. Her nipples pressed against the deep-blue hue and stood at attention under the drape of fabric that swooped and rested against her breasts.

And, ah, her lips.

So full.

So damn sure.

A grin that announced the game was won and dinner was ready all in one lazy, long predatory stretch. Part of his body throbbed in response. The rest of him was pretty damn annoyed.

Wasn't she the one who had suggested they keep it PG? Was she playing games?

Justice's eyes, soaked in velvet onyx and framed by midnight lashes, narrowed. "Okay, I give. You eat me up with your stare and then you hesitate. What is it with you? Do you have something against strong women?"

Sandesh snorted. "For someone so direct, you are seriously clueless."

"I'm clueless? Buddy, you have no idea of the opportunity for friction and fun you are passing up right now."

He had to laugh. Had to. Not just because she was quick and funny, but because she was all of that—not afraid to speak her mind, heat and energy, and the promise of friction and fun.

His fingers left the edge of the cold espresso and sought out her hand. He needed to feel all of that energy and fire pressed up against him. "Okay. Let's dance."

She didn't resist. Another surprise. She'd taken his hesitation personally. He'd thought she'd make him pay for that. But she didn't. She simply bequeathed him with a that's-more-like-it smile. Seriously, this woman was scorching hot.

"At this Moment" by Billy Vera and the Beaters played through the speakers. Not what he would've expected here.

He pulled her to him as they hit the empty dance floor. She curved into him, drawing a sound from his throat that was as involuntary as breathing. She purred into his ear.

"That's one."

His hand slid along the silk fabric of her dress, down her back to her smooth, round, and hot-as-hell ass. And there he went. Zero to sixty. He cleared his throat. "One?"

She ran a tongue over his earlobe and inside his ear. That warm, wet stroke sent tremors zinging low into his body. Her sultry voice meshed with that teasing tongue and vibrated through him. "I'm counting how many different ways I can get you to moan."

He growled, a raw, desperate sound that even to his own muffled ears sounded like raging intent.

She laughed. "Two."

Okay. Definitely time to divert the conversation. Complex math, anyone? Or a subject destined to slow down any hot moment. "Have you spoken to your mother about our progress here?"

She laughed, as if she could see him wrestling control from the moment. She moved her mouth close enough that he could feel her breath on his neck. "No. But I'd like to meet *your* mother. You've met mine. It's only fair. What's she like?"

"You'd like her. At least who she used to be."

"Used to be?"

"She's been sick for a few years. Early-onset Alzheimer's. She's at a care center. I have friends and family scheduled to sit and read with her every night I'm away."

"Oh. I'm sorry." She looked past him for a moment, then returned her gaze to his. "So what you're telling me is that while you're away on your humanitarian mission, you've organized it so your mother will always be watched over by a close friend or family member. You do realize I already want to sleep with you. You don't have to sweeten the pot."

He laughed. Only this woman would think talking about his mom—meant to cool things off—was sexy.

"Sandesh, I'm serious." She began to roll her hips. His eyes rolled back in his head.

That. Felt. So. Fucking. Good. Nothing like a violent hard-on to give a woman the upper hand. Her hand. His hard-on. Settle. Settle.

Fuck it.

His lips came down on hers. There was an instant and

overwhelming zing of electricity. Mindless of where he was, he tasted her, tickled, and teased her mouth open. Her wet response, the moan against his lips as his tongue played back, caused fire to erupt down his body.

Dubdubdub, *dubdubdub*, pulsated through him. He couldn't tell what throbbed faster—his cock or his heart. He deepened the kiss. She opened wider, accelerated the roll of her hips.

Time to go. Time to get her off the dance floor and into his bed. Or her bed. Which room was closer?

The phone in his pocket buzzed. Justice stiffened in his arms. She pulled her sweet mouth away. "You should answer it."

He tightened his grip on her. He ran his nose down her face, inhaled her lavender-warmed-by-the-sun scent.

"Ignore it." Please. God. Ignore it.

"Your mission." Justice shook her head. "I can't do that."

Oh. Shit. Not happening. He looked into her eyes, her endless depths, midnight-and-mystery eyes. She was serious.

She stepped back.

Fuck.

He answered the phone. It was Salma. The tremor in her voice doused the fire in his body. A tsunami would've had less impact.

"Sandesh, please, I need your help."

Chapter 18

SALMA PULLED SANDESH FROM THE TRAILER THAT SERVED as the training facility for the refugee women. He entered the connected, smaller tent filled with a gurney and medical equipment. This was where Salma, a doctor, had originally started helping refugee women.

She'd created Salma's Gems after finding medical intervention wasn't enough. That was shortly before he'd reached out to her.

Salma pushed some medical equipment out of her way and sat on a steel stool. "We have a problem. Word is spreading that we have a place here for abused women rescued from ISIS. Your funding has made it possible for us to take in many more women. I have already negotiated a larger place, one left by departing aid workers. There, the women can sleep and work, receive therapy and care."

"That's a problem? It sounds good." Not such a big deal to drag him back out here, refusing to even tell him why. "Except I don't want you being overwhelmed with requests. We're not set up for volunteers yet, and I'm worried the expansion might bring about threats."

He'd already seen the attitude of a few people, mostly men, toward the former sex slaves, and he didn't know how it would go when more women were brought in. "Do you think you can hold off for a few weeks? Until I get my volunteers here?"

Salma shook her head. "This is out of our hands now. This is blessed by God. Not a coincidence."

The woman was getting to a point, he was sure of it. "What do you mean?"

Salma grabbed her right hand with her left and squeezed. Nervous? "I have word from some friends in Syria. A large group of women, Syrian and Yazidi, were being sold to an international criminal organization."

"*Were* being sold?"

"Kurdish and resistance fighters intercepted the bus. Even now, they are hiding from their pursuers. They need a safe place to send these women. More importantly, someone with pull, with backing to bring them here."

Sandesh nodded. The pull and backing was the sudden and generous donation of Mukta Parish. It didn't matter where you went—Wall Street or a tent in Zaatari—money moved mountains. "When?"

"They are doing evasive maneuvers and plan to meet us later tonight at an abandoned village. In addition to your support, I was hoping you could help me to pick up the women. Would you be willing to drive a truck into Syria?"

He had no idea what Mukta or Justice would think about him diverting their humanitarian cause. But he'd started this charity and he wasn't going to start asking for approval now.

"Yeah. Let's get organized. But can we keep this between us? I don't know how my backers would feel about the risk."

Chapter 19

EVEN A FEW HOURS AFTER SUNRISE, THE DAY WAS SWELTER-
ing hot. In Jordan. Go figure. Didn't help that Justice
had gotten no sleep. Her hair was plastered to her skull
in thick strands of sweaty goo. Her clothes looked like
she'd been living in them for two years. Her face was
smeared with dirt.

Good thing Sandesh had gotten that call. Justice
doubted that what had been going to happen between
them would've left her much time to get into position
here.

Until the produce had arrived at dawn, she'd been
hiding in the alley, under the black bumper on the squat
loading dock. Now she hid among the produce crates
stacked outside. She had to pee. Her bladder felt like it
weighed ten pounds.

Might've been all that water she drank.

The laundry-service truck backed up to the loading
dock with a slow *bEEp*, *bEEp* tune that sounded some-
what off to her American ears.

The stench of oily exhaust mixed with the nearby
kitchen odors of cumin and bread saturated the loading dock. Justice moved farther back among the crates.
Hopefully, no one from the kitchen would choose this
moment to get the produce.

Her hands fingered the small electronic device that
would cut off the stream from the security cameras. She

only needed a minute. Not enough time to really send up a security flag.

The driver, dressed all in white, clambered onto the loading platform. He was a young man, lean. He arm-wrestled a white handle and pulled. The rumble of steel wheels against pockmarked steel treads echoed as the door slid open. The driver disappeared into the truck and strolled out a moment later, pushing a dry-cleaning rack filled with staff uniforms draped in plastic. He stopped as someone from the hotel came out with an electronic pad.

They greeted each other. They chatted. About Jordan. About the violence in Syria. About the increasing violence in Iraq. And the heat.

While they spoke, Justice pressed the device that shut off the cameras and slipped from between the crates. She crept forward. Silently, she found and unhooked the correct staff uniform, balled it up, and shoved it up under her abaya.

The driver took the e-pad, signed, and handed it back.

She slipped backward as he reached for the rack. Her foot hit the edge of a crate. She stumbled, grabbed for leverage, and knocked over a stack of peppers.

The reverberation of the crate hitting concrete faded. There was silence on the platform. The men rushed to the area, stopped, and stared at her.

To them, she must've looked like a refugee—tired, hungry, and dirty. The hotel man moved toward her. She loosed her bladder. The urine soaked her feet and the cement of the loading dock. The driver's face pinched in disgust. The hotel man jumped back and began to yell at her in Arabic.

He didn't dare come at her, for fear of the urine. She jumped down from the dock and ran down the alley, holding her clothes in place against her stomach as if she were pregnant. He yelled curses after her.

Chapter 20

A DUST-COATED MILITARY TRUCK, MEN WITH RIFLES hanging from its slat sides and a group of veiled women huddled inside, rumbled into the burned-out village.

The crumbling walls of abandoned buildings and large piles of debris dotted the landscape as the sun bowed against the blue-black edges of night and relented control of the sky. Sandesh and Salma had been here over fifteen hours. He'd mapped every inch of this place.

The truck pulled to a stop. The driver, a man in his twenties, jumped out and approached. His fellow freedom fighters kept their rifles pointed at the horizon.

Every hair on Sandesh's neck stood on end. He kept his weapon pointed down. These were the good guys. Back when the war here had started and the resistance was made up of moderate rebels—the secular Free Syrian Army trying to overthrow the brutal dictator Bashar al-Assad—he and his team had armed and taught men like these. Men who'd defected from Assad's own army, disgusted by his treatment of the Syrian people.

That was before the FSA had splintered and those with more radical views had decided Assad going wasn't enough. They wanted a strict Islamic state. That gave ISIS the opening they needed. They joined with the rebels who were of like mind. Now the FSA, which served as an umbrella name for many moderate groups, fought ISIS and Assad. And too often Assad sat back and watched his enemies destroy each other.

Of course, Assad helped in their destruction. He bombed any hospitals and schools that the FSA or ISIS relied upon. He made no distinction between the two. And maybe the world had forgotten too.

Salma spoke with the man from the truck for a brief moment. They broke off. And then the man turned to the others in the truck and began issuing orders. The truck tailgate was dropped as men jumped off and began helping women out.

Salma turned to Sandesh, "We have to hurry. The traffickers pursue them."

Sandesh went into action. He began to lead the women from the large military truck into the pickup.

He did a double take on seeing a pregnant woman. Salma saw his reaction and put a hand on his forearm. "No honor among thieves. This Yazidi girl was a favorite of an ISIS commander. His wife, a facilitator on this transaction, was jealous of her."

Sandesh's stomach soured.

He gently guided the pregnant woman to the passenger side of the truck's cab. The moment he opened the door, there were a series of clangs. Bullets hitting steel.

They were under attack.

Sandesh rushed the pregnant woman into the front seat. She was bleeding. Salma climbed in after her. He slammed the door closed.

The other women ran past him and began to climb into the truck as the soldiers provided cover fire.

He pulled his gun from his holster and moved toward the back of the truck to reinforce the other men.

"Go. Go!" one of the Kurdish soldiers yelled.

He jolted, looked into the truck filled with women. What the hell had he been doing? He told the seated women to hold on and pushed closed the heavy steel tailgate. He jogged to the driver's side, jumped into the cab, hit the gas, and took off.

Chapter 21

JUSTICE ARRIVED ON THE FOURTEENTH FLOOR SHORTLY AFTER Walid and Aamir's scheduled dinner. She wore the crisp white shirt, black vest, white gloves, and sleek tie of a maid as she walked down the hallway lined with exclusive suites.

Even if she hadn't had the room number, she'd have known the room. Two bodyguards stood outside the door.

Her heart sped up. She took in and let out a slow, controlled breath. She tried to appear harmless—just maid service here to shut the curtains and turn down the beds.

She plastered a smile on her face, grateful for the prosthetics that made her nose and chin larger. That, the change of eye color—she'd gone with Egyptian gold—and the addition of braces and wig made a decent disguise.

One of the guards waved her to stop. She noticed the bulk under his jacket. Both guards were armed. In Spanish-accented English, one asked her what she wanted.

She pointed to her mouth. She opened her mouth and showed them her braces and her damaged tongue. The men cringed.

As well they should; that bit of F/X hurt like hell. The steel wires holding down her tongue pinched her gums at the metal bracers attached to her teeth. Still, it didn't hurt as badly as her Arabic. And even if she'd known they understood English, she wouldn't have wanted to be remembered as someone who spoke English.

One of the guards commented to the other that it was "disgusting."

The other guard nodded as he patted her down, thoroughly. In some countries, probably this one, that pat down would have been enough to consider them married.

He waved toward the door. "Go."

Stepping forward, she used the key card Momma had provided.

One of the guards, touchy-feely, walked in behind her. Expected.

He called to the interior guard, and they exchanged information. The inside guard had a Russian accent. Okay. Did anyone in this country still speak Arabic? The hall guard exited.

The thin, angular interior guard watched her move across the central room, the living area. It was opulent, even by Parish standards. With thick velvet drapes that extended floor to ceiling, a large chandelier, velvet couches, a dining table, and a full bar.

She closed the drapes, found the engraved silver lighter behind the bar, and lit the candles along the dining table, then moved into the bedroom.

The guard didn't follow her but told her to leave the door open. She did.

The guard's interest flitted from her to the other bedroom and back to her. She turned down the bed, then, spotting a pair of brown shoes on the floor, she shook her head as if lamenting men and their barbarous ways. She walked the shoes into the closet.

Once inside, she reached under the wig and pulled out the slim packet that contained the poison. She handled the pod with care, though she knew it would take more than just squeezing it to open. It required something sharper.

She left the closet and slipped into the bathroom. Fiddling with her braces, she removed the metal wire. Her hands, covered with the traditional white gloves with rubber gloves underneath, began to shake.

Instinctively, she held her breath, though the poison needed to be ingested. She squeezed a small drop on the only toothbrush present. It seeped quickly into the bristles.

Now came the hard part. She palmed the wire and the packet and moved to the bedside table, careful to keep her back to the man. She finished turning down the bed.

One more.

She walked into the living area. The Russian guard now sat at the bar. He turned to her as she crossed to the other bedroom. "Be quick in there," he said. She nodded.

It wasn't until she was in the room that she realized why the guard wanted her to be quick.

The shower was on. It went off while she stood there. Justice's heart lurched forward and began to pound. The bathroom door opened. Steam wafted out along with Aamir followed by a girl with long, damp, blond hair.

Hope?

No. Not Hope. Hope was dead. And the man who had killed her, who had raped and murdered her, stood here now. Naked.

And the girl. She couldn't have been more than

twelve. She was naked too. She shook, kept her eyes down. Aamir smiled when he saw Justice, smiled as if shame and evil didn't really exist. He strutted past Justice and told the girl, who hesitated at the bathroom doorway, to get into the bed. The girl made a small, despairing sound, then obeyed.

Aamir didn't cover himself. Justice didn't move. He raised one eyebrow. He passed close enough that she could see the water droplets on his eyebrows.

In Arabic, with his creepy British accent, he said, "It's okay. We're married."

Mother. Fucker.

She grimaced. All teeth and temper.

Chapter 22

THE GLIMMERING RESTAURANT WAS DULL TO WALID. THE expensive meal, oysters heavy with cream and exotic truffles, tasted empty, like regret in his mouth. He was not proud of himself, not proud of his anger or of taking Aamir's best men out of spite.

Although spite wasn't the right word—more a need to validate, prove that, despite his dismissal, Aamir still cared for him.

It was Aamir's rejection that stung.

He'd watched Aamir, watched the way he'd folded the girl's hair over his hand, as if it were spun gold. And then noticed the distinctly annoyed tension at the corner of his brother's eyes when Walid had asked him why he was not yet ready for dinner. "I am on my honeymoon, Walid. Surely, you have some appreciation for that?"

Walid had had to stop himself from stamping his feet like a child. "We have such a short time together. There is much to discuss."

"We spent the day discussing things. We have seen to the shipment, met with the smugglers, and secured the routes."

"I had hoped to discuss the threat to us."

Amir smiled. "So your FBI man has come up with new information?"

Walid felt the sharp sting of retribution. "No. He is

working on it. But he has yet to uncover any leak in my organization."

"Then what is there to discuss? As you know, my men are closing in on the informant's digital trail and will have more in a day or so. There is nothing we can do until then."

Furious, Walid had slammed his hand against the doorway of his brother's room and stormed out. He picked up his wallet and motioned to his men—two Colombians as out of place in Jordan as giraffes on ice skates.

Aamir had followed, his eyes shrewdly evaluating Walid's guards. He'd already told Walid they were not well trained and would need to be replaced. So it shouldn't have come as a surprise, or a relief, when Aamir, as was his way, took control.

"No." He'd pointed to each of Walid's two guards. "You and you stay with me." He waved at two of his own loyal guards. "You two go with him."

Angry about being made second to a whore, Walid had refused to acknowledge his brother's kindness. He let the guards trail him.

As he'd passed out of the hotel suite doors, he'd heard Aamir tell his men, "Protect my brother as you would protect me. For if his heart were to stop beating, mine would as well."

How was it that Aamir could make him feel so unworthy of his love? And so childish?

Perhaps because he had been childish. Perhaps that's why Aamir's guards, seated at a different table, huddled together. Were they discussing him?

Walid sipped his white wine. Aamir was a man with very specific tastes and desires. He accepted it. Thought he'd accepted it. The way Aamir accepted Walid's own rough needs.

Enough. He would eat this. He would not let guilt ruin his night.

One of Aamir's guards, they were practically the same man—big and disappointed-looking with hooded eyes—came over to the table. "We have news."

Walid tossed his pronged fork onto the plate. He couldn't eat anyway. "Go on."

"The men we sent after the digital warning located the source. A man. Late forties. Early fifties."

Walid sat up. "Contact my brother."

"We've already tried. No answer." Aamir too involved with his child bride. But this was good news. Worth going back upstairs to discuss with his brother. "Have they found anything out from him?"

"He wasn't in the apartment. They found a computer there. It was tracking a GPS signal. We believe the signal is the assassin."

The assassin? "Why would you think that?"

"Because the signal is in Jordan. Here. At this hotel."

Walid stood. "Contact my guards immediately." He lurched forward and whisked through the tables, out of the hotel restaurant, and toward the elevators. His heart wailed like a siren in his chest.

Chapter 23

AN ANGRY BUZZING—LIKE AN ALARM WAKING YOU TO A hangover—built in Justice's head. It was thick with memories and pain and hatred.

"Care to join us?" Aamir grinned at Justice with his oh-so-slick smile, his can't-be-stopped surety, his nothing-you-can-do-about-it cockiness seeping from the pores of his skin that mocked Hope's life. Justice adjusted the sharp thread of metal.

Not for nothing, as Tony would say. She stepped forward. He spread his arms out. Another invitation? She had no idea. She slammed the sharp wire up and through Aamir's ribs. It pierced him like a dart. He jerked taller, as if someone had just woken him the fuck up.

Not enough. She smashed the pod into his mouth. He spit it out. But that much concentrated poison caused an instant reaction. Foam spilled from his lips as he lurched backward and fell halfway between the bedroom and bathroom. His head thudded against the marble bathroom floor with a wet slap.

Justice carefully rolled off the gloves and shoved them into the sealed pocket inside her vest.

The girl screamed. In warning. Or fear. Either way, it served as warning.

Justice pivoted and snapped a roundhouse against the guard's neck. He staggered right.

She stepped forward, fisted his shirt, and kneed him

in the balls. He tucked tail, dropped to his knees. She bent and grabbed his sidearm. Silencer. Nice. His eyes widened, hands came up. She smashed the gun against his skull, hard enough to crack sanity. His eyes rolled back. His body gave out.

The girl screamed again.

Fuck.

Justice removed her prosthetic tongue with a jerk that made her teeth hurt. In Arabic, she instructed the girl to stop screaming.

No go.

The girl, all bony knees, elbows, and long, blond hair slick against a skeletal back ran screaming into the main living area. Justice followed.

The suite door opened. One of the two exterior guards came inside unhurriedly. Little girls screaming? Just another day at the office.

He didn't draw his weapon until he came far enough into the room to see his boss's body.

Too late. Justice shot him in the head. *Crack*. He dropped like a puppet whose strings had been cut. She ran over and pretended to be helping him, using his big body as cover. The second guard entered with weapon drawn. His eyes locked on her.

She shot. Hit him in the leg. He caught himself on the doorframe, kept his gun raised. There was a crack and the *thuck* of a bullet hitting the dead guard's back, and a split-second later, the phone in dead guard's pocket began to play Ritchie Valens's "La Bamba."

How typically inappropriate.

Justice crouched lower, sighted, squeezed the trigger again.

The bullet drove into the last guard's chest. In almost a lazy, casual way—like a B-movie actor—the guard slumped against the door and slid to the floor.

Justice ran into Walid's room, then slowly approached the girl. Since Justice's Arabic sucked, a simple explanation would work best. "Women are fighting back. I am here to rescue you. I need you to get dressed. Fast."

The girl swallowed. Her blue eyes filled with tears. She spoke English. "I'm Amal. I'm the one who prayed for you to come."

––––––––

With her throat tight with panic, Justice grasped the girl's sweaty hand. Amal shook so hard the tremors in her hand felt like a mini earthquake. She squeezed tightly. Together, they moved out of the room and down the hallway.

The kid was as determined as she was scared. That made two of them. But the girl's quick responses as she'd gotten ready and listened to the plan had given Justice a little more surety. Innocence was something only unused children got to keep.

At the end of the corridor, two hotel security guards waited by the elevators. They had their weapons out, but they were already looking past Justice. Amal did and said exactly what she was supposed to. She cried out for help, waved behind her. "The men are all dead. All dead."

She began to sob. One of the hotel guards hustled Justice and the little girl behind them. He told her to stay and that others would come soon.

The two guards began down the hall. Justice knelt

before Amal, blocked her from view, met her eyes. Justice hunched closer to the girl, tried to appear weak, small, a nonthreat to the reinforcements. The elevator dinged. Her mouth went dry. Her heart prepped for takeoff.

The elevator doors opened. She angled her head to see the men from the corner of her eye.

Not reinforcements.

Walid came out followed by two guards. The men spotted hotel security advancing and began to follow them down the hall.

They didn't even register Justice and the girl. Or they had in some part of their brain that told them they were harmless.

Amal began to tremble. Her head and body leaned toward the open elevator.

Walid stood feet from them. Justice could shoot him. She could. Her gun was hidden. He was so close. But she'd risk Amal.

He followed his men down the hallway. The elevator began to close.

"Go." Amal pushed Justice toward the closing elevator. "The elevator."

Walid looked then. His eyes fell on Amal. His eyebrows rose. A few feet ahead of where he'd stopped, his guards turned too.

Justice yanked Amal by the arm and darted into the elevator, half dragging her.

The guards dove forward, dragged Walid down, covered him. One of them swung his gun toward Justice and shot. The elevator doors slid shut.

Purposely trying to mislead anyone watching the elevator numbers, Justice pressed buttons for multiple floors, but not the floor she needed. The elevator stopped. Justice and Amal walked out.

Justice picked up her pace toward the stairs. Amal followed.

Inside the stairwell, Amal didn't complain or ask a single question. But for the sound of their footsteps echoing as they ran, she was almost spookily silent. Two floors up, they exited and moved quickly down the hall.

Justice struggled to remember her training. That was bad. Training should just kick in—like coughing when you'd swallowed water incorrectly. But that wasn't happening. It might have something to do with being shot. The ache in her side. The pounding of her heart. The weight of the gun in her right hand. The fragile feel of Amal's small hand grasped within her own as Justice tugged her to keep up.

They made it to the room, and she pulled out the key card. When she'd been doing recon, she'd spent a whole day arranging a room here. Leaving her hotel down the street, changing at a restaurant, then coming here in disguise with false ID and credit cards. It had seemed overkill. Now, she was glad she'd done it.

Time wasn't on her side. They'd already be looking for her, scanning the cameras.

With a push of her hand, the room door swung open. Without a prompt, Amal slipped inside. Following, Justice closed the door and hurried to the bathroom.

The bathroom light flicked on when she entered. Wiping the blood and sweat off of her hands and onto her pants, she grabbed a towel and used it to stanch the wound on her side.

Her body was tense with adrenaline. Her mind racing. Digging the tips of her nails under the wire in her mouth, she yanked off the last piece of metal from her teeth. It gave way with a pop. She ran her tongue over her teeth, tasted blood.

Inside the hotel room, she found the suitcase she'd brought.

It contained three airtight packages and clothes, but nothing that could be tied to her. Except the locket Cooper had given her, which she quickly put over her head. With the last bit of metal pinched between her fingers, she pierced each of the three packages.

Air entered and they expanded. Amal gave a small squeak of surprise. Justice told her it was okay and pulled the plastic away. A noxious chemical smell filled the room as the sponges expanded more.

Two of the sponges in one hand, she walked to the bathroom, placed them on the sink, and stripped off her uniform. In her underwear and bra, she tore the sponges with shaking hands then tossed them, her hotel uniform including the vest, and the poison into the tub. Back at the sink, she washed her hands and hustled into the room.

The last sponge had expanded to the proper size. Good. The straps attached to this football-shaped sponge secured it to her midsection. Over this she slipped an abaya, and on her head a niqab. One pregnant Muslim. Check.

Amal watched this transformation with eyes growing larger by the minute. She probably would've been less stunned to see a car turn into a Transformer.

The suitcase she'd brought had a small pair of

scissors. They'd do. Tossing the white bedding off the plush bed, she cut a square strip from the sheet.

"Can you make this into a niqab?"

Amal held out her hands, then went into the bathroom and did a fairly good job of it. Justice straightened it a little, tucked the sides under. Not perfect. Not with that blue dress. But it would have to do.

That done, Justice grabbed a towel and wiped down any surface she might have touched, including her suitcase. Back in the bathroom, she tossed the towel in the tub.

She stroked the wheel on a lighter she'd brought and put the flame to the flammable gel padding. It went up with a *whoosh*. She threw in the lighter. The material would burn to ash quickly, so it wasn't a danger to the guests, but it would destroy the evidence and create enough smoke to set off the fire alarm.

Her heart fluttering in her chest like a bird against a cage, Justice grasped Amal's hand and kept her other hand holding the gun within the sleeve of her abaya.

She gave final instructions to Amal. "When the alarm goes off, we head out, down the stairs, and out the front door with the other people."

The fire alarm sounded.

Chapter 24

BENEATH A DULL STREETLAMP THAT LIT ONLY A SMALL section of the dirt road through Zaatari, Sandesh cleaned up the bloody strips of cloth from the planks of the truck. He tossed them into the refuse container outside Salma's headquarters.

Salma's grandson had taken the rescued women to the new, larger facility they'd finished setting up yesterday. Originally used for aid workers, it had easily morphed to fit the refugees. They'd deal with the medical and psychosocial needs tomorrow.

Reaching for the bag of weapons, he hesitated, flexed his hands. He didn't need them. With a purposeful mental shove, he walked back into the tent.

A dull light hung down from the wooden support rafter over a small gurney. Basic medical tools sat on a steel table. The tent resembled a clinic. Salma used it to give medical assistance to the women and girls. He avoided looking at the small, blue corpse atop the metal cart. A boy.

The Yazidi woman had been taken to the French hospital. Soon, an official would arrive to take the corpse.

He picked up a jug of water, poured some into the basin on a cart in the corner, and washed his hands. Blood didn't usually bother him, but the brutality of the birth and the loss of the woman's son had lodged like disease in the creases of his knuckles, the tension of his fisted hands.

Salma's skills as a doctor had saved the woman, but only because she'd been pregnant. The baby had taken the brunt of the gunshot.

Damn. Everything in him wanted to protect the softness he'd seen in that bleeding, terrified teenaged girl. But that wasn't his job. He was here to aid those who were injured, not to bring injury to others.

"You have dealt with conflict for so long, Sandesh," Salma said, "that you can't even find peace within your own mind."

Her brown eyes glistened with knowing intelligence. She was right. He nodded. "I almost told you to take the truck and leave me to fight."

Her eyebrows rose. "That would've been a problem, as I don't drive."

He laughed, but somehow that made him feel better. He wiped his hands on a towel and placed it beside the basin. "How do you do it, Salma? Work here, witness what happens, knowing you can only save the moment for someone, leaving them alive in a violent and unfair world to save all the succeeding moments for themselves?"

"What would I do differently? I heal. That is my mission. And when given the chance, I speak of healing, speak of their pain, and open others to the possibility of soothing the ache that too much anger and too many ideas of God's justice has done to our delicate minds."

Delicate minds? That seemed an oversimplification. Or was it? Was it as simple as not allowing certain beliefs to take root, make patterns in the brain that caused kneejerk reactions?

Salma's clever eyes seemed to reevaluate him as she

cleaned up the area around the gurney. "Why start this venture if you aren't willing to risk yourself?"

Risk? Did she think he regretted helping those women? "I'm not sure I understand."

"You have to risk your, uh, perhaps in English *ego* fits best?"

"Fits best for what?" God, the whole room smelled of blood.

"You are trying to change the way you see yourself. And tonight, you came face-to-face with that reinvention. Stay. Fight. Or pick the other path, the one that helps without violence. You chose a different path. You needn't beat yourself up for that. This time, it was the right choice."

A swish of the tent flap and Sandesh turned toward the opening. A pregnant woman in niqab and black abaya, holding her side, staggered into the emergency tent.

A young girl, her daughter perhaps, supported her. The girl looked at him with eyes much too old for a child and whispered, "Help."

He rushed to the woman, caught her just as she fell. He lifted her easily and carried her to the gurney. Salma moved quickly to the woman's side. "Are you in labor?"

Standing by the gurney, the girl took charge. "She's hurt. Her side. She speaks English."

The woman proved this by speaking English. "We're being followed. Please hide the girl. Amal."

Sandesh knew that voice. Justice?

Salma reacted with a speed that indicated she'd been here before. She directed the girl to hide in a steel cabinet. Amal, who couldn't even have been a teenager yet, darted into the cabinet and shut the door with a metal clang.

"Justice?" It was her. Justice, but with eyes like

honey. Contacts? What the hell? Justice had been injured. Justice had a daughter. No. That was panic speaking. "What's happening?"

"I think I'm being followed. Sort of. I don't understand. They were here when we got here."

What the hell was she talking about? Sandesh tied down the dog of war that wanted to break whoever had injured Justice. He needed to stay calm. Why would someone be following a PR hack? "Who?"

The tent flap was tossed open. Two armed men entered. They began yelling, asking who the woman on the table was.

Sandesh slipped toward the first man, preparing to disarm him so he could take down the second.

From her place at the bedside, Salma waved her bloodied hands at the men. "Get out. Can't you see that she has lost her baby?"

The men hesitated. The stillborn baby lay lifeless and purple-blue inside the metal pan.

Sandesh took her lead. "Outside, outside." He waved with his hands. "She has lost much blood and might die."

On the table, Justice began to moan. The confused men turned on their heels and left.

Sandesh waited five seconds before he glanced outside. He saw the men move away, take out a cell. They'd be back.

Salma had already pulled up Justice's abaya and located the wound. She patted Justice on the hand. "There is a piece of metal in your flesh. Not deep."

"Not a bullet?"

Salma's eyebrows rose. "A bullet? No. I am going to pull out the metal. Do you understand?"

"Yes. Quickly. Please."

He returned to the bedside. "Salma, what do you need?"

Salma looked up at him. "The men," she said. "How long?"

"Not long."

She nodded. They both understood the risk. Soon this tent would be filled with anger and accusations. Their choice was to turn Justice over to those men and keep the charity clear of the violence. Or save her.

"Quickly." Salma began to tear at the dress.

Justice put her hand on top of Salma's. "I need this dress."

Justice tugged the abaya up with one hand. Sandesh came over and helped, exposing delicate pale skin, black lace lingerie saturated with blood, and a deep gash, an inch wide, below her hip.

A slice of metal filled the wound. What the hell? And Justice had a gun? She hid it under the sleeve of her abaya while her other hand clenched the scaffolding of the bed.

Salma wiped the blood from the wound. Justice flinched. Salma had snatched up a pair of forceps. She bent close to Justice. "A tiger stalking, no sound, brave one."

Justice nodded. Digging into the skin, Salma plucked at the edge of the shrapnel, once, twice. Her face locked in concentration, Justice seemed to put herself somewhere else, like someone accustomed to dealing with pain.

The only sound from her was slow, deep breathing. Sandesh cursed to himself. What the fuck was going on? Could she be some type of operative? Salma dug in again, grasped it, twisted, then pulled it out.

Justice let out a sharp breath. Tears rolled down her cheeks. "Is it over?"

"You need stitches."

He handed Salma the alcohol, and she cleaned the wound. With steady, learned fingers, Salma sewed quick stitches.

Justice inhaled and slowly exhaled. Again and again. She did not cry out.

This was not a public relations specialist.

Outside, Sandesh could hear voices. One of the men talked on the phone.

Justice sat up. He put a hand on her shoulder and steadied her. She winced.

"Did I hurt you?"

She shook her head. She didn't meet his eyes. "No. Don't worry about me. Take care of Amal."

Salma bent under the counter and spoke with Amal. She began directing all of them in Arabic. "I will hide the girl with a family I know here. Take her." She motioned toward Justice, who had her legs under her a lot more than she should have. What kind of training had this woman been through?

"No." Justice supported her own weight. "I've risked you enough. I can get out from here. But take care of Amal. She has a family she wishes to return to. I can arrange—"

Salma waved away the words. "I will arrange it. This is what I do. But you cannot go alone."

"Sure she can," Sandesh said, his anger building. He'd been a total idiot. "This is no woman accidentally hurt. She is an operative. Her backup is probably on its way. I'll help you deal with the men she's brought here."

He shouldered Justice toward the back of the tent and steadied her. She looked haunted and vulnerable, and he wanted nothing more than to hoist her up and carry her to the nearest safe place.

No. He'd been enough of a sucker.

She wasn't what she appeared. She wasn't helpless. And she wasn't a PR specialist.

He leaned into her. "I'm going to find out who you're working for, and I'm going to have your ass."

She smiled then, wicked and full. "Flirting at a time like this, Ranger?"

She winked, ducked under the tent side, and walked confidently into the night.

Chapter 25

JUSTICE STAGGERED DOWN THE DARK DIRT LANE. *MUST NOT fall down. Must not fall down.* Ugh. This sucked.

To her ears, she breathed heavily enough to make the people in their trailers think death itself stalked the streets. Her side hurt like hell.

She staggered quickly, because she knew, even as mad as he was, Sandesh would help if he saw her vulnerability. And she needed him there for Amal and Salma.

Okay. That had to be far enough. She grasped her side and let out a breath of pain. Really, not shot?

It hurt like she'd been shot. Her skin felt like it had been twisted in a vice and sewn up with hot metal spikes. Could that just be thread?

Fuck. How did Walid's men follow her from the hotel? How did they get here *before* her? The only way was if Walid had already had men in the area, and somehow figured out she was coming here. That made no sense. Unless, someone from her family…

Could she have been betrayed? By who? She hadn't told any of her team she was coming. Unless…unless someone on her team had checked her GPS. Every family member was required to have one implanted.

Usually that information was only monitored for missions by Leland, his security team, and Momma. For this mission, only Leland and Momma had had access.

But the truth was it wouldn't have been that hard for

someone in the family to figure out how to gain access to that information. Especially since they'd had similar tech implanted in themselves.

Had someone in her family, one of her siblings, informed on her and almost gotten her killed?

If so, did the traitor care? Did the traitor hate her that much? What had she missed? *Who* had she missed?

Stop thinking about it. Focus. Let go of the failure. One of the two Brothers was dead. That meant something. Too bad the other was well and truly pissed and might have access to the GPS that would let him know exactly where to find her.

She needed to get out of this camp. This country. And then she needed to make another plan. Walid wasn't going to just give up and go away. She needed to get to him, take him out before he found her family and the school.

Chapter 26

INSIDE THE MEDICAL TENT, LIT ONLY BY A SINGLE DANGLING bulb, Salma prepared Amal for what would happen next. Meanwhile, Sandesh checked out front again. He looked down the road both ways. A few locals, but not the men who'd busted in here. Why hadn't they come back?

Salma walked over to him. "You must go after her." She pointed out the back way. "She is in need."

"No. Justice has people. I guarantee she's already with them. You need me."

She shook her head, clutched a blood-soaked rag. "These men will let me be. They will not harm a Jordanian woman, a doctor, a devoted Muslim with ties to this community. One of my sons is on his way here. He works for the government." She held up her cell phone. "Those men will not want that trouble. They want Justice."

She began to push against his chest, guiding him toward the back of the tent. He would've laughed at her pathetic attempt if it wasn't so damn frustrating.

"No." He refused to give another inch. "I am here for this. I changed my life to be here for you, for this cause, for people who want to make things better."

Salma let out a frustrated sigh. "You are a good man. But stupid. Her cause and ours are the same. No matter whom she works for or why she has done what she has done. Do you not see?"

"Salma—"

"No." She held up a hand. "When the leaves fall, you will see further. Take the advice of someone who has lived longer. Destiny isn't always the path we have chosen for ourselves. It is the one that most clearly matches the values we aspire to protect."

The crack of distant gunfire punctuated her meaning. Gunfire? Could that mean the men really weren't coming back? Could that mean they'd gone after Justice?

He stared at Salma for a wordless second. She shoved the truck keys into his hand. He kissed her on the cheek and bolted outside.

Chapter 27

CROUCHED INSIDE THE CAB OF A RUSTED TRUCK THAT, judging by its rounded grill and the holes in the floorboard, had been around since the fifties, Justice checked her ammo. Three rounds.

She was going to die.

She was going to die in a truck that smelled like goats.

She was going to die in a truck that smelled like goats on the Jordan–Syria border after failing her most important mission.

Who had betrayed her? Gracie, Tony, Dada, or Bridget? She didn't want to die without knowing. Which meant, she wasn't going to die today.

She threw out her senses, tried to hear beyond her little bit of street. There was only one way they could be tracking her. They were in direct contact with someone who knew exactly where she was. And the only way to know that was by the GPS in her wrist.

She'd take it out, but it required hands much steadier than the ones she now possessed.

Plus, kind of useless now. The group of men hunkered down outside the truck knew where she was.

Of course, they'd wait her out. Walid wanted her more than just dead. He wanted her in pain. She'd taken the one person the man actually cared about.

She knew the Brothers' story. Two boys, orphaned on the streets of India—granted they'd made themselves orphans—and afterward they'd been trafficked to a man in England. They'd killed him too and taken over his business. Together. Two brothers with equally evil souls.

Now one was dead. And the other wanted her in pain. Normally she'd think of that as a bad thing, but now it meant opportunity. When they came for her, she'd have a chance to distract, deceive, and deliver her own special brand of justice.

Shit. She was really losing it. She hated puns that involved her name.

One of the men called out to her in Arabic, "Come now. You are endangering the people here. Come out. We will take you some place to talk."

Oh. They just wanted to talk. Silly of her to think otherwise.

"How's Aamir?" she called back. "Did I break his heart?"

They began to fire at the truck.

Chapter 28

SANDESH COULDN'T ALLOW HIMSELF TO THINK OF JUSTICE IN any way but as a target that needed to be acquired. He rolled down the truck's window. She had to be close. Things were quiet here.

Most nights, men patrolled, but women and children had learned not to be outside after dark.

Tonight, with the gunshots, it seemed no one walked the dirt roads. He drove around with his lights off. The moon and some lights in the camp let him see enough.

He swung Salma's old pickup around a corner.

His heart clenched with regret. He shouldn't have let her go. He'd been so angry. And, he hated to admit, hurt. She'd lied to him. And so had Mukta.

Her mother had to know. It was the only thing that made sense. Or did it?

If Justice had people, if her mother knew, why wasn't anyone coming for her?

There. Gunshots. He drove between tents and parked. He got out, scanned the area, and crept forward.

He stuck his head around the corner of a metal trailer.

The *bam bam* of gunfire. He ducked, though the fire hadn't been directed at him. It had been directed at the rusty truck sitting twenty feet to his right.

He had no doubt Justice was in that truck.

What was it Salma had said about destiny? He could

have gotten closer to where Justice hid only if he'd been airlifted in.

Justice didn't fire back. Probably had low ammo. That might be a good thing. It was a huge city, where gunshots didn't usually bring authorities, but a firefight might draw them over.

He doubted Justice or the IPT could afford whatever exposure came from messing with the Jordanians.

Weapon drawn, he belly-crawled along sandy dirt, dug his elbows into the gritty soil.

The crunch of tires on sand drew his head up, and the flash of headlights dropped it down. The truck rolled down the dirt street. Reinforcements or the authorities? Or some gang here to clear their territory?

A spotlight came on and began to sweep the area. The authorities. The light hit the men crouched on the other side of the street. With gun in hand, someone got out of the truck and called to the men.

This was his chance. And apparently that was exactly what Justice had been thinking.

She swung out of the cab. Crouched, she darted his way. He got to his feet, held up his hands. "It's me. Me, Justice."

She pulled up short, lowered her gun. Wordlessly, they ran.

He leaned closer to her. "Salma's truck. There."

They turned the corner in sync. He jumped into the driver's seat and she into the passenger's.

He backed up. The truck with the authorities swung around the corner; the spotlight landed on them.

He turned the wheel, threw the car into drive. *Bam.* The back window erupted.

Justice jerked and looked down. Tear gas began to pour into the cab. Before he could tell her what to do, she picked up the canister and tossed it out the open window.

They both started to hack. He wiped at his nose, tilted the wheel, and swung the truck down a side street. It was nearly impossible to hide here. The whole thing was a grid.

When she held out her hand for his weapon, he passed it to her. She fired through the back window. Once. Twice.

There was a crash, and the spotlight winked out. Nice shot.

Sinuses burning, he tore down the road. His eyes strained to make out any movement.

This was a shitty place to try and escape. Penned in like a damn prisoner on all sides, where people could pop out anywhere, and the boundaries of who worked for the government and who worked for themselves were murky. So said the fact that the authorities had joined with the others and were now chasing them.

Justice bent over, clawed at her eyes, took out her contacts, and flung them away. She spit into her hands and rubbed her eyes. "We can't go out the main gate."

"No shit." He'd just rescued her ass. A little respect or "thank you" would be nice. He shook himself. Christ, he was still that guy.

With less bite but louder, since the wind whipped about them, he said, "How did you get inside?"

"Under the fence. I can show you."

"Okay. Let's ditch the car."

She nodded, slid to her window, turned, and aimed her gun. After a moment, she coughed, spit, and said, "Slow down. They're not following."

He slowed and pulled over. "Why not?"

She bit her lip near in half, then, nodding to herself, held up her wrist. "I think…I think they're pretty confident they can get me outside of this place. They're tracking me. There's a device under my skin."

She picked up a penknife lying in a cup holder, along with a small woodcarving. He grabbed her hand. "Don't. Let's think about this for a minute."

"Think about it? What's there to think about?"

He rubbed a hand across his face. Tears and snot. Beautiful. He couldn't believe he was about to say this. "Could they have ties to whoever put that thing in your arm?"

"Maybe. I think. Maybe. Someone betrayed me."

"Someone? How did it get in your arm?"

She stiffened. "I was born with it. Like an electronic birthmark."

He'd expected the lie and the sarcasm. "Okay, well, not telling me gets you nothing. And that someone might have betrayed you is not really the answer either of us is looking for. Someone *is* betraying you. Present tense. Someone is, at this moment, tracking you and reporting the information to whoever is chasing you."

She flinched. Nodded. She looked shaken for the first time. "So we destroy it. We take it out. Toss it."

"Not so fast. Let's take a guess on what would happen. If you destroyed that thing or took it out, the bad guys would go straight to the Mantua Home."

She flinched, brought a hand to her heart, clasped something under her abaya. "Suggestion?"

"We could set up an ambush."

Her eyes rose in shock. He'd actually surprised her. That shouldn't have pleased him.

"You'd do that? Help me?"

Yeah, he would. And he had no idea why. Scratch that. He had a good idea why. And it wasn't because the galaxies in her eyes held him as surely as the universe holds the sky. But because that girl she'd brought into the tent had been rescued. Justice and whatever she was into weren't self-serving. It was a small comfort. But he'd take it.

"This one time, Justice. Then we go somewhere quiet and you answer every question I have." He brushed his hand along her wrist. "Including how you got this."

Her eyes, which had softened with his touch, narrowed.

She was going to fight him on this? Really? Chick had teeth. He was her only fucking lifeline here. "I could walk away, Justice. And you can avoid these men. Until they follow you home."

Her eyes widened—which is to say they swallowed him whole—and then her rich lashes lowered. "Come on. I'll show you the way out."

Chapter 29

OUTSIDE ZAATARI, AT THE START OF A LONG ROAD THAT connected the refugee camp with the desert, Justice found another truck. It probably belonged to the Koreans. They had a tae kwon do academy set up a short distance from here.

So many people had been drawn here to help. Like Sandesh. She hoped he could still help these people. She'd do whatever she could to make this right.

Removing her niqab, she used it to cover the butt of her gun. She was about to smash the window when Sandesh cleared his throat. She glanced back. He mimed trying the door. She did. It opened.

Huh. Trusting sort, those Koreans.

Sandesh had a big, not-my-first-rodeo grin on his face. Cocky. She dropped inside the vehicle and began to hot-wire it.

She sensed more than saw Sandesh reach inside, flick down the visor. A jingle, and keys dropped onto her hip, tumbled to the floor. She picked them up and refused to look in his direction. She could hear him smiling.

She put the keys in the ignition. She fully expected the car not to start. It started.

Really? They deserved to have their vehicle stolen. Sandesh tossed the large, black bag with whatever weapons he'd brought into the back seat, then started toward the passenger side.

No way. She couldn't shoot if she was driving.

She waved him back to the driver's side. Without objection, he reversed course. She climbed into the passenger seat, and he slid inside and began to drive toward Syria.

The truck's headlights cut through the night like cones of yellow glass. The road was deserted. Not much call for traffic into Syria from Jordan these days, especially this late.

Except for the wind whining through the old weather strip, it was as quiet as a tomb in the car. Justice didn't need a whole lot of empathy to feel the fury that rocketed off Sandesh. Even in the dim light, she could see his hands clutch the steering wheel. Yeah, the road was bumpy, but not that bumpy.

She wasn't sure she wanted to know what he was thinking. He kept randomly hitting the steering wheel.

Anger at her seemed like it might be a good bonding experience between Tony and Sandesh. Note to self: Make sure that conversation never happens.

He probably expected an explanation. And the thing was, she really wanted to explain things. Unusual for her in many ways. First: She was brought up in a secret society of vigilantes. Not an open group. Second: She didn't do relationships.

She bit the inside of her cheek. Something had to be said to fill the silence. Well, if he was anything like Tony, she knew how to get him to talk. "Stop pouting."

He waited a beat or two. "Pouting? No, Justice. You don't get to put this on me. I want an explanation. What are you doing here? Who were those men? Why were they after you?"

"I can't answer those questions."

Sandesh swung the car to the side of the road. She slid along the seat. Her wound shot off hot protestations. He threw the car into park. Plumes of gray dust mushroomed over light streaks from the headlights.

He turned in his seat. His blue eyes stabbed her with ice and steel and accusation.

"Actually, you have no choice. Says the only guy who can get you out of this desert alive. I need to know what I'm up against."

Whoa. He was playing a dangerous game of chicken. If they were going to implement their plan, they needed to keep moving. She shifted, rolled her shoulders. The vast cold of the desert night quickly seeped into the truck. Sandesh kept staring. He really wasn't going to budge. She shivered. "Drive. I'll tell you what I can."

He turned in his seat, shifted into drive, and kicked up sand as he accelerated onto the road. Justice listened to the wheels eating up ground.

"Let's hear it, Justice."

Oh hell. "I do what Salma does. Sort of."

"Sort of?"

Her chest ached like someone had taken a scalpel and cut strips called loyalty from her heart. "Well, she goes after the girls who are being lured or sold or tricked into sex slavery. I go after the men who are doing the luring, tricking, and selling."

In this instance, anyway. The League was just as likely to go after men who stoned women, burned them with acid, beat them, gang-raped them. Wherever society let bad things happen to women, the League was there. No need to tell him that.

He breathed out a sound that was part curse. "She saves girls. You aren't saving these men."

"No. I'm saving many girls and women by killing the men."

He tapped the steering wheel. She wasn't sure if she saw disgust or curiosity on his face or maybe something more complicated.

"Your mother obviously knows. Is this what she does? Is this why she covers her face?"

"No. She was a teenager, a preteen really, burned by acid. That man picked the wrong girl to attack."

"I read she was adopted by two wealthy women. Brought to America. It would seem the happy end to a sad beginning, but she wasn't satisfied. Was she?"

So not going to answer that. Subject change. "The men who chased us work for a sex-slaver called Walid. Earlier tonight, or I guess that was yesterday now, I killed his brother. Wish I'd gotten them both. The way they run their business. Stupid. It really is get the head of the snake and the rest collapses. I would've gotten away clean but for the girl."

The sound of the tires spinning against the road filled the cab as they lapsed into silence.

"I wondered why your mother would fund my charity."

Dude was like a dog with a bone. No matter how she tried to steer things away from Momma, he went back there.

"A start-up with no reputation. Obviously, that's

exactly what she needed. Give them money, use them, control them. And I played right into it. Idiot."

Now she knew he was disgusted. With himself. She hated that she'd used him. She didn't want him to be this angry. To feel suckered.

She glanced at the side-view mirror, at the darkness behind them. "Remember what I told you on the plane about Hope?"

A long pause. "Yeah."

"The man I killed tonight. He killed Hope."

Silence. She could practically hear him realize what happened tonight was very personal. A lifetime of plotting, planning, and pain. "You're seeking revenge."

"No. I'm seeking redemption." She wanted to call it justice but wouldn't. "So if you think about it, our goals aren't really that dissimilar. You kind of want redemption for a military life."

Sandesh scratched roughly at the back of his head, clearly annoyed. "Redemption? No. Redemption indicates I thought what I did in the military was wrong. I didn't. I don't. And I don't expect you to understand right now. You're in the thick of it. But the kind of anger you have, the kind of anger I had, it doesn't just go away when you take off the uniform or put down the gun."

Justice leaned back and tilted her head toward him. She was so tired. "What do you mean? You've never struck me as too angry."

"Trust me, if we had met a few years ago, it would've been one hell of an explosion. Because when I first left Special Forces, I had an excess of anger."

He did? She knew the feeling. "I know that excess. I use it."

"Sure. I get that too. As a Ranger, I had a place to direct it, a need to direct it, stoke it, but when I got out… it became wild. Everyday normal encounters would escalate. I'd find a way to fight my way through. Even if it was some dude trying to bring twenty items through the ten-items-or-less aisle."

Justice thought about her day-to-day. How she yelled at people, her sisters, Momma, Leland. She fought a lot too. "Sometimes you have to fight."

"Sure. And I know there's a place where you can't give an inch to the enemy. I've stood on that line. I've defended that ground, refused that inch, with every ounce of strength and courage and determination I possess. But once I no longer had to do that, I ended up trying to fight my way out of anger."

"Can you fight your way out of anger? Is there an end?"

He looked over at her, must've read the sincerity in her face, because he shook his head. "No. I got out of it the opposite way."

She waited for him to expand.

"A few months after leaving the service, my friend, the guy who'd eventually help me start the IPT, Victor Fuentes, asked me to go down to Louisiana and help in his childhood neighborhood. They'd been hit by a hurricane.

"From the moment I had boots on the ground, I felt useful. It was kind of amazing, seeing so many people with no idea what to do. But we were soldiers, we knew how to organize, keep calm, work in tough situations. I helped for weeks. Never once did I feel rage.

"That's when I realized that part of me, the boy who'd tried to save the life of a dying bird, who thought that being a hero didn't mean crossing lines, needed…" He paused for a moment. He released a breath and maybe some anger. "Does it make sense to you if I said he needed air?"

Oh. Man. Yeah. It made perfect sense. Her childhood self, the one that had stood by helplessly, needed air too. "Yeah. It makes sense. But that's exactly what my anger needed, what Hope was denied: air. It was choking me."

"And that's your choice. I'm not judging. But I'm done with that chapter. I'm done walking through each day with my hands balled in fists. I'm done questioning when the violence I did helped, when it hurt, when it made a difference, when it fucked things up, fucked me up, saved people, or let people down. I'm done with that." He paused. "Or I thought I was."

He didn't say it accusingly, didn't even glance her way, but Justice felt remorse like a hot brand against her chest.

She wanted to tell him that she'd do everything to make it right and get him back to where he should be. But she thought the promise would sound hollow. And that wasn't how it felt to her. "I'm so sorry, Sandesh."

He looked over at her. Something in him seemed to soften. "Do you feel better now? Less angry?"

If he had said it with an ounce of sarcasm, she wouldn't have answered, but he hadn't. He was sincerely interested. Which made her think about the question.

A cold chill worked its way up her back. "No." She placed her head against the window. "But I've never been this tired before."

Her body gave out in a rush. She was so damn tired, but she heard Sandesh whisper as sleep overcame her, "It's the adrenaline backfire. Murder does that."

Chapter 30

THE ABANDONED VILLAGE IN SYRIA WAS MORE RUINS THAN town. Crumbling structures of stone so deteriorated they seemed to be dissolving into sand.

The truck rocked and jolted as Sandesh maneuvered it inside the remains of a bombed-out building that had only three sides. He parked with the truck's grill pointed out the open back, making it easier to start up and get going.

The building provided some cover but did nothing for the cold. Downright chilly. After they'd arrived and prepared the area, Sandesh had announced he'd keep watch. So Justice had curled up in the back of the truck to try and get some sleep.

But it was too damn cold to sleep. She sat up in the back seat. Pain tapped and jerked muscles in her side. She'd thought it hurt last night. Turned out that was just the opening act. She climbed out of the truck cab. Stretched. Ouch.

Stationed in a high stone window in the front wall, Sandesh scanned the darkness with night vision goggles.

This was the big test. If Walid's thugs showed up, it could only be because they'd followed her GPS.

She and Sandesh would fight as hard as they could against any danger that showed up, but nothing could stop the pain of knowing one of her beloved siblings had betrayed her. And wanted her dead.

She moved around the front of the truck and over to Sandesh. Stiffness locked his shoulders at her approach. She hadn't been going for stealth, but she was still impressed with his awareness.

He turned to her. She handed him up a water bottle. "I can watch if you want to get some rest."

He drank, wiped his chin with the back of his hand, handed the bottle back. "I'll sleep when we're in Israel."

She took the bottle without challenging his statement. She could feel the storm of determination he built with every passing hour. He wanted what she wanted. To end this here. Tonight.

Walking away, she checked the bandage on her wrist where Sandesh had taken out the tracker. No matter what happened tonight, these men wouldn't be able to follow her farther than this village. Sandesh had some skill. Her wrist didn't hurt near as bad as her damn side. Not shot? Really?

They'd left the tracker in a building across from them. Though she doubted they'd be able to pinpoint exactly which building—or maybe they could; the cell service here was surprisingly good, and that building was the logical place for people to hide. It was the most intact.

"Justice?"

She felt his voice in her body, a hook that seemed to latch on to her, pull her toward him. She looked over her shoulder.

"Can I ask you to take that off?"

Her eyes must've widened, because he smiled. She didn't even have the heart to flirt. She tugged at the abaya. She'd forgotten she'd had it on. "I don't have anything else to wear."

He shifted against the window, and small rocks tumbled down. He lifted himself onto the balls of his feet, rifle across his lap, reached down, and brushed stones from under his fine ass. "Check the side pocket of the weapons bag. There are clothes. And a bulletproof vest."

She shook her head. "You wear the vest."

"No. You'll be the one out in the open. Put it on."

She didn't bother to argue. His tone said it would be useless. She hated that tone.

She wobbled back across the rocks and demolished concrete. Her ankles twisted in her rubber-soled shoes, and she righted herself with a quick step.

Back at the truck, she opened the door—they'd disabled the light inside, so it stayed dark. She lifted off the abaya and pushed it into the back seat. She groped around and pulled out the weapons bag with a jerk. Her stitched side yelped in protest. She sucked in a breath.

Sandesh's head whipped toward her. Without even seeing him, she could tell he watched her scantily clad ass through his night vision goggles. When she'd hauled the bag into the back of the truck, she heard him turn back to his job.

She took out and put on a too-big shirt and rolled the sleeves up as tight as fists. Over the top of that, she added the bulletproof vest, then slipped on the much-too-big pants. She rolled the pants at the ankles and then folded them twice over at the waist. She took the KA-BAR combat knife from the bag. Whoever had packed the bag had thought ahead. She cut a series of holes underneath the rolled-up waist.

When she was done—grateful she hadn't stabbed herself by the yellow moonlight—she used the knife to tear a strip off her head scarf, then threaded the strip through the holes she'd created.

She tied the strip tightly, making the pants snug enough that she'd be able to run without them falling off. Then she made sure her beggars-can't-be-choosers Glock 20—hello, future carpal tunnel—had a full clip.

She heard the movement on the road a split-second before Sandesh's warning. "They're coming."

She'd expected it. Of course, she'd expected it. So why did it hurt so badly? Why did it feel like one of her siblings had just stabbed her in the back?

Lights from the approaching vehicle bounced between the gaps of stone. She ducked around the truck. Sandesh slid from the window. He held up two fingers. Two cars.

She crept forward and crouched beside him. They watched the scene through broken gaps in the wall.

The cars slid to a stop, one behind the other. The first blocking the second from their sight line. That made things difficult.

The four men in the first car exited and went toward the building. The men in the second—impossible to tell how many—stayed put. Cautious fuckers.

Justice leaned toward Sandesh. He smelled like action, as if the molecules under his skin had bounced off each other, flung outward, and coated the air in an excited combination of sweat and intent.

She flicked her head to the side. He nodded.

Taking a breath, she slipped away, past the truck, out and around the building. Outside, she crouched, kept to the path she'd cleared earlier. She stopped by a mountain of debris that dammed the entire street. The barricade had been erected at some point in this country's sad history.

She gave Walid's men time to get deep into the building. Controlling her breath, she took out Sandesh's cell and punched the number. They'd rigged her burner phone to the explosives they'd found.

That was the good thing about being in a war zone: abandoned ordinance. This place had a small stockpile.

Something was wrong. She held her breath, put in the number again. *Come on*. Nothing. *Okay. Stay calm. Backup plan*.

As she ducked down, her heart refused calm like a bull refusing a rider. She sprinted forward and wove down the barrier of blasted cement and stone.

Her feet teetered over rocks and debris. She kept her balance only because she'd practiced the route. Once across the street, she paused. Sweat rolled into her eyes.

The second car was diagonal to her position. They had their front windows down. One of the men inside the car used what was probably night vision to scan the remains of the building Sandesh hid inside.

Two of the men who'd gotten out of the first car watched the rigged building. How many had gone inside?

Shit. Not enough.

Snake-on-a-hot-road fast, she scurried to the wired building. Swiping the sweat from her eyes, she crouched so her back—and this so didn't feel right—was to the men in the cars. Fingers shaking, she pulled out the lighter Sandesh had given her. Her heart squawked and clucked like a chicken sensing a fox.

She jammed her hand into the fire hole she'd made.

It was deep, but she still covered the area with her hand and her body.

Her hand shook as the small, orange light met the sharp point of the fuse. The fuse hissed and spit.

Rolling away, she looked around the side of the building. She heard the men talking, heard them say something about checking the side of the building. One of them came toward her position.

She broke cover, firing, because it was a short fuse, and things were going to explode.

Her eyes tracked poorly in the dark, but she kept firing until she made the relative safety of the barrier. She skidded down behind it, then loped forward like a spastic hairy Muppet. Hotfooting it over the rocks, her ankles screaming with each unexpected loss of balance.

Gunshots hit the top of the debris barrier. It erupted in tiny explosions of sand, grit, and powdered stone. Bits of stone pelted her.

From his place, she heard Sandesh return fire. The gunfire above her ceased, but she heard a car start up. Rev.

Fuck.

Blow up, already!

The explosives detonated.

A plume of smoke and dust and an ominous moan, like from an ancient warrior who'd taken one too many arrows. She hit the ground. A wave of heat pounced over the barrier, bringing a hot spray of gravel that clawed at any exposed skin.

Dust and grit steamrolled the air, embedded into every pore, coated her lashes, rushed into her throat, and clung to her esophagus. She coughed and hacked and crawled forward. Blind. Blinking. Eyes tearing. Her ears rang. Her head spun.

Smoke and gray dust meshed with the air, keeping her from seeing the headlights until they crashed over the barrier and nearly on top of her.

Gravel and debris landsliding down. She pinched her eyes shut, then cracked one eye open enough to see the wheels of the car spinning. The car rocked at the top of the barrier, vacillating like a seesaw, front wheels beating against air. Two blurry shapes flung themselves out.

She pointed her gun. Shooting with one squinty eye. She heard bullets hitting metal. She fired again as she ran.

Chapter 31

CROUCHED BY THE SMALL SNIPER HOLE, SANDESH FIRED AT one of the two men who'd flung themselves from the car. He hit him in the gut. The guy tumbled down the barrier. The other guy dove back behind the car.

Damn. His sight line was blocked. He kept up cover fire, shooting at the car to keep the man down.

A spray of bullets hit near his hole, and he flung himself backward.

Justice tore from around the building, motioned to him, and climbed into the truck cab. He put the tip of his rifle through the cement wall and fired to disguise the truck starting.

He ran, threw himself into the driver's side of the truck, hit the gas, and sped forward while breaking the bad news. "Five. Likely six left."

She shook her head. "No fucking way. I killed more than that."

She wasn't lacking in the self-confidence department.

The moment the front of the truck came around the building, they took fire. Bullets ricocheted and dinged into the steel hull. He jammed the gas.

"Left, hard left," Justice shouted.

He spun the wheel. She turned, aimed, shot. *Boom, boom, boom.* "Got one."

Got who? A shot like that, in motion, no way. He

floored it down the street, dodged a chunk of concrete. The second car came out of nowhere.

Sandesh banked. Justice had her arm hooked around the headrest as she took out the pin on a grenade, leaned out, and tossed it wild-thing style.

Ba-boom. He gripped the wheel. The truck jerked forward. Through his rearview, he spotted the car lit by orange flames.

He looked over at her. "You hit them."

She leaned back against the seat, black eyes slick with velvet confidence. "They weren't that far away."

Chapter 32

SEATED AT THE DESK WITHIN HIS MEXICAN COMPOUND, Walid clicked off his phone. The ache in his lower back—which had started at the hotel when he'd been flung down to avoid the assassin—screamed. And outside, the rain came down in buckets. Thunder cracked against the sky. Lightning painted the mountains with white streaks.

Walid needed a voice like thunder, needed to shake the world from its axis.

Whoever was behind his brother's murder had sent a woman.

A woman.

It would not stand. For this woman's actions, many other women would suffer. He would dedicate his life to putting them in their place. To overturning the imbalance. The awful imbalance where a great man, with vision and courage and beauty, could be destroyed by a creature that history knew aligned with snakes.

He slammed his fist on his desk again and again and again. Pens shifted. The computer password screen flashed on. His phone bounced along the blotter. His back barked with pain.

He welcomed the pain. The anger. He needed his rage to distract him. He would grieve later. After everyone responsible, especially the one most responsible for his brother's death, were brought to him.

A knock sounded against his door.

Walid adjusted himself in his seat. "Enter."

Dusty, former FBI and his current right-hand man, walked into the office. Typically American, he wore a baseball cap emblazoned with *USA*. He was a big, broad-shouldered man with a confident stride and an almost brutally handsome face under a field of wavy brown hair.

Despite his casual smile and the lilt of his Southern accent, Dusty was a complete professional, a man who inspired loyalty from his men. A skill Walid had treasured along with his many other skills.

Dusty nodded as he came forward. "These new guys you've brought in are a real pain in the ass."

Walid's eyes swept over Dusty and the two "pain in the ass" men who had searched Dusty and followed him inside. Aamir's men, the very ones who'd saved Walid. Men so devoted to his brother that their loyalty had passed to Walid like an inheritance.

So the American thought of the addition of the men as an insult. Good.

It had been Dusty's men, the ones he'd hired, who'd allowed the assassin to enter Aamir's suite. If he had the energy, he'd explain to Dusty how lucky he was to be alive.

"What word do you have of my brother's killer?"

"The supplier in Jordan has tracked the stolen product back to a charity at a refugee camp. The same one that sewed up our assassin. It's run by a Jordanian woman, a doctor. She has ties to an American charity run by a soldier, former Special Forces."

This pierced the rage-armor, but only for a moment.

"Name?"

"Sandesh Ross."

Walid leaned forward. His back complained. "Are you saying this man, this Special Forces soldier, uses a charity to funnel women? Could he be the one who sent the original warning to us, who told us to come to Jordan?"

Had they walked into a trap?

Dusty tipped back his baseball hat. "We don't know that. We don't know what the woman, Salma, knows. She's shut down operations. And he's disappeared."

"She knows something, if these women have scattered like roaches. She could tell you who has taken my brother's"—he almost choked on the word—"wife."

"Probably." Dusty cursed. "We'll find out. Just give us some time on that."

Walid's head snapped up. He could barely contain his rage. But he kept his voice very soft. "We do not know where the stolen women went. We do not know who sent us the warning. We do not know what role this Special Forces man played. We do not know who the leak is among your men. Enough. I need answers."

Dusty rolled his shoulders. His expression said he was fighting hard to stay in control. "It has to be someone outside of camp personnel. Someone not directly tied to us. There is no other explanation."

Walid considered, seriously considered, killing Dusty. But. No. He still needed the man. Dusty was the one who had the loyalty of the men here. And until Walid could focus his attention away from his brother's killer, he needed Dusty.

"I think it's time we assign this task to another." He motioned to Aamir's man. The man nodded. And Walid felt mollified by the instant agreement and by the way Dusty took obvious affront. To drive home the point of his demotion, Walid directed Dusty, "Take the guard down to the cellar. The one who let the assassin into Aamir's room. I want to see what he remembers."

Chapter 33

JUSTICE SAT ON THE EDGE OF THE LUMPY BED, CROSSING AND uncrossing her legs as she kept the recently acquired burner cell pressed to her ear. The headache-inducing scent of overly bleached sheets didn't help her nerves. She couldn't even pace inside the claustrophobic Israeli hotel room.

But she was safe. Sandesh's partner, Victor, had a contact that had gotten them over King Hussein Bridge and into the West Bank. He'd given them food and water and even clothes.

Well, he'd done his best. She currently wore men's white boxers and a T-shirt. This wasn't exactly the Ritz. The sound of Sandesh in the pipe-rattling shower nearly drowned out Momma's voice. "Justice, I need to know what you've told this young man."

"He knows nothing about the League." She swallowed what felt like a lie. He didn't know about the League, but he wasn't an idiot.

Momma made a stern tsking sound. "M-erasure is painless. Harmless. And in this case, we only need to alter his memory very slightly. Not removing actual events, but shifting only those moments of heavy suspicion and distrust, where he suspected you and our operation. When he thinks of it, he will dismiss his suspicions and be reassured it was the price of doing business in the area. Nothing more."

Harmless? Really? Momma would see it that way. But just because you employed and trained some of the greatest scientists in the world, women who could not only implant memories but erase them, didn't mean you should use that power.

Not on Sandesh. But she'd deal with that threat once she got back home. "Did you take care of security at the school?"

"Of course, I increased it. But we already have the best security of any school in the world."

Momma. She didn't mess around. "How long until you arrange to get me out of here?"

"A few days. I'm working on covering up your abrupt departure."

"Am I a suspect?"

"No. You did good going to Zaatari. There is no one to connect Justice Parish with what happened at the hotel."

"And Salma? Is everything still okay there?"

"Yes. Sandesh has taken care of her. He mobilized his volunteers at a speed that I envy."

Justice had to agree. Sandesh and his IPT cofounder, Victor, actually managed to locate and organize two former soldiers fighting with the Kurds. Even now, they were protecting Salma and the women she'd rescued in a secure location while they waited for the volunteers from the States to arrive in Jordan. And he'd done it while keeping Justice's secret.

Which is why she wasn't giving Momma anything on Sandesh. She owed him her life.

The running shower switched off. "Okay. Thanks for all your help. Got to go. Love you."

"Love you, Daughter."

Justice listened to Sandesh moving in the bathroom. She could hear him grab a towel and dry off. There had been only one towel, so he was using the one she'd used.

She couldn't help smiling at the idea of him wiping himself down with a towel that had been against her body. She tried not to imagine him all sexy, wet, and naked. Whoops. Too late.

Crossing her legs again, hair still damp from her own shower, she familiarized herself with the threads of red and brown in the hotel room's carpet. Things were getting crazy.

Even though Amal was safe, Salma had had to close up shop. Damn. She never should've involved Sandesh and Salma. In one fell swoop, she'd crippled a charity that had been doing a lot of good, turned an honorable man into a fugitive, and brought attention to the League they couldn't afford.

Ugh. Don't think about that. Or about those women Salma's charity helped, so eager to learn, so excited and joyful despite the pain and uncertainty of their lives.

She rolled onto her side, stared at the closed shower door, and tucked her legs into a fetal position. She had to remember she'd killed Aamir. She'd done it.

So why did she feel like such shit?

She'd thought once the man who'd killed Hope was dead, she'd feel better. Something like relief. Something like she'd earned the sacrifice of Hope's life.

But now the pain of losing Hope had only been added to by the regret of destroying Salma's and Sandesh's good work and putting her family in danger.

The bathroom door opened. Sandesh walked into the

room, bringing the smell of hotel soap and warm steam. He wore only boxers and had the abs and pecs of a man who needed no help getting laid. Damn. He worked out.

He stopped on seeing her checking him out. A grin spread across his face. "'Shall I compare thee to a summer's day? Thou art more lovely.'"

He'd left out the "more temperate" part of that line. She smiled, very much aware that her white cotton undies and tee did little to cover her. "So in addition to being smoking hot in boxers and providing expert cover fire, you also recite Shakespeare. Guess that's not something you learned in the military."

He walked to the bed. His eyes jumped along her body, caught the curve of her hip, followed it up. He shook his head. "As a kid, my mom read poetry and Shakespeare to me."

His mother. Justice had heard him call to check on her a short time ago. "Was she okay when you called?"

"She's doing the same. My partner at the IPT, Victor, goes over nearly every night and reads Shakespeare to her while she eats dinner. He says sometimes she likes it."

"Victor of the many contacts sounds like a good guy."

"He is. Most of the time." That last seemed almost like a warning. His eyes, which had wandered again down her body, traveled back up to her face. "He would like you."

"What about you? Do you still like me?"

He sat on the bed. It dipped with his weight. He was close enough that she could feel the moisture and heat on his skin, see the sky-blue of his eyes grow serious, detect a subtle tightening along his sharp, kissable jaw. That couldn't be good.

He put one arm back, supporting himself with his hand. "You're a vigilante. And you've started a war."

Okay. They were going there.

She raised herself up on one hand, so they were eye level. "No. Men started the war. I'm just defending my sisters."

"Men? Not me. I didn't start this war. You dragged me into it."

He had her there. "But you're a good man; why not fight bad ones?"

His lips pressed together then relaxed. "Because I've tried that way. Tried it until I didn't recognize myself. And that's not my job anymore. There has to be more than that, Justice. That can't be my only choice."

He was right. Her eyes charted the muscles in his forearms, the length of his fingers, the spread of his hand. Strong and gentle. "What made you decide to do this, start a charity? Was it just that experience you had helping Victor? Was it your mom?"

He stiffened, started to get up. She put a hand on his thigh. It was muscle and tension. He looked at her. Spent a long moment staring into her eyes.

He ran a thumb along her brows, across the edge of her eyes. He whispered, "Your eyes…endless."

He dropped his hand. "Partly that. But my mom getting early-onset Alzheimer's made me realize I wanted to create more good memories. I saw what the bad memories did to her. The terror of an abusive relationship she escaped too late, one that is now part of her waking nightmare. But it was also…my own nightmare."

"The one from the plane?"

He nodded. She waited, didn't want to ask him to share. He had to know she'd listen if he wanted to tell her.

"You have your own shit, Justice. You don't need to carry mine around too."

What? That's why he hadn't told her? "So what? I burdened you when I told you about Hope."

He startled, as if he hadn't thought of it that way before. Men. Sometimes they got such a bad deal. Don't share. Be tough. Sheesh. He took another moment and then said, "I was on a mission in Syria."

"Not Iraq?"

"We went all over the Middle East. This was the end of my tour. Before things in Syria imploded. We were training the FSA."

"FSA? Free Syrian Army? The good guys, right?"

"They weren't the good guys, but a whole lot better than the Syrian president, Assad. Trainees usually met us in Qatar, but we'd been sent into Syria. We were close by when Assad dropped a barrel bomb filled with chemicals on the local girls' school."

He scratched hard behind his ear, as if digging out a memory. "Someone had a hose out trying to wash the girls. The kids were screaming. Frantic. A young girl came running at me. I mean directly at me. She'd been stripped of skin and clothes. I didn't even think. I just picked her up. Her skin sloughed off in my hands."

Justice's stomach turned over. "Oh God."

"Yeah. I didn't know what to do. Nearly vomited. One of my team had called for an extraction earlier. He alerted me to the helo. I started to walk toward the LZ. Thought I could get her to safety. I was so tense with anger I could feel it harden my veins. The kid was shaking like a leaf in my arms. But she reached up to me. The bones…the little bones in her hand visible." He rubbed at his eyes. "Before she died, she said, 'Poppa, don't be angry. There is more.'"

More. More than violence. More than pain. He was looking for the pot at the end of the rainbow. Maybe not something clean, but a way to feel something other than anger. And didn't he deserve that? Didn't he deserve the other side of the coin? He'd fought enough.

Something in Justice's chest, a kind of hopeful ache, moved forward as if seeking him.

"What did it mean when she said that? The more part?"

"It could've meant nothing to me. And in that moment, it should've. But I knew exactly what she meant. She was telling me that as total and awful and fucked up as that moment was, it wasn't all there was to life. She was telling me to keep going. Reminding me my life wouldn't end that day. For me, there would be a lot more than the moment of violence that ended her life, even more than the violence I'd participated in.

"And she was telling me it was okay for me to have that more. So now, I'm trying to make my more be a way to help others, kids like her."

Aw, hell. She rose to her knees. "I'm sorry, Sandesh. Sorry I dragged you into this. I'm going to make this right. I promise."

She ran a hand along his jaw. He'd shaved. It was smooth and still damp. She kissed him there, sucked the moisture. His breath caught. It smelled minty, like toothpaste. She kissed the side of his lips.

He sat deadly still. But he wanted her. So said the

hardness expanding his boxers. She kissed his jawline until she met that soft place below his ear. She licked.

"Justice." He sighed her name. A plea. A prayer. A promise.

She swept her tongue inside his ear and breathed a sultry sigh. "Sandesh."

He moaned, a sound so hot it could have burned away walls. He turned his head toward her. "Justice."

The invitation was there. She took it, put a hand around his neck, tugged him forward, and leaned back.

He rolled so she was solidly under him. He rubbed his hard cock against her already-wet core. His eyes searched hers for an answer.

She arched, letting him know with the rise of her body that she needed and wanted this. And even though every signal told him to proceed, she still knew he'd ask.

He closed his eyes. His breath heavy. His body pressed so intimately she could feel the pulse in his cock. "Justice, let's share details. I'm clean. Had a whole workup before I left the States. I don't have a condom. So?"

He battled his own need as she writhed under him. Damn, his control was the hottest thing she'd ever seen.

And that shouldn't seem like an opportunity, but it did. She gripped his ass and made soft pleading sounds. He shook his head. He tried to lift off her. She put her arms around his waist, held him.

He closed his eyes. "One of us has to think here, and it's getting really difficult for me to think with you rocking under me."

She put her palm against his face, waited for him to look at her. He did. He stared at her like it would cause pain to look away.

"I'm clean. Tested regularly. And the GPS isn't the only thing implanted. I'm on the pill. Long-term. But I don't want you to stop thinking. I want you to think. Be aware of this moment, with me. Feel it with me. Don't let go of this day, this room, us. Stop talking. Be with me. Please."

She kissed him on the lips, drawing it out, sweeping her tongue into his mouth. She probed their slick, soft connection with gentle eagerness, then a teasing softness, then a raging, wild desire.

He responded in kind.

She wanted to shout with the pure, electric joy of him against her. The exploration of their tongues and hands—filled with heat, igniting every inch.

Skin. She needed… She pulled at his boxers. "Off."

They stripped. The seconds of separation felt like an eternity. They reunited hot skin against hot, smooth skin. Glorious. She was wet and crazed with the need to have him inside her.

She reached for his cock. "Please."

He smiled against her mouth as he pushed himself against her hand. She whimpered.

"I want to taste you."

Oh. Okay.

He kissed his way down, sucked her breasts, her stomach, moved to her center. She arched expectantly as he brought his lips around her clit, sucked and licked and stroked. Her head fell back.

His tongue danced along her edges, dipped inside her, stroked her clit until she lost her mind. She threaded her hands into his hair, pressed herself against him.

The pressure built. She could feel the orgasm so

tantalizingly close. She wanted him. She needed him. Inside. She grabbed for him, pulled at his broad shoulders. "I want to come around your cock."

He growled. Approval. Need. He shifted over her, his cock between her legs. He lowered his head, kissed along her cheek. Pushed inside her.

She cried out. He filled her, hot and dense, the most perfect feeling ever.

He thrust. Deep. Oh. Better. So…much…better.

He began to thrust and retreat, deep then shallow, deep then shallow. She rocked her hips, kept pace, made desperate sounds of want and need and please-don't-stop.

He responded, thrusting harder. Faster. And she was thanking him and moaning and pumping her hips to meet the slam of his thick cock. The orgasm tensed her core, tighter, tighter, impossibly so. Then it broke open. Tremors released and pounded over and through her.

"Sandy, yes. Yes. Don't stop."

She tossed her head. Waves of shuttering vibrations kept her moving, grinding. So good. She was distantly aware that he watched her, drank in her writhing curves, slick with sweat.

She slowed her frantic pace. Her body melted as her nerves celebrated the last little shocks and tremors.

He kissed her lips, teased her mouth open as he put his hands under her ass, scooped her up, and slid his knees under her. He draped her legs one and then the other against his chest. Her ankles up by his ears. The elevated position gave him better access. And her less control.

"Justice. Watching you come is the sexiest thing I've ever seen."

He plunged thick and heavy inside her. Air broke from her in startled grunts. He moaned a rough oath, a gritty promise followed by the single-minded declaration in the slap and slam of his body.

He thrust deep and fast, but not mindlessly. He watched her, watched so that the action of his hips met the sighs on her lips. His hard body responded, sliding against her pleasure points, teasing helpless cries and soft moans from her.

His own desire lined his brow, tightened his jaw, parted his lips.

When a second orgasm crested, she could see the knowing in his eyes, feel it in the arch and increased speed of his hips. *Oh. God.*

The sharp muscles of his stomach coiled. The line of his biceps stood out as he squeezed her ass, bowed her hips, drove into her.

The pressure built, rolled up tight. She rocked with him. It was too much. The electric, hot feel of him stretching her.

She came again.

The swell and roll of the orgasm wracked her body, sent her heaving against him, whimpering and calling out his name. It felt like dying, like nothing existed but the trembling, hot push of his body into hers.

He responded to her cries with a groan. Then he lost himself. Thrusting without rhythm, almost uncontrollably, he broke hot and heavy inside of her.

For sweet seconds, his slick heat pushed within her, then with a final moan that sounded like willing surrender, his thrusts naturally slowed, and he stilled.

Panting, he disentangled himself from her and collapsed beside her, one leg partially on top of her.

His leg was heavy, so warm. She didn't need him to move, but he did. He moved his leg, kissed her forehead. A line of semen followed him, dripped across her hip. He drew her to him.

He brought his mouth to her ear, nuzzled her.

The sound of their heavy breaths filled the room for quiet, comfortable moments. And then she heard him chuckling.

Okay. Apparently, she was amusing. He said, his voice a whisper of hot satisfaction, "The way you move—all gyrations and fury. Damn. I can't get enough of it."

"And that amuses you?"

"I love how carried away you get."

Uh? What? Doesn't everyone? "You have had sex before, right?"

He chuckled again, moved his head down on the pillow so his mouth was closer to her ear. "I'm not saying it's a bad thing. It's a good thing. You're easy to read."

"I'm easy? Careful, charmer." She grinned at him, enjoying this part. Who knew pillow talk could be fun?

He used his thumb to brush a strand of hair from her cheek. "You tell me what you want with the double-pump action of your tits and hips. And those fuck-me-harder sighs and the way you beg. Oh God, the way you beg me not to stop. Like I have a fucking choice. Like seeing you moan and grind into me does anything but make me too crazy to do anything but lose myself fast and sloppy inside you."

She still didn't get why he was so amused, but it didn't seem a bad thing. "So, you're saying you really like having sex with me. Like, it's the best sex ever. And you're helpless under the spell of my hot, heaving body."

He grunted. "I'm saying…" He stopped. Thought. "You asked me earlier if I still like you. I do. A lot. More than I have any other woman in a long, long time. Maybe ever."

Whoa. That was so sweet. Too sweet. Made her feel guilty that, as soon as her transportation was arranged, she was going to ditch him and get back to run interference with Momma.

But it was for his own good.

Momma's words, "M-erasure is harmless," chilled her through and through. She wouldn't let Momma take advantage of him anymore. No. He'd sacrificed enough for her mission, a mission that was in no way his. He was a good man and should be free to do his good work. Which meant keeping him away from Momma.

But first she was going to fuck him until his eyes rolled back in his head. Fuck him until he couldn't do anything but pass out. She'd leave him satisfied. And sans passport, visa, and identification. Good luck getting out of Israel, buddy. No point telling him that. He wouldn't understand.

She snuggled closer. "Get some sleep. In a little while, I'm going to wake you up so you can show me again just how deeply you like me."

He snorted. She kissed the crook of his arm and fell asleep inhaling the musk of him.

Chapter 34

THE SUN MADE ITS LAZY WAY THROUGH THE BLINDS AND across the bed. Sandesh rolled onto his side and watched it play across the soft curves of Justice's sleeping body.

The few stitches in her side had bled through the bandage at some point. The bloodstain was dry and dark now. She had other scars here and there. Some savage. Some delicate.

They told a story. Survival and sadness. She was amazing—more complicated and interesting than any woman he'd ever been with. His cock grew hard. He pressed it into the side of her smooth leg. She smiled but kept her eyes closed.

He pressed deeper. She giggled, turned, so that her sleek, wet core met him. That was more like it. "Oh, Sandy, did you want something?"

"You. Back. Front. Over. Under me."

She laughed out loud. He wasn't sure he liked the sound of that. He knew enough about Justice, had learned it through repeated exchanges, that the girl liked to joust. Sometimes her jousting involved games of teasing. He did not want to be teased right now. He wanted to fuck.

He ran a hand over her breast. The tip sat up. She bit her lip, then made an "oh" sound. She grabbed his hand, pushed it aside.

Shit. Girl wanted to play.

She batted her big, dark, "screw me harder, deeper,

yes there" eyes at him and began to sing. That song. From *Grease*. Boner killer. Nearly, anyway.

"'Stranded at the drive in. Branded a fool. What will they say Monday at school?'"

"Stop that."

She sang faster, louder. The stanzas weren't even in the right order. "'Oh, Sandy, baby, someday when high school is done. Somehow, someway, our two worlds will be one.'"

"You're bringing up painful childhood memories."

She giggled. And, of course, kept singing. Jokingly, he covered her mouth with his hand. She reacted like he'd whipped out a knife and held it to her throat.

She knocked his hand away, rolled on top of him. She glared down. "Don't ever do that."

Boundary alert. Fuck. He was an idiot. "Sorry. I wasn't thinking."

She waited. He had no idea for what. He didn't dare move. He felt awful. And what did it say about him that he still really wanted to have sex? Preferably soon. She began to sing again.

No way.

Now she was just challenging his manhood.

He drove his hips up so hard and fast she lifted into the air. He shot to a seated position and caught her carefully in his lap. They were face-to-face.

She cursed. It would really help if Justice pissed off wasn't the hottest thing he'd ever seen.

And if her cunt wasn't pressed against his cock.

He put his hands on her shoulders. "Stop squirming, Justice. I just want to talk." Preferably about how we could go back to being friends. And then fuck.

She was having none of it. Her left fingers snapped out, jabbed him in the neck. Damn it. He began coughing. She pushed him flat onto the bed, so she straddled his middle. Her eyes were on fire.

How the hell had this happened?

She pressed her knees onto his biceps and her hands onto his wrists. She watched him. There was a challenge in her face. And rage.

What had started out as playful wrestling took a turn that bordered on testing. She put her face within inches of his. "What are you going to do?"

Yeah. Justice was very much interested in testing him.

Every instinct screamed for him to use his strength to easily flip her over. His cock and fists were equally hard. But instinctual reaction didn't override his reason. Logically, he understood. He'd challenged her. She felt vulnerable.

He knew this not by the way she rolled her ass across his hard-on—that was her way of egging him on—but by the strength she put into holding him down. Her hands tighter around his wrists than was necessary. Her forearms so tensed he could see her veins.

For her, this had stopped being a game. She needed to know he would not take advantage of superior strength even though she taunted him, even though they both knew he wanted to overtake her.

She was asking if she could trust him. Any other woman, he'd probably just get up and tell her to fuck off. But this one… He wanted her to know. He would never cross that line. Not emotionally and certainly not physically—unless she spoke the words and gave the unequivocal signal that that was what she wanted.

And then it would be playing.

He gritted his teeth. Her ass rolled across the tip of his cock. Fuck. She was going to torture the shit out of him. His breath became ragged. The sound of it filled the room.

She stared at him. Her dark eyes teasing and serious as he walked the edge of wanting and fury. "You were saying?" She began to hum that song as the softest part of her body, the moist wetness, gyrated against him. This might have been the hardest thing he'd ever done. Literally.

He wanted to roll her over. He wanted to fuck her.

She increased the friction, humming that damn song louder. His body responded automatically, adding moisture to accompany her rhythm. He didn't follow his instinct. More than anything, he wanted her to trust him. He watched her, waited for her to get it.

A well-worn Shakespeare phrase filtered through his head. "If you prick us, do we not bleed? If you tickle us, do we not laugh? If you poison us, do we not die? And if you wrong us, shall we not revenge?"

He had the good sense to keep quiet.

A long moment of sweet friction that felt as much like losing as winning. Damn fucked-up ego. She eased up. She smiled, as if they'd reached some kind of understanding.

She lowered her face to his. "I like you." She kissed him. It was long and deep and set his body thrumming. "I really like you."

Her soft lips pressed his, then slipped to his chin, his neck. She kissed the hollow at the base of his neck. Her hands came off his wrists. She stroked his biceps, his chest. Her hips rolled faster against his cock.

She kissed down his body. Her core lifted from his cock. He fisted his hands in the sheets so he wouldn't grab her. She was in the driver's seat, and he wanted to see where she'd ride him.

She moaned, sucked on her pinky finger. Then her hot lips trailed soft, sucking kisses down across his abs. Her mouth. Shit. She was going to…

She found the tip of his penis and sucked it inside, without her hands, which were busy doing other things.

The pinky of her right hand slowly circled and entered him from behind. Shit. So smooth and sweet. She knew what she was doing.

Her tongue moved against the head of his cock. Her mouth ground lower, putting pressure and releasing. The pace was excruciatingly good. He moaned and bucked into her mouth.

She began to stroke the base of his cock with her other hand as she sucked him off and gyrated the soft tip of her finger inside his ass. Goddamn.

He'd had blow jobs before. Had amazing blow jobs before, but he had no idea how anything could feel so fucking good. Her pace increased. He had to calm himself, get some control. No chance. She sucked and rolled and pumped. The orgasm slammed into him as hard and unexpected as a summer storm.

"Fuck. Yes. Justice. Fuck!" He rocked into her mouth as his cock exploded. She sucked him down, swallowed his come as her dark eyes dipped closed.

When the final shocks of pleasure receded, his body collapsed back against the mattress. She sat up and wiped her mouth on the back of her hand.

He wanted to move, grab her to him, but she'd

absorbed every bit of energy and need out of him. He was too satiated to stir. She flopped on top of him, grinning like she'd won, had the trophy, the blue ribbon, and the crown. Damn. Yeah. He'd give her that.

She smelled of his musk. And like Justice. He closed his eyes. He kissed the top of her head. He found his voice. Barely. "In two hours, I'm going to wake up and return the favor. Then I'm going to roll you over and fuck you until you scream my name."

She chuckled. "I'll set my clock."

Chapter 35

TWO HOURS ENDED UP BEING FOUR, BUT IN EVERY OTHER way, Sandesh was as good as his word.

Electric zings still ricocheted inside her from the orgasm that had sent her screaming his name.

Now, his strong hands gripped her sides and flipped her over. He stood, pulling her over to the side of the bed. She obliged with a happy little raise of her hips. She still wasn't high enough. He was tall. He positioned her on all fours, slapped her once on the ass.

She looked back at him. He grinned and slipped his hard cock into her. She gasped. Was there anything better than the feel of him entering her, filling her?

He grasped her hips, tightly grinding her onto his cock as he drove slowly into her.

She moaned. Oh. Yes. That. Much better.

She began making yes-more-now-please noises. His body picked up the pace. His cock was so hard. The friction so good. Her body began to hum as he slapped hard into her.

The heat and pressure built. A coil of energy pulled at her core. The heat rose, lowered, tightened. He reached around and pressed his thumb against her clit.

She cried out. She rocked frantically back into him, slamming against every demanding thrust. Sandesh began to lose his tempo, cursed hotly, gained control, and kept his pace for her. His thumb insistent against her. Her orgasm broke over her, racking her inside and out.

He let out a groan that was part relief, part single-minded intent. He grasped her hips, his fingers digging into her hip bones. He pushed wild and hard, sending the tingles of her orgasm rippling through her. His pace shattered.

"Justice." Her name on his lips sounded like a declaration. And he came inside her with a thick heat that felt a lot like confirmation.

He pulled out of her, and she crawled up onto the bed, leaving a space for him. He joined her. She pressed herself to his front, and he snaked his arms around her.

He stared at her for a long moment as the space between them heated with their heavy breaths. His eyes turned serious, caring. "In all the things I've seen, places I've been, women I've known, you are so solely unique that I feel driven to pay homage to you." He traced her lips, nose, cheek with his finger. "If I were a writer, I'd use words. A sculptor, clay. An artist, paint." He ran his hand along her body and cupped her ass. "But I'm a soldier, and all I have is my allegiance. So that's what I'll use to worship you."

He kissed her on the ear and wrapped his arms around her again, squeezing her body hard to his chest. "You're not leaving this country without me."

She'd been drifting asleep, but that woke her. Whoa. Was she that easy to read? "What do you mean?"

"I mean, you might've started this war, but I'm in it now. The IPT's mission in Jordan is compromised. Salma's Gems are in hiding. Walid is still out there." He ran a hand along her cheek. "Someone has betrayed you. You're in danger. And if you think you can ditch me, get back to the States before me, do whatever it is you do, and not have me by your side, think again. You go. I go."

They stared at each other.

His eyes softened. He looked at her as if seeing something wondrous. He looked at her as if she had killed him. And saved him. He looked at her as if he understood and accepted her.

And she felt him everywhere. In the heat between her thighs. The moisture in her mouth. The beat of her heart. The pull of her thoughts. The scent of him on her body. Everywhere was Sandesh.

Chapter 36

SANDESH KNEW HE WAS ALONE THE MOMENT HE WOKE TO the sun streaming in through the hotel room window. She'd gone. She'd fucked him into a coma and then she'd gone. He flung his arm over his eyes.

It had been absolutely worth it.

He knew where she lived. And he'd been expecting this.

He reached over and grabbed his cell. He checked his email for the confirmation on his flight. He had a couple of hours.

He rolled out of bed and saw his jeans scattered on the floor. He wasn't a neat freak, but this room was compact enough that if he'd left them on the floor, he and Justice might have tripped on them.

Shit.

He ran over, picked them up, checked the pockets. Fuck. Fuck. Fuck!

He was going to kill Justice. She'd taken his ID, passport, and multi-entrance visa.

Did she think she could throw him off the trail of what her family was? Did she think a couple of days stranded here would keep him from asking the questions he needed answered? From stepping up to help her against Walid? He spiked the jeans into the floor and dropped back onto the bed.

He was part of this battle now, in whatever war

Mukta and Justice had conjured up. More importantly, Mukta Parish owed him the truth. Not just what Justice had shared, but what he had his deeper suspicions about.

The Parish clan was notorious worldwide. They were all so driven. You couldn't open a paper without seeing one of them somewhere—a foreign country doing aid work, lobbying for reforms, or visiting world leaders.

Could this be part of deeper, hidden activities? If he did research, would he find Parish family travels mirrored darker events in certain areas? Events aimed at taking out men or those who'd harmed women or women's rights? Hmmm. He was going to better acquaint himself with Parish Industries and Mukta Parish.

He rolled onto his side and took a deep breath. Justice. The sheets and pillows buzzed with her unique, spicy scent—distinctly female.

God. He wanted her. Even now.

He was in it deep. Had no idea when it had happened. When he tried to find the exact moment, a dozen vivid images of Justice tortured him.

Justice pushing boldly into her mother's office.

Justice's hand opening to his on the plane.

Justice's eager responses as he thrust into her body. And his overpowering need to get deeper, closer. And an orgasm that had felt like surrender. And finding home. And purpose. And more.

Which made no sense, because at this very moment, he couldn't recall ever being this pissed off at anyone. He had a group of women in hiding in Jordan, women saved from a man who still had money and power enough to make their lives a misery. The IPT's mission was in jeopardy there. Hell, globally. And until he handled Walid, he couldn't press on like nothing had happened.

He'd told her that. And she'd still taken his shit and left. Odd that the pillow smelled so sweet when the woman herself was frustrating as hell.

He shoved off the pillow, grabbed his phone, and pressed the preset for Victor. If Justice thought she could sneak out and he would just stay put, wait for her to solve his problems, to take out the threat while he was trapped in Israel, she had another think coming.

Chapter 37

HAVING SLEPT VERY LITTLE ON THE PLANE—GUILT DID that to you—Justice drove her Jeep up the winding hill to the Mantua Home. The L-shaped mansion sat atop the highest hill on campus. It overlooked the entire Mantua Academy.

Justice swung around the stone fountain and parked.

She got out of her car. Stretched. Her side still hurt. But not as badly. The Mantua Home. Just home. Special not because it had thirty thousand square feet, or mullion- and tracery-arched windows, or any of the historical stone etchings, but because of the people. And the memories.

A pit of doubt rooted in her throat. Something had changed. In some way, it hurt worse than any prior betrayal. It had taken her a long time to find trust again after what her father had done.

Gracie. Dada. Tony. Bridget.

One of them had given Walid the ability to track her. One of them had almost gotten her killed.

Above the house, the last blush of departing sun winked away. The lights along her home's exterior popped to life, as did the lights along the cobbled driveway. The air smelled of spring, freshly turned earth and the bright perfume of the early-flowering hawthorn that dotted the extensive and expert landscaping.

That smell brought sharply to mind spring jackets

and childhood memories. Testing boundaries and getting in trouble. How many times had Momma warned her, "Justice, there are some lines you cannot cross"?

She'd crossed those lines. Repeatedly. And paid the price. She'd never had a problem facing the consequences for her actions. But now it involved more than her.

Sandesh knew and suspected things he shouldn't. And she'd pay her price for that, but she'd protect his memories.

She took the front steps, thick slabs of red stone, two at a time. Pushing open one of the exotic front doors, she stepped into the grand foyer. This opulent expanse held as many memories for her as the always-present fresh flowers on the pedestal table and the *Gone with the Wind*-style staircase.

She closed the door.

Home. But not safe. Who was the traitor? She tossed the question aside as the comforting noise of her big family enveloped her. It was never quiet here.

Upstairs, two girls argued. The sound echoed down the wide hall and mixed with the training session in the gym to her right. She smiled. Only her family would put a gym, not a library or a sitting room, off the entryway.

The explosive grunts and forceful "hiyuhs" reverberated through the open gym doors.

As she strode past, she looked inside. Bridget was training. When she saw Justice, she waved her to come over.

Traitor?

She probably wanted to grill Justice on the mission. By now, they must all know. With Walid still out there and a new mission looming for her unit, Momma had had no choice but to come clean. Well, partly. They'd know about her failure. Know how she'd snuck out behind their backs. Know how she'd had to rely on someone who wasn't family. And that now they all needed to band together to form a new plan. But not the whole truth.

She kept walking.

She felt grimy and used up and pissed off and sad to her soul. She walked purposefully toward the end of the long, ornately decorated corridor, past the sunken library, and toward the elevators.

"Justice?" Tony popped out of the arched, open doorway that led into the library. She jumped.

He grabbed her, hugged her. He held her tight enough to crack ribs. He smelled like Tony. Like celery juice and ginger. Could he have told Walid where to find her in Syria? Her heart shrieked denial. Not Tony. Not him.

"Justice. I thought…" He broke off. A large, disbelieving smile cracked half his face. Damn, some orthodontist had gotten so carried away with Tony's braces. She doubted even in Hollywood you could find a better smile. No need to tell him that. She squirmed free.

"Nice smile, Tone." She pushed at his shoulder. "You could actually double as a Muppet."

He opened and closed his mouth in exaggerated delight. Like a Muppet. Tony. Not easy to offend.

"So funny, J. Now tell me what the fuck happened? Forget shutting us out or lying to your unit. You don't do recon anymore? You pop into Jordan and attack the Brothers like you were taking down a massage parlor in the middle of nowhere?"

Sheesh. Even when he wasn't on a mission, he critiqued her. And she hated lying. But until she knew who had betrayed her, she had to keep the truth from all her siblings. Even the one she trusted the most. She went with the story Momma and she had concocted. "I was sent to do recon. I went rogue. I saw an opportunity and took it."

He raised an eyebrow—disbelief or something else? He lifted his shoulders, spread his hands wide like someone describing the big fish that got away. "You left one brother alive. That fucking sadistic, crazy-as-shit one. Y'know we gotta go after that fucker now, right?"

Gawd. It sounded so much worse when summarized with curses, hand gestures, and South Philly. "Yeah. Well, at least he wasn't the smart one. Any thoughts on how to get him in Mexico?"

He jerked back as if she'd physically hit him. "You mean other than the detailed plan I laid out to Momma about getting the Brothers separately? The plan I put in a heartfelt letter and sent her before you even left?"

He glared. "Did Momma even tell you?"

Oh. Fuck. Tony was so sensitive about what he saw as the family ignoring his opinions.

She hadn't seen it, but she really didn't want to get into it with him. "It was my mission. I said all along we had to take them out together to keep one from alerting the other."

"Yeah. Well, that worked out great."

"I know, Tony. I was there. And so was Sandesh. And right now, I have to talk to Momma about him." She ran a hand through her grimy hair and a deep breath through her agitation. "Sorry. I'll catch you later. Okay?"

His eyes became suspicious. Or hurt. "You really like this guy?"

She looked away, shook her head. "Not really."

Without meeting his eyes—no need to see if her lie had landed or missed the mark—she continued down the long hallway and turned right.

Once out of his line of sight, she exhaled and leaned her shoulder against the wall by the elevator. At this time of day, Momma would be home and in her office. She slammed the up arrow.

She wasn't going up.

The elevator dinged. Opened. She stepped inside. Four yellow, round buttons indicated there were three floors and one basement level. Not exactly accurate. There were two other floors. The doors slid shut.

She lifted her wrist above the number pad. Nothing happened. Oh. Right. That would take some getting used to. She'd inserted a new microchip on the plane. She lifted her other wrist. The one that didn't have a scab on it.

There was a beep of recognition. Yes. Welcome back to elevator-X. "Subfloor 4B."

The smooth feminine automation responded, "Access is not operational. Two unauthorized personnel remain on this level. Please enter via another route."

Oh. Hell no. "Override."

"Wait for verification."

She did.

"Override accepted. You have been processed and cleared for subfloor 4B. No cameras, cell phones, or unauthorized electronics."

She braced her feet wide. The waist-high handholds

were a deep temptation, but it had been a challenge since childhood not to hold on. The elevator intoned, "Proceeding."

She took a deep breath. The elevator plunged. Her stomach slapped into her esophagus along with her heart. She clenched her teeth. Sheesh. No matter how many times she prepared for it, the violence of this drop made her stomach twist.

After the sinking free fall, the elevator slid to a weighted stop. Her legs buckled, and she locked her knees into place. The elevator intoned, "Subfloor 4B. Welcome, you are being monitored. Entering unauthorized areas will result in immediate expulsion."

She stepped out of the elevator and into a spotless, windowless hallway. It was an authoritarian prick of a corridor. Unauthorized areas meant any of those accessed through the large, misted-gray glass double doors to her left. Not a problem.

She went right. She had nothing against internal security rules, but she'd learned a healthy respect for them as a child. They were the cops of her adolescence, led by Leland, and she steered clear of the numerous offices and security centers behind those doors.

It was a line she rarely questioned. Well, not after that time with Gracie. She shuddered. Being a teenager with an attitude hadn't been easy.

The muffled feel of being underground was compounded by the sound of the rhythmic humming breaths of the ventilation system. It smelled like forced air. Manufactured and new-car clean. She preferred the floor above this, 4A. And not just because the gym and gun range were there. But because it wasn't so stiff.

She knocked on Momma's office door and entered before getting a response. Momma's office made up for the lack of decorations on this level. It testified to the colorful soul hidden beneath her damaged skin.

Thick, hand-woven rugs splashed with garish, bright colors; ornaments of every conceivable hue; lush, gold damask wallpaper; sub-Saharan artwork; elephant lamps; brightly painted masks; and a delicate, hand-carved desk of bleached wood.

Wearing a silver silk niqab, Momma sat working at her desk. And before her, in one of the two robin's egg-blue chairs, sat Leland—working on an iPad. Probably monitoring the many security cameras. Though he usually did that from his office in internal.

Momma raised her head. "Justice. Welcome home."

"Momma, I need to talk to you."

As dapper as the silver suit he wore, Leland stood and put the iPad on the desk, then walked around and sat on the corner of Momma's desk, as if to highlight the point that they were a team.

No need. These two were spookily coordinated. Seriously, her niqab almost matched his suit. What was with them?

So hyperaware of herself, her senses, that she could feel the fibers in her socks, Justice shut the door behind her and walked across the room. She kissed Momma on her silk-lined cheek. She smelled like Momma, like that flowery, earthy richness of Une Rose.

Justice nodded to Leland, who indicated the chair he had just left. "Please sit down."

Please? Okay. That was different.

She sat in the chair, still warm from Leland. Hot even.

Huh. She was in the hot seat.

Shit. That wasn't funny. She inhaled, held her breath, released.

"Yeah." Justice crossed, uncrossed her legs. "I know you want details on the mission, but I need to talk to you about Sandesh."

Leland shook his head. "First, you listen."

Okay. Again different. Usually, after a botched mission, they wanted her to talk.

Her mother tugged at the fabric draped across her shoulder. "Yes. We need to discuss your young man."

Her young man? She didn't like the sound of that. She looked each in the eyes in turn. "Momma. Leland. I won't stand for you taking his memories. I won't."

"Calm down and listen," Leland said. "Sandesh is with Gracie."

"Gracie!" She jolted to her feet. Nightmare. "Where? When?" Poor Sandesh. She had to rescue him.

Chapter 38

SANDESH STEPPED OFF THE ESCALATOR AT THE PHILADELPHIA International Airport with a chip on his shoulder. He adjusted his too-light backpack across his shoulder. The overhead fluorescents by the baggage carousel gave off enough light to see clearly but not enough to seem warm and friendly. Ah, Philly.

He moved past the baggage claim and outside, toward the cabstand.

What the hell?

He blinked until he was sure that he understood what he was seeing. A redhead. Red hair pinned back in an angry little bun. A pissed-off redhead, as hot as she was angry-looking, holding a sign with his name.

This would be Gracie. What was it Justice had said about her sister? Something about never wanting to be on her bad side. Looks like that's where he'd started out.

The redhead, Gracie, sauntered right up to him. She didn't just wear her attitude; she was cloaked in it. That attitude made her bland, black suit seem threatening and imperial.

She pointed at him, then hitched her thumb toward a limo. "Let's go, big guy. We need to talk."

Chapter 39

Momma waved at Justice. "Sit. He is fine."

She sat. Her legs felt dull and heavy against the chair. Her sister had her... What was Sandesh to her? "Great lay" sounded a bit cold. "Why Gracie? She could be behind all this."

"If she is," Leland said, "she won't like the fact that we're bringing a man into the organization. Your man. Especially when we made her give up hers."

Fuckers. So manipulative. They were putting Sandesh in the line of fire with Gracie. And Tony. After being excluded from the Jordan mission, Tony would be so pissed if Sandesh was... Wait. What? "You're bringing Sandesh in?"

Momma shifted in her seat. "Yes. It is imperative for his safety and our security."

Oh. That was good. Wasn't it? "What do you mean?"

"The Brothers Grim, or I guess we can call him the Grim Brother now, believe that your *friend* Sandesh has a deeper connection to our mission than he does. Probably because he and Salma intercepted a shipment of women bound for Walid and the Americas right before he helped you escape."

Looked like Walid had put one and man together and come up with the wrong conclusion. Way to stick to character.

Dude had no idea how very wrong he was. "So, what?

You'll use Sandesh to flush out the traitor, then dangle him in front of Walid as bait, and then after he's served his purpose, you'll M-erase him?"

Momma sat up straighter. Offended? Good. Leland put a hand on her raised shoulder. She relaxed.

"Justice. I am allowing Sandesh his memories, so he is aware of the threat and can defend himself and his charity."

"How totally selfless of you."

Momma slapped angry hands together. "Would you have me throw away opportunity? Yes. I am sending a message to whoever betrayed you, us. That person might now grow angry and careless. And yet will fear revealing more information to Walid, knowing that doing so will bring them more easily under our scrutiny. But at the same time, I am giving Sandesh a chance to prove himself. Perhaps we can continue this business relationship."

She brought her masked gaze directly onto Justice. "Can you say you have dealt as fairly with him?"

That hit home like nothing else. She was right. Her mission had jeopardized his charity, and she'd then left him to put the pieces back together while she took on Walid. And Momma.

Heartsick. That was the only way to describe the feeling in her chest. Like her heart had a fever, the chills, and was curled under the blanket of her chest, moaning in pain. Oh, Sandy, I'm so very sorry.

She schooled her features. "And you're going to trust him? You're going to allow him to know our secrets?"

Leland shrugged. "That wasn't our choice." His eyes took her in, accused her. The sudden rush of blood to her cheeks heated her face as a wave of cold dread settled into her stomach.

Leland continued his stare down, as if weighing Justice's thoughts and emotions. "Besides, trust won't be an issue. First, because he has more to lose than us. Second, because you are going to stick to him like glue. And third, because he's being brought here to be tagged."

She cringed. "He's agreed to have a GPS implanted under his skin?"

Leland waved a hand. "We expect you'll handle that minor detail."

Chapter 40

THE REDHEAD WITH THE I-CUT-GLASS-WITH-MY-UNYIELDING stare leaned over the desk toward Sandesh. Under the black business jacket, she had a Beretta Tomcat. A tiny little thing that easily hid its real potential for danger. Telling.

They'd been in this windowless, colorless, almost airless ten-by-ten room for hours. His neck hurt. His ass hurt. Apparently, this was the way the Parish family treated potential suitors. They sat them at an Amish-crafted wood table, on a schoolmarm-straight wooden chair, while accusing fluorescent lights glared down at them.

Not that he thought Justice would ever consider him a suitor. Damn. He'd settle for "I won't screw you into a warm, satiated coma and then abandon you without your passport in a foreign country."

He'd need more than luck for that. He didn't even know where she was right now. Didn't even know where he was. He had some idea, though Gracie had blindfolded him. After he'd agreed.

That seemed to be a big deal for her. Asking if he'd mind her blindfolding him and taking him somewhere.

It had taken them three hours to get here, but he suspected that was to throw him off. The Mantua Academy was eighty minutes from the Philly airport. Where else would they take him?

The limo had seemed to drop down at one point, like

into an underground garage. And she had taken him into and down an elevator that felt more like a ride at Great Adventure.

So he was down deep. And there was a muffled feeling that came from being surrounded by earth. He sat back, stretched.

Gracie grinned at him. "So when was the first time you and Justice had sex?"

Sandesh blinked. That was a turn in a whole new direction. They'd spent hours discussing Jordan and now she wanted to get personal. Curiosity? Or some weird suspicion? "That's not significant to this discussion."

"It is to me. And since you need our protection—"

Sandesh laughed. "If you didn't get the memo, I did just fine protecting myself. And your sister. Unlike your supposed group of professionals."

Gracie's green eyes narrowed. Her pale skin reddened. Sandesh had never been a fan of blushing, but he was bored and angry and had to keep himself from taunting her to see if he could provoke a deeper skin tone.

"So you don't care if Salma and her family are in trouble?"

He lowered his arms. Clenched his hands into fists. "What are you saying?"

"Well, tough guy, you rescued a group of enslaved women and girls on the same night Walid's brother was killed. He followed the trail of those women and it led to Salma and you. He's convinced you and she are his enemy. Which is part of the reason I took so long to get here. You're on the Mantua Academy campus. Had to make sure Walid's men weren't following you."

He let that sink in. Not just the statement—how the hell did she have access to that information?—but the domino effect. Salma's organization, her safety, the safety of those they'd freed, the IPT's mission, all compromised. And the final domino. The big one.

He was being bribed. Stay in line. Do what we say. Keep our secrets. And we'll protect your friends and business. Mob-like practices. He kept his face impassive. He'd give her nothing. Not even a sense of his annoyance.

"What do you want?"

Gracie jerked her head sideways, as if cracking her neck. Frustration? "What do I want? Or what does Momma want?"

"There's a difference?"

"A big difference. Momma wants your help taking out Walid. She wants you brought into the family, into our inner circle. I have no idea how they can possibly think that you're worth it. When other men, good men, are…lost to us."

Brought into the family? This fact pissed her off enough that she'd told him about the offer before her mother had even made it. She must be seriously pissed off. People made mistakes, revealed things when they were angry. *Good men lost to us?* "So you don't have sex yourself. Is that the reason you want to hear about your sister's sex life?"

Her face heated. She took a step back. "Justice spoke to you about me?"

Damn. He'd only been guessing, but he'd struck bone. And she looked anything but annoyed or suspicious. She looked hurt.

Sandesh pushed back in his chair. It creaked as he

tried to snap his spine into better alignment. "Let's say I agree to help you."

He brought his hands up. Maybe a bit too quickly. Gracie flinched, reached under her jacket.

There was a moment of silence. His heart thudded in his chest. She drew her hand back out without the gun. Damn, were all these women just waiting for the entirety of the male population to go berserker on their asses?

He desperately wanted to ask her that, ask her if she thought he'd be putting up with this bullshit if it weren't for her sister, but he didn't trust her. He sensed she hid more than she said. And he didn't need to give her any more information.

The whole reason he'd agreed to come here, to be blindfolded, to talk to this lunatic, was to keep Justice safe. Although Justice was scarce on details, someone in this family had betrayed her. He intended to find out who. And make sure they couldn't do it again.

"I'm in. For as long as it takes to find and take out Walid. But that's it. Justice and I have a personal relationship. If she wants you to know more, ask her. Or you can steal into her room at night and read her diary."

Gracie laughed. She quickly schooled her features. "You're kind of a bad boy. A bad boy who likes to do humanitarian stuff. Is that your story?"

"And I'm sticking to it." Though the whole bad-boy thing made him sound like a thug and not a trained professional. He had better things to do than throw down over poor word choice.

Gracie sat on the edge of the table, close enough that he could smell her perfume. It smelled like fruity candy. He kept his eyes locked with hers. She leaned over, showing much more cleavage than he was comfortable not noticing.

He pushed up from his chair and stood. Justice had some messed-up family. She eased off the table and followed him. He stepped back. She stepped forward.

"What are you doing?" If he didn't think she'd bring out her gun, he'd have put his arms out to impede her. She was practically pressed to his front.

"Come on. I saw you checking out my backside."

He laughed out loud. Backside? She had to be joking, right? "I want to speak to your mother. The sooner the better. And like you, I look at a lot of people. Evaluate them. It's reflex."

She stopped, tilted her head. "Momma was right. You are a good man."

Seriously? "So what, you were using your looks to try and manipulate me into revealing what a dog I am?"

She shrugged.

No. Not good enough. "First, my actions aren't that involuntary. I don't knee-jerk fuck women. Second, and this I really don't get, how can a group of women dedicated to female equality use their own sexuality to gain position? Isn't that what you're fighting against?"

Gracie slapped a hand to his chest. "If you're stupid enough to fall for those things, if you can't overcome your own programming, please don't think that I'm dumb enough not to use that to my advantage."

Damn, these Parish women were as scary as hell.

—∿∿—

After escorting him through a set of double doors and down a bland, gray-and-white hallway, Gracie led Sandesh inside a brightly decorated office. Mukta Parish's office.

The moment Gracie showed him inside, Sandesh knew he'd be doing whatever they wanted.

Justice.

She stood up, turned. Those eyes—a deep darkness that captured pinpricks of light and turned them to stars—beamed. Like he carried something she'd been waiting for. Something she desperately needed.

Damn. He wished he could be angry. Forget this woman who'd told him her nightmare as a way to offer comfort. Forget that she'd risked herself for a child. Forget the seamless nighttime eyes that had launched the grenade that had saved them. Forget the lost and broken parts. The way she'd sung to him. The way she'd threaded her hand through his. Threaded her body around his. Threaded herself around his heart.

He should have been angry. He wanted to be. But he understood her too well. And he understood that leaving him had been her way of protecting him.

But he didn't need her protection.

He walked to her. What had they done to her? She looked so…shaken. Behind her, Leland and Mukta exchanged glances. He didn't care. If they wanted his cooperation, they'd have to put up with him being here. For Justice.

Her dark eyes. So beautiful and intense he had to swallow the pain in his throat.

She lowered her eyelashes. "You looked so peaceful sleeping. I didn't want to disturb you."

The corners of his mouth twitched. He held on to the smile. Barely. "I appreciate you leaving my passport at the airport. Kind of you."

She whispered, "You don't have to join my family. This mission."

Oh hell. He wrapped his arms around her. "It's done, Justice. I'm in it with you."

She put her hands around his waist, tugged him closer. He could feel the entirety of her—the spread of her hips, the bend in her shoulder, the length of her neck, the muscles in her arms, the tip of her nose, the lay of her forehead against his cheek. Everywhere she touched left an impression of her as sweet and powerful as her kisses, her sighs, her tears, curses, laughter.

He loved this woman. Not going to tell her that. Not here. At least not with words.

He tipped her head up and kissed her.

He'd expected her to hold back. Family in the room and all. But she didn't. She dipped her tongue into his mouth, tasted him as unconsciously and fully as if they were alone.

Sharp heat knifed through his body. He should walk away. Protect his heart. Not just his heart, but his charity. Too bad his programming, as Gracie put it, didn't work that way. They broke apart. A moment longer and it would've gotten really awkward.

"Tagged and tailed," he said, rubbing his nose along her proud forehead.

Justice stepped back. Her eyes widened. "You're okay with inserting the GPS?"

He didn't know how to answer that. Okay with it? Not at all. But he'd learned to be okay with sacrifice, the kind of sacrifice that could only tilt the scales toward justice.

His eyes scanned the others in the colorful office: Mukta and Leland. They'd manipulated him into a spot where he was forced to cooperate. Well, they'd be forced to do things too.

"Of course, I'm going to need some things in return. Like Mukta agreeing to fund the IPT startups for the next ten years."

Mukta and Leland exchanged another glance. Their eyes conveyed messages only two people who were genuinely close could read. He wondered if they suspected the truth.

He really didn't want any ties to Parish Industries or their covert operations. Not for ten years. Not for two.

But he knew people like Mukta and Leland. He knew that they'd figure his attraction to Justice wouldn't be enough to keep him in line indefinitely. His offering them part of the IPT assured them that he was in this for the long haul. Another cog in their giant wheel of using peace operations to secretly kill and maim in the name of a higher cause. But until he was able to extricate himself and the IPT from that, he needed them to believe he was part of it.

Mukta nodded thoughtfully. "We could discuss such details."

"Mukta?" Leland said. "Is it wise to tie the school to the IPT right now?"

Sandesh couldn't help the bitter laugh. "So let me get this straight. You compromise the IPT's name, organized crime is now after me, and when I ask for a little reimbursement for the charity you've all but destroyed, you take issue with my reputation."

Leland put a hand on his waistband. Yep. Carrying.

Justice stepped slightly to her left, more fully between

him and Leland. "Enough," she said. "We're connected. This is just money."

Leland arched a brow at that.

"Done," Mukta said, ending all objection. "I owe you, Sandesh. You saved Justice and kept our secrets. I might not know much, but I know that decency deserves my respect."

"Funny, the last thing I feel is decent. In fact, I'd like to go home and get a shower. If you don't mind." He stepped past Justice, held out his arm for the tracer.

Leland reached into an ivory box on the desk. He opened it and pulled out an instrument that looked like a weapon to Sandesh, but he guessed would insert a microchip.

"This tracking device will give us an update on your location every fifteen minutes." The message being that he would be constantly watched. "As head of Internal Security, I can see your exact location at any time."

He loaded the device with a silver cylinder. "With this, you'll have access to this home and to areas within. Justice will show you around. But when she's not here, you'll know when you don't have access, because those doors won't open to you."

Leland placed the cold barrel of the instrument against Sandesh's wrist and pressed. There was a pop and a sharp stab of pain. Heat spread along his skin. He looked at his arm. For one moment, he saw the outline of something. Then he flexed and released, and the chip sank away.

Justice reached out to him. Her hand shook as she traced over his wrist. Her fingers brushed back and forth. Her thick eyelashes lowered, fanned across her skin, blinked, and lifted. Her eyes, those fall-into-deep-waters-after-a-storm, those cool, sunless depths invited him in. "Ready to be initiated as a warrior woman?"

He huffed. "Sounds incredibly painful."

She laughed, winked at him. "Actually, it all started with your elevator ride. How did you feel about going down, Sandesh? Want to go again?"

He wished he could've controlled the shocked laugh that broke from him. Or the heat in his face. Or the instant surge of lust. But this was Justice. And some things were just out of his control.

"How's tomorrow? I need to check in on my mother."

Justice cocked her head. "Stop trying to seduce me."

Chapter 41

JUSTICE STOOD IN THE HALLWAY OF THE CONSHOHOCKEN apartment building and took out her cell. She added a contact, assigned a speed dial number. The only person she'd ever done this for. She pressed that number—one.

He answered on the fourth ring, his voice fuzzy. "Justice? It's"—he paused, probably checking his clock—"seven a.m."

Oh, he sounded so vulnerable when he was sleep deprived. Just the thing a girl could take advantage of. "Open up. I'm outside your apartment door."

"What? Security didn't call me."

She snorted. Someone doubted her stealth skills. "Still here."

She hung up, smiling. A moment later, the covering over the peephole clicked open and then closed. The door swung wide open, his body positioned behind it, so she was offered unfettered access.

Trusting.

She walked inside. The apartment had an open floor plan with natural wood floors. Kitchen with a breakfast bar. A two-person, bar-height table by a sliding glass door that led to a balcony. A gray leather Chesterfield sofa with thick scroll arms and a high back, flanked by two equally deep upholstered chairs. And a huge flat-screen TV stationed on the wall over a fireplace with a green-marble mantel. She liked.

She turned at the sound of the door closing.

Whoa. So fucking hot. Disheveled hair. Shadow-lined jaw. That just-woken-up confusion in his bleary, blue eyes. And, hello. At least one part of him was awake. She grinned. "So, you sleep in the nude."

He moved like a panther, grabbed her by the waist and dragged her up against his hard-on. He kissed her, skilled and insistent, as if the time they'd spent apart had been years and not days. His need, his wordless hunger, took her breath away. And set her on fire.

She arched into him. He smelled so good, like sleep and man. Warm, velvety liquid saturated her panties.

His demanding lips worked against hers. His stubble scratched against her. His hot hands traveled up her body. He pulled out her hair tie, tangled his hands in her hair, and angled her head so he could deepen the kiss.

Man knew how to kiss. Their tongues, wet and hot, and their lips, soft and needy, reacquainted themselves. Their breaths grew strong enough to force them to break apart.

His breaths ragged, his hands grasping her hair tight enough to hurt, he said, "Take your clothes off."

That was an excellent idea. Too bad she didn't have enough air to say that. She guided his hands from her hair, stepped back, unbuttoned her shirt, tossed it, undid her bra, freed her breasts. He groaned out loud.

Loving the stark need on his face, she unzipped her black jeans, turned her ass in his direction, and lowered pants to ankles. Without bending her knees.

"Dear God."

What man didn't appreciate a good thong? She took

her time unlacing her boots, flicked them off, wiggled out of her jeans, and made a show of losing the thong.

When she stood, he came up behind her, pressed his hard body against her ass. He ran a hand over her breasts, squeezed and fondled them. "Fuck, Justice. I need you."

Good to know.

He reached down to her clit, stroked her silky wetness, and grunted in male satisfaction. Two long fingers crooked inside her, nearly causing her to orgasm. She was strung that tight, so ready.

He slid his fingers in and out, the palm of his hand rubbing against her clit as his breath raged loud in her ears.

"Sandesh. That feels so good."

He pumped his fingers faster, pressing his other hand flat against her stomach, pulling her tight against his hard-on. With him behind her, his hot breath in her ear, his arms stretched across her front, she felt enveloped by him. He was so big and warm and solid.

Her body tightened and tightened. The tension built and strengthened. She panted hard. Trembling, electric pulses rode over her, shattered her. She curled her toes, arched her head back into his shoulders, and dug her hands into his biceps. "Oh. Sandesh. Sandesh."

He whispered to her as she came, "Watching you come. Can't get enough."

The aftershocks tingled through her as he slipped his fingers out. She turned to him instinctively, seeking the hardness of him between her throbbing legs. They kissed, wild fury, crazed excitement.

She broke from him. "Ride me hard," she said.

He grinned, gazed around the room. "Lady's choice."

Oh, yes and yes. She pushed away from him and went to the end of the couch, draping herself over the tall scroll arm. Cushiony.

She put her hands flat against the seat, turned her head, and raised an eyebrow at him. "How's this?"

He didn't answer right away. He licked his lips. "Prettiest sight I've seen in my entire life."

He moved behind her, rubbed a hand along the curve of her ass, squeezed, spread her cheeks, and thrust into her wet and throbbing core.

She cried out at the insistent pull and stretch. Deeper and deeper he went, until the tip of his cock pressed against the wall of her cervix.

With a steady exhale, he began to pull out. Slowly.

He was torturing her.

She was about to tell him so when he slammed himself back inside her, fast and rough. She gasped. Her hands slipped. She re-braced against the cushion, panted at the increase in speed and friction.

Her core trembled and tightened around his thick thrusts, and she watched him, the beauty of him, reflected in the glossy blackness of the TV screen.

His long, muscular frame with one palm pressed flat against the curve of her back. His head tipped down to watch where he entered her, a look of exquisite need on his handsome face. His perfect ass tight and hard as he pumped into her.

He thrust so rapidly her clit began to rub against the couch. Still sensitive from what his fingers had done, this caused an intense reaction. "Oh God."

Caught between him and the couch, the friction so

delicious it took only a moment of pure bliss for her to come again. She cried out as electric pulses crashed into her. The tremors obliterated awareness of everything but the overpowering, exquisite release.

Panting, the muscles in her arms tense, the jolting aftershocks of the orgasm made her wiggle and squirm under Sandesh as he pumped hard into her.

She pressed the tips of her toes against the floor, raising herself up, giving him greater access.

"Justice," he said. And there was no doubt that he meant it as a warning. He wouldn't last much longer.

She'd already had two orgasms, but he was angled just right. And the walls of her body tightened and squeezed as the pressure of his cock rode into her, stroked and pumped, rubbed against her G-spot.

The thick width of him plunging with frantic abandon…the feel of him… So good. "Yes. Yes. Don't stop."

Greedy, sure. But it felt so damn good.

He grunted something that might've been, "So fucking beautiful," then slapped himself into her again and again and again.

She whimpered and moaned and shuddered beneath him as another wave of pleasure rose and rose and crashed through her.

Nearly on top of her shout, he came inside her with a drawn-out groan so scorching hot it singed her ears.

The rub and tug of her final orgasm slowed with his pace. Breathing like he'd run a four-minute mile, he slumped over her, kissed her on the back of the neck. Her body was so charged with energy, so tender to the touch, that she jerked.

He smoothed a knuckle across her cheek. "You okay?"

Was he kidding? "I love this couch."

He barked a surprised laugh, helped her up, turned her to face him. He kissed her long and deep, then put his hands on her shoulders, pulled back from the kiss, and turned her toward what she assumed was the bedroom door.

He bent to her ear, smacked her on the ass. "Get going. I'm going to teach you what getting up at a decent hour means."

Her ass tingling, she looked back at him. "A little bossy now."

"Get into my bed, Justice."

She shrugged. Turned out, right now, she liked bossy.

Chapter 42

With the curtains drawn and dim light in his bedroom, it was hard for Sandesh to imagine a more perfect morning. Not every day a hot woman broke into your apartment building, asked to be let inside, and ordered you to: "Ride me hard."

Got hard just thinking about it. Then again, she wasn't just any woman. She was one of a kind. And his heart was as tangled up with her as she was in his sheets.

Justice, deep in the softness of his bed, snuggled up to him, her lips to his ear, whispering soft sounds of appreciation. Not that his ego needed that, but he liked making her happy. His eyes drifted closed and his body relaxed.

"Why Sandman?"

He pried open his sleepy eyes. "Huh?"

"You said they called you that in the military. Sandman."

He yawned. She was so warm against him. Felt good. "Are you a morning person?"

"Yeah. Didn't you notice that in Israel?"

"That room was so dark I lost track of night and day. We barely ate."

"True." She began to rub a hand across his chest. "Answer the question. Why Sandman?"

He turned his head toward her. Her eyes were velvet night sky. A deep dark that demanded soft confessions.

He couldn't fight it. What man could? "Remember when I said in Israel that I liked you?"

She smiled. "I believe you said you liked me a lot. Maybe more than any woman ever."

He cupped the back of her head, pulling her close enough that their foreheads touched. "No maybe, Justice. None. I've never felt this way before about anyone. Ever."

"Oh." They were so close, he could feel his own breath mixing with hers. She kissed him softly. "You're my speed dial number one."

He smiled. He knew just what she was telling him. No one used speed dial anymore. It was symbolic. "Sandman," he said, closing his eyes, "because you can sleep easy if I'm on guard duty. Got great hearing. If something's out there, I'll know about it way in advance."

"Funny, I thought it was because you liked to sleep. You seem really sleepy right now."

Oh. Man. "You're not going back to sleep, are you?"

He felt her shrug. "I have a traitor to catch. Kind of hard to sleep."

That woke him. "Anything new?"

"I got news from internal security this morning. A secure email sent around four a.m. There was no electronic trail or any evidence that someone in the family had asked for GPS information on me."

He brushed a hand along her shoulder. "Meaning?"

"In order to get GPS information, you have to go through three layers of security: password, the inserted chip, and facial recognition. There is no evidence that anyone in the family did that."

He knew what she was getting at. She'd told him that

her sister Gracie was into computers. She ran a cyber-crime unit all on her own from her club. The information she obtained was used to rescue girls and track down predators. "You think it's Gracie."

"She'd be the only person with the ability to do something like that."

"What's your plan?"

"I want to interview her. This morning. And I was hoping you'd come."

Gracie was not a fan of his. Probably the point. "You think I'll throw her off?"

"That and you might spot things I might miss. Same with the rest of my family. But I'd like to tag team them."

"Meaning?"

"I'll hit them first, this afternoon. You come by for dinner later and take a second crack at them."

It would be as good a place as any to start. "Okay." He rubbed his eyes. "I'm up. Is it sexist to ask you to make me coffee?"

She squinted at him. "This isn't a situation where I can't, so no. And, baby, after triple mind-blowing orgasms, I'm pretty eager to please. Coffee, no problem."

He laughed, reached over to the nightstand. "Go. Make coffee. I'm putting you as my speed dial number one."

Chapter 43

JUSTICE PULLED INTO THE PARKING LOT BEHIND CLUB When? and hit the brakes. Maybe a little too quickly.

In the seat beside her, Sandesh jerked. The coffee in his hand spilled onto his suit pants.

Whoops. "Aw, and I took such care getting you clean during our shower."

Heat flushed his face as he placed his cup in the cup holder, leaned back, and wiped at his pants. "I'd think you'd worry more about the suit you insisted I wear."

"Suggested not insisted. And trust me, if you're coming to the house later for dinner, you'll be glad to be in a suit. Momma does not mess around with that stuff."

"I'll keep that in mind."

Beyond Sandesh, through the window, sat Gracie's car. He must've caught her looking at the white, hail-damaged Ford Fusion. He hitched a thumb toward it. "Gracie's?"

"Yeah." She hated that her voice sounded so hurt. But it did hurt. All of this hurt. "You know, we used to be best friends. We shared a room together, our first drink together, our first sneak out of the house. Not an easy thing when you have armed guards around your home."

"What happened between you?"

"The Tasmanian Devil, a.k.a. Gracie's bio-mom, came back into her life and took her here, to the club. They started and ran the club together. After that, Gracie was different. Now, she hates taking money from Momma, even for the work she does. Reason number one to suspect her."

"Actually, I'd say that falls second to the other thing you told me. About her ex running away after finding out about your family."

Justice halted with one leg out the open door. "Yeah. Coming from a family of vigilantes limits the dating pool."

Sandesh snorted. He climbed out of the Jeep and strolled with her across the gravel to the back of the club. She liked the feel of him at her side. It was nice.

Though it was barely eleven, the club was already open for lunch. An eighties Prince song pounded out into the lot.

Sandesh didn't seem to be a fan. He dug at his ears. "Prince?"

"Club When? changes musical eras every six weeks, so you might not know until you get inside what decade or date or Boston Tea Party you'll find. It must be the eighties this time."

He nodded, getting it.

The music, which had sounded loud outside, hit her with a punch once inside the small, crate-stacked back corridor. Her eardrums pulsed with base vibrations. And her stomach rumbled at the smell of fried onion rings and fish.

Justice expertly avoided the food-carrying waitress, and with Sandesh following, rounded the corner toward the upstairs offices.

She bit into a steamy onion ring. Sandesh looked at her. "How did you get…?" He trailed off as she offered him the rest of the onion ring.

With a shrug, he took and ate it. She put her code into the steel number pad by the security door. It beeped. She waved her wrist and her newly implanted chip over the pad. It beeped, and a shrill warning sounded.

She motioned to Sandesh's wrist. "You have to do the same. It reads the number of people out here and won't open if everyone doesn't have clearance."

Still chewing, a lot less cheerful, he put up his wrist. The pad beeped again and clicked.

She pulled the door open with a heave that brought her onto her heels. The steel-plated, heavy-as-a-tomb door crashed shut behind them.

"Blast proof?"

Dude did not miss a trick.

"Yeah."

All club sounds went silent. Their footfalls echoed up the stairs.

At the top, they entered a hallway. A series of steel security doors lined with security cameras. Information systems, computers, and servers for the underground railroad and its operations were behind those doors.

Maybe she was being paranoid, but she could feel Sandesh taking note. She shouldn't have brought him.

She knocked on Gracie's closed office door. Waited. Sandesh cleared his throat. She really shouldn't have brought him. She knocked harder. Come on.

"Behind you, dork."

Ahhh! Justice spun. Gracie stood there. Full lips cocked back in a smile. A smile echoed by Sandesh.

"You're all kinds of ninja, Gracie." Justice bent and threw her arms around the petite redhead. She smelled like watermelon Jolly Ranchers. Totally normal for her. She squeezed her sister tight, trying to see if she felt different, like a traitor.

Gracie stiffened. That too was normal. Since losing John and Tyler, girl hated to be touched.

Gracie stepped away. "Why are you here?"

Justice went with the lie she and Sandesh had concocted. Which wasn't really a lie since she was genuinely interested. "The kid. Cee."

Frowning, Gracie eyed Sandesh. "And you? Why are you here?"

"I'm a prisoner of love. And your crazy-ass family."

Gracie raised an eyebrow at the word *love*. And, truth, it'd made Justice's heart skip like a kindergartener during recess. She knocked her shoulder into Sandesh. "He's the Scully to my Mulder."

"I think you have that backward," Sandesh said.

Justice shook her head. "I was going by personality."

He flicked his head to the side in a I'll-give-you-that-one gesture. Hard to argue with the truth.

Gracie unlocked her door with a wave of her wrist over the small black pad. "Come on in."

Gracie's office was as neat as a pin. And modern. White bookcases lined the wall behind a bleached white desk. In the corner stood a white grandfather clock with a round, white face. And in front of the desk, two modern, white Belgian linen chairs.

Type A, party of one.

Gracie's neatness made Justice nervous. And she wasn't the only one. Sandesh brushed at the coffee stain on his pants before sitting. Gracie stared at him like he was a walking germ. Girl had mad OCD.

Justice sat, crossed her legs ranch-hand style, right foot on left knee. "What's the holdup with Cee? You haven't even given her a psych eval yet."

Gracie sat in her white leather chair and leveled direct, all-business eyes on her. Sheesh. She wasn't that much older. Why did she seem so freaking ancient?

Maybe it was the way she pinned her hair back—tight little bun, to go with her tight little body. Or the way she carried her loss, high-shouldered, like her back was pinned to the past. Maybe it was the suit. A charcoal-gray Ann Taylor original with matching silk blouse.

Gracie put her hands on the computer mouse and clicked something open. "Who shot the sex-slaver in the distribution center?"

Whoops. Justice stared down at her flats, watched as her toes curled and uncurled, bowing the cheetah-print fabric. "The kid did."

Sandesh's head spun toward her like a rock from a slingshot. Yeah, she'd forgotten to tell a few people that part.

"And you ask me what the holdup is?"

Justice raised her eyebrows. "So she took matters into her own hands. Sounds perfect to me."

"Sounds scary to me."

Scary? "Who else could she depend on? How many times have we seen raids go down at these places and the slavers go free and the women end up punished? Besides, even you can't deny she's got real potential."

Gracie's eyebrows crashed together, like two red lines intersecting to form a stylish V above her nose. "To be adopted as a sister?" Gracie shook her head. "No. She's rejected. She's way too old."

"She's fifteen."

"Possibly sixteen. We don't adopt that late."

"She saved my life."

"Yes. And you should be grateful. And more careful. But that doesn't mean I'm going to go through the trouble of giving her a psych eval, making sure no family is out there, and then washing her to make her look like a legit adoptee. No. She has too much history. Besides, I don't need a psych eval to tell she's messed up."

"Not all of us can be adopted from the cradle, Gracie. Some of us are used, abused, angry, and messed the fuck up."

Gracie crossed her arms under her chest, exposing cleavage, a brown freckle, and a lacy, black bra totally at odds with her bland suit. "Don't belittle my life, Justice. You know what I've lost because of the League."

Yeah. Justice knew. And she didn't want to get into this with her. Not when Sandesh was here, obviously knowing about the family. Not when she was asking her to make room for a kid who was about the same age as the son Gracie had let go.

But Cee deserved better. "She asked, Gracie. You know how rare that is? They never ask. Do you think she's just going to forget about us?"

"No. I'm going to M-erase her."

"You bit—"

Gracie slammed her hand on the desk. "Don't, Justice. I won't put up with that."

Sandesh looked over and mouthed, *M-erase?*

Clenching the seat's arms, Justice shook her head but did her best to keep him up to speed with her next question. "Tell me why you're threatening to erase the memory of a fifteen-year-old girl?"

Because you're a traitor and secretly hate the family and the sister that loves you?

Gracie reached over and took out a watermelon Jolly Rancher from the bowl on her desk. She unwrapped it quietly, expertly. The grandfather clock *tick, tick, tick*ed the seconds away. Gracie put the candy in her mouth. "I've never encountered a rage like hers before. Not since…" Her eyes shifted away from Justice. Her face reddened.

"Yeah. I'm angry. I've always been. I think I punched you in the face the first time we met."

Gracie smiled. "Because I called you my sister. You told me your sister was dead and punched me. But that was different."

"How? How is my childhood anger different from hers?"

Gracie clicked the candy between her teeth, turned it over, sucked it back in. "Don't you have enough, Justice? Isn't getting first Tony and now Sandesh into the League enough? Now you want the kid indoctrinated too?"

Indoctrinated? Justice dropped her foot to the floor with a thud. She sat forward, close enough to see how fast Gracie was breathing. "This isn't about Cee. This is about Momma, our home, the League. You think you know better. You think Cee can do better."

"Yeah. Fine. It's about the way we were raised. The way I was raised before my mom came. Being a Parish, having all that money, having your values and knowledge filtered through the school messes you up. It's different for me. I see things differently."

Justice bit down on her bottom lip. If she had to hear one more time about Gracie's miraculous transformation into worldly woman and how the rest of them were sheltered for too long, she'd lose it.

"You can't use your injury to injure others, Gracie. I'm sorry about John. I'm devastated about Tyler. I wish things had been different. But he left, he chose to get out."

Gracie worked the candy in her mouth and glared like only a redhead with green eyes can—all spit and fire. "God, Justice, you really are the baby of our unit. Grow up. John would never have done that."

"What are you saying?"

Gracie rubbed at her eyes. If she had worn a stitch of makeup, that would've smeared it. But Gracie had no interest in dressing up. Face or body. Her biggest fashion accessory was her incredible body.

She got that from her devotion to the Cambodian martial art of Muay Thai.

And genetics.

"Leland found out John knew about the League."

"Yeah. I remember the shouting. And?"

"And when he found out, he told me there were three choices. The first two involved killing or M-erasing John."

Justice paused for a long beat. "Leland threatened John?"

"The last choice?" Sandesh said.

"I made John go to save him. Told John I chose the League over them." Gracie's voice hitched. "Told him I'd fight for full custody if he ever breathed a word. He left. Stayed silent. Stayed alive."

Gracie stared at Sandesh for a long, complicated moment before licking her lips with a tongue coated unnaturally red. She turned her gaze to Justice. "You asked me how your anger was different from Cee's. You were six. You wanted love and kindness, even if you couldn't admit it. Cee just wants to hurt people. The League is bad enough without adding people like that."

Justice suddenly couldn't breathe. She hurt for Gracie. She did. She couldn't imagine the kind of pain her sister had to carry. Or the rage she must have been holding against Momma and Leland.

A sinking feeling pulled at her stomach. A tremor of doubt convulsed in her heart. The traitor could be Gracie. It could.

Chapter 44

THE HEADQUARTERS FOR THE INTERNATIONAL PEACE TEAM was in a suburb outside of Philly. It was a beautiful building with a sunlight-fed, plant-filled, tree-lined, decorative atrium.

As he entered the Conshohocken building, Sandesh loosened his neck noose. To his mind, ties were a way to make men uneasy, reminding them to choke back any spark of individuality.

He made his way over to the elevator. The phone in his pocket rang. He pulled it out, looked at the screen. Leland. "Yeah."

"I see you are at the IPT."

So this was how it was going to go—weighty reminders that he was being watched. How *I Know What You Did Last Summer*. Sandesh wasn't in the mood. "Yep. I'm at my place of employment, my business." Because he wasn't a prisoner as much as these people wanted to think he was. Bad enough he had to keep looking over his shoulder for Walid and his men.

"What are you doing there?"

"Actually, I was just headed upstairs to prepare my press statement on global covert Parish family activities. Can I get a statement from you?"

There was a pause hard and solid enough to feel like a punch to the gut. "Don't let this get messy, Sandesh. We care about Justice. We'd hoped you did too."

Was that a threat to Justice? Sandesh swallowed the instant gonna-eat-you-up-and-spit-you-out fist rising in his throat. "Look, Leland, we both understand the situation. I'm on your side." For now.

Another weighty pause. Like an orca circling a seal. "Can you still make it to dinner tonight?"

"I've already got it penciled in on my company calendar as a meeting with the head of a secret society."

Leland actually snorted what sounded like a laugh, then hung up.

Sandesh looked at his phone. Before this call, he was wavering on doing what he was about to do, but Leland's threat to Justice, even as mild as it was, sent his defend-and-conquer genes scrambling. He was going to find out everything he could about this family.

The elevator jerked to a stop at his floor. The doors opened, revealing a wall of steel-framed black-and-white photographs. And Victor.

Brown hair buzzed down to military attention, khaki slacks, and a screen-printed T-shirt with a colorful logo of a woman twirling, arms outstretched. Victor had the sleeves rolled up to reveal biceps that meant business and a Death Before Dishonor tattoo. He whistled at Sandesh's suit and winked. "Oh, Sandy. If I were into discipline, I'd be all over you."

Sandesh shook his head. What was it with his bisexual friend? He flirted like he had an agenda to make everyone in the world shake off their uptight restrictions. "I appreciate the love, man. Especially since I pretty much abandoned you for two weeks."

They turned together and walked down the hall into the suite of offices.

"Forget it, Sandman. How's things with Momma Warbucks?"

"Actually, we're going to need to talk about that." He gave Victor a look. "In my office."

Inside the blue-carpeted reception area, seated at her half-moon desk, their receptionist, Myrtle, was on the phone. Sandesh nodded hello but didn't slow down.

The moment he entered his corner office, Sandesh realized the office wasn't as he'd left it. Clean.

Three gray-and-red-striped chairs pulled out around a table with two tablets and multiple files scattered across it.

Sandesh's U-shaped desk was also covered with files. Looked like much of the staff had been here late yesterday organizing volunteers. Sandesh had no idea why his office was the one people gravitated to, but apparently it happened even when he wasn't here.

Victor put a hand on Sandesh's shoulder. "Okay, big guy, that's a lot of brooding silence. Should I pull a fire alarm?"

He really hated to do this to Victor, who'd already done so much for him. "I know you're the last person I should be asking, but I need a favor."

"Hey, my currency is favors. But tell me this isn't about one of those Parish sisters?"

Sandesh slipped behind his desk, put his keys and personal cell atop a stack of files, and plopped into his leather swivel. "No. I mean. Yes. I guess."

Victor tugged at his pants and sat on an edge of Sandesh's desk. "Which one?"

For a moment, Sandesh's mind went blank. Which

one? The only one that mattered. He stared through the thick glass windows that muted the sound of cars on the Schuykill Expressway as they shot past on their gleaming way to the city.

"Dude, tell me it's not that mad scientist Kenyan. That chemist chick has a patent on some sort of mind serum shit. She's selling that to the government."

"You're paranoid." At least he hoped he was. "And no. It's Justice."

"Oh. The hot Native American chick. I'd let her beat my war drum."

Sandesh swiveled toward Victor, held up one finger. "Don't."

That was it. One word. Victor's entire demeanor changed. He met Sandesh's eyes and nodded. Warned. Backing off.

Good.

Sandesh didn't want Justice compressed into anything. Not into a race. Not into a woman. Not into a hot woman. Not into anything that identified her in a way that let her be simplified.

It seemed wrong. Like calling the Pope a religious guy.

Victor had the oddest smile on his lips. What was that about? Sandesh scowled. The grin disappeared. Victor busied himself by picking up the bronze Wounded Warrior statue from the desk, turning it over.

"What favor?"

"I know you have connections." Victor grunted. Yeah, it was like saying Bill Gates had money. "So can you see what you can dig up on Mukta Parish and the Mantua Academy? And four of the Parish family?"

Sandesh began to write down the names of Justice's suspect siblings. Gracie topped his list. Chick didn't trust anyone. To his mind, that was a trait of someone who couldn't be trusted.

Victor raised a hand to take the list. Sandesh pulled it back. "Can you make that five?"

Though he wasn't a sibling, Leland went on the list.

"Yeah." Victor took the paper. "Easy enough. I know someone. Former NSA. She owes me a favor. Or six."

Sandesh pointed at Victor's shirt. "Is that one of ours?"

Victor put the list down and nodded. "Yep. The screen-printing equipment arrived and the women are busy making shirts in Jordan. It's beautiful, right? A Syrian woman designed it, got only one arm. One fucking arm."

"Yeah. I know. I met her. She's incredible." And she wasn't the only one. All of the women there had been fixated on the opportunity to make things better. Turned out Syrians didn't give up easy. He was glad Salma's work was still continuing. "So they're okay at the warehouse?"

"Yeah. You were right about Mukta. First she helped shut down and evacuate Salma's entire operation—and you have to tell me how you managed to get yourself kicked out of Zaatari—then she rented a warehouse in Amman under the guise of a bakery. We're planning on selling the shirts online. Now that we have the funds to begin manufacturing."

Sandesh felt the weight of this entanglement settle in his chest. They'd been at this for a year. And he had no problem with volunteers. No problem with organizations to partner with. But he hadn't been able to get the attention and funding they needed until Mukta.

And now, that gift horse might just screw everything else up.

Sandesh put his hand on the sleeve of his jacket, over his SF tattoo. A scar cut it in half. He'd gotten it during a jump gone wrong. It reminded him that sometimes you had to battle your way to the battle.

Chapter 45

ELEVATOR-X SLID TO A STOP ON 4A. GYM, FIRING RANGE, and lots of secret society–type classrooms.

The doors opened soundlessly as the astringent smell of processed air and show-your-pores-bright fluorescent lights glared down on Justice. She walked along the hall. Tinted glass walls ran along one side of the corridor, showing the firing range. The thick walls muffled the sounds.

She saw a few siblings, but no Tony.

He'd be in the gym, waiting for their scheduled training session. Which is why she'd changed into her workout clothes. Black leggings and T-shirt. Dark clothes to match her mood.

Unlike the gym upstairs, a sensor at these gym doors read her upraised wrist. With a low click, the massive doors whooshed open. A *ping, ping* registered her presence. Her shoulders tightened. Being tracked hadn't bothered her before. Now it made her feel exposed.

As she entered the massive auditorium, she felt that bone-deep sense of pride.

The gym was state-of-the-art. From treadmills that read your vitals, advanced weight machines, trampolines, punching dummies that calculated the force of impact, an area set up as a dojo, a roped-off boxing ring, and at the farthest end—shudder—the Devil's Gauntlet.

The DG had balance obstacles, salmon ladder, cargo

net, warped wall, spider climb, and impossible ledges and agility leaps. It was the League's own version of *American Ninja Warrior*. But the League had had it years before the show made it cool.

Thirty or so people filled the gym, along with their grunts, slaps, clank of weights, and treadmill thuds. She skirted the training mats. The speaker system came online, announcing her and Tony's sparring session.

Right on time.

Shirtless, shoeless, wearing only his well-worn white gi pants, Tony did a double backflip, then sprang off a trampoline, landing with an eager smile.

The best time to talk with Tony was while fighting him. He loosened up. So damn loose and talkative. It was like trying to hit a cross between Stretch Armstrong and Elmo.

They met in the center of the mat.

Usually, they'd run through pattern practice, a series of training skills, and then do a bit of free sparring. But she decided to get right to the fun stuff. She used her outstretched arms to distract him. "Tony. How's my favorite sister?" And sent a spin kick at his ribs.

Tony dodged like water—like water sliding across ice. Her toes skimmed his skin.

He danced back, lean, flexible, and a bundle of muscle. He rubbed at his rib, in the general vicinity of his *All for One* tattoo. "Old moves, J. Rib still pings from last time."

Huh? She was that predictable. "Holding on to a grudge, Tone?" She charged in close, grasped his neck, trying for a neck lock.

He blocked, got control of her arm, trapped it. Fuck.

That hurt. She sent an elbow at his head. He dodged, loosed his grip. She broke away, backed off, shook out her arm.

He flashed pearly, straight teeth. She was pretty sure she could get her entire fist in that mouth. While he ate an apple.

Other than that great smile, he was all deadly charm and South Philly. "Did ya know female ducks got a hidden uterus?"

"What?" He was trying to distract her. But… "Like a covert uterus?"

He sent a front kick at her. She grabbed his heel easy enough. Guy had big feet. He one-leg jumped toward her, shoved a hand up under her chin, forced her head back, ripped his leg free, looped it around hers, tripped her to the floor. She rolled, bounced up.

They were breathing heavy now and starting to sweat. "Know how some animals go all-out, plumes and whatnot, even dance to impress the females?"

He kept an arm's length away, but she watched the spread of his hands, the shift of his hip, and the slide of his feet against the cushioned mat.

"Yeah, so?"

"Well, male ducks ain't goin' for that shit. They just up and rape the females. Fact, they do it all the time. So the female's anatomy adapted. Not only are their duck vaginas ridged like a screw—going the opposite way of the male penis ridges—"

"Ouch. You're makin' shit up."

He threw a right. She blocked with one hand, struck with the other, hooked his leg, flipped him to the mat, and dropped on top of him.

They grappled for a moment. "God's honest," he said, nearly in her ear. He had no shirt and was slippery with sweat, but she managed a leg lock. She put pressure on it. He tapped with his other hand. Enough. She rolled off and bounced back up.

He got to his feet, smiled, danced back. "And their vaginas are like a labyrinth. Fake little offshoots for the sperm the female don't want."

A labyrinth? She blocked his kick with her shin. They exchanged a series of strikes and counterstrikes, and he came in close, got control, forced her head down. She made a move toward his balls, and he dodged. They broke off the exchange.

She wiped sweat from her face. "So what you're saying is a species has developed, through the violence of their own kind, physical ways to prevent rapists from procreating with their rape victims. Wasn't there a weird senator who claimed a human female's body did the same thing?"

"Yeah. Dick. Like women are raped as much as ducks and evolve that kind of shit."

"What? No. I meant he was compa—"

He hit her with a series of fast, hard strikes. Too fast. Not just fast, angry in a way she hadn't expected, that wasn't even close to the playful way they'd been sparring.

She jerked away. He kept coming. She lost her footing, staggered. He swept her legs out from under her. Her head bounced against the mat.

Cushioned or not, that shit hurt.

She stayed down, stretched her legs out in front of her. Tony came over and offered her a hand.

Huh. Accept his hand, or use it to retaliate?

Why had he changed the tone of their sparring? Ah hell. She knew to expect the unexpected. She reached for his hand.

When he pulled her to her feet, she slammed into him, then plopped back on her heels.

"Charming story, Tone."

"It's easy with you, Justice. You bring out the charm in people."

Whatever. She preferred blunt to charming. "So some kind of lesson in that story?"

He walked over and grabbed the floor cleaner. When he returned, she noticed something dark and heavy seemed to weigh down the usual lightness in his hazel eyes. "The lesson is that even the cold gaze of evolution knows when something is wrong. And so do you. You need to be honest with that guy."

"What's it to you?"

"It ain't right. Admit the truth. Admit what we both know. Momma's using his organization. And you're flirting. You don't do boyfriends. And you won't shit on the League's greatest strength, our closed ranks, for a guy."

"Not so closed. He's in. Or didn't you get the memo?"

"Really? So you're going to keep using this guy's humanitarian missions to do global ops?" He held out the floor cleaner. Loser had to clean the mat.

She glared at him.

"So that's a no," he answered for her. "And are you going to quit the League? Help him with his humanitarian work?"

"I'm not quitting the League. Ever."

"No shit." He gave her a smile so crooked it looked

like he'd tasted something sour. "That's what I'm saying. Bad enough you fucked with this guy's business. Don't fuck with his heart."

Justice's shoulder blades drew together. Her neck tensed. Tony. What did he know? She swiped angrily at the mat as Tony's next session was announced. "I can walk and chew gum, Tone. I can have him and the League. Fuck your advice."

He looked at her as if she'd slapped him. "J." His voice was tight with hurt and more than a little angry. "Fine. Go the way of Dada. Make that colossal mistake."

"What does that mean?"

"It means Dada has spent more time mooning over her informant than doing the job. Ask Jules."

Another set of toes had appeared. Neat and trimmed. And painted black. Justice looked up. Juliette, a.k.a. Jules.

Justice creased her brow. "Don't you usually train with Dada?"

Juliette looked down at Justice. Her hands fisted at her sides. "She says she's sick, but I just saw her pigging out in the break room." Juliette pointed at Tony. "So I get to train with Monkey Man. Again."

Tony put a hand to his chest as if insulted. "Monkey Man's gonna kick your ass, Jules."

Break room? Dada had to know Tony already had his hands full with Jules's twin, the other half of the dynamic duo, Romeo.

God, those names. Some parents were so fucked up.

The twins, Romeo and Juliette, had been adopted eight years ago. The second male adopted into the Parish fold. Tony loved the kid.

A quick visual sweep, and she spotted Romeo. Rome.

He worked the heavy bag. He was a big kid. Muscular. And though Jules's twin, he shared little in common with her. She was blond and golden-skinned. He was dark-haired and pale-skinned.

"I'll talk to her," Justice said.

Jules turned her head slightly, as if to avoid a bad smell. Yeah. Lame. What else could she say? Justice finished wiping and stood up.

"Monkey Man has a next victim," Tony said and let his arms drag to his sides. He began making monkey noises. Jules looked terrified. And pissed. "Tell Dada she sucks."

Will do. One, "you suck, Dada" coming up. Subheadlined with, "What's this I hear about you and your Brothers Grim informant?"

───∽∽∽───

Still a sweaty mess, Justice heel-toed her way to the break room. What the hell was up with Dada? You didn't just abandon your little sister like that. And what was it with her and her informant?

After waving her wrist over the door panel, there was a series of high to low beeps, then the overly feminine-sounding computer program said, "Authorization for forty minutes in lounge B. No weapons allowed. Do not abuse this privilege. Thank you."

Sometimes security was too damn much. Like all the slackers would be tempted to hang out in a boring break room watching CNN. Can't get enough steel cubbies and plastic seats pushed up against round, white-laminate tables.

She walked inside. The whole room smelled of

marinated steak and freshly baked bread. The red spikes of Dada's size-nine Jimmy Choos were propped up on the smooth, white table, near a balled-up wrapper of white, crinkly paper and a bottle of imported water.

Her indigo skirt had slid up, revealing long, glossy, black legs.

Dada waved at one of three flat-screen TVs on the wall. "Look, Justice, Fahid scored. Isn't he beautiful?"

Justice slid into the seat opposite from her sister. Dada developed crushes on soccer players the way teenage girls developed crushes on characters in books.

And maybe on informants. "What does your informant do for the Brothers Grim?"

Dada sat up, fingered the thick, woven-leather bracelet on her wrist.

It was a nervous habit and the only jewelry Dada wore. If not on a mission, where it was part of an image, she stayed away from jewelry. Jewelry reminded her of her childhood. Her bio-mother had dressed her in jewelry right before she sold Dada's body. The first time, she'd been eight.

Mukta had found Dada four years later inside a brothel. She'd been giving birth. The bracelet was for the child. The boy who had not survived.

"He provides documents. That is how I knew the Brothers had changed locations. He isn't involved with them otherwise."

"Oh. Okay, so he just helps the slavers get around."

Dada's gold eyes widened, then narrowed. "Juan became involved before he knew of their business. Now he is trapped."

She seemed to know a lot about this man. What else did

she know? "Why do you think the Brothers picked Jordan? A place where we have so few resources? Coincidence?"

"I have an informant, not access to their brain waves."

"If you had to guess?"

"If I had to guess, I'd say the Brothers Grim were informed that this was an ideal place to get away from an imminent threat and still proceed with their meeting."

Justice flinched. Looked like the cat was out of the bag. And peeing all over the bed. "Could your informant have—"

"No. He knows nothing of us."

"But—"

"I am not a novice. I know how to manage an informant."

"Really? How much time do you spend managing this guy?"

Dada's eyes dropped. "If you are asking if I am sleeping with him, the answer is yes."

Whoa. What? If she was willing to admit that, admit the violation, she must be in it bad. Or guilty. "What the fuck? You've risked the League. This guy, this informant, has obviously told them about—"

"First, you have no room to talk. You revealed secrets to Sandesh. You—"

"That's not the same—"

"No. It is worse. But Juan is not being brought into the family and welcomed. He does not have a charity Momma can use as cover."

"Sandesh risked himself—"

"Juan risked himself. He provided us with secret information. He told us of Jordan. He cares."

He cared? Well, she obviously did. What would Dada

do to keep Juan safe? Could Dada have actually tipped off the Brothers in order to get the change of venue, create an opportunity for Juan to run?

If so, had he run? Only one way to find out. "I'm going to need Juan's help to get into Walid's Mexican compound."

Dada recoiled. "Those men are aware now. Anything he does could draw suspicion. They are already attempting to find him and us."

"All the more reason for him to help."

"Justice"—Dada slapped her hands together—"the nature of the work is covert. We need to work on covering our tracks. If we wanted to be heavy-handed killers, we wouldn't need preparation and subtle manipulation."

"Wrong. I know of many brutal retaliations carried out by the League with minimal prep. And more exposure."

"By our sisters in arms in poorer countries. In places where the myth is necessary, where men can be scared from their abuse. But we are talking about going on the offensive against organized crime. At their home base. When they are ready. This is not something done with a cudgel or by slicing off someone's balls."

Justice stood up and headed for the doors. "I'm going to need Juan's help."

Dada pointed a finger at Justice. "Not everything is simple. You can't always use your temper to shape the world to your desires."

The doors slid open at her approach. "Actually, that's kind of our company motto."

Chapter 46

BLOOD SATURATED THE CEMENT FLOOR AND ITS SCENT permeated the chill air of the underground chamber.

At times, Walid thought the world was full of people who did not want to listen. Or learn. His hands ached from trying to get this man to listen to reason.

Walid flexed his sore hands. "Juan, we already know that you are sleeping with a woman. We know that you have been giving her information. Why will you not admit to this? Why must you make me beg not to hurt you? Please. Tell me who she is. Who is behind her?"

Juan sniveled mucus and blood. "No. Not me. Didn't."

Walid furrowed his brow. What he had done to this man was beyond what most could endure. It made no sense that he still held out. Could Dusty have been mistaken?

He called to his man. The former FBI agent entered through the arched doorway with a face as blank as a freshly cleaned chalkboard.

Walid pointed to Juan. "Are you sure this is the one?"

Dusty's eyes didn't drop to the man. He obviously knew better. Some images stained the mind. The control Walid had over his own mind was not common.

"It's him. Like you asked, your brother's men over-saw the entire process. They went through everyone. Not just current employees and contractors, but former."

Walid heard something in Dusty's voice: Annoyance? Disgust? Jealousy? "Yes. They are good men. They also located the digital trail and have men attempting to get information from the go-between."

They hadn't succeeded yet, but he didn't need to know that.

Dusty's eyes opened. "You didn't tell me?"

Walid cleared his throat. That was something. His realizing he'd been demoted. "Why would I? I am master here."

Juan pulled against the straps holding him to the dentist chair. A surprising burst of energy. "Let me die."

Dusty's eyes did drop then. "Let me finish him."

Walid's anger surged. "I need this information. Or do you think my brother's death a minor matter?"

Juan's momentary burst of energy left him. He dropped his hands against the metal supports and began to weep. "Let me die."

Ah. Now they were getting somewhere. Walid bent over him, smoothed a hand along the man's sweat-soaked scalp. "Do you think I want to see your pain?"

Juan cough-laughed through tears and blood. "You like this."

Walid looked toward the door of the underground chamber. He was glad to see his man, Dusty, had shut it when he left. He didn't like his men to witness these moments.

"All you must do is tell me about your woman and who is behind her. And then, I will kill you."

And her. And anyone who rose against us. With great fanfare.

Chapter 47

THE LINE OF FOUR GIRLS AND ONE BOY THAT RANGED IN ages from thirteen to seventeen shifted and squirmed on the dojo floor before Justice and Bridget. If Cee was adopted and added to this group, this would be the biggest unit ever.

Bridget had the floor, but no one's attention. They were nervous about dinner. If you weren't on time, you skipped dessert. And they still had to go upstairs and get dressed.

Bridget tried the Momma clap. A few ears perked up. "Please remember the three moves we showed you are quick defense. And only part of what you need. Remember what I said about keeping your eyes open, your spirit open, always noticing the world, even if it's uncomfortable. In fact, if it makes you uncomfortable, pay even more attention."

A few nodded, but most had their eyes on the door. Justice gave her too-kind sister the look. Bridget sighed, and with a wave, gave Justice the go-ahead.

Yeehaw. "Sisters!"

All heads snapped up. Romeo's eyes narrowed.

Huh.

Sensitive.

With a too-high opinion of himself. Probably because of his looks. That striking, tapered edge to his large, amber-brown eyes. As if somewhere buried within his

Slavic ancestry was a long-gone relative from China. She didn't bother to correct her word choice.

He'd learn.

"All for one and one for all isn't just a motto. Trust us. If we hold you here longer than necessary, it's because this matters more than dessert."

They quieted. A few looked abashed. Some angry.

She watched emotions play across their faces. A difference in skin tone, eye color, height, weight, and yet they all had the fire; they were all family.

Bridget took over again. She met the eyes of each, bowed at the waist. "Namaste."

Five teens tore up and out.

Bridget frowned. Justice hid her smile. She couldn't count the number of times she'd been trained here and had waited while an older classman went on and on about stuff that seemed irrelevant.

She turned to Bridget, watching the others go with that frown still on her face.

What was that about? Hmmm. "We should get the Troublemakers to rename that unit."

Justice inclined her head toward the stampeding teens. At the landing, one of the girls used the banister to slingshot herself up the next staircase. "They're more *Fast and Furious* than *Vampire Academy*."

Bridget smiled. "Yeah, but we nailed the Troublemakers. Those three. Sheesh. They need meditation."

Justice picked up her towel and cell phone. "Or Xanax."

Bridget laughed. Her eyes turned contemplative. "Whoever started the idea of letting the older unit be in charge of naming the unit directly below them?"

Huh. Who had started it? Momma had been adopting lost girls since she was twenty-three, for over forty years. The first unit, Fantastic Five, Momma had named. Justice's unit was the third of seven. "Momma, I guess. But we have the A-Team to thank for our awful name, Spice Girls."

Bridget shook her head. "God, Tony hates that."

"You mean Sporty Spice? Yeah. He does. I still think the youngest unit has it the worst. Really, the Lollipop Guild. I guess it's all part of having a big family. Teasing."

Bridget frowned. "Things have gotten a bit contentious in these past years. More fights. More issues."

They exited the gym and stood together in the front hall. "Yeah. I guess. I mean it's a mansion full of kids. A mansion full of kids, sorted into units based on age, not when they were adopted. We have our own freaking culture. Do you think that's the problem?"

In the hall, the echo of *Vampire Academy* teens running around upstairs crashed down the steps. Whoa. Bulls at Pamplona up there.

Bridget glanced up the steps as if she could see the offenders. "I don't know. Do you think we're doing right by any of them?"

What? "We saved them. Taught them to fight. Taught them not to be victims. Yes, we're doing the right thing."

Bridget's face heated. "I know. I know that. It's just...the violence."

"They have a choice. We all have a choice."

"Do they?"

A buzzing reminder of Bridget's earlier words zipped through Justice's head: *If something makes you uncomfortable, pay more attention.*

What the hell was up with Bridget? Could she be trying to undo the school, expose it or make it feel threatened enough that covert ops were stopped?

"What would you have us do, Bridget?"

Her lips thinned and tightened, like the boom gate falling across a train track. For a moment, Justice was sure the conversation was over, but Bridget's lips unclenched. "It's like with the yoga. I mean, the Sanskrit. Words matter. It's brain food. So if you give a child thoughts that are like junk food, you have to expect they're going to have bad reactions. Thoughts can destroy us, Justice."

"So, what? We should teach them only good, happy thoughts?"

"No. That's not... Maybe we should teach them how to do a mental detox. The same way we tell them to avoid bad food, we can teach them how to step away from thoughts."

Oh. Boy. How come when people went all cosmic interface, they forgot what was weird? "Bridge, we're a school. We can't go around teaching kids how not to think."

Bridget's lips tightened again. A firm, disappointed line on a face that was usually bright and open. She fiddled with the black belt around her gi. "You know, I get that a lot of times you and the others make fun of me. Act like what I do makes me a pie-in-the-sky hippie, but you're wrong. Meditation allows me to see a macro-view, not just of my own thoughts, but of the thoughts of people around me. It's incredibly enlightening. It's almost a superpower."

A cold knife of fear unsheathed itself and pressed to

Justice's throat. That was very *Pinky and the Brain*. "So, you're smarter than the rest of us?"

Could macro-viewpoint Bridget have plotted against the family to show them the error of their ways?

"Not smarter. Just less attached to the thoughts that might keep your mind looping, keep you from seeing the bigger picture."

"Keep me from seeing the bigger picture? Like we should just hold hands with sex-slavers?"

Bridget looked down. Shook her head. "It's like with your humanitarian—there are other ways to help."

"He's not *my* humanitarian."

"He's not? But he's okay with all of this? With what you do?"

"He's implanted, so yeah, I assume he's okay with it."

Bridget's eyes slid sideways toward Justice. "You should definitely ask him."

She walked away, leaving Justice to stand in the hallway contemplating doubts and bad choices and bad decisions she would never be able to take back.

Chapter 48

SANDESH'S TRUCK IDLED BEFORE THE MANTUA HOME'S front gate. Armed guards checked his credentials. They had some serious campus security. How could people not realize just how serious? Did every school act like they expected an attack by armed gunmen? Okay. Stupid question. Every school in America probably expected armed gunmen.

Still, none of this mattered if the threat was already inside. His cell rang. He picked up. "You ready for my family?"

"Ready and willing." Knowing their phones had end-to-end encryption, he asked, "What'd you find out today?"

"Dada's sleeping with her Brothers Grim informant."

Maybe he should take back the ready part of his statement. "Can't be good."

"Yeah. Betting money's on her or Bridget right now."

The guard approached his truck. "One sec, Justice."

The guard handed back his ID and a printed pass with a barcode, and told him to put it on his dash. He did.

Another guard withdrew the mirrored pole she'd used to check beneath his truck. They waved him inside.

He entered slowly, necessitated by the speed bump, and came to rest at a stop sign. To his right, the campus stretched over rolling hills. Brick school buildings, dorms, the library, and cafeteria hub, and winding

among all of them, walkways lined with elegant street-
lights. The overcast and misty afternoon couldn't lessen
the beauty of the campus. Of course it would be beautiful. A school this prestigious had a reputation to uphold.

Girls of varying ages walked here and there. They all
looked so young. Innocent.

Was it possible for Walid to find his way here?
Sandesh tightened his grip on the steering wheel. No.
Mukta Parish had kept this school safe for forty years.
He had to remember that.

"So we're not thinking Gracie?" Having to send away
your son and the love of your life because he found out the
family secret could be a reason to try and expose the group.

"I don't know. Bridget said some weird things today.
She thinks she's got some kind of super-brain that can
tell what people are thinking. Or something like that. It
was really weird."

That was strange. Turning left on School Drive then
right on Parish Court, he headed up the hill to the big
house. BIG house. "And your brother, Tony?"

"He thinks the League is reverse sexist. He told me
that he'd given Momma a plan before the BG mission,
to take out the Brothers separately. She never brought it
up to the team. He seemed pissed about it."

"Have you seen the plan? Could we use it to get Walid?"

She paused as if that hadn't occurred to her. "I'll
reach out to Leland. Ask to see it."

He crested the top of the hill. "I'm out front."

"Almost ready. Be down in a sec." She hung up.

He pulled around the fountain and parked in one of
the few open spaces. He turned off his truck, got out,
and surveyed the 1914 stone mansion.

He'd heard they'd done a massive renovation thirty years ago, but he couldn't tell the old from the new. The three stories, finely crafted cornices, arches, and long, elegant windows fit together seamlessly.

With enough money, you could do anything. Even run a secret society of vigilantes in your huge mansion.

A lean, sixtyish woman with a military-straight posture, shiny silver hair, pale-blue eyes, paler-white skin, black suit, and a jagged scar across her nose approached him. A butler?

She greeted him with a brisk, "Welcome, Mr. Ross. My name is Martha. I'm head of home security. I'm here to show you to the dining room."

Okay. Not a butler. Head of home security. So, if he had it right, there was home security for the house, internal security for underground ops, and external security for the grounds and the school.

Huh. Seemed pretty damn secure.

———⁓———

In many ways, going to dinner at the Parish residence felt like going to a dance at an all girls' school.

Lots of beautiful dresses. Not a lot of guys.

Sandesh matched Martha's brisk stride down the richly carpeted hall. She led him to a long dining room that looked more like a banquet hall, complete with multiple doorways.

Martha gestured toward the table. "Would you like me to show you to your seat, or would you prefer to wait for Justice?"

Seemed wrong to sit without her. "I'll wait."

She nodded and moved away.

Inside, the rectangular runway of a room had to be three thousand square feet. Multiple smaller side tables, with seating for two or four or six, flanked the walls. A thick-legged wooden beast of a table that could seat at least forty dominated the room.

Above this fortress of a table, old wood beams crossed a fifty-foot vaulted ceiling. A gleaming row of mismatched crystal chandeliers hung from the central beam and ran the length of the Goliath table.

Thick, hand-carved chairs abutted the table, which was dressed with crystal glasses and yellow roses and gold-edged plates.

Mukta and Leland were already here, walking around the table, addressing children here and there, directing others to take certain seats. They then took their own places, two seats at the head of the table. How very royal of them.

Girls of varying ages, and one out-of-place teen boy, slipped past Sandesh like he was a rock in a stream.

He watched as the groups, what Justice had told him were units, automatically sat together. No one acknowledged him. He felt almost unwelcome, standing at the doorway of a banquet room with heavy chandeliers and ceremony and community.

A warm arm slipped around his waist.

The heat that shot through him was answer enough, but he looked down anyway.

She wore an apple-red, juicy-as-sin, off-the-shoulder, like-a-second-skin dress. Damn memory was so inadequate when it came to this woman. His arm went around her, drew her to his side.

Justice rose up and whispered hot into his ear, "Hungry?"

The message delivered within the waves of heat milking his body had nothing to do with food and everything to do with the feeding of his lips against her skin.

Yes. Starved. His eyes feasted on the pert, juicy curves. He swallowed. "Where do I sit?"

She winked at him, winked at him with lashes so lush they seemed made of silk and sleep. Looking into her eyes reminded him of the dark. Of the dark covering bodies. Of the dark covering their intertwined bodies.

She grabbed his hand and pulled him after her. "Keep looking at me like that and we'll never make it through dinner."

Chapter 49

JUSTICE TUGGED SANDESH, WHO STILL WORE HIS YUMMY BLUE suit, through the room. She explained the seating arrangements to him as they walked.

"We have five units here tonight. Mine." She pointed toward the head of the table near Momma and Leland. She leaned closer to him, close enough to whisper. "We'll sit across from them. Concentrate on Bridget."

He nodded. Justice slid to a halt as a child raced by. "That would be Bella. She's one of the two members of the Lollipop Guild."

"You think more will be added?"

"Oh, definitely. And unfortunately, the youngest unit always sits near Momma, gives the nannies a break, so you'll get plenty of time to become acquainted with Bella."

The Troublemakers' Guild, capital *T* for Trouble, caught Justice's attention. They had already scored some vino. She introduced them to Sandesh. They waved hello, almost like normal people, but as she and Sandesh walked away, she saw the trio eyeing Sandesh's backside appreciatively. Cue eye roll.

She introduced the teens of *Vampire Academy* and the tweens of *Lost in Translation*—not a one of them had spoken English or even the same language when they'd come here—before leading him to the head of the table.

Momma welcomed Sandesh. He greeted her and Leland coolly. Still some anger there.

Justice pulled out a chair for him directly across from Tony.

Looking amused as she held out his chair, Sandesh sat and said hi to the munchkin on his left, Bella, and nodded to Tony and Bridget across from him.

Justice slid into her seat beside him. He leaned all his beautiful, blond self toward her. Her heart approved by doing a yeehaw high kick followed by a hot-damn jig in her chest.

"Is it rude of me to ask—"

She leaned closer to him, inhaled. "Let's hope so."

He laughed and brushed the hair from her bare shoulder. He seemed unaware of how intimate the gesture was. She wasn't.

Maybe Bridget had been right. And Tony. Should she make it clear she was never leaving the League?

He waved at the large dining table with its usual mix of loud and louder. "How do you keep everyone straight?"

Her turn to smile. Not twenty minutes ago, she'd called one of her siblings by the wrong name. "Sometimes it's confusing. But mostly it's like keeping your extended family's names straight."

He didn't look convinced. "My extended family isn't that big." He took a sip of water from a gold-ringed crystal goblet. "What about getting to know them all?"

"Yeah. That's harder than remembering names. Dinners like this help. It's expected for each unit, if in the area, to show up once a week."

"Unit? You said that had to do with when you were born not adopted, right?"

"Yep. It's an age range. Kids from birth to seven.

Eight to twelve. Thirteen to eighteen. Like that. They share a bathroom. Share a floor. Share a tutor."

Share covert training.

"So Gracie was in your unit? Who else?"

He knew who else. He was asking to get a better feel for the potential traitor and so they could engage with the people across the table from them. She could use the help. Right now, it seemed like it could be anyone.

"I was raised with Dada and Gracie." She looked around. Gracie never came, but where was Dada?

"Hey, Tone." He looked up from his seat across from them. "Where's Dada?"

"Sick."

Again?

She pointed at Tony. "Tony and Dada are the oldest in my class at thirty-four. Say hi, old man."

Tony's eyes swept over the two of them. They stopped on Sandesh. For a moment, Justice thought Tony would say something embarrassing. Like, *Dude, she's using you*. She transmitted a warning to him through slit-serious eyes. Tony smiled, nodded at Sandesh. "Hey."

Sandesh acknowledged him with a return nod.

Phew. She pointed to Bridget, next to Tony. "Bridget's the middle kid. And our local yogi." Who apparently had super mind powers.

Bridget waved.

"But of course, you already know the best."

Sandesh leaned into her, brushed his lips against her ear.

Oh. Yes. That. Felt. Great.

"Is it Gracie?"

She covered her mouth and smothered her laugh.

What. The. Hell? She wasn't a girl who covered her mouth. Or giggled at a guy. But she'd done just that. Hadn't she?

He smiled along with her, and the heat in his eyes was as playful as it was deadly serious. She could feel Tony and Bridget gaping at her. Good. Let them feel off-balance. Maybe it would shake something loose.

"Are you in love, Justice?"

Holy shit!

The midget sitting next to Sandesh had asked the most embarrassing question known to big sisters everywhere. The five-year-old Russian with big, brown eyes and a long, evil grin jumped up and down in her seat.

Turned out the younger kids' group name was dead-on. Like the Lollipop Guild from *The Wizard of Oz*, they should've been cute, but they were scary as hell. And so was her newest sister. She'd have to make a point to get to know the evil monster better.

And teach her some manners.

"For a little whiles anyways," Tony said and grinned at Justice.

Gawd. Tony and all his South Philly.

Sandesh didn't look the slightest bit concerned. In fact, he looked like he was enjoying himself. "Love takes time, Bella. But I hope Justice and I can spend as long as it takes." He winked at Justice. "And then some."

Aw, seriously, that might be the cutest answer ever. And her own damn heart told her she didn't need even one more minute. What was that about?

Sandesh dipped down to Bella's level. He stage-whispered, "How long do you think it's going to take me?"

And…that was it. The room erupted with speculation.

Chapter 50

OUTSIDE AFTER DINNER, THE NIGHT WAS COOL AND THE AIR smelled of the rain shower that had just passed. Sandesh followed the motion of Justice's hand as she buttoned up her jacket, outlining the soft curves and the dress that made him swallow hard.

They descended the stone steps and walked down the driveway, past his truck and the row of cars gathered there. He tucked his hands inside the pockets of his slacks.

She looped her arm through his. "You really enjoyed it? That dinner? Despite all the giggling and talking and squeeing?"

"Squeeing?" The cobbled driveway gave way to the paved drive, and they stepped onto a sidewalk. Justice's heels clicked against the concrete.

"It's a sound girls make when they're highly pleased."

Wrought-iron lampposts lit the way. He found himself angling his walk, as if drawn to her body. Truth. He'd had worse targets. "I think I've heard you make that sound before. But it was louder and involved more sighs."

He winked at her. Good thing he knew exactly how to follow up sexual banter with action. He unhooked his arm from hers and put it around her.

She leaned into him. "Sandesh, truth, if I didn't have to sneak you past my little sisters, I'd take you up to my room right now."

His heart picked up speed and expectations. He

wasn't sure what he was supposed to say to that, but doubted, *I can scale the side of this house into your bedroom* would be appropriate. So he settled for, "I'm good with my truck."

She laughed, snuggled closer. After long, easy moments of silence, she said, "Did you get any vibes?"

He let out a breath. He'd had some vibes for sure. Tony. There was something there. But he didn't know enough about any of them. Yet. "I'm going to withhold judgment. For now."

She lifted her head off his shoulder and her eyes to the skies. "Guess it was too much to hope we'd be able to sort all of this out in one day."

He smiled. She was obviously joking. "We have some time. Whoever it is has to be a little afraid. Afraid enough to hold back from any activity that might draw attention to them."

She pointed ahead on the path. "That way. I want to show you something."

They walked down lanes with elaborately carved shrubs, then stopped at a grotto lit by two spotlights. A series of iron candleholders with white candles sat along the perimeter. The sign on the outside read, BEFORE US, YOU.

Along the inside of the grotto were statues. Women with baskets on their heads, others bent as if to gather a harvest. A woman carrying a child stood off to the farthest side; another child clung to her dress.

At the center of these statues was a lone figure on her knees. Her arms thrown wide, her head thrown back, wailing to the heavens. None of the other statues faced her, so she seemed alone in her grief.

"This is my favorite place on campus. Besides the gym." Justice bent, grabbed a long match from a lidded tin, lit it from one candle, and transferred the flame to another candle.

"What is this place?"

She stood up, blew out the match, and passed it through a slot in a small silver box. "The Grotto of Shoulders. I light a candle for my sister Hope whenever I pass it."

"Grotto of Shoulders?"

She gestured at the statues. "These are the shoulders of the women we have stood upon. All over the world, women who were strong so others could benefit. This is why I fight. So other people can stand on my shoulders." She pointed to the candles. "The candles are lit in memory of them. Can I light one for someone you know?"

He felt his throat grow tight. Though he'd seen her just this afternoon, she hadn't been there. Not mentally anyway. "My mother."

She nodded, reached over, and took another long match from the tin. She bent and lit another candle.

When she was done, he held his arms open. She walked into them without a second thought.

He wrapped her up, held her tightly, securely. He kissed her soft, black hair. "I'm so sorry, Justice. I wish I could spare you even the memory of that pain, that basement, your sister's death."

She took a deep breath, let it out. "The memory is my strength. I need it."

"No." God. No. "That's what we tell ourselves, but it's not the memory of pain we need, it's the good stuff. Like me and you."

She grabbed the front of his shirt, fisted it, and leaned her forehead against his chest. He brushed the back of her hair, uncertain. After long minutes, she looked up at him. "I'm not serious here. I can't be."

"What?"

"I just want you. Physically. Just sex. Okay?"

Nope. Too late for that. "Where is this coming from?"

She scrunched up her face, grabbed tighter to his shirt. "I'm not quitting the League. Ever."

So that was it. "Look, Justice, I get it. You. This place. The kids here. Before I came here, I didn't understand. I get it now. It's more than war. A lot more."

Her breath hitched. The worry in her eyes eased. She ran her hand along his jaw. "I bet you're like some kind of grotto gigolo, making a move on the women as they swoon over the candlelight."

He laughed. "That's it exactly. Ready to drop your panties yet?"

Of course, he remembered a second too late that he was dealing with Justice Parish, and sexual banter was more like a pole dance than a subtle striptease.

"Maybe I was unclear earlier. Basically, you could take me behind that tree and have me."

She pumped her eyebrows. He was seriously growing to love that gesture. She eased closer, lifted onto her toes, and angled her head. "I'm serious."

God help him.

Chapter 51

JUSTICE SIGHED DESPERATE RELIEF AS SANDESH'S MOUTH dropped and slanted against her lips. She slid her tongue inside. Oh. His mouth was so hot. His strong, slick tongue so skillful.

Her eager exploration quickly raged into hot, open-mouthed, frantic kisses.

He grasped her at the waist, pulled her decisively against his hard-on. The tight ache of need sped up her heart, flushed her skin. She wiggled against him. He moaned.

She pulled away, kissed her way to his ear. "Cameras. The trees."

Their mouths collided again. He lifted her, cupping her ass with his large hands. He carried her back behind the trees.

Damn the security cameras. Like a horny adolescent, all she could think about was the cover of darkness and his hands under her jacket.

She pulled at him, his clothes, urged him deeper into the woods. Hidden by trees and darkness, he thrust her back against a tree. His body was hot and hard against her.

The taste of his mouth, the tingle of his tongue made her entire body scream for him. More. Closer. Skin. She needed skin.

Trembling, frantic hands explored under his jacket,

his shirt, found his skin, muscles, and warmth. She stroked and rubbed the sharp lines on his abs.

His hands undid the buttons of her jacket. She slipped out of it, and he pulled down the strap to her dress, releasing a breast. He expertly teased the taut, hard nipple with nimble fingers. Oh. That felt good.

His cock was so hard she could feel him throbbing against her. She rolled her hips. His breath hitched. He let it out on a moan, a deep and wild sound, a deep and wild promise that would've buckled her legs if the press of his body hadn't pinned her so firmly against the tree.

She grew so hot and wet and ready she couldn't wait. She broke the kiss, arched against him, reached for his pants. "Now."

He smiled against her cheek. He rubbed and excited her nipple with one experienced hand. She drew in a breath, tossed her head against the rough tree bark. "Please."

"Not yet." He pushed her dress and underwear down, letting them drop to her ankles, and helped her step free. She was naked in the moonlight and should've been cold. She wasn't.

He teased the curls of hair. His fingers dipped between her legs. He murmured in appreciation. "So soft. So fucking wet."

His fingers stroked her wetness, increasing the friction until she went mad and began to grind into his hand. He rubbed her clit with his thumb. She gasped, spread her legs wider. "Yes. That."

She was on fire as he pushed his fingers inside. She approved, saying words in a language that she'd thought she'd forgotten long ago.

"Damn. I can't wait to feel all this softness around my cock."

Oh. Good. She loved that too.

"After I taste you."

Oh. And that.

He kissed her neck. Her collarbone. His mouth descended and sucked her hardened nipple, then his tongue did something that made her cry out.

He moved lower, kissed her stomach. Her thighs opened in the moonlight. Opened for him.

He dropped to his knees, teased her clit with his tongue. Electric sparks shot through her. He sucked slow and deep. Hard and fast. Alternating. Devouring. She whimpered, threading her hands through his hair.

His fingers slipped inside her, moved in and out.

Oh. God. His fingers gyrated inside, against her. She cried out. How was he doing that? How was he...?

That lovely wet tongue. Those bending, snaking, strumming fingers. Her core tightened around him. She writhed and moaned.

His tongue played against her sweetness faster, faster. His fingers played inside her, quick and nimble, as if he'd played this instrument a thousand times and knew the exact chords.

She came. Released with a cry of pleasure. A throaty, "God, don't stop. Don't stop."

Chapter 52

JUSTICE SHOOK AND CAME AGAINST HIM WITH A DEEP AND insistent cry that had Sandesh's cock so hard it was painful.

She writhed and convulsed and shuddered. He licked and tasted the most sensitive part of her, hot and warm and salty in his mouth. So good. So sweet.

When she was done, when her hands released the stranglehold she'd had on his hair and the last throb and pulse died against his tongue, with her body still sensitive and waiting, he rose.

She kissed him, long and deep. He loved that she liked to taste herself on his tongue. He unbuttoned his slacks.

Justice was there instantly, pulling them down, releasing him. She grasped his shoulders and jumped. Though he hadn't been ready, he caught her. His hands firmly under her ass. She wrapped her legs around his waist, lowered down as he thrust inside her.

He buried his mouth in her neck. "Justice."

With his help, she began to ride him.

A physical whir from above alerted his system, cut through his lust. He stopped. She made a whimpering sound, began to move again. He leaned her back against the tree, held her there. "That sound."

"What?" She was breathless. Her voice fuzzy.

His head cleared only slightly quicker. He knew that sound. "Do you have drones here?"

"What? No."

A concussive bang ricocheted through the trees, through his nerves.

A bomb.

———✺———

Sandesh tripped out of the trees and onto the path, zipping up his fly.

Justice followed a moment later. Dress in place, eyes wide. She grasped his elbow. "Was that an explosion?"

"Yeah. Come on." He grabbed her hand and pulled her toward the red glow in the distance. Smoke rose into the sky. The fire alarm sounded. Only to be quickly silenced and replaced with a warning for everyone to seek shelter. Several blue strobe lights began to spin along the path.

She pulled against his hand, stopping him. "This way. It's faster."

She dropped his hand, flicked off her heels, and ran through the trees, despite twigs and branches. He followed.

She grabbed the hem of her dress and darted through the night and trees as well as any trained soldier. Better. She knew this place. Adrenaline and a real fear for her and her family meant his heart pounded in his chest like a boxer on the heavy bag. He kept up, learned the land by paying attention to her footfalls.

After a minute of full-out sprinting, her lean frame leapt over a hedge of shrubs and landed on the main road, School Drive. He was right on her heels.

To their left was the big house, which seemed to have every light on. In the distance, he spotted the gatehouse that served as the main campus entrance.

It was on fire.

Stones and rubble were strewn across the entrance, blocking it. One guard was helping another one hobble away from the destruction. A third guard yelled into a two-way radio. A fourth was outside the gate, beyond the stones, weapon drawn, scanning for approaching danger.

Sandesh increased his pace, pulled up next to Justice, bent to her ear. "Drones. Someone dropped a bomb. Might be more. Nix the warning system. It's too loud."

Her eyes were wide and worried, but she pulled to a stop and took out her phone. She punched the number. "Security. We believe there are drones—"

Another explosion behind. And another. He and Justice crouched automatically. Fires started in the distance.

Sandesh jumped rubble, ran over to the gatehouse and the security personnel. "Can you light this place up? Turn on every light, floodlight, you have?"

The woman, who'd been speaking into her mic, clicked it again and relayed the information. In seconds, lights began to go on all over the school. Even lights inside classrooms and all along the walk. They were seriously tied in here.

The warning system went silent.

"There, there, there." Sandesh pointed at the sky, turned the guard by the shoulders. She shook her head, uncomprehending.

Justice sprang up next to them. "I see it."

As if she'd handled as many weapons as he had over the years, and she might have, she removed the guard's sidearm. The guard objected. Too late.

Justice aimed, pointed, and fired repeatedly. *Pop. Pop. Pop.*

The drone exploded in the air. Fiery fragments rained down as it slammed into the ground. Pieces scattered in all directions.

The guard looked over at her, skimmed Justice and her gown. "You just hit a drone from the sky. At night. In a ball gown."

The guard and Justice stared at each other. Justice shrugged. "I'm going to keep your gun."

She turned to Sandesh. "We need to get organized. You're going to have to leave."

Chapter 53

JUSTICE HAD TO BALL HER HANDS TO KEEP FROM SHOVING Sandesh through the gate and off the property. If his car hadn't been up the hill, she might have.

Sandesh's entire demeanor changed from ex-soldier taking control to ex-soldier digging in his heels. "You want me to leave? Now? In the middle of this? No. Hell no."

"I have to find out what's going on. I need to… And the police. Sandesh, this is the last thing the IPT needs to be connected to."

He grabbed her hand. "You're not thinking." He drew closer to her, whisper close. "My truck is here. I signed in. There are cameras all over. Us going into the woods, Us running. You shooting a drone. Think. We need to tone this down. You can't run around with a gun right now. You're panicking. Think, Justice. Let the security here do its job."

He motioned to the security guard watching them. Shit. He was right. External security, unlike internal, did not know about the League. They protected the school and the campus, not the main house. They had no idea what went on in its depths. She let out a breath. The cops were coming. Probably the FBI. All the camera footage would be looked at. She looked around.

Two other guards stared at her. She had already fucked up. Shot the drone from the sky. She could cover that. Tell the cops that her Special Forces boyfriend had taught her to shoot.

She handed the gun back to the guard. "I'm sorry."

The woman took the gun with a look that said she wasn't sure an apology was necessary. "No problem. We got this, Ms. Parish."

Justice turned to Sandesh. Letting the adrenaline backlash do its job, she began to shake. She put a hand to her head.

Seeing her playing a part, Sandesh quickly put an arm around her as if to hold her up.

Would this be enough to counter her rabid-dog routine the guards had just witnessed? A vine of panic and anger in her chest had grown sharp offshoots, twisting barbs and thorns that spread out, hooked and tugged her skin. Go. Go. Act. Do.

But Sandesh was right. The school, the League, had never faced this big a threat. A threat to all they had subtly and secretly accomplished over forty years.

She wanted at Walid. No doubt this was him. She wanted to find out what the fuck was going on. And which of her dumbass siblings had turned monster overnight.

She could feel the vines tighten. She tucked it all down for now. But she was already plotting how to get her vindictive ass to Mexico.

"Let's get back to the house. Check on my sisters."

———— ⁓⁓⁓ ————

Back in the main house, things were crazy. Her sisters, girls rescued from war zones or who'd seen violence firsthand, were at extremes. Her siblings were gathered in the family room, a large room connected to the dining room by an arched opening. It was filled with comfy seating arrangements and a large fireplace.

Her sisters either cowered by the fire or they'd grabbed the nearest object and stood watch over the others, ready to fight.

The twins—a.k.a. Jules and Romeo—held fireplace tools.

Whoa. Those two were a little scary. Especially the boy. He had a chip on his shoulder Atlas couldn't have carried.

"Okay, all. Deep breath." She pointed at the twins. "Put the irons down."

Jules did. Romeo hesitated. His eyes darted to Sandesh. After a second of some internal debate, he complied. Kid was strung tight.

The nannies had done their best, getting them all into one room and trying to calm them, but they needed family. And Justice was the only family here over eighteen. Her mother had gone to meet with the police. Leland was handling internal, shutting things down to keep off the authorities' radar, assessing damage. Tony and Bridget had gone to the dorms to handle the situation there. Who knew where the Troublemakers had gone?

She assumed they'd left to investigate, figuring the girls in the main house were being trained for combat and being groomed by the League, so they could deal. She got that. The dorm kids had been sent by their families to an elite boarding school. They knew nothing about covert ops and should be treated with kid gloves.

But seeing her sisters huddled by the fire while the tougher of them stood guard, she couldn't help but be overcome with memories. And anger.

Walid was going down.

The clink of fireplace tools shoved into the iron stand was followed by the sobs of five-year-old Bella. She launched herself at Sandesh. Her tiny, trembling arms latched on to his legs.

Sandesh hoisted her up. "It's okay."

She buried her face in his shoulder. He turned to the rest of the family. "If you can all sit and listen, I'll tell you what's going on."

Damn. The man was perfect. Or at least knew the perfect thing to say. Bella squirmed out of his arms. She padded across the room and joined the others around the fire.

Romeo sat by the fireplace tools. Jules stood behind him.

When everyone was absolutely still and quiet, Sandesh said, "First, I want you to know that you are safe." Justice felt her heart loosen and lurch toward him. Drawn instinctively to his strength and kindness.

Not only had he recognized that they'd needed a mission or goal to get them settled, he'd also realized that more than anything, they needed to be assured of their safety. He was good.

"The police have arrived. They are checking every inch of the grounds. Beyond that, the security at this school is top-notch. And all the campus staff are on alert." Justice raised her eyebrows at this, and he winked at her. Yep, not a stupid man. "In addition, the school is on lockdown. New measures are being put in place to make sure this type of attack doesn't happen again."

"Who attacked us?" Rome asked.

Sandesh spread his hands wide, "We don't know that yet. We know someone flew a few personal drones over the school and dropped small explosive devices at the gym, tennis courts, and on the gatehouse, which was empty at the time. Falling debris injured one of the guards."

"It doesn't sound like they were trying to hurt anyone," Rome said. "If they'd wanted to hurt people, they'd have dropped the explosives somewhere with people. Not the school gym. Or the tennis courts."

Jules pinned her lower lip beneath her teeth, then released. "Do you know what kind of ordnance they used? Timed? Or did it go off when it hit?"

Good question. It had gone off when it hit.

"How did they get past the cameras?" Jules said. "There are only a few places--"

Sandesh turned surprised eyes on the twins. Because, yeah, the kids had practically pointed out that it was an inside job. Who else would know the hidden camera layout?

Jules and Romeo exchanged a look. Juliet's face reddened. She'd realized what she'd suggested. She didn't try to overcorrect, either with rambling or embarrassed explanation. She stayed silent and let the warm blood rush into her cheeks. Smart. Sometimes talking made things worse.

Justice patted Sandesh's arm, felt his coiled bicep. Somehow, that strength comforted her. Huh, must be some sort of primal response. She'd have to excise that.

Sandesh bent to her ear. "I have an idea. A way to help with PR."

"I'm not sure all the PR in the world will be able to fix this."

He opened his mouth to expand when one of the staff came into the room. "The police are looking for you, Ms. Parish. And you, Mr. Ross."

Great. Time to lie her ass off.

Chapter 54

JUSTICE'S PUBLIC RELATIONS OFFICE IN THE MANTUA Academy's administration building was a tiny room that should've held brooms and mops. It was an afterthought at the very end of the guidance counselor's corridor. Right now, it felt two sizes too small. The room equivalent to *had too much turkey and pie at Thanksgiving and now have to wear my stretchy pants*.

Twenty-four hours after the attack, Justice's office was a hive of activity. All this attention could go to a girl's head.

Or straight to her trigger finger.

How had Momma ever thought that putting her in a situation where she had to be diplomatic and courteous to irate people was a good idea?

The phone kept ringing with furious and concerned parents—people used to ordering others about—and the administrative staff, including her siblings, came and went with their hair seemingly on fire.

And the media attention was out of control. She'd been answering phone calls and questions since five a.m. It was now almost six p.m. She'd felt less exposed during gynecological exams.

For forty years, the school had dictated how people saw it—an excellent but stuffy place to send your daughter. A place of diversity that gave scholarships to deserving children, a place that taught the brilliant

Parish children, women who had become leaders and scholars and scientists and business people.

Now it had become the target of intense and blistering scrutiny.

Really not a good thing when a covert operation that housed the world's most elite group of female vigilantes existed underfoot. Or had existed.

No one was going anywhere near the League until the authorities combing this place had left. For now, all necessary research would be done aboveground or at Gracie's club. Momma and the academy's principal had also decided to close the school early for the summer.

They'd analyze and increase security during the off-summer months.

Finals would be given online. They'd circled the wagons and battened the hatches. Necessary when the FBI was up their ass with questions and demands. They'd searched the entire grounds with a fine tooth comb.

Justice shifted the list of numbers she had to call behind the list of online media journals to reach out to. Ugh, she sucked at this. Pretending to be a PR specialist, with her family under suspicion, the campus on lockdown, the possibility of another attack looming, a traitor among them, and there went the phone again.

She picked it up. "What?"

The person on the other end paused. "Tell me that's not how you're answering the phone."

"This is my cell, Gracie. I can answer it any damn way I please. And just so you know, I am being extremely courteous to every idiot reporter who calls me."

The landline on her desk rang. She glared at it, tucked her cell next to her ear, reached over, and unplugged the cord. What Gracie didn't know wouldn't hurt her. "What do you want?"

"I want to know about this story in the paper. The one that suggests the school was attacked because of its support of the IPT. What the heck is that about?"

Justice thought of shutting the door, but spun her chair away from the office doorway instead. A split second later, she heard the secretary walk in with another pile of messages.

Justice waited. Gracie waited, understanding even though Justice had said nothing. She knew the drill. The swoosh of papers hitting the desk was followed by the swish of the woman exiting. She left behind a disgruntled scent trail of Tom Ford's Velvet Orchid.

Justice waved away the perfume, lowered her voice. "You read the paper. What do you think it's about?"

"I think we're blaming our support of Sandesh and the IPT's work in order to distract from the League and their operations."

"We're supporting the IPT. They are going up against some bad people. Those people might have struck the school in retaliation. And that is the FBI's theory. Not mine."

"Sure. But you jumped on it. You're using Sandesh and the IPT. I thought you cared about this guy. Or was that a trick to convince him to join the League? Use him and his business to perpetuate our global interests while always having a scapegoat? Really, that's low, even for Momma."

Using? No. It had been Sandesh's suggestion. He'd presented it, rather subtly, to the FBI. Sandesh had merely mentioned he had a history of confronting sex-slavers in Jordan. It was a good plan. If the FBI found any link to Walid, this would make the most sense. "Again, Gracie, the FBI thinks it might have something to do with Sandesh's work in Jordan. Maybe militants."

"Really. How interesting. Wonder when they're going to claim credit."

Whoa. Gracie was great at heavy sarcasm. And making a valid point. "I don't have insight into the workings of terrorists."

"Sure. Well, let me know if you decide to follow the message this bombing has conveyed."

She sat forward, elbows on knees, head cocked to the right, phone clutched in a sweaty hand. "What message?"

"It's obvious, isn't it? This is Walid forcing us to keep our heads down. Stay in our school."

Is that what had happened? It could be. Having the FBI and local law enforcement running around the school handicapped them. Limited access to intel and the specialized equipment belowground.

Gracie seemed to have drawn some interesting conclusions about Walid's mind-set. "Why would he want to scare us into circling the horses?"

"I think this first attack is meant to clear out the school, so Walid can launch the real offensive. Reveal the League and take out those responsible for his brother's death."

Fuck. That made sense. The sound of an engine firing up and a car fasten-your-seat belt *beep*, *beep*, *beep* let Justice know Gracie had gotten into her car. "Hmm, good of you to provide Walid's motivation and his future plans. Do you have a date and time you think he'd like me to go after him?"

"Nice, J. I'm not setting you up. Just because I lob

a common-sense grenade, make some obvious connections, you practically accuse me of being the traitor—and, yeah, I figured that out too."

"I'm not the one living at the club. I'm not the one who separated herself from the group. I'm not the one who mysteriously provided insights into Walid's plan that are not *obvious*."

I'm not the one who would love to see the League go down, so she could reconnect with her son. Maybe even rekindle an old romance.

Gracie let out a long breath. "You know, I think I like this new suspicious Justice. You can learn the lesson I learned long ago."

"Which is?"

"Trust no one."

Chapter 55

HEARING MOVEMENT IN HIS ROOM, SANDESH WOKE UP confused and disoriented. Where was he?

"Sorry to wake you."

"Leland?" Oh, that's right. He had spent the night in a guest room at the Mantua Home. "Tell me you don't have a thing for blonds."

Leland laughed. "No. Definitely not my type. And I know you haven't gotten a lot of sleep, but I have a favor to ask."

Sandesh looked around. It was not even five a.m. What was with this family and waking people up? Truthfully, he preferred the way Justice woke him.

He sat up. The room was still dim, but he could see Leland clearly enough, standing at the foot of the four-poster bed. The whole room looked as if it belonged in Victorian England.

"No problem." Sandesh rubbed at tired eyes. He'd gotten only about two hours of sleep. "What do you need?"

Leland shifted, let out a breath. "What do you know of Justice's father, Cooper Ramsey?"

Her father? "Not much. He left Justice to an abusive grandmother. He's a drug addict."

Leland moved to the chair by the vanity. He pulled it out and sat. "That's true. But more important, we suspect he is working with the family traitor."

Sandesh swung his legs out of bed. This seemed like

a big admission on a normal nine-to-five schedule, but at five a.m., it was pretty obvious where this was leading.

"Where does he live?"

—⁓—

Wearing jogging gear donated by Leland, Sandesh ran with steady ease down the wide blacktop of the Schuylkill biking trail.

He wouldn't have pegged Leland for the mesh-shorts-and-Glassboro-hoodie kind of guy. The brown hoodie was big—big enough to conceal and carry. Helpful.

The sneakers were a good fit, though not Sandesh's style. Expensive. White. With too thick of a sole. He felt like he was running on a loaf of bread.

When Leland had woken Sandesh this morning, he'd brought the shoes, the clothes, and a mission. Though the security cameras had spotted very little of the drones, Leland's security team had scoured the camera footage along the campus perimeter from the last few days.

They'd spotted Justice's father outside the school taking pictures. Leland wanted Sandesh to look into it, because, well, thanks to his own ideas and a few well-placed suggestions in his FBI interview, the feds suspected Sandesh's connection to the school had caused the bombing.

If he were caught investigating the bombing, it would only draw more attention to Sandesh and away from the school. After last night, he'd jumped at the chance to help. He didn't mind being used.

He should mind. But he'd always had a problem with giving a shit about petty crap like what the FBI thought of him when he was trying to save people's lives.

Even with the friction of the gun harness against his chest, it felt damn good to move. He let his body stretch with each stride, enjoying the pace, the breeze. It was a beautiful trail. Trees budding, the sun out, the river to his left, and the river houses on stilts with their boats and careless yards.

He wouldn't mind a house like that. Waking up beside Justice with a cup of coffee and easing out onto the deck before starting their day.

As the trail angled up, the river dropped down, and the apartment complex came into view. A series of five-story red-and-tan buildings.

He circled, doing recon on the place and the area. Outdoorsy. Pet friendly. He passed a woman with two wiener dogs. She scolded one as they walked along the trail.

From what Justice had said of Cooper—a drug addict who'd sold his own children—this place was not what he'd expected. Did painting houses pay this well?

He eased off the trail and onto the grass in front of building 7. Sandesh stopped and stretched.

When a man with a dog went inside, Sandesh followed. The man held the door open. Yep. A nice neighborhood. Sandesh said thanks and dipped his head, petted the dog to avoid the security cameras, slipped past.

The elevator was open and waiting. He got in and pressed the button for three. And quickly hit the "close door" button as the man with his lab went to get his mail.

At Cooper's door, Sandesh knocked. After thirty seconds of no answer, he squatted, took the light tools from his pocket, and picked the lock.

Checking the empty hallway, he palmed the edge of

his sweatshirt, turned the handle, pushed open. A huge, slobbery, black-and-white Newfoundland bounded out at him.

Sandesh cut him off with a sweep of his body, guided him back into the apartment. He kicked the door shut, knelt, and petted the big dog, whose entire body vibrated with joy. And slobber. Sandesh cringed. Lifted his hand up.

Not just slobber?

Blood.

He wiped his hand on the inside of Leland's sweatshirt, took out his gun.

He swung his Ruger as he scanned the front hall and into the main living area.

Jesus.

He moved past the dead man strapped in a chair wrapped in bubble wrap, past the kitchenette, and into the bedroom. Empty. As was the closet. And bathroom.

Back in the bedroom, the dog watched as Sandesh checked under the bed.

A white box. He slid his leg under and kicked it out. A drone box, an empty drone box. He went back into the living area. The dog followed.

Judging by the long, black hair and distinctly Native American features, not to mention Justice's exact nose, the corpse strapped to the artist chair was Cooper.

He'd been tortured to death.

Under the plastic wrap, chicken wire pierced Cooper's face and down the flesh of his naked body. His mouth split in small red fissures at the creases, chafed by a thick leather ball gag. Cooper's head lay to one side. Blood pooled beneath the chair. A dog-sized bloodstain saturated the beige carpet beside the chair.

The apartment had a lot of windows, but all the metal blinds were closed.

He took out his cell, hit Leland's preprogrammed number.

Leland answered on the first ring. "And?"

Not even a hello? "Found Cooper. He's dead. Someone did a nice job of torturing him. I'm not sure how this is going to go down with the authorities. Justice's father murdered a day after the school was bombed."

There was a very long pause. "Clean off any of your prints. We'll be there in twenty minutes."

Leland hung up.

Sandesh holstered his gun and went into the kitchen. Keeping his hand covered by his shirt, he opened a couple of cabinets, found the dog food. He opened two cans and slapped them into the empty dog dish by the fridge. The dog was eating big, sloppy mouthfuls as Sandesh refilled the water bowl. When he was done, he surveyed the main room.

There was an easel and paints in one corner. The easel contained a painting of a Buddha in front of an orange, red, and yellow Buddhist temple. He recognized it. He'd passed it on his way to the Mantua Academy campus. It had caught his eye because of the bright colors and because there weren't a lot of Buddhist temples in Pennsylvania.

So Justice's father had been a Buddhist? And was now a suspect in the school bombing. And had been tortured to death.

Could Cooper have been a go-between? Someone the traitor had recruited to help?

Maybe.

And after Jordan, Walid might've been able to track him here.

So he came here, tortured Cooper to get information. Maybe to figure out who'd given him the warning about Jordan. How much had Cooper known? Had Walid been told about the school and then gone to bomb it? If so, is that why Cooper had a single drone box here? Had Walid's men set up camp here?

Cooper wasn't exactly swimming in enough luxury to be buying drones to mess around with. Other than the easel, the chair with him in it, a small, round kitchen table, and an abused, brown suede couch, there wasn't any other furniture.

There were a lot of decorations. Well, paintings.

He'd never seen a picture of Justice as a child, but he knew the portraits that took up nearly every wall were of her. And the girl beside her, the one Justice had her arm slung across, was most likely her sister. Hope. And the woman? He'd take a guess, since she resembled the blond girl Justice had her arm around, and say that was the mother.

The portraits were repeated again and again all over the walls. Like the man had played one moment, one loop of thought in his head for the last twenty-five years.

So Cooper painted not just houses, but people. And not just any people but Justice and Hope and their mother. Over and over again. The same picture. Dissected down to the smallest detail.

And those details were so clear. Freckles. Blue eyes. Dark eyes. And the dark shadow over every painting, as if the artist foreshadowed the days to come. Or asked where it had all gone wrong.

Chapter 56

JUSTICE ENTERED THE HOUSE AND WASN'T SURPRISED TO SEE it filled with family members who usually worked or trained belowground. She maneuvered around them and down the hall. Where was Sandesh?

After his late night being interviewed by the FBI, Martha had found a room for him. Justice assumed he'd been here sleeping this morning when she'd left for work, but it was now almost six. She turned into the library.

A few of the oldest sisters, Fantastic Five, sat at a long reading table, sipping coffee and eyeing her speculatively.

Sheesh. Intimidating bunch.

Justice headed for Tony and Dada. They were huddled together at a small corner table pressed up against a black suit of armor.

Huh. They looked so chummy. Coconspirators?

No. That was paranoid.

Those two couldn't plan a lunch together. She slipped into the only available seat.

Tony leaned back. "Justice. What do you think? Drones over the school." He gestured with his hands. Tony used his hands like a conductor used a baton to convey the tone of his emotions, but still, Justice couldn't figure out what he meant.

"Huh?"

Dada shook her head. "He wants to put drones in

operation over the school. Ridiculous. Do you want to draw even more attention here?"

"Attention? Didn't you hear about the attack that has parents lined up outside waiting to drag their kids outta here?" He walked his fingers across the table to demonstrate parents fleeing.

Dada *tsked*. "Your fear has made you reactionary."

"Not reactionary. I've seen the footage."

"You've seen the security footage?" Justice said. "How?" Right now, access to those videos was limited to those underground. Had he been down there? Impossible. Leland had completely sealed off the lower floors.

"I was in the control room when everything went down. I stayed after the strike and ran the tapes."

He'd left Sunday dinner and had gone to the control room? "What's the footage show?"

Dada shifted toward Justice. "According to him, the footage shows nothing."

"Exactly." Tony's whole body jumped forward. His weight slapped against the flat edge of the square table. The table slid forward and knocked into Dada.

She shoved it back and put her hand protectively over her stomach. "Careful. Idiot."

Tony frowned. "The drone avoided detection by our cameras, 'cause we didn't have anything to patrol the sky."

Dada pulled the edges of her lips into an incredulous grimace. "Why would we have done such a thing?"

"It's called security, daddy-o. You need to outthink and outplan your enemy."

"Do not call me that. I dislike it." Dada's mouth tightened. She looked a little gray. And worn. She looked like shit. Was she worried about her informant? Justice assessed her sister. Her illnesses. Her hand resting on her stomach. Could she—

"Justice?" Justice jumped at Leland's voice. He stood at the entrance to the library and beckoned her with a crook of one insistent finger. "Would you please accompany me to the next level?"

Silence. Every eye in the room turned to her. She was being summoned to a level no one else was permitted to go at present, not even the older sisters. Tension rippled across the room.

Justice stood and walked across the silent room. *Damn, this is so awkward. Someone cough or something.*

Behind her, Tony, loud enough for everyone to hear and with a tone that bordered on tragic, said, "And we never saw her again."

The room erupted in laughter. Leland shook his head. Tension broken. And that was why Tony was her favorite sister.

Chapter 57

SANDESH COULD NOT GET USED TO HOW ARTIFICIALLY bright Mukta's lower-level office was. And colorful. The space insisted on merriment. But Sandesh couldn't forget it was also the center of dark pain and anger and plotting.

He also couldn't forget this dual nature had been the upbringing of the person he loved, the person looking a bit wary sitting on the seat next to him.

Leland stood behind Mukta, who leaned cupped hands against her desk. "Justice, we have some bad news to impart."

Justice put up her hands in a *stop* gesture. "If it's worse than 'your school was bombed by one of your traitor siblings,' I don't want to hear it."

Leland, his usual ramrod straight posture, ran a hand through military-short silver hair and cleared a throat that did nothing to ease the rasp in his voice. "We believe your father is involved with the traitor."

What? That was the way they were going to go? Not, "Justice, we're very sorry your father has been murdered."

Justice shook her head. "Cooper? He's drugged out. Not capable of conspiring with anyone."

Mukta slid a bracelet up her arm, then another. "He's capable of following instructions, coming to see his daughter, and reporting back to the Brothers. He's capable of meeting with one of your siblings, following their orders, and getting in touch with Walid."

Justice reached for the locket around her neck. She clasped it. "You think Cooper helped whoever betrayed us?"

"More than that," Leland said. "We think he was a go-between, informing Walid and taking money for the job. We also believe he helped orchestrate the attack on the school."

"The attack? You think he worked with Walid?"

Damn, these people liked to keep stuff to themselves.

Mukta Parish shook her head. "No. All signs suggest the attack was an inside job. Few would have the knowledge to avoid security. And though the traitor could have passed this information to him, I sincerely doubt Walid would target areas devoid of people."

"In fact," Leland said, "we believe the drone attack was the family member's plan."

"What proof do you have it's not Walid?" Justice asked. "Gracie thinks this is all strategic. Keep us in the school. Keep us busy. Get rid of the kids. And then Walid can move forward with a second attack."

Mukta and Leland shared a look. Mukta uncupped her hands, laid them flat on the desk. "I believe our gentle Bridget is behind everything. There was written evidence in Cooper's apartment, communications between them. Not only that, she and Cooper were part of the same Buddhist temple. And she has implicated herself with prior statements and by repeatedly advising her siblings to resist training."

Come on. They were really laying a lot on Justice right now. This seemed cruel. This was not how he'd have handled this. Give her a chance to understand Cooper was dead, then break it all down.

Justice drew in a sharp, pained breath and shook her head. "Coop. Bridget and Coop? Are you sure it's her? Dada is sleeping with her informant. Tony is so angry. And Gracie practically gave me Walid's plan of action. She's also a tech genius. Could easily access computer info like my GPS. And how did Bridget operate the drones?"

Leland tugged at the button on his suit coat's sleeve. "According to the FBI, the drones were preprogrammed. She could have hired someone for that. As for the GPS, we don't know."

Justice shot to her feet. "This isn't horseshoes, Leland. We find out. We bring Bridget and Cooper in. We question them."

Enough. What was this game? Sandesh grabbed Justice's hand. She looked down at him. "He's dead, Justice. Cooper was killed. I found him tortured in his apartment. Most likely by Walid."

Justice sat with a pained sigh. "Tortured?" She stared at him, then her eyes narrowed and turned on Leland. "You dragged Sandesh into this?"

Sandesh put a hand on her knee. She was shaking. "I was asked to go. No dragging involved. And no danger to me. Leland had the place cleaned. Made it look like Cooper had taken off for good."

The tension around her eyes didn't ease. In fact, it tightened. "Cooper. I almost believed him. And now he's taken another of my sisters."

Technically, it wasn't Cooper who'd started it all. But it was probably easier for her to blame him than her sibling.

Justice bent forward, hands against her stomach. "I hate him."

It might not sit well with her, but she should know what he suspected about Cooper. Sandesh got out of his chair and dropped to his knees. He smoothed out her hair. "Justice. Judging by his condition, Coop resisted interrogation. And you should know, he painted pictures of you and Hope. They were all over the apartment. I think—"

Her head shot up, nearly hitting him. "Don't. Don't say it." She wiped angrily at her eyes. "He was an asshole. And Bridget. Bleeding heart. She brought Coop here. Probably hoped we'd have a relationship. Macro-view. Like she has more of the bigger picture than anyone else. Please. She's so much into peace that she won't even eat dairy from a cow. That has to screw with your head."

Macro-view?

Leland moved around the desk, pressed a button on the phone. "Tucker, where is Bridget Leigh Parish?"

There was the clicking of a keyboard, a moment of silence, and then, "In her office."

"Have someone bring her to Mukta's office on 4B. Posthaste."

He clicked off. Leland exhaled a sound coated with age and regret and acceptance. "While we wait, I think we should discuss how we're going to eliminate the very real threat Walid still poses."

Chapter 58

JUSTICE APPRECIATED THE LIFELINE LELAND HAD THROWN HER. He knew that action was better for her than the silent brooding of waiting for Bridget and thinking about Cooper.

Cooper.

Dead.

Tortured.

She'd never understood before that saying about people who weren't "comfortable in their own skin."

Now emotions sliced worries across raw nerves. She had always known what was right: her family. And what was wrong: those who went against her family. But damn it to all hell, losing Bridget felt wrong. She wanted to scratch at her arms, legs. Anything other than endure this helpless, aching hurt.

Cooper dead.

Bridget a traitor.

Enough. Focus on Walid. And sarcasm. "Going after Walid with all the school scrutiny going on right now will be super easy."

"Easy or not," Sandesh said, his voice military sharp, a knife honed to its finest edge, "we have to assume Walid knows who you are, Justice. So we get him."

Overprotective? "Think the FBI will want to tag along?"

Sandesh laughed.

"About that," Leland said, "Sandesh has a good idea about how to get you out right under the nose of the FBI."

Justice's heart jumped up and cheered, doing the splits, pompoms and all. "Oh, Sandy, you've been busy."

"Well, the first part was easy. Your birthday."

Her birthday? Her stomach turned over. "We're going to have a party?"

The hammer of condemnation left a loud gong of silence. She didn't care. This was crazy. Having a party after all this shit.

The jingle of Momma's bracelets disrupted the stillness. "This is what we do, Justice. Distract with one hand, so no one looks at the other. In this case, the FBI will have their hands full with the guest list and the party. They won't pay attention to your antics."

"My antics?"

Leland and Momma exchanged another look, this one slightly uncomfortable. Probably some kind of silent signal, because Leland took over. "You do have a reputation as a party girl. One of the Parish Princesses."

Gag. She hated that. "Yeah. So?"

"So you make a show of getting drunk. Grab the mic. Thank people for coming. Say it was your best birthday ever. And then say something about Sandesh. Some innuendo. The two of you dance. Make it obvious you are going to leave and be together. Alone."

Leland. The man couldn't be direct.

"Basically," Justice said, "dry hump Sandesh on the dance floor, make everyone uncomfortable, so when we leave, they assume we are going to fuck and not going to Mexico to take down a sex-slaver."

Sandesh coughed into his hand. She looked over at him. A red flush covered his face. What? Something she said? "Come on, Sandy. You know you love it."

"I'll admit I like your version better than Leland's."

She smiled. Her chest still felt tight, but better somehow with him here.

"But how about once we get there? How do we...? Leland, Tony mentioned something about a letter. One in which he outlined a plan to take the Brothers out separately. He said he'd figured out how to get into the compound."

Leland's broad shoulders tensed.

Okay. "You know what I'm talking about?"

He sighed. "The letter was a rather senseless rant at your mother for perceived wrongs, and also gave his plan for the BG operation. He wanted it brought to a vote."

Momma turned her face to him. "But now, the plan might work."

Leland, implacable Leland, reddened. "Perhaps. If we can get Dada's man to help bring our agents inside."

"She'll do it." Justice was sure of it. "But we have to promise to bring Juan out with us."

Someone knocked on the door. Everyone in the room froze.

Bridget.

No one spoke. No one moved. No one breathed.

If Justice could have put a knife to the tension, it would probably have snapped back and killed someone.

Justice got to her feet and moved so she stood by the side of the desk. Sandesh did the same. Momma stood with help from Leland.

Finally, Momma managed, "Enter."

———※———

Standing in Momma's inappropriately whimsical office, Bridget looked like a cross between a yogi and a math nerd with her lopsided bun and dark-framed reading glasses. Her face held a serene expression.

Justice wanted to slap her. She'd just accused the woman of betraying their family, of conspiring with Cooper, and she stood there as if purity itself.

"What the fuck, Bridge? Say something."

Bridget eased her shoulders back. She had great posture. "I am ready for whatever punishment you see fit to give me."

"You admit this?" Momma leaned a hand on her desk. Her eyes, always so clear, seemed cloudy and confused. "Tell me, Daughter. This is important. If you have any reason to cover for another, you must not. We need to be able to trust the others."

Bridget turned her head. "You don't have to worry about the others. You can trust them."

Justice's stomach rolled, hit a guardrail, and plunged over a ravine. She wanted to walk over and shake Bridget. Ask her what she ever did to deserve that kind of hatred. But she put that shit on hold. Sort of. "Why? Why did you do it?"

Bridget shook her head. Her eyes darted back and forth between her and Sandesh, Momma and Leland. "It was done to keep you safe. To keep all of you safe."

Justice pointed a finger at her. "Safe? Telling Walid I was after him in Jordan, giving him step-by-step directions to track and find me, to kill me? How was that to keep me safe?"

"That wasn't how it happened. Cooper was a go-between. Walid's men tracked his digital trail, found a computer in his apartment that was being used to track you."

Tracking her? And Bridget was worried about Justice's soul?

"How was it tracking her?" Leland asked. His normally gruff voice even deeper, sounded like he'd eaten a razor blade.

A hot flush crept across Bridget's cheeks. "Using a copy of the software the League invented to ping and track the GPS. That way, the risky act of checking League computers was unnecessary."

Justice's stomach rolled again. The locket felt suddenly hot against her skin. Not a locket. It was a miniature of her father's betrayal. She walked to her sister, stabbed a finger at her chest. "You deserve to lose your memory of this place. You deserve to no longer have any of this."

"I'm willing to accept that. Would you be?"

What? Was she seriously going to turn this into some kind of lesson? "No, Bridget. I wouldn't. But I would never do what you did. I would never choose to betray you."

Bridget looked down at Justice's raised finger, then over at Sandesh. She shook her head. "You did betray me, us. If you hadn't, Sandesh wouldn't know about our operation."

Bridget stared at Sandesh. For his part, he stood at military attention, silent as he watched the family falling apart before his eyes. "Everyone makes mistakes. But only a chosen few are given a second chance. Cooper loved y—"

"No, Bridget! You don't get to talk to me about love or mistakes. What I did, what I revealed, came from being backed into a corner. Something that happened when I tried to rescue a girl. Someone who never would've been saved if not for the League. What you did almost got me killed, and you did it because you no longer believe in the League."

Bridget's chin lowered the slightest bit. It was the only sign in her straight-backed, light-me-on-fire-and-I-won't-blink posture that let Justice know she might have struck pay dirt. And she wanted pay dirt. She wanted Bridget to feel something. All that equanimity shouldn't mean she couldn't be properly punished. Or hurt. Like she'd hurt Justice.

Bridget lifted her head. "You're wrong. I never stopped believing in the League. It was the League that stopped doing what it was designed to do. It was founded to rescue people. Ask yourself, are the kids here rescued? Or are they warped warriors being trained to break the law?"

"Warped? The laws are warped. The laws don't work. Or haven't you watched the news? Men everywhere see us as evil. They see our normal emotions as something that need to be repressed. And apparently you do too. We can't all suck up the pain, Bridge. We can't all cut ourselves off from the world."

"I do none of those things." Bridget seemed pissed now. She breathed slow and carefully. "I pay attention. I look for opportunities to advance our cause. I do this without violence. And it works. Mostly."

Mostly? What a joke. "Bridget, the 'mostly' is what we're worried about. The girls like Cee and Juliette and that little Russian kid. They need us to fight for them. Do you think that men are going to suddenly stand up for us? Do you think…?"

She stopped. She couldn't finish. Men had stood up. Men like Sandesh, who had kept her secret, gone to find Coop, and now stood beside her while she railed. Men like Tony and Leland. And men raised in a world far away from the League. Like Gracie's John. Like Dada's Juan.

Bridget stared at her knowingly. "It could work. Not just a band of sisters, but all of us, together. Men and women working to change the laws or see them enforced."

"You want us to give up covert ops to concentrate on lobbying? And what about in other countries? If we'd done what you wanted, Bridget, a twelve-year-old girl would, at this very moment, be a victim of the man I killed. But she's free and safe. And you are wrong. So get out. You're wasting my time. I need to plan another soul-fracturing murder that will set free women in need of rescue."

Bridget wavered. Her eyes swept over to Momma. Her shoulders finally slumped. "I'm sorry for my lies."

She walked to the door and opened it. A member of Mantua Home Internal Security, Eugie, stood there. She would isolate Bridget and keep her from any more of her bullshit. Until things were clear with the FBI, until they could find a way to M-erase her that eradicated League information but allowed her to keep family memories.

Sandesh walked over to Justice. He put a hand on her shoulder. "You okay?"

"Yeah."

He wiped moisture from her cheek. "Are you sure?"

She swallowed, felt it overwhelm her, and broke down. He took her into his warm embrace, hugged her close, and held her until she had no more tears, no more strength, no more energy for rage.

Chapter 59

STANDING IN THE DOORWAY BETWEEN HIS WALK-IN CLOSET and his essentials-only bedroom, Sandesh undid his bow tie. It looked like crap.

Damn. He was nervous. He hated the idea of using Justice's party to publicly sneak off with her.

It wasn't a bad idea. He just wasn't into making that kind of spectacle. The party would be filled with feds and people and paparazzi. He and Justice getting hot and heavy on the dance floor and sneaking off together would start a lot of press and rumors. Fortunately, not one of them would suspect that they'd really run off to Mexico to kill a human-trafficker.

He turned his head. "Don't eat in my bed."

Sprawled out across Sandesh's gray comforter, Victor dug into the bag of Lay's salt and vinegar chips. "Chill, dude. You want the information or not?"

Beautiful. Tied it wrong again. "Yeah. What did you find out?"

Victor shoved a handful of chips into his mouth, chewed. He shrugged. "On Mukta. Basically, what you'd expect. Attacked with acid, then adopted by two aid workers, a wealthy lesbian couple. They trained her in the art of business. She's got a shit ton of degrees. Maybe she got interested in all that science when she was a kid. She had a couple of serious surgeries on her face. That's where she met her right-hand man, Leland."

"Really? She met him in the hospital? Was he sick?"

"No. Had a younger sister with leukemia. She was at the Children's Hospital of Philadelphia when Mukta was there having one of her surgeries. Leland and Mukta met then."

"The sister?"

"She survived. Gotta love CHOP. Anyway, fast-forward a couple dozen years. Sister marries. Has a kid. Has a couple of domestic disturbances on record. Nothing major. Then one day, she up and goes missing. The police suspect the husband. No proof. The husband takes the kid and disappears."

Sandesh moved into the bedroom. "This guy killed Leland's sister? What happened to the man? What happened to the kid?"

Victor dusted crumbs from his shirt, which fell all over Sandesh's bed. "Well, this is where it gets interesting. The father disappeared with the kid, but he resurfaced six years later when he reported his son, then eleven, missing. The kid had run away from home. Six months after that, the father is dead. Suicide. Apparently, his conscience had gotten the better of him. In his suicide note, he admitted to abusing his son and killing his wife. He told the police where to find the sister's-slash-wife's body. Later, the kid was found and adopted. By the Parish family."

Sandesh felt goose bumps down to his toes. "Tony? *Tony* was the kid. But Justice told me she was responsible for his adoption. She'd found him in an alley."

Victor stopped with a chip midway to his mouth. "Why lie about it to her?"

He wasn't sure. But this was the kind of shit that

made him crazy. Did Tony know that Leland was his uncle? "Maybe because he was the first boy. They probably figured he'd be accepted even less if people knew he was related to Leland. They're big into unity."

Victor stuck the chip into his mouth. "They're big into something."

Sandesh met his eyes, waiting for the other shoe to drop. "Meaning?"

"The records on the father's suicide suggested he had been in a fight earlier that day. Apparently, there were bruises all over his body."

Sandesh froze. He knew exactly what Victor suggested. Maybe the reason the family had lied about Tony was because they didn't want to be associated with the death of the father. Could be right. And he didn't feel right telling Victor otherwise. He was his partner and as much in this as Sandesh, though he knew little. "So what do you think?"

"Yeah." Victor reached into the bag. "Well, I think the Parish family is into some strange shit. And I have to wonder how long it will take the FBI to start piecing it together. After the attack two weeks ago, they're still investigating the school, right?"

"Yep."

"Does this have anything to do with why you were chased from Zaatari?"

Sandesh waited a moment before responding. "Do you really want in on this?"

"No. No I don't. Do you?"

Sandesh detected a splinter of annoyance in Victor's voice. Couldn't be helped. He was crossing all kinds of lines here.

Victor crunched down on another chip. "Why you going to this party?"

"Why wouldn't I?"

"Forget the fact that there were bombs dropped on the place not too long ago. And that the students flooded out faster than water from a broken damn. Getting caught up with these people endangers the IPT. The mission."

Sandesh shook his head. "What I'm doing is necessary to keep the mission safe."

Victor put the Lay's bag on the nightstand. "It's not worth the money, man. Walk away. Learn whatever the fuck you needed to learn. Get back to letting go of the bad shit and back to making some good shit happen."

The tie was as good as it was going to get. Sandesh pulled on his tuxedo jacket. He ran a hand through his hair and disregarded the judgmental look on Victor's face. "Look, Justice is the good shit. And her family… most of her family are the good guys."

"Is this love or business?"

Both. And more. "I've got to go."

"Sure. Hurry along. Chase after that chick like a groupie tailing a tour bus. But you better hope that bus isn't lined with explosives. Because this kind of stuff gets a guy killed."

The night doorman held open the front door as Sandesh exited his building. "Good evening, Mr. Ross. Your limo has arrived."

"Thanks, Al." Normally, he would've driven himself, but Mukta had insisted on sending a car. And she'd made a good point. He didn't want his own car hanging out on campus while he and Justice flew to Mexico.

Sandesh skirted construction tape—they were always doing some construction here—to get to the limo.

He introduced himself to the driver, slipped inside the car, and closed the door.

The driver walked around the car and got in. Sandesh eyeballed the guy behind the partition. A limo driver who trusted his passenger to shut his own door? It was a new day in America.

The driver pulled away from the building. Interior limo lights cast a faintly bluish glow on the sleek leather interior. Sandesh rolled his shoulders. Damn he was tense. There wasn't much that could get under his skin, but being compared to a groupie pretty much did it.

Victor didn't know the truth though. He'd never sat at dinner with a bunch of kids rescued from impossible situations and given chances for better lives. He'd never seen those kids, even in the face of a school bombing, empowered and strong. Who would they have been if not for Mukta? Who would Justice have been? Would she even be alive?

Victor didn't know. If he did, he'd understand.

Honestly, it would be a hell of a lot better to be led around by his dick. At least he'd have single-mindedness. Right now, every doubt in his mind played Russian roulette with his determination. Was the plan good enough? Would it work? Was there another way?

He shook himself from his thoughts. Where was this guy going? He pressed the button to lower the partition. "Driver," he said, "You missed the turn for 76. Has the venue been changed? I thought the affair was at the Parish home."

The driver didn't answer right away. After a minute, he said, "Sorry, sir, we have one other guest to pick up before we get there."

The partition went back up.

Okay. Weird. Not that he cared, but he was fairly certain when you sent a car for someone it didn't turn into a bus ride. Still, Mukta did things differently. He liked that about her. And having someone to share the ride might actually make the drive less about what was going on in his head.

The driver turned toward the Ben Franklin Bridge exit. Sandesh leaned forward. This was wrong. Courtesy be damned, there was no way Mukta would send a car that had to circle this far back in the wrong direction.

Sandesh pressed the partition button. Nothing happened. The car sped up. His heart rate increased. He shifted into the seat opposite of him, lifted his hand, knuckle knocked. "Hey, buddy."

Nothing.

The car slowed for traffic. Sandesh reached for the handle. Locked. He reached into his pocket and pulled out his phone. No signal. *Oh...kayy.*

If this guy did work for Mukta, his night was about to suck royally.

Raising his foot, he drove the heel of his shoe into the side window. He hit it one, two, three times. It splintered like a web.

Security glass. Barely cracked.

Rubber-soled pieces-of-shit shoes. His leg ached. Damn. He longed for the days when leaving his home without a gun would've felt as comfortable as leaving the house naked during a snowstorm.

He kicked again and again.

The limo banked to the right. He slipped sideways. He braced himself. The limo veered off the exit and into a run-down area close to the docks. Place could double as a landfill.

Rusted metal fence. Trash everywhere. Large, dented storage containers. A bulky, bolt-rusted, four spread-legged crane, with a precariously dangling claw. The thing looked like one serious wind could push it over.

As they veered around equipment, Sandesh noticed a car followed close behind them. This was getting serious. What was it Gracie had told him about Walid? He thought that Sandesh was the key to everything.

The attack on the school had switched Sandesh's focus from worrying about himself to the school. Stupid. Should've done both.

The limo jerked over a pothole and slammed to a hostile end alongside a steel storage container.

The crunch of tires sliding against stones, and the car pulled up behind them. Two men got out. They stalked toward the limo with a ready-to-bust-heads set to their shoulders.

Chances they were friendly? *Nada*. Each headed toward a different door. Wouldn't be easy to fend off two attacks. But it was even harder to coordinate two attacks.

One of them would be first.

He looked around for a weapon. A wayward glass. A bottle from the mini-fridge. A toothpick. Nothing. Damn it. The limo-driver released the doors with a click.

Sandesh loosened and readied. Both doors flung

open. But not simultaneously. The faster man came inside, led with his gun. Mistake.

Sandesh grabbed his wrist, locked his gun arm, pulled. He twisted the gun hand, aimed, fired at the second guy. The guy had already jumped back.

The first guy yanked. But Sandesh had secured his feet on the doorjamb. Using the leverage, he jerked the guy forward and head-butted him.

Crack. The guy's nose broke like an egg. Hot blood poured out. Sandesh's stomach gave a reflexive roll. *Fuck. Gusher.*

Gusher guy made a whiny, distressed sound and loosened his hold on the gun. Sandesh punted up with his pointy, worthless, POS-soled shoe. The guy grunted, released the gun, fell across his foot. Sandesh kicked him off. The guy stumbled back.

Rolling out of the limo, Sandesh crouched, kept the long car as a barrier between him and guy two.

Where was guy number two?

The limo took off. Raising the semiautomatic, Sandesh shot at the back window. The glass barely splintered.

Guy two still nowhere to be seen. Guy one on the other hand?

Hands covered in blood, Gusher charged. Sandesh was painfully aware of the amount of pressure he put on the trigger—next to nothing—the snap of the shot—loud—the recoil that rode up his arm—forever.

Gusher went down.

The driver spun the limo around with a squeal of tires and burnt rubber.

Sandesh darted left. The limo swung in the same direction.

It followed him the way a dog follows a sheep. Slow. Leading. They obviously wanted him alive.

At the last moment, the limo veered past him, doubled back. It came straight at him this time. Still slow.

There was a ladder on the storage container. Taking a running leap, Sandesh vaulted up. He slammed into the steel container. His fingers latched on to the ladder. The rusted metal sliced his knuckles.

At the top, he got a knee up, pulled himself onto the container. Both of his hands bled. Barely noticed. He crawled to the center edge, took out his cell.

The limo had backed up and now headed straight for the container. He was going to smash it?

Sandesh spread out like an *X*, held on.

The limo hit with a slam that rocked his body. And a vibration that shook his skull. *Stupid fuck*. What good did that do? He rolled. Just in time to see the guy suspended by a crane fire the Taser.

Chapter 60

THE THIN SPIKES OF JUSTICE'S LOUBOUTIN PUMPS *TAP*, *TAP*, *tap*ped against the marble floor. The sound echoed in the wide hall as she made her way to the gym.

With each step through the main corridor of the Mantua Home, the energy increased. Electric anticipation warmed by the promise of rich food, rich conversation, bubbly drinks, and the anything-can-happen vibe.

Though it was early, barely eight, the house was a hive of activity. Caterers buzzed in from the kitchen, through the dining room, into the hall and gym. The gym was set up with lights and music like a high school dance to delight the kids. The main celebration would be out back on the lavish patio.

The serving staff, dressed in black-and-white uniforms, familiarized themselves with the home's layout. Six bartenders were already set up, some inside the house, most outside on the patio.

Her sisters flitted around here and there, many in flowing ball gowns, but some in shorter dresses. Three in tuxedos. Well, Tony, Romeo, and the youngest girl in *Vampire Academy* wore tuxedos.

Everyone had their marching orders. Dance. Mingle. Strike up conversations. Ask questions. Meet eyes. Shake hands. Be polite. Don't leave the party without permission. That was typical. Momma was big on courtesy to guests. No wallflowers here.

Music played softly through the entire house, even in the gym. The music made the room seem even more high school prom. Momma had let the Troublemakers pick the playlist. Kind of surprising they liked the acoustic stuff.

The overall effect as her feet clicked against the wood gym flooring was theatrical. Bright and warm and full of opulent promise. Sort of perfect. If you were into that kind of thing.

Tonight, she was. But only because of whom she waited for. She was aware of her every movement in her gown. Silk swept her legs. The same blue silk that plunged at the back hugged her breasts and butt. Long slits up both sides made it easy for her to move. Never knew when a girl might need to run. Or leave herself open for groping.

Sandesh was going to love this dress. That thought made even her jaded nerves tingle.

Speaking of Sandesh. She peeked out one of the long windows as guests arrived in droves of sleek, black limos. It was like watching the Academy Awards. Drivers escorted ladies and gentlemen from polished limos. The people gathered out front chatted, commented on the home, laughed, flirted, looked hot and wealthy and successful for the hired photographers.

The warm night was growing cooler. Many of the guests milled about in small groups before making their way into the house. Leland and Momma stood outside the large front doors, at the top of the stone stairs, welcoming everyone. Leland looked sharp and handsome and confident in his tuxedo. Momma looked elegant in her silver-and-turquoise gown with matching niqab.

The little Ruskie, Bella, had grabbed a fistful of

Momma's ten-thousand-dollar gown and clung to it like a lifeline. Momma didn't protest or try to drag the girl away. Her hand merely directed her guests around the little girl as she greeted them. From where she stood, Justice never saw her once ask Bella to engage anyone who came inside.

Unusual. Momma had a thing for making sure each of her daughters interacted with the outside world in a forthright and open manner.

The fact that Bella got special treatment meant that her story, more than any other Momma had ever heard, prompted a great deal of sympathy. Sometimes new adoptees were quick to tell their stories. Sometimes not. Justice wasn't sure she wanted to know Bella's story.

"Looking good, J." Tony strode up to her. She turned from the window. He wore a black tux. His dark hair brushed back, hazel eyes playful and amused.

"Right back at you." She ran a hand down the front of his tux. "Planning on getting laid tonight?"

He grinned. "You offering?"

"Gross, Tone. We're practically twins."

He shook his head. "Last I checked, you're an American Indian and I'm Italian."

She cocked her head at him. Was he serious? Where had this come from? She leaned in close, smelled his breath. Vodka. "You drinking already?"

He took a step back. His shoes shuffled against the wood floor. He averted his eyes. "You see them?" He gestured out the window, then around the room, and toward the hall. He didn't say feds, but she knew.

"Yep. They kind of stand out. But it's to be expected."

The attack had rattled the government and the locals. She took a longer look around. Lights low, disco balls, streamers. And though most of the people in here were kids, both family and the children of guests, she spotted the outsiders easily. Stiff. Capable-looking. Dressed nice but not too nice. Muscular and thin, like they ate nothing but knowledge and worked out as a matter of survival.

These were the people she and Sandesh would have to fool. Not a problem. If there was one thing she could do well with Sandy, it was let sparks fly. Her insides fluttered.

The plan was for her to take the microphone in one of the outdoor tents and give her speech thanking everyone for coming. She'd say something embarrassing, slur her words as if drunk, mention how hot Sandesh looked, then drag him out to the dance floor. *Yeehaw*. She kind of liked the idea of being the center of attention that way.

But Sandy wouldn't be here for a while. Ah, well. She'd have to entertain herself with Tony. "Okay, Brother, let's show our siblings how it's done."

She grabbed his hand and threaded her fingers through his. He didn't complain or pull back as she led him out of the gym, down the hallway, past the library, dining room, and entrance to the kitchen.

They exited through french doors held open by well-dressed servers, past a bartender bent over stacking crates, and the event coordinator aggressively speaking into a headset.

Outside, the air smelled of the numerous flowers that now decorated the patio.

Music played over speakers.

Stone clicked under her heels. Tony made some comment about her birthday present being a pony now that she was thirty and a big girl. She laughed as they descended the three-tiered stone patio.

"Shut up and keep up, old man," she said as they walked down the walkway and through the garden maze to acres of open expanse, better known as the "bunting."

She suspected the name had something to do with the numerous ceremonies held here that were often decorated with triangular flags.

Heaters ringed the area. It had warmed up this week, but the nights were still cool. Huge tents were set up on the bunting, one with a makeshift dance floor. They walked inside and stepped out onto the floor.

Lights were strung along the inside of the tall, circus-like tent. The beat of the music thrummed under their feet as they circled the dance floor. Some couples were already dancing.

Tony put a hand at her waist and drew her closer. He was warm. Even his smile was warm. He grinned from ear to ear. "J, remember when we'd play wedding when we were kids?"

She laughed. "Yeah, I remember."

When Tony had first been adopted, she'd told him they were going to get married one day. She'd forced him to practice the wedding. He'd been an extremely patient twelve-year-old. He'd never complained or tried to reason her away from her delusions. It was Gracie, sharp as nails, who clued them into the harsh realities.

Justice increased the pitch of her voice, clipped her words like Gracie, and said, "You can't get married. You're related. Losers."

They laughed. Tony pressed closer. "But we aren't." He looked away. "Not like Jules and Rome." His voice lowered. "Or me and Leland."

"What?"

Tony twirled her around, avoided her eyes. After a moment, he said, "Manipulative fucks."

"What are you talking about?"

"Last year…"

His voice trailed off. His eyebrows drew together. He flicked his chin at something coming up behind her.

She spun, searched for what had caused him to freeze. Gracie. The redhead strolled across the dance floor. She wore a deep-red gown. Her hair and body might have been on fire as fast as she moved.

Justice's heart leapt, skipped, and avoided the next beat. As if it could leap, skip, and avoid the truth. Something was wrong. Gracie was on the dance floor? She hated dancing. Hated touching people. She was headed right toward Justice and Tony.

Gooseflesh. Like someone had ghosted past her window, screamed in the night.

Tony sensed it too. His body tensed. "What the hell is she doing?"

Gracie neared.

"My turn," Gracie said and swung herself at Tony. He was so shocked he nearly bobbled her.

His arms came up even as they released Justice.

Gracie laughed. She turned her head away from Justice but gave directions most definitely meant for her. "Don't panic. Go to Momma and Leland's office."

Already panicking, Justice threaded her way through the growing crowd of dancers. She noticed some of the agents along the perimeter moved too. Her heart picked up speed. Her feet did too. No one had to say it. She knew.

Sandesh.

Chapter 61

JUSTICE DARTED INTO MOMMA AND LELAND'S SHARED HOME office on the main level of the Mantua Home. More sedate than Momma's office underground, it was twice the size, had two desks with chairs opposite them. And two sitting areas, each containing a couch and four leather chairs.

Justice's hands were slick with sweat. Her heart so high in her throat she could barely breathe. Her eyes darted around the room.

Leland.

He was on the phone. She stepped over to his desk. He looked at Justice. Held up one finger. *No. Way.* That phone was going out the window. She reached toward him.

Someone cleared a throat. Justice turned.

Bridget?

She was dressed in a loose gold gown cinched at the waist by a belt of faux flowers. It looked like something a Greek goddess might wear. Traitor. They let her come to the party. Of course. They needed everything to look normal. It wasn't normal. And soon Bridget wouldn't be normal. She'd be M-erased.

"What's going on?"

"Justice." Bridget used her customary let's-get-calmed-down-and-seated-before-we-proceed voice.

The familiar tone, the normalness of it, hurt in a way Justice hadn't anticipated. A physical ache in the center of her chest. She shoved it away, shoved all the pain into a box. "Don't fuck with me right now, Bridget."

Leland put a hand over the mouthpiece. "The limo we sent for Sandesh was found abandoned. The driver dead in the trunk."

The driver? Lewis? His poor family. Justice straightened her shoulders, lifted her head, clenched her stomach, readied for the next punch. "And Sandesh?"

Leland raised a curious eyebrow. Paused as if listening on the phone. *Come on*. She could barely fucking breathe right now. "Leland."

Leland hung up the phone. "They took him."

Justice didn't faint. She would never in a million years faint. Her legs though, it turned out, could forget to keep her standing. She sat. Plopped right on her ass in a chair in front of Leland's desk.

It was Walid. It had to be. She turned to Bridget, glared.

Bridget shook her head. "I know nothing. Maybe Dada. Her contact, Juan."

That made sense. "Leland, tell Dada to get her ass in here."

"I am here, abrasive one."

Dada, wearing a cream gown with black brocade and capped sleeves that showed off her toned arms, strolled through the double doors. Justice stood. Wet noodles had more strength than her legs, but she pushed past the chair.

The doors opened again as Tony and Gracie entered. Tony had undone his bow tie so that it hung around his neck like a loosened noose.

"No." Leland waved a hand at them. "We need to have actual family members out there entertaining."

Tony spread his hands in an are-you-serious gesture. "Trust me, we got an extra twenty or so." He came up to Justice, put his arm around her. "I'm sorry, kid."

She shrugged him off. "Sorry is something you tell someone when they have no choice but to deal with something. I've got a choice, Tony. I'm going after him."

He nodded. "I'm with you. Remember that."

Justice could feel the twitch in her eye and the tremble of her lip. She looked away, toward Dada. Dada clasped her hands around her cell and let them fall protectively in front of her.

Justice would not take it easy on her. "You know things. You have a contact there. Find out where they fucking took Sandesh."

Dada held up her cell. "I just texted Juan."

The doors swung open again. Momma entered. She took one look around the room and made the only play that would've calmed Justice down. "I don't think they would hurt him."

She didn't add what they all knew. Yet. Eventually, they'd take him to Walid. And the torture would begin.

The thought hollowed her stomach. She had to get out of here. Do something.

Dada's phone chirped. Justice fisted her hands to keep from grabbing it. Dada looked down, cleared her throat. "He's on his way to Mexico. My source." She paused, lowered her eyes. "Juan confirms this is so."

"I don't trust this guy," Gracie said. Despite the fact that she was so much shorter than Dada, Gracie still commanded attention when standing beside her.

Dada stiffened, looked down at Gracie. "He has proven himself by getting us this information. And when he could have run, *should* have run, when another man was tortured and killed in his place. But he hasn't. And, more important, you can trust him because we have his son."

Dada put a hand on her belly.

Gracie gasped, literally gasped. Then her mouth tightened. Her eyes grew hard.

Shit. Dada was pregnant. And though she'd suspected it before, now that she took a good look, she could see the swell of Dada's belly. Gracie looked sick to her stomach.

The room went silent. After a moment, Tony said, "'Bout time you admitted it."

Bridget let out a breath. "Strategically, considering the League's goals, the secrecy, this is good news."

Everyone turned to look at her. "Not the pregnancy. I mean, that's good. Congrats and all. But I meant Mexico is good. Doable for our government. By now they know Sandesh has been taken. I saw some agents scurrying out of here. We'll find a way to pass on the information of where. They'll go after him. They'll assume it's all related to his work with the IPT."

She had to be kidding. "We are not leaving Sandesh in the hands of that sick bastard while the government makes up its mind whether or not to go in there."

"She's right," Leland said. "Even if the authorities did get him out, there would still be the issue of Walid and what he knows of us. We need to get him before that happens. Which means we have less, not more, time."

Cold dread lined Justice's bones. She felt brittle and frozen.

A memory of she and Sandesh in that small room in Israel, of him holding her, his warmth, and her telling him that she didn't believe there was such a thing as a real hero.

What she hadn't told him, what she'd kept to herself, was that she respected the men in the League, but in her mind, all the heroes were heroines. Women. And to find that decency in a man, someone outside the League, a soldier, it had shaken her to her very core.

She hadn't recognized before what Gracie had been trying to tell her, about how many preconceived notions she had. About the world. About men. Now, she wanted to go back in time and erase them all, replacing them with the strength and warmth that was Sandesh.

She wrung her hands, looked around. She wouldn't ask them without telling them the truth. *Crap*. How had this happened to her? "I love Sandesh."

She heard the whisper of disbelief from her siblings but kept her eyes on Momma. She'd never felt more vulnerable. "I'm going after him. But I'm not willing to make that choice for anyone but me."

Gracie raised a hand and a devilish eyebrow. "I'm in. I like Sandesh. Apparently not as much as you."

"You know I'm in," Tony said.

Dada shook her head. "Juan can get you inside using the plan he and Tony devised."

"I can help," Bridget said. "I can—"

Justice held up a hand, stopped her from talking. "Not you. Traitor."

"We'll have to revise the plan," Leland said. "It never called for a rescue."

Momma touched her niqab, nodded. She gazed around at the others in the room. "And if I'm not mistaken, the original plan called for a second man. Justice, you'll have to choose someone from internal, unless you have another idea."

Chapter 62

SANDESH WOKE UP WITH THE HALF-LIDDED GAZE OF A MAN drugged. He blinked repeatedly. Didn't help. Total darkness. He had a pounding headache. He could feel dried blood on his forehead. It pinched his skin every time he blinked.

The thin materials of his tuxedo shirt and pants weren't enough. The stone floor was ice cold. Stone cold. He sat up. Promptly slammed his head into the ceiling.

Mother…

That explained the blood on his forehead and the pounding headache. Although either could have come from the fight. He doubted it. He had a feeling that had happened days ago.

But right now, that wasn't the thing that really had his attention. The manacles did. He raised his hands. He couldn't see them. Couldn't see anything. But he heard the clink of metal and felt the cold weight of steel. The pressure grated his wrists and ached against his bare ankles and ice-cold feet.

He looped his hands around the chains and pulled.

Sharp coils of pain, twisted into wrist, skin, bones. He pulled. Again and again. The manacles clanked. Pain jolted up his arms.

Shivering all the way down to his ass bone, he felt along the gritty stone and traced the outline of a ring. It was embedded deep into cement.

He lifted a hand so frigid his knuckles felt arthritic. He traced along the chips and flakes of the stone ceiling. Cold. Rough. Pitted. A stone coffin. Or if you happened to be a prisoner in France during the Middle Ages, an oubliette, a place of forgetting.

Forgotten would not be his fate. No. They'd brought him here to torture him.

They thought he was the one who'd organized the Jordan hit.

That meant pain. Lots of pain. They might even ask him a question or two. But mostly, they'd want to hurt him as badly and for as long as they could.

"You're quiet."

Sandesh jumped. His head slapped stone again. *Fuck*.

The voice had sounded as gritty as sandpaper. He peered into the darkness. "Who's there?"

"The one you sentenced here."

A Russian. He'd sentenced a Russian here? Great. The guy was a nutjob. He hoped his hands were manacled too.

"Sorry, buddy. You've got the wrong guy." Maybe the wrong century. How long could someone stay alive down here? Or was he speaking with a ghost?

The man shifted in the dark. Metal scraped against metal. Not a ghost. And chained too. Good.

"Liar. The woman you sent to kill my bosses caused this."

Sandesh laughed. It was that damn funny. Funny enough to overcome his pounding head, the rough tongue, dried throat, and manacled hands. That damn funny.

"Like I said, wrong guy." Hell, wrong gender. Still, keeping him talking might get answers. Like where they were. And if this guy was any kind of threat. Or a plant. "But we've got time. Tell me about it. How long have you been here?"

The Russian gave a humorless laugh, dull and pitiful. His laughter dissolved into tears. His tears broke into coughing. Gunshot-loud, hacking coughs ricocheted off the stone. The man was close. The space was small. Maybe ten by ten. Sounded like he was across from him.

The man stopped coughing. He wheezed, took a few wet, careful breaths.

Sandesh waited for him to catch his breath. And then softly, soft enough to evoke a response, said, "I'm Sandesh. What's your name?"

"Dmitri."

Dmitri. The man had obviously been one of the guards for the sex-slavers. The brothers Justice had called the Brothers Grim. Well, at least one of them deserved to be imprisoned and tortured here. Best not to mention that. "Where are we, Dmitri?"

"Mexico. The woman"—he coughed and made a wheezing sound—"Justice." He practically twisted the word on his tongue. "I find her name ironic."

Girl was getting a reputation. "You and a lot of other people."

He moaned. A deep, pained sound. His every breath was laced with moisture. "I'm dying. It hurts."

"That's been going around."

"Sandesh?" He whispered it. Almost as if it were an entire question and not a name. His breath was labored. He *was* dying. "Will you kill…him?"

"Who?" Sandesh shifted his legs. The shackles on his ankles clinked.

"The man who begs but never means it. Walid."

Great. A poetic Russian. What were the chances? "Not sure I'm in a position to make that promise."

Dmitri coughed again. His coughs sounded more like sobs. "They will bring you out. Strap you…to a chair. The first time…you still have strength. Act then. Don't do as I did." He coughed and fell into a long moment of gasps. Sandesh cringed at the wetness.

"I thought to satisfy him and live." He laughed as if at another person, a dumber person who had done something naively amusing. His laughter erupted into coughs.

He wheezed. It was so dark that sound was the best way to tell the guy was still alive. "Walid tortured you? Himself?"

"Yes. Him. He likes it."

He must. It had been weeks since Jordan. Not good.

"Describe the room. The instruments. Tell me as much as you can."

Chapter 63

TWO HOURS AFTER JUSTICE'S PLANE HAD TOUCHED DOWN AT A private- -meaning seedy, rundown, and secluded—airstrip in Mexico, she stood inside a nearby hangar with her team.

Landing on the dilapidated runway had been bad. But their prospects of getting into the ranch were even worse.

Which was why the mood inside the hangar—a rickety metal structure so dented and rusted it looked like a toddler having a bad day could kick it down—was tense.

And awkward.

Dada's informant, boyfriend, baby-daddy, Juan, had followed through on getting them onto Walid's estate. Well, some of them.

Victor and Tony.

Problem was, they had to pose as mental-air-quotes-around-the-word *entertainers*.

Turned out Walid got off on pain—specifically, inflicting pain, then watching pain inflicted by men having sex, sadomasochism. He was some kind of fucked-up torturer-voyeur. Guess she shouldn't have expected the morals bar to be too high with this guy.

He had a routine. Torture captives. Down to business. Live sex show anyone?

She should be grateful that Juan had done anything. Grateful that they knew for sure where Sandesh was and that at least the talent, Tony and Victor, had a way to sneak through the security.

But she really didn't like it.

Victor seemed at ease in his black speedo. Guy could roll with anything.

Tony hated it. Not for modesty. Conceited idiot. In the gym, he'd been known to break into a spontaneous striptease. He'd Magic Mike you until your eyeballs bled. But wearing a leather jock thong, even with the sex toys tool belt—a pronged collar and some other handy devices attached to his waist—to a potential gunfight was scary as hell.

"I don't get how strippers do this vulnerability thing," Tony said. "I feel so fucking exposed."

He moved his hands around, trying to find some place to rest them. Not happening. Not with what he was wearing. A heavy gold chain around his neck and the leather jock thong that created a *W* of his ass. The front sock part practically carried the imprint of his thingamajigger. Classy.

Not that she'd looked.

Okay. She had. But it was unavoidable. Still, she hadn't said a word to him. Not one uncomfortable word.

"What are you complaining about?" Gracie said. "I wish this guy preferred women. At least you're not being entombed inside a gaudy Mexican Cadillac."

Entombed. Not a good word choice.

"Hey," Victor said, smoothing a hand over his contact's lime-green Cadillac. "Don't knock the car. That space is ingenious. Took me forty minutes to find the thing, and that was with instructions on where it was."

Gracie didn't look impressed. Justice wouldn't have been either if she'd had to ride stuffed into a secret compartment that made up the car's back seat. But Gracie was the only one small enough. Sucked to be a shrimp.

Justice would provide cover from atop a nearby hill. Not a shrimp. And she was the best shot anyway. She'd have to hike through the woods tonight to get there. Which meant she'd be dropped off a few hours before everyone else.

"Don't sweat it, Gracie." Tony swiveled his hips. "You couldn't pull off the male sex-appeal part. Besides, the guards probably have your photo—probably have most of the Parish kids. I never let the media near me. I'm discreet that way."

"Please," Gracie said, "I'm never photographed. And you're like a hermit. No one is even sure you exist."

Tony smiled. "Yeah, I'm fucking bigfoot."

"You're big something," Victor said and winked. Tony flipped him the bird.

Victor had no mercy when it came to flirting with Tony. But he was a great addition to the team. He was all kinds of connected, gutsy as hell, and smart. And devoted enough to Sandesh that he hadn't hesitated when asked to help.

"Does everyone know their part?" Justice couldn't help her nerves. This whole thing seemed too risky. "Do you know what we do if it doesn't work?"

Everyone turned to look at her. Yes, this wasn't the first time she'd asked. And, yes, she did understand that Dada had gone to a great deal of trouble to arrange this, but…

Tony fingered the thick gold chain around his neck. "Look, Walid is on a sex, drugs, and torture bender."

Justice cringed. She needed to get to Sandesh. She couldn't stomach the thought of Walid getting his groove on by torturing him and then doing some hardcore, live-sex-show shit.

"I don't get why either," Tony said.

Gracie waved an explanatory hand. "He's trying to convince himself life is still worth living and he's in complete control."

"Ah the lies we tell ourselves," Victor said. He sounded as if he'd been there. Lying to himself.

"Yeah, well," Tony said. "Works for me. Excluding the ball gag and that whip, the tools on your belt will make taking Walid out a hell of a lot easier."

"If it's too risky," Justice said, "stick with the patch."

The League's latest invention—a poison patch sewn within a protective tag onto Tony's G-string. It worked like a nicotine patch. This stuff absorbed through skin.

Meanwhile, Gracie would be tucked in the secret compartment inside the car. She'd break out and get to the control room, where she'd use her cyber skills to take out the fence and run a ten-second, nothing-to-see-here loop on the cameras.

Justice would pack up her equipment and make her way to the back of the property, where Gracie would help her get inside. They'd make their way to the elevator that led underground.

Juan said there were only two guards with Sandesh. *Easy peasy.*

"Stop looking at my ass, Victor," Tony said, scratching said ass.

Victor laughed. "Just window shopping, amigo. Trust me. Learned my lesson from Sandman. You all got mad skills, but that ride comes with one hell of a price tag."

"Fuck off."

"Speaking of price tags," Gracie said. "What if I do get found? Shouldn't I have some kind of cover story?"

"Like what, Red?" Victor said.

"Like maybe you wanted to try and add me to your show, broaden Walid's experiences."

Justice nodded. It was a good idea. Except... She looked around the desolate plane hangar, raised her hands. "We're shit out of eight-hundred-dollar bras, and there's no Agent Provocateur in sight."

Gracie's face heated. She bit her lip.

What was that about? "Out with it, Gracie."

"Well, I don't think I'll need a costume."

Before Justice could even process what that meant, Gracie was stripping down to her skivvies. And that might have been the sexiest underwear Justice had ever seen. *Seriously?* Rhinestones?

Justice burst into laughter. Tony sputtered until he began to cough. Victor whistled long and loud. "Damn, Red, if I'd known you were hiding that, I would've been nicer to you."

"What's that supposed to mean?" Gracie thrust her lavishly tattooed hip out. *Great*. The last thing Justice needed was for these two to be at each other's throats.

Justice stabbed a finger into Victor's chest. Like stabbing chiseled concrete. "Knock it off."

"Joke." Victor held up his hands. "Getting involved with one of the Parish clan is as smart as hiring your own hit man."

"That's a job I'd be willing to consider for you," Tony said.

Justice rolled her eyes like a fistful of dice. They came up snake eyes. *Enough*. "Let's get to work."

She bent and took her steel-cased smart pad from her backpack. She punched in the clearance code. The screen showed satellite images of the ranch and surrounding area.

"This is Walid's home." They huddled around the screen, though by this point, they all knew the plan and the layout. She just wanted to get them to focus. "The land is fairly open, but there's a hill lined with trees that I'll use to set up surveillance."

She pointed at it, then at the stables—practically up against the fence. "This is the easiest place for me to enter. Assuming Gracie disables the cameras and electric fence, this barn will provide cover for my entry." She moved her hand from the barn to the old mineshaft. "The home itself is close to seventeen thousand square feet, but three thousand of that is underground, accessed through this old mineshaft."

"Seems like a Parish kind of place," Victor said.

Gracie's head snapped up. "I'm not a bottom dweller. I live in the real world. Got it?"

She waited for him to answer her.

Gracie. So sensitive. Like the guy had any idea of their underground facility. Not everyone got the whole Parish-culture thing.

Thankfully, Victor seemed to have bigger fish to fry. Namely, helping free his friend. "Sure. No problem, Red."

Gracie opened her mouth.

No. Nope. So sick of this shit. "Gracie, get over it. The guy doesn't have to instinctively know your issues inside and out. He just has to help."

Silence. Silence as heavy as ten mastodons encased in ice. Gracie and Tony stared at her. What? They acted as if she'd never stuck up for someone outside the League before.

Chapter 64

SANDESH WAS STRIPPED OF HIS SHIRT AND HIS HEAD WAS forced down. His hands bound behind him. A Taser was held to his neck. Two men steered him through a hallway. One on either side. They teased and mocked him, tried to trip him up, but he kept his legs under him. A miracle of willpower, considering how thirsty, weak, and dizzy he was.

The walls and floor were pitted red brick with the memory of dark bloodstains, as if many bleeding victims had been dragged down this hall. The stains increased as they proceeded.

At the threshold to a chamber, the sour, defeated smell of torture and blood twisted his gut. Apparently, Walid knew the most important thing about torture—fear.

He hoped that's where his experience ended. But judging by Dmitri's story, he doubted it. Fortunately, he wouldn't stick around long enough to find out. Even with his head forced down and his hands bound behind his back, he knew what to expect.

Not much, but it gave him something to think about other than the stench. He mentally prepared himself for what was coming.

According to Dmitri, the room was large, with several torture stations and a stone bath. The guards would secure his feet before they unbound his hands. Sandesh would rather have waited for that moment to attack, but

Dmitri's account of the room and the element of surprise forced him to act before that happened.

The edge of the stone bath, cracked and crumbling gray cement, came into view. The moment he spied it, he planted his foot, twisted the energy up and out. His foot snapped back, slammed Taser Guard's ankle. An audible *crack*. The man jerked, cursed, and fell.

Sandesh spun, rammed his lowered head into the second guard. He drove him left. Into the spikes. The man stumbled, tripped. He fell against the metal wall. Sandesh threw himself left to avoid the same fate. He half fell, half rolled up and out of the way.

Damn. The blood. The second guard had fallen at an angle. His body mostly on the ground. His right arm and shoulder stabbed with spikes. Blood ran in crooked lines down his chest. His lips were moving. Maybe in prayer.

According to Dmitri, Walid didn't appear until the guards secured the prisoner, stripped off his pants with a sharp knife meant to intimidate, and made the call. He'd be expecting the call.

On his feet, he crossed the room to the first guard. The man had rolled and had the Taser up. Sandesh dodged. The man fired. One spike landed in Sandesh's leg. The other went wide. *Not good enough, pal*.

Sandesh brought his knee down and landed all his weight on the guard's neck. The man's hands flew up, tried to push him off. Tried to roll his leg under him. His eyes bulged. Must've forgotten that leg no longer worked. He gurgled, wheezed, went slack. Not dead. But out of the way.

Squatting over him, Sandesh fished the keys from the man's pocket. He undid his cuffs with a practiced hand.

Sweating and breathing heavily, he crossed the room—a well-used torture chamber with a dentist's chair, chains from the ceiling, spikes coming out of the wall, and several blowtorches. He bent to the stone bath. The water was foul. It had probably been bathed in by miners a hundred years ago. He was so damn thirsty. He didn't dare drink it. He dipped his head in and rubbed the blood from his eyes. He stood, shook off the water. That nearly did him in. So dizzy.

The room had no windows.

Of course not, it was at the bottom of a coal mine on a large compound. According to Dmitri, Sandesh couldn't escape the compound. Unless he took Walid with him. And he would. One way or the other.

Chapter 65

WHEN JUSTICE HAD IMAGINED SECURITY AT THE FRONT gate of a British national sex-trafficker, born in India, living on a ranch in Mexico, she hadn't once pictured an American guard. Well, a guy who looked American, like he'd stepped straight out of Blackwater and into a more lucrative profession.

He wore a baseball cap with *USA* lettering, dark sunglasses (at night), a .45 snugged in a chest holster over muscles so jacked they strained his T-shirt, and a stay-ten-feet-from-my-person-at-all-times vibe.

Gotcha. She'd shoot from here. Here being the top of a tree-lined hill overlooking the fenced-in compound of Rancho de Grim y Grimy. She was stretched out along a natural depression, with her head behind a shrub. Forearms tensed on the scratchy ground, finger on the trigger. She watched the guard through the night vision scope on her rifle.

The lime-green Cadillac drove down the road toward the front gate.

Justice's headset clicked. Gracie. Again. "How much longer, Justice? I'm roasting."

"Please, you've been in there for two hours. People smuggled out of Mexico stay in that compartment for days."

"Yeah, well, not me. If my cyber skills weren't

needed to rescue your boyfriend, nothing could get me into this *Dante's Inferno*. Nothing."

Yeah, it was a shit place to be. Telling Gracie that would only make it worse. "Chill your white privilege. You're almost inside the compound."

Her earpiece clicked again. Even the click sounded angry. Justice kept her focus on the gate, but listened to Gracie vent, responding here and there, mostly to encourage her—better anger than the fear it covered up.

When the car pulled to a stop before the guards, Justice silenced Gracie with a play-by-play. "There's a big *American Ninja Warrior* security guard talking to Tony and Victor. He seems to be in charge of the five men at the gate. He's gesturing our boys out of the car."

Tony and Victor got out. Victor exited, did a cute little pirouette that showed off his finely toned ass, and threw his head back with laughter.

Ninja Warrior shook his head, motioned them both to the side. They obviously had no weapons on them. And, at this point, were chilled to goose bumps. Unlike Gracie, who must be holding her breath down there, sweating and miserable.

"They're going to check the car."

With Tony and Victor away from the vehicle, huddled together like two men used to each other's intimate company, Ninja Warrior motioned two men to check the car.

Justice's heart rate, which had been elevated already, launched itself to top speed.

While the vehicle was searched, Tony and Victor were held under armed guard—guy looked maybe twenty, with a scruffy mustache that didn't pass machismo. Justice kept her eye on him.

She held her breath. Let it out. Don't find her. Don't. The guard got into the car. He crawled into the back seat. Holy shit. He was practically sitting on Gracie.

The guard inspecting the car climbed out. She couldn't take any more of this. *Yes? No? What?*

They cleared the car. The guard got out and into the front seat, backed the car up, and drove it down the road a little ways. They weren't going to let it inside.

Gracie must have felt the car reverse. "Justice—"

"Fuck. Parked it outside the compound. You're like twenty feet from the front gate." She clicked off, then back on after Gracie assured her she could still get inside. "You're east of the guard tower."

A golf cart was coming down the driveway. Looked like they expected Tony and Victor to ride in it up to the house.

Tony and Victor were motioned forward. Justice kept her finger poised on the trigger. Her boys were scanned and frisked. Like they could hide anything on their person that wasn't already visible.

They were motioned forward through the gate. Justice held her breath. Sweat beaded on her forehead. "Gracie. They're in. They're—"

A nerve-rattling alarm punched a hole right through the fabric of night and the thinnest of bad plans.

And hell, which had been biding its time waiting for the exact moment to royally fuck them, broke loose.

Chapter 66

DRAGGING FEET THROUGH THE UNDERGROUND CHAMBER, Sandesh listened to the general chatter on the two-way he'd boosted from the guard after he'd used the room's equipment to handcuff the man to a wall.

An American with a Southern accent spoke on it a couple of times. Alternating between English and Spanish, he seemed more interested in sharing stories. *Clown*.

At least he kept Sandesh in the loop. And it helped to have that voice to focus on. As if somewhere, someone thought this was just another day at the office.

God, he was nauseous. He hadn't realized just how damn sick he felt. His body was feverish and his steps sluggish. To top it off, he'd gotten lost in this medieval stone-and-shit tunnel.

Twice.

He'd only found his way this far thanks to Dmitri, whom he'd backtracked to get. Good thing the keys he'd taken from the guards he'd handcuffed had worked on the oubliette.

"I can't walk," Dmitri said.

Yeah. Sandesh had already figured that out. Using one arm, he dragged the guy—whose naked body was riddled with injuries. They sounded like shuffling zombies. Good thing the guy now weighed next to nothing. And that no one else was down here. The two guards he'd taken out seemed to be it.

"I'm dying. Let me die."

Not likely. If he could've gotten out of here on his own, he would've left the guy to die in peace. "Which way?"

Dmitri moaned. "I told you." He broke into a fit of coughing. He wheezed. "Down to get up."

Yeah. That was the crazy-ass shit directions that hadn't helped. And all that talk of uneven stones. "A little more specific."

Dmitri raised a trembling hand, as pale and bony as a concentration-camp corpse. "There."

Where? The stone corridor was lit with caged lights spaced haphazardly along the ceiling. They didn't do dick. And… Wait. He did see.

A brick a little larger than the rest with a white streak down the center.

He dragged Dmitri forward, used his shoulder to prop him against the wall, and hit the brick with his elbow.

The wall slid open. *Hallelujah*. Sandesh blinked at the brightness. Stairs? Stairs leading down. And…shit.

He grabbed Dmitri, pulled him back. A camera. *Damn*.

Leaving Dmitri, he crept around the side, used the wall to support his gun hand, aimed, shook, steadied his hand, aimed again, and took out the camera.

He picked Dmitri up—guy was practically unconscious—and hoisted him into a fireman's carry, leaving one hand free for his gun. He stepped down the first step.

Three things happened at once. Dmitri began to convulse. An alarm sounded. And two armed guards appeared at the bottom of the stairs.

Chapter 67

JUSTICE KEPT HER SCOPE ON THE SCENE AS NINJA WARRIOR reacted to the alarm. He immediately told Tony and Victor to get out of the golf cart and get down on their knees. They did.

The guard with the gun trained on Tony and Victor began to shout. He looked jittery.

Fuck.

He lifted Tony onto his feet and got in his face. Had they identified Tony? This wasn't good. Her finger twitched. Don't shoot. Wait. Wait and see.

Ninja Warrior stepped forward, hand on his gun. He was shouting too. The guard screaming at Tony dropped one of his hands, began to pull out his weapon. Justice took a breath. Held it. Focused. Aimed her scope.

Shot.

Snap. The bullet struck the temple of the guard holding Tony. The guard's head jerked. She didn't wait to see him go down. She swung the rifle left. Aimed. Shot another guard straight in the face as he'd turned toward her position.

Justice could feel the adrenaline flood her system, feel it make everything slow. She rode the hyperawareness, found Ninja Warrior scrambling away. She shot. Missed. Shot. *Shit.*

She returned to Tony and Victor and let off a round of suppressing fire as they bolted.

Meanwhile, Ninja Warrior, understanding where the danger was coming from, had zigzagged to the Cadillac, ducked, and swung his gun in her direction.

His first shot missed by a mile. He needed a rifle.

She fired at the car, forced Ninja Warrior to stay down but kept clear of where Gracie hid. The car was bulletproof, but no need to take chances.

She hoped Ninja Warrior wouldn't notice Gracie. Had he opened the car door? Damn tinted windows. She shot again. Keeping him hunkered down, though he'd probably give instructions via two-way.

Yep. A black Land Rover with dark windows tore out of the gate. It raced up the hill, over brush and stones, toward her. She fired at it. Seriously, was the whole country bulletproof?

Someone in the car fired at her. The dirt in front of her burst up. She ducked her head. The shots stopped. She took two deep breaths. *Fuck this*.

She surveyed her escape route, then spoke into her mic. "Gracie?"

Gracie's voice came through the headset, clear but soft. "Go. I've got American Ninja Warrior."

Justice didn't need more encouragement. She unhooked her night vision goggles from her belt, put them on, crawled backward, rolled, and ran at a crouch.

Chapter 68

HIDDEN AMONG THE TREES AND DARKNESS, JUSTICE adjusted her night vision goggles and watched her pursuers. The Land Rover stopped at the edge of the woods.

A group of men got out.

She ran, pinning the stock of her rifle with her forearm, aiming the barrel safely away. Her lean legs stretched out as she skirted through the trees, and her mind sifted through her catalogue of satellite images. From this hill, the ground sloped and became even and flat, a straight and open shot to the barn.

She heard movement behind, men dispersing into the woods.

Shit. She ran faster. Not good. If she ran toward the barn, breaking from the cover of trees, someone would spot her.

Stumbling on a root, she worked her feet to regain balance. *Nope*. Holding out her weapon like a chicken wing, she slammed into the ground. Dirt, broken tree limbs, and a muffled *umpf*. Way too much noise.

Someone shouted. Her head began to buzz. Her heart rate doubled. Her ears thrummed. She got to her feet, double-checked her rifle, focused her hearing, sought out identifying sounds, determining location, distance, and intent.

They were close. Time to do the unexpected.

Resettling her NVGs, she began to backtrack. It was a gamble, but she had an idea. Or the memory of an idea.

Years ago, when she and Gracie were teens, they'd gone down to Philly and had gotten into what Momma would later call an "unacceptable altercation." Basically, they'd gotten into trash-talking a group of older kids, after one had whistled at them outside a convenience store.

Even back then, Justice had had a way with words. Enough of a way that one of the kids had pulled a gun on them.

Being younger, unarmed, and slightly inebriated, they'd run. The four kids jumped into their broken-down Expedition and gave chase.

Using a bit of evasive tactics—Gracie's idea—they'd led the gang to a nearby apartment complex. At the complex, Justice hid while Gracie let them see her darting into a narrow alley. The driver had slammed on the brakes. They'd all gotten out and sprinted after Gracie. They'd left the car, as expected. The girls' plan had been to try and hot-wire it, but the guys had left the car running.

Justice, who'd backtracked, jumped into the car and took off. She picked Gracie up at a prearranged spot. Being fifteen and having had two beers, they'd made it a few blocks before she'd crashed into a parked car.

Lessons learned: Don't drink and drive hijacked cars. And if you leave your car running, because you may need to give chase, station a guard.

Keeping her breath controlled, she slowed near the Land Rover. Hoping. Praying.

All four doors open. Lights on. No one home. Car idling.

Same state. Different city.

She ran in a crouch alongside the Land Rover and slipped into the front seat. Seat warmer. Nice.

———~~~———

Switching off the Land Rover's lights, Justice headed down the hill and straight for the stables. She clicked her mic. "Gracie?"

There was a long pause, a pause where she imagined her sister climbing out of a leather seat and being shot by a huge idiot wearing a USA baseball hat, a pause in which her throat dried and her heart froze. And then her sister's voice, slightly garbled. "In mine shaft. Fence down. You close?"

Gracie had gotten inside? She'd gotten inside and turned off the fence. Whoa. Take that, American Ninja Warrior. You're no match for a half-naked redhead with mad cyber skills.

"Almost."

Static. "ETA?"

"Ten. Copy."

The crackle of a mic. "Can't wait."

Fuck. "I'll catch up."

"Roger."

Justice clicked off, slid her body down while steering over bumpy ground and closer to the gate. She'd probably be shot at. Good thing this thing was bulletproof. If someone did shoot, her best bet was to drive straight through the fence.

Sure it would attract a lot of attention, but she wasn't exactly in stealth mode right now.

She neared the fence. There were no lights on along it. No one shot at her. Her heart rate picked up. She had the craziest feeling, the most insane idea. She could still sneak inside.

She slowed, parked the car, got out, pocketed the key. She looked around. It was quiet. No guards. The alarm had stopped.

Was that Gracie's doing? She definitely couldn't hear the hum of the fence. She drew closer. Not that she didn't trust her sister, but someone could've turned it back on.

She chucked a bottle of Benadryl she'd found in the glove compartment. It hit the fence and rattled to the ground. Fence still off.

Okay. It could go back on at any moment. She could end up at the top, legs straddling either side when the juice came back on.

"J. Over here."

Flicking up her NVGs, she looked through the fence. At the end of the stable, Tony stood, dressed in a guard's uniform. He waved to her. "Come on."

He stepped back into hiding.

Tony. Brilliant, wonderful Tony. He'd taken out a guard, stolen his uniform.

Slinging her rifle on her back, she took a running leap, hit the fence with a *clang*, and scrambled over. She landed like she'd been training for this her whole life—she had—and sprinted forward.

She ran around the side of the stables, her nose prickling at the smell of manure, and spotted him. She reached for Tony's hand. He reached for hers. She skidded to a stop.

Walid.

Walid stood behind Tony with a group of armed men.

"Get down!" Quick as boiling hatred, she brought up her sidearm. Tony stepped up, intercepted her hand, pulled her forward, twisted her wrist into a lock. She cried out, dropped the Sig.

He caught the gun, released her. "You need to come with us."

It took her a minute. It took her a lifetime. It took her breath away.

"You?"

Chapter 69

THE MEN AT THE BOTTOM OF THE STONE STAIRS FROZE. Blinked. They were looking from light into darkness. Perfect.

Sandesh rolled Dmitri off his shoulders, dropped, and shot. Missed.

One of the men, the better trained, belly-crawled to safety. The other stayed in the open, reached for his gun.

Poor guy.

Sandesh shot. The man fell.

The alarm thrummed against the walls like a stone heartbeat. On the step behind him, Dmitri stopped convulsing. Sandesh reached over to confirm what he strongly suspected.

Surprise. Dmitri still had a pulse.

Getting his hands under Dmitri's armpits, he dragged him back around a corner and sat him against the wall. "Dmitri, Dmitri, is there another way out?"

Sandesh listened to the calls coming through the two-way to see if the guard below called for backup. Lots of noise. People checking in. But most of it had nothing to do with him or the guard he'd left handcuffed.

The real problem was at the gate. The ranch was under attack. Two guards had been shot. Shot from a distant hill. Hell of a shot by the sound of it.

Warmth rolled into his chest. Justice. His mother had

always told him a man shouldn't keep his woman waiting, so he better get moving.

He patted Dmitri on his shoulder. The Russian was
as good as dead. Even with the best and most immediate
medical attention. And he wasn't getting either. "Rest,"
he said. "There is more."

Dmitri's eyes flashed open, cleared, and focused on
Sandesh. "Kill Walid."

His eyes dropped to half-lidded, dulled, and froze.
And the once-real human, the broken and tortured body,
seemed nothing more than an empty reminder of too
much pain and anger.

Sandesh closed the lifeless eyes. The two-way
squawked to life beside him, and the guy with the
Southern accent, in a voice a hell of a lot less cheerful,
said he was handling, "That mess in the mines."

They were coming for him.

Ready or not.

Ready.

Crouched behind Dmitri's body, by the only exit, the
one that led down and then up, Sandesh wasn't sure if
the silence was a good or a bad thing.

Actually. He was sure it was bad.

The guards had organized. They'd changed frequency
on their two-way. He wished he knew how many guards
were in the camp. How many were coming for him.

He had two semiautomatics, full clips, taken from the
torture guards. He'd wait, wait for them to come through
that damn door.

Too bad his fight-or-flight reflex sang so loudly it

was hard to stay put. Waiting was never fun. It never felt like you were being proactive.

But if he tried to go down that tunnel, the one that led to some kind of elevator—he'd heard the thing creaking to a stop a short time ago—he'd be killed.

He forced himself not to respond to the nerves that told him to fight, fight, fight. He let out a breath. *Calm. Reason.* He emptied his mind. He aimed his gun.

The stone wall swung open with a *whoosh*. Wait for a visual. Justice was here. It might be her. It might. Wait.

It wasn't. A man, a huge guy with a USA baseball hat, stepped out, weapon down. *Down? USA?*

A woman's voice came from behind him. "Don't shoot."

Sandesh hesitated. USA turned to the side as if to push someone back. The person shoved him in the ribs, stepped in front of him.

"Gracie?" What the hell was she wearing? "You're rescuing me in your underwear?"

Gracie shrugged. "All the cool kids are." She eyed Sandesh—shirtless, pants ripped. He wasn't exactly styling. Gracie elbowed USA in the ribs again. "Don't shoot this guy. He's with me."

Sandesh lowered his weapon and climbed out from behind Dmitri's body. "What's going on?"

Gracie jerked a thumb at the big guy. "This is American Ninja Warrior." She gazed up at him. "I don't trust him."

The big guy grinned down at the feisty redhead. Sparks flew. Temperatures rose. Global warming increased. He shook his head, reached a hand out to Sandesh. "Better known as Agent Leif McAllister of the FBI. You can call me Dusty."

The FBI working in Mexico? And he had a Southern accent. Sure. Why not?

Gracie stepped forward. "Sorry, Sandesh, there's really no time for a debrief." She tilted her head back. Her cheeks were flushed. Excitement? Nerves? Something else? "This guy has gotten me safe this far. And he says he can get us out of here so we can reconnect with the rest of our crew."

"I can get you out, if you follow my rules."

She stopped, bit her lip as if remembering an important detail. "After we kill Walid."

Sandesh eyed the two of them. Shrugged. "Kill whoever you want. I'm only interested in finding Justice."

Dusty laughed. "You and half the world's population."

Chapter 70

YELLOW LIGHTS PERCHED ALONG THE BARN CAST A BROKEN shadow across Tony's face, making him look two-faced. Appropriate. Tony's eyes seemed a thousand years old. "I can explain."

He could explain? Explain betraying the League? Betraying her? Betraying the entire family? Letting Bridget take the blame for his actions?

No. Her brain stuttered over the idea, confused. So confused. Because his eyes, Tony's eyes, stayed on her, stayed locked on her, and they said, *Trust me. This isn't what you think*.

Disbelief and panic clasped hands around her neck, trapping her heart in her throat. Her training kicked in. *Assess the situation. Assess options*.

Four armed men stood behind her brother. They had guns on her. Her gun was on the ground.

Okay. Only one option kept her alive. She held up her hands. "What do you want me to do?"

Tony let out a breath. He said softly, so softly his voice seemed to float like the airborne seed of a dandelion to her ears, "I have to search you, J."

He kept his hands out as he approached. A chill ran down her body. She wanted to step back. Every instinct in her body told her not to let him touch her. She stayed put.

He began to search her. She ground her teeth.

Betrayer. He didn't speak. But his face came so close to hers, she could see the regret in his eyes.

He felt along her arms, her back, her butt. He took the knife strapped to the outside of her leg, took the rifle hanging at her back, but left the knife strapped on her calf under her pant leg.

What was going on? He'd obviously felt it. Hell, he'd given her the knife when they'd been getting ready. He stood up. His eyes seemed to be telling her something.

What was going on?

She swallowed.

Tony stepped back. "She's clean."

He handed the weapons he'd taken from her to a guard. It was then that she processed and understood that Tony wasn't armed.

What. The. Hell?

As if given leave to move, to animate, Walid, and the two big guards flanking him, stepped forward. He smiled. He had some really nice teeth. Like he'd taken the money from selling women to be broken and used, and had gone straight to the most expensive dentist in town.

Had Hope's life paid for those teeth?

She wanted to tear that smile out one tooth at a time.

One of the two men flanking Walid said, "I think I should search her. I don't trust him."

Walid considered. He nodded. "Search her."

The guard moved forward. Tony put a hand to the guard's chest and shook his head. "No one. And I mean no one is going to touch my sister."

The man froze, glared. "I'm going to search her."

Tony kept his arm against the guard's chest and spoke over him. "Walid, if you want what I have to give you, if you want your brother's murderer, you will stay the fuck away from my sister."

Walid licked his lips. Other than that, he stayed composed. A man who'd faced a thousand tense situations, a thousand desperate moments, and who had survived them all.

Walid waved his hand to indicate his guard should withdraw. He stepped back to Walid's side, shaking his head.

"You see," Walid said. "Nothing means as much to me as getting my hands on my brother's true killer. Mukta Parish."

Chapter 71

ORGANIZED WITH TONY AND WALID IN THE LEAD AND JUSTICE in the middle of four armed men, the group walked past the stables and toward the house in the distance.

Justice walked with her hands raised. Her jaw couldn't have been tenser. Tony. Tony, who knew what it was like to be used; Tony, whom she loved, whom she had begged her family to adopt, had conspired with Walid. Against her. Against their family. Against Sandesh, who had wanted nothing more than to help people.

It was a good thing armed guards surrounded her.

In front of her, Tony walked side by side with Walid, like a friend, a confidant, a brother.

She wanted to jump on his back and smash his face into the piles of horse dung saturating her senses. Then pounce on Walid.

They passed onto the porch of the main house, an expensive villa with a dry fountain and a thousand ruined lives paying for every spectacular piece of architecture, handcrafted item of furniture, and enough luxury to satisfy a tycoon.

They went through a set of arches, down a red-brick-lined corridor, and into an expansive office.

The brightly lit room had a Tuscan-ranch feel with terra-cotta tile flooring, exposed beams, leather couches, and heavy, parchment-colored drapes.

Two stern-faced guards accompanied her, Tony,

and Walid into the room. One of them—he seemed in charge—had ordered the other men to go help someone named Dusty.

Completely comfortable and at home, of course, Walid sat on one of the two red-leather couches. A little awkwardly, Tony sat beside him. *Sure, let's all get comfy.*

Justice eyed the room, the layout and possible escape routes, as Walid's two personal guards positioned themselves.

The first, in-charge guy, who had a thick forehead and matching neck, stood directly behind Walid and Tony on the couch.

The second, smaller neck, colder eyes, stood behind Justice and kept his gun on her. He stayed far enough away that he'd be able to shoot long before she made it to him.

Plan B? Create time to make a plan B.

"So, Tone," she said. Tony looked up at her, met her eyes with a cringe. "You're friends with human-traffickers now?"

"Not so much friends as enemies with a common interest."

Something in her spine snapped to attention. Her hands fisted at her sides. Her bones fused into one giant club of anger. "Which is?"

Tony met her eyes again. And this time there was no regret. Only rage. "Stopping Mukta Parish, so that she never warps another child's mind. Never takes a kid from the street and turns them into a killer, into someone who can never be good enough, someone allowed only two emotions, anger or shame, someone forced to hate his own gender."

Justice's heart lurched, split, and broke in half. Unbelievable, stunning vibrations of pain shot through her. She doubled over.

Walid laughed. "Women. They are the most devious of sexes. If not controlled, they will poison the world. With complaints. With excuses. With the vagaries of being female."

Justice rallied the muscles in her spine and torso, ordered them to straighten. *Fuck Walid. Fuck Tony.* Anger boiled in her cells. She pushed it down.

She needed to stay calm and look for the opportunity to save Sandesh. She locked eyes with Tony. She saw them flicker, once, toward the couch across from him.

Fucker.

He wanted her to sit. *Oh, sure, Tone, why not? You'll turn on Momma, but you'll help me. You shit.*

She pushed aside her feelings. She couldn't afford them. She'd deal with it later.

Legs like steel, unbending and tense, she walked to the couch. Cold eyes kept his gun on her as she moved, but remained stationed where he was. There was a sharp crack as her weight hit the couch. Truthfully, she more fell than sat.

Justice didn't need Tony's eyes to keep traveling to his left, toward the window. She saw Victor almost immediately, standing behind one of the heavy drapes.

Victor's mostly naked body only slightly reflected in the window. And only because of where she sat. She made a point to keep her eyes focused on Walid and not give Victor away.

Tony knew Victor was there, so he must've told Victor to be there. What was going on?

"So this has been about Momma? You couldn't have, oh, I don't know, told us how you felt? Brought it up over an awkward Thanksgiving dinner like a normal person?"

Tony laughed. Sarcastic. Hurt. And laced with hundreds of thoughts and questions no one had bothered to acknowledge. "You mean like write a letter? A letter that told everyone—everyone in my family of female fanatics—exactly how I felt?"

Female fanatics? What letter? The one with the plan for dealing with the Brothers Grim? She'd never seen it. She hadn't—

Not now. Deal with it later.

Victor had a gun. She saw it glint off the glass. He had it raised. Was he waiting for some kind of signal? Or maybe just the right moment? Hmmm. "Tone, you don't think the League is doing the right thing?"

It was Walid's turn to answer. "The bitches!" His outrage and disbelief made his words drop low and sound heavy. "They are trying to overturn the natural order of things. Women are to be bedded and fed and kept out of the way."

Tony laughed. He turned his body so that he faced Walid. He put his hand on Walid's shoulder. He placed a thumb on Walid's neck, rubbed it back and forth. "That's the kind of shit that gets everyone in trouble."

Walid knocked his hands off. Too late. Justice knew. Tony had affixed the clear poison patch.

How long until it took effect? How long until the guards noticed there was something wrong with Walid?

Once they noticed, they'd figure out who did it. They'd shoot Tony. He'd die, and she'd never understand why he'd done any of it.

She needed to do something. Now.

She had a weapon. If she could get Walid close enough, she could use the knife tucked in her pants. Victor could probably take out the guard closest to him, the thick-necked one behind the couch where Tony and Walid sat.

That left Cold Eyes for her. Okay. Kill Walid. Keep the knife, chuck it at Cold Eyes. Hope Victor took out Thick Neck.

Not for nothing.

She crossed her legs, ranch-hand style, right foot on left knee. Her pant leg rose up her calf. "I need to pee. About as badly as your brother did when I shoved that little piece of metal into his heart."

The room went quiet. Walid's face turned crimson angry. "You will piss when I dig my knife into your gut."

Tony grabbed Walid by the shirt. "Knock it off."

The guard behind Tony put his gun to Tony's head. By the look on Tony's face, he'd finally registered the shit he'd gotten them into. Huh, it had only taken a gun to his head.

Not really helping.

Walid knocked Tony's hand away, stood up, flicked open a knife. He stalked toward her. "Your brother can cry over your corpse as I did my brother's."

"Come on then, Wally," Justice taunted. *Please, Victor, understand the signal.* "Let's go!"

Chapter 72

THE RICKETY MINE SHAFT ELEVATOR ROCKED TO A STOP with a *pop* that spit out coal dust and congealed mechanical oil. Even the throat full of water Sandesh had chugged from Dusty's flask couldn't keep him from coughing.

He wiped his mouth and blinked his eyes clear. The short tunnel leading out to the compound was lit by a single, old-school light bulb. A group of four men stood at the mouth of the mine shaft with weapons drawn.

Dusty used his Glock 22 to motion Sandesh and Gracie out of the metal box and to the side of the wood-beam-supported tunnel. Sandesh shuffled out, head down.

Gracie did a good job of strutting out like she didn't give a damn. Although Sandesh strongly suspected that was an act.

The waiting guards kept their weapons drawn, watched her more than Sandesh, but they really watched Dusty.

Whoever he was, Dusty had the respect of the men who worked here. He strolled out with an almost good-natured casualness. Of course, he pretended that Sandesh and Gracie were his prisoners. And though it wasn't easy for Sandesh to trust this guy's plan, if it got him closer to Justice, he had to take the chance.

Dusty spoke in Spanish to the men. He asked what was going on in the camp. They told him that Justice had been captured, captured because her brother had lured her into a trap.

Gracie made a small, pained sound. Sandesh's hands clenched into fists. Fucking traitor. He was going to kill Tony.

Dusty didn't miss a beat. With a flow of Spanish almost too quick for Sandesh to keep up, he told the men that he had a confession. He sort of felt bad about it, but facts were facts, and he still worked for the FBI. Yep, he told them, things were going to get very bad very quickly.

Guy had balls. Telling a group of men with guns trained in your direction that you'd basically lied, infiltrated their ranks, and tricked them wasn't how Sandesh would've played it. Dusty even made sure to emphasize that the kidnapping of an American was a serious crime.

Not giving them time to consider shooting, Dusty appealed to their sense of self-preservation. He told them he didn't want them in trouble, so he'd give them a chance to leave before the rest of his people showed up. In helicopters.

Dude was a good liar. The guards began to talk among themselves. Dusty didn't let up. His Spanish was much better than Sandesh's. "You boys will have to leave those weapons," he said. "I can't help you if you're caught with them. If you're caught without guns though, I can get them to let you go. No questions asked."

Dude was a great liar.

The pressure built as the men began to argue. Dusty turned his gun on them. "Don't be stupid. Leave the guns and go."

Sandesh was pretty sure the air in the tunnel had gotten a lot more congested, what with the size of Dusty's balls taking up so much space.

The men froze. Sandesh readied himself to act. A long, tense moment passed. A Mexican standoff, of sorts.

"Boys." Dusty shook his head. His voice was the same casual, good-natured stream. "Come on now, get going."

Slowly, the men placed their guns down on the packed dirt and backed out of the tunnel. Dusty turned to Sandesh and Gracie. "Let's give 'em a little while to spread the word before we head out."

Shaking his head, Sandesh bent and grabbed a semi-automatic rifle from the pile. "I'm not waiting."

Tony was a dead man.

The shreds of his tuxedo pants flapping around his ankles—flimsy things weren't built to take any kind of real movement—he stepped out into the night.

Chapter 73

"COME ON THEN, WALLY. LET'S GO!"

Everything seemed to happen in one horrifying time-lapse instant.

Justice reached for her knife. Victor broke from the curtain, shot the thick-necked guard behind Tony.

With a slap as loud as the bullet that'd killed him, the guard slammed against terra-cotta tiles.

Still by the door, Cold Eyes jerked his weapon around and shot Victor. One, two, three times, hitting him in the torso.

Victor fell against the curtains, grasped at the gold sheets. They slid through his hands, and he slipped down in a bloody mess.

Justice's knife sailed past Walid as he had the good sense to drop down, slamming his knee against a marble coffee table.

Walid was back on his feet in an instant. Guy must have a huge pain tolerance. He motioned Cold Eyes not to shoot and hobbled toward Justice with a sneer as vindictive as it was certain.

God. If he got his hands on her, she was going to die. In pain. Now would be a really good time for that poison to kick in.

Sensing the gun at her back, Justice braced her feet and spread her hands wide.

Walid's eyebrows rose. He stopped short and grunted.

The knife in his hands dropped. He reached over his left shoulder where Justice's knife jutted out like an insult.

Holy shit. Tony had stabbed Walid. He'd hidden behind the tall fucker and stabbed him in the back of his neck.

Walid cursed, a bloody rumble like earth shattering against earth, then began to convulse. He crashed to his knees, lowered his head, vomited, and curled onto his side.

The remaining guard shot at Tony. Tony jerked to the side and dropped. The guard swung his gun at Justice.

Reinforcements burst through the doorway, three guards.

No. Not guards. Sandesh and Gracie with…

American Ninja Warrior?

Bam. Bam. Bam. Sandesh shot the guard who had his weapon aimed at Justice. He didn't stop shooting until the guy was on the ground. Dead. Dead. Dead.

Sandesh moved into the room. His weapon now aimed at…

Tony?

Uninjured, Tony had faked his fall, crawled around the couch, and picked up the dead guard's assault rifle. He now stood.

Tony and Sandesh had some serious weapons pointed at each other.

And Walid, whose nervous system was closing up shop, convulsed at the foot of the couch. A knife deep in his neck.

Gracie took charge. "Stand down, big guy," she told Ninja Warrior who, Justice now noticed, also had his gun on Sandesh. "This is between family. Keep an eye on the door."

To Justice's utter shock, Ninja Warrior nodded once and said, "Okay, darlin'," and did as she said.

What had just happened?

Gracie glared at Tony. "Drop the gun, traitor."

Tony swallowed, put the gun on the floor, took three steps back, and held up his hands.

Sandesh rushed over to Justice but kept the rifle trained on Tony. "You okay?"

He was worried about her? He clearly hadn't looked in a mirror recently. His face swollen, bruises over his ribs, his pants torn, his lips cracked and dry. "Did he... did they hurt you?"

Sandesh shook his head. He bent, ran his nose across her cheek. "Justice, are you okay?"

Warmth crawled across her skin and down into her muscles. Was she okay? "Yes. But..." She looked over Tony's shoulder. "Victor."

"Victor? Victor is here?"

Sandesh started forward. Justice stopped him. "Give me the rifle."

Chapter 74

SANDESH HANDED JUSTICE HIS WEAPON WITHOUT HESITATION. How the hell was Victor here?

Justice pointed the rifle at her brother's chest. "Move to the side so Sandesh can help Victor."

Sandesh walked across the room. Once clear of the couch, he saw him. Victor, dressed more scantily than Gracie, curtains cushioned his torso, blood covered his body.

Sandesh fisted his hands to keep from attacking Justice's brother. He was well aware of the man's eyes on him, the anger and frustration there. That made two of them.

"Fuck, Victor," Sandesh said, dropping to his knees. "What are you doing here?"

Victor was conscious. His gun still gripped in his hand. His eyes widened. "Got shot."

Sandesh nodded to acknowledge this was indeed true. Gracie was there instantly, handing him a bottle of vodka she had grabbed from a small rolling bar.

He poured the contents over his hands, washed them like a raccoon in a stream, then poured vodka onto Victor. Victor hissed.

"Don't move, Tony."

Sandesh looked up to see Justice had stepped closer and threatened her brother. Tony shook his head. Sandesh pulled Gracie's attention from her siblings.

"Gracie, could you get Walid's knife, cut strips from the curtains, stop the bleeding?"

Gracie dove for the knife Walid had dropped, then rushed over to the curtains and started cutting one into strips. She made quick, tidy bandages and handed them to Sandesh.

Once he got the big bleeder tied off, he could see the wounds better. He patted Victor's shoulder. "It's actually not so bad."

Victor made a fuck-you face and then said, "Fuck you."

"Where's he shot?" Justice said, having come around the couch. "I can't see anything but blood."

Gracie answered. "Thigh, skimmed, superficial. Arm. That's bad. Some muscle damage. But it won't kill him. And one into his hip. Barely bleeding, that one. He can make the plane ride back."

"Hip bone," Victor moaned. "Oh. I need that thing." His head lolled back and forth against the tile. "I really need it."

Sandesh patted him on the shoulder. "You're going to live. And fuck. And samba."

"Samba?" Victor said. "Racist much?" The slurred words ended when Victor closed his eyes and passed out.

Gracie and Sandesh continued to work to make him comfortable and stop the bleeding.

Dusty stuck his head inside. "The grounds are clearing out, but we need to get moving. I'm going to go look for a vehicle."

He left. Gracie stood up, looked toward the doorway. "I don't trust him. I should go with him."

Justice reached into her pocket and tossed a key at Gracie. "Land Rover. Behind the stables."

Gracie caught the key but shook her head. "It's not big enough."

Justice kept her weapon on Tony. "He's not going with us."

Gracie nodded and left the room.

Tony's head fell forward. He let out a breath. "I'm so sorry, J."

Sandesh was pretty sure *sorry* wasn't what Justice was looking for.

Chapter 75

HE WAS SORRY? OH, WELL. NO PROBLEM THEN. "I DON'T give a shit how sorry you are. What the fuck did you think you were doing? You betrayed us, the League. Momma. You betrayed the woman that rescued you from the gutter."

"No." He shook his head. He lifted his eyes to her. "She took me from the streets and made me kill people. That's not saving me."

"So what, you decided to join forces with a human-trafficker to teach her a lesson? Even if it meant betraying me?"

"No. I wanted to keep you safe. Take out these fucks myself." He closed his eyes, opened them. "Momma. I told her you were too emotionally involved to execute the operation. She ignored my letter."

"What?" The fucking letter. The thing must've been ten pages long. A fucking manifesto.

"Had to stop you. Then I'd do my plan. Take 'em out separate. Understand?"

She was beginning to. She didn't like it. "You warned the Brothers Grim about us, sent them to Jordan to keep my mission from moving forward?" He nodded. "When that didn't work, you sent the drones, so Momma would become afraid, let you move forward with your plan?" Again he nodded. "When that didn't work, you gave them Sandesh."

His shoulders tensed. He looked down at Sandesh then shook his head. "Dusty—the guy with the USA hat—tried to stop that."

Dusty, a.k.a. American Ninja Warrior. "How the hell did you develop this bromance with that guy?"

Tony crossed his arms. "He's legit." He began speaking quickly. His south Philly rising. "FBI. Met him by accident. At a bar. Believe that?"

No. She didn't. She'd look into it later.

"So you joined forces with some FBI guy. You had money. He had skills?"

"Basically. He was sick of traffickers getting ignored for drugs. Took what the government calls a hiatus. Came to work for me. He got in here. Worked his way up. Helped keep everything running. Until that shit at the massage parlor. After that, Aamir, the smart one, stepped in. He knew Walid had a leak here. Still, I thought I had it covered. I thought it would all end with Jordan. Only an unfeeling, uncaring lunatic would send her daughter to Jordan without back up, knowing the Brothers were suspicious."

He spit the last. Literally. Spit flew from his lips. He was furious. And not just at Momma. At himself.

"You're saying you did all of this—betrayed our family, my trust, the woman who rescued you—to keep me safe? But why?"

"Why?" His dark eyebrows scrunched together. "'Cause you're the good one, Justice. With you I can laugh, feel, breathe. And that woman…that monster you call Momma—"

"Watch it, Tony. Watch it. I'm still not sure I won't shoot you." Her hands tightened on the rifle.

He began to laugh. "I wish you would. That'd make it easier." He let out a long gust of air, sucked in an even longer breath. "She was gonna let you get yourself killed."

He swayed, leaned a hand against the back of the couch. "It's like you didn't matter. Well, fuck, you mattered to me."

Tears started to fall down his face. He was shaking. Angry. Sad. Broken?

"Really? You and Bridget conspired with Cooper, tracked me, and left the computer with a drug addict. That bit of brilliance almost got me killed."

He shook his head, worked his lower lip between his teeth like he was going to bite it off. "Tracking was my mistake. Bridget didn't know I'd set that up."

Bridget. Justice had never suspected it could've been the two of them. Never.

"Needed to keep track of you. To not risk you, the family, the school. Know how hard that was? How much I had to work? I even saved that Juan guy for Dada. I did that."

"Oh. Well. Brava. Way to go. Would you like your silver star pinned to your chest now, or would you like to wait for the ceremony?"

"Smart-ass," Tony said. And he said it like it was a compliment, like it was love.

"And Coop? You brought him in on this knowing what he did. Knowing he was a drug addict?"

"Cooper?" He seemed confused now, groggy. "Told him he was helping. Told him it'd keep you safe. He was really trying, J. You know he was sober, right?"

He lifted his head, met her gaze. His hands shook against the couch. He fisted them.

"No. He was high as hell every time I saw him."

"Nah. Think I'd of let him within a hundred feet of you if he was still using? No f'in way." Tony's eyes slid over to Sandesh, then back to her. He sighed like he had nothing else to lose. "I love you, J. Loved you from the moment you rescued me."

Justice felt something in her chest crack. She held it back, held back the pain. No. Tony was a liar. "Like the way Cooper loved me? He left me to be tortured. He left Hope to die."

Tony shook his head. "Lies. That's what she does. Makes it so you only want the League. But your dad wasn't all bad."

He had to be kidding. Or crazy. "Yeah. He was. All bad."

"No. Didn't you ever wonder how Mukta found youse? Some rich woman in the Northeast found two girls in Virginia?"

"The League."

Tony leaned heavily on the couch. He was really trembling now, like a sudden fever had overcome him. "Come on, you know better. The League isn't all power-ful. Coop went to her. After being forced to leave you with his mother-in-law."

"Forced?"

Tony's eyes drooped. Then his head. He shook himself. Head and eyelids rose. "Court gave her cus-tody. Man didn't have a chance. An American Indian drug addict versus a white middle-class woman. No contest."

What? Her father had been forced to leave her? To give her to that crazy woman? It didn't matter. It didn't change things. "He could've taken us. He could have run to the reservation. He knew what she was."

Tony shook his weary head. "Wouldn't a worked. Did what he could. Drugged as he was, found his way to Momma, a woman he knew adopted kids. And Leland. Told 'em about you."

"Cooper? Cooper was the one who told Momma about me and Hope?"

Tony nodded. His eyes told a thousand things, a thousand secrets she had never guessed. She'd had it all wrong.

He sniffed. Coughed. "Yeah. He hung outside her office for three days, begging her and Leland to help. They finally listened. A day too late for Hope. But not for you. My. Justice." He reached over and hit his chest. "This tattoo. 'All for one.' Is for you. You're the one. You with the good heart. You really want to save people. Not Momma. Never her."

Justice had to force her throat to swallow past the root of growing panic. "She rescued us. She rescued you."

"No. You did. They set it up. They took even that from me. But you didn't know that. You did what they knew you would."

"What? Who set it up? Took what from you?"

Her throat went into lockdown. Alarms sounded in her head; doors closed in her heart; prisons sprang to life in her soul.

She lowered her gun. The salt of her tears kissed her lips. "Tone, why are you shaking?"

He looked up at her. He blinked. He jerked his head. "Oh. The patch." He waved his hand. "Smeared it. Got no reason to live anyhows."

He stumbled left and fell over.

Justice screamed. She ran to him. "What did you do?" Skirting the dead guard, she fell to Tony's side. She grabbed his shoulders. "What did you do? You stupid idiot!"

Sandesh reached across Tony, pulled her hands away. "Careful. Don't touch."

"He's got your back." Tony tucked his hands into his armpits. He gasped for breath. He'd landed oddly. His right leg bent back, caught under his ass. His body began to convulse. His teeth to chatter.

How did she fix this? How did she stop it?

Tony looked up at her. "I did good too? Right, J? Not all bad." His hazel eyes, the haunted eyes that had once looked out from the face of a starving twelve-year-old boy, pinned her. Begged her. Her heart broke into a thousand irreparable pieces. It hurt to breathe.

"Yeah, Tone." She spoke over sobs. "You did a lot of good. You were my best friend. I love you. I will always love you."

He closed his eyes. "Don't cry, J." He smiled. A smile that twitched at the edges, then went flat.

Chapter 76

THE ENERGY IN SANDESH'S APARTMENT HAD CHANGED. NOT subtly either. Though he couldn't think of the perfect word for it—this shift in atmosphere since Justice had begun staying there.

There was probably a French word for the buzz of warmth, the charged peace, the surge of contentment, the electric joy of waking up every morning beside the person he loved.

All he could think of was...*blessed*.

That sort of fit. But it still didn't describe the thrill of falling asleep with her in his arms. Or the jolt of awareness he felt, like right now, with her warm and asleep against him.

Or the way his heart lifted every morning when she rolled over and kissed him. Then fucked him until he fell back to sleep in a satiated heap.

Or the pleasant way it hurt when she disentangled herself from him and the sheets and left the bed in the morning.

Or the way his heart jumped, *hip-hip-hooray*ed in his chest when she returned, carrying a cup of coffee as hot and dark as her eyes.

Blessed just didn't cover it.

He hated the idea of her going back to her house. Not that they'd talked about them shacking up together. But she'd been spending every night for a month, every night since Mexico. She'd told him she couldn't face her house yet, knowing Tony wouldn't be there.

So the move in had just kind of happened. Of course, they'd returned to the Mantua Home many times, for dinner, to work out, to hang out with her siblings. She seemed to be getting more comfortable back there, less consumed with bad memories. He was beyond grateful for the easing of that pain.

But that didn't mean he wanted her to go back there. She'd turned his apartment into a place he now considered a home, not just the place he paid rent on. He didn't want that to end.

Sandesh shifted with that sweet touch of regret as Justice, buck naked, climbed out of bed and sashayed out of the bedroom with a promise to return, "With coffee."

God, he loved her. He waited for her to get far enough away that she could no longer see into the room before he jumped out of bed.

He yanked the sheets and blankets straight. Made the bed in record time, military tight. Then he got the box he'd stashed under the bed. Rose petals, a hand drawn sign that read *Our Home Sweet Home*, and a black bow tie.

Couldn't say he wasn't classy.

Not enough? Should he have…

Fuck. He'd thought of this a thousand different ways. He'd decided to make it simple, offer to share himself, his life, with her.

He sprinkled the rose petals across the bed, hung the sign across the headboard, put on the tie, and laid his naked self strategically across the bed just as he heard her making her way back.

Shit. Almost forgot. He sat up, reached into his nightstand, pulled out the hand-carved wooden box, and settled back into position.

She walked in, fingers looped around the handles of two coffee cups, the other hand holding an iPad. She was staring at the tablet and didn't look up. "Cats can pretty much escape anything."

Cats? "What are you looking at?"

"This video…" She shook her head, laughed. "It's…"

She looked up, a beautiful, seductive grin spread across her face. "That's the hottest thing I've seen in my entire life." Good. It was already working.

He was actually sweating. Though he'd decided she wouldn't want anything too traditional, should he have gone for a ring?

No. Dada had told him—nothing she'd have to take off for missions. It would bother Justice, doing that. And nothing too expensive. To her, it would mean less. Dada had given him another idea. He opened the box, revealing two smooth garnets and a series of light and dark leather cords.

Justice came closer, placed the coffee cups and iPad on his nightstand. She peered into the box. "Arts and crafts? Kinky. I can definitely use the leather cords."

He tried to bite back his eager smile. Tried and failed. He cleared his throat. "These stones are from Syria. From a jeweler I met in Zaatari. They represent hope and strength and perseverance. And they're red because Choctaw brides traditionally wear red."

He stopped, tried to judge how she was taking this. She pumped her eyebrows at him.

He swallowed. "And the leather, light and dark, for

good times and bad, for us to braid together, to braid the gems into. I wanted something that represented us, symbolized us. Something you could wear on your wrist. Something...." God, stop babbling. "That's if..." *Don't be a fucking coward.* "Justice, will you marry me?"

She launched herself onto the bed without warning, causing him, the flower petals, and the box to bounce. She took the box and moved it gently onto the nightstand, straddled him, kissed him.

Heat shot through his body. "Yes," she whispered against his lips. "Fuck, yes."

She kissed him, long and deep. She pulled back, stared at him. Stared at him with eyes like a cool, starless night, so endless not even the gods could imagine the edges.

"I want to meet your mother."

Not exactly where he'd thought that was going. "Okay. It's just—"

She shook her head. "I get it. But you've met my family. I've met your dad—"

"Most awkward lunch ever."

She laughed. "Yeah. But I'm serious."

"Okay."

"Okay?"

He nodded. For her, anything.

"I love you, Sandesh."

"I love you, Justice."

She grinned, squirmed on top of him. "Oh, I can feel that."

"Cocky." He rolled and she cried out. He maneuvered himself so she was under him and he was pressed hard against her. "Pun intended."

She laughed, lifted her head, and kissed him until his head spun and his body raged.

Fucking blessed.

—∿∿—

It'd been a good day. A great day. Any day spent entirely in bed with Justice, eating, having sex, talking, laughing, making jewelry—while she cursed like she'd stubbed her toe on a cement block; woman was not crafty—was a great one.

His hand tightened around hers as they walked up the stone stairs to the private nursing home where his mother lived. His heart picked up its pace. He wanted the two women he loved most in this world to meet. But he couldn't be sure Justice would get to meet Mom. She might be someone else today. Scratch that. She might be *somewhere* else today.

"Don't do that, Sandesh."

He looked over at Justice. Her eyes serious. Clothes casual, black jeans and a button-down top. Hair pulled into a long ponytail. "What?"

"Worry."

"Just don't expect much. I can never be sure how she'll be with a stranger. Sometimes, it can be hurtful. But she's…she's a good person."

She squeezed his hand. "I know enough of you, the man she raised, to know that however she appears now, she is a good person. She provided the shoulder you rested on, the heart that comforted yours, the soul that taught you to love. The disease might keep her from us, but it can't diminish who she is in my eyes. Ever."

A sudden, weighty presence lodged in his throat.

Made it hard to swallow. They pushed through the front doors and entered the brightly lit corridor. Didn't matter what time of year it was; this place always smelled of pinecones and cinnamon.

After they stopped at the front desk and checked in with security, Justice pointed to the hall lined with amateur paintings. "It's rather elegant. Are these done by the people living here?"

He'd stopped seeing the paintings long ago. This hall had become a place filled with worry and sometimes dread. "Yeah. I brought Mom here after I met the head of the community. A kind woman who knew I was concerned about Mom's quality of life. On the day I met her, she said to me, 'Talent, joy, love of life, and creativity don't have an expiration date. That's a limit placed by smaller minds.'"

Justice grimaced. "Sometimes pain makes you feel that way too—limited."

He brought her hand to his lips and kissed it. She meant her own pain over Tony's death. And her father's. The further they got from the shock of it, the more she was able to talk about it. He liked that she trusted him with her memories of her brother, her regrets, and how his death had changed her. Changed the whole family.

She asked questions too. She didn't remember a lot about their escape from Mexico. Shock and grief could do that to a person. He had to admit, for a long time, everything had felt unreal to him too.

The escape from the compound had been rushed. And awful. Justice rocking, sobbing over Tony's body. Then Gracie had returned, taken in the scene, and had totally lost it. Her screams...

Crap. It had been all he and Dusty could do to organize them and carry out Victor, who'd been passed out.

Dusty had turned out to be a good man. He'd stayed behind to take care of Tony's body. Since then, Justice occasionally asked questions about how they'd escaped, questions that let him know she remembered very little. But she never asked where Tony was buried. It was like she didn't want to know.

Not that he could've told her. He had no idea what had happened to the body. Or Dusty, for that matter. He strongly suspected the guy had gone underground.

"Sandy!" His mother's voice whooped through the hallway.

Justice pulled her hand away. Made sense. Best not to confuse Mom with their relationship until they got a feel for how she'd react. In truth, he'd forgotten he'd been holding it.

Sandesh grinned as his mother shuffled down the hall with a fist full of balloons bobbing above her head. In one hand she clutched the string. In her other she held a stuffed teddy bear.

He bent and greeted his mother's frail body with a gentle hug. "You look great, Ella."

She kissed his cheek. "Did you see my balloons?"

"I did." He stepped back. "Did you see my friend?"

Ella let out a delighted squeal, tossed up her hands. The balloons flew into the air. Justice grabbed the string and brought them down with a flourish.

His mother clapped and Justice handed the balloons back to her.

His mother yanked the string away. "The balloons are mine." Justice nodded her understanding and Ella's face became sly, almost predatory. "So is that young man. So treat him right."

Sandesh moved to intercept the awkward, to guide the conversation, but Justice cut him off. "I will, Ella. In fact, I'm taking him to a family dinner tonight. As my date."

His mother smiled. "He's very handsome, isn't he?"

Justice gently kissed her cheek. "Yes."

His mother, his mother who had been lost to him off and on for five years, flushed. Her eyes grew slightly more aware. "What's your name, dear?"

"Justice Ramona Parish."

She nodded. "Justice Ramona Parish." She repeated it as if chewing on it, tasting it, savoring it. "See, Sandesh? I always told you there was Justice in the world."

Sandesh's eyebrows shot up his forehead and he laughed—hard. She had. Repeatedly.

Justice reached out and hugged his mother, laughing softly. His mother laughed along with her. And the two of them…

He had to tell his heart to settle. And then tell it twice more.

Didn't work. How had this happened?

How had a gun-wielding assassin, a smart-ass vigilante with a nose for trouble and a yearning for intrigue, captured his heart so completely?

Maybe that's just the way blessings worked. Mysteriously.

Chapter 77

"SHE'LL GIVE IN," JUSTICE REASSURED HER SCORCHING-HOT and somehow doubtful fiancé as they strolled hand in hand through the Mantua Home's wide, sunlit corridors. "It's a wedding present."

"China is a wedding present. A toaster oven is a wedding present. Hell, a wedding is a wedding present. You're asking for her to allow you to return to Jordan. With me. For the IPT. Something that could lead to a deeper investigation of your ties to that mission in Syria."

She smiled, kept pace with him as they walked. "Yeah, you people at the IPT are trouble."

"I'm serious, Justice. Why draw more attention to your time there? The feds are already suspicious."

Understatement. But they were the suspicious sort. And, sadly, not stupid. Kept asking after Tony. The party line was that he'd simply run away, disappeared.

A big coincidence that Sandesh had also been released by his captors. All of this was why Leland wanted them to stay away from Jordan and Syria until things quieted down.

It felt wrong. "I don't need dishes or a toaster oven, not even a wedding. I need to fix the things I've screwed up." She cringed, thought of Tony, thought of how she couldn't fix everything. She looked up at Sandesh, at all his blond, beautiful self. "As much as I can."

He started to say something, maybe about how she

hadn't screwed things up, how everything had worked out, how he didn't hold her responsible—all of it, but he simply nodded. And that, right there, was another reason to love him.

Every day added one more reason.

She pulled up short before the wide, arched doorway leading into the library.

Inside the brightly lit room, Romeo sat at one of the long tables in front of a computer, typing like a lunatic. Maybe feeling her eyes on him, he glanced up. Such a cute kid.

She smiled at him. "You available to train tomorrow, around noon?"

He turned left and right in a *Who me?* kind of way. No one else in the library, kid. Registering this, his lips twitched into an uncertain smile. He gave her a tight nod.

Yeah. Couldn't blame him. She turned away, met Sandesh's alert, blue eyes. He bent and rubbed his nose against her cheek. "It's a start."

He was right. She'd continue to reach out to Romeo, make sure he was okay, find a way to talk to him, so that he knew—no, so that he *felt* he was respected here.

She'd read Tony's letter. Finally. He'd spoken of his pain, never feeling accepted, never feeling good enough, listened to, cared about. Reading it had changed her as much as losing him had. Things here had been unfair to him and to Romeo.

Sandesh squeezed her hand. "You okay?"

The flip thing to say would be, "Yeah." But it wasn't the real thing to say. She swallowed the regret and sorrow. "I'm going to make it up to Tony. He might not be here to see it, but I'm going to. And you and Salma and the IPT. Got it?"

"Yeah. But if your mother says no—"

She shook her head, continued down the hall. He kept up. "She won't. Trust me. I can convince anyone of anything. I am a kick-ass public relations specialist. Remember?"

Sandesh snorted, bit his lip, and nodded at her, nodded like he wanted to say something else. He didn't.

Smart man.

They moved down the hallway, passing an intersecting hallway, the one with the elevators. Someone called out, "I see it worked."

Justice startled. Dada. So stealthy. And gorgeous, especially with a baby bump. Wait. "What worked?"

The elevator doors opened and Bridget stepped out. She took in the scene with a raised eyebrow. Dada pointed at Justice's wrist, at the braided band of light and dark leather with the garnet woven within it. "Look. It worked."

Bridget smiled at Sandesh. "She said yes?"

He nodded, not looking half as guilty as he should have. "I appreciate the suggestions from both of you."

Seriously? She should've recognized Dada was in on the whole weaving bracelets thing. "So, what, is this some kind of conspiracy proposal?"

Bridget flushed; she actually looked bothered. That didn't happen every day. Or ever. Huh. She felt guilty. Looks like letting her keep her memory had another upside.

Dada moved closer, lifted Sandesh's hand to examine his band. Ugh. Justice cringed. She'd made his. He'd made hers. His band was more roughly woven than hers. By far. Who knew arts and crafts were so fucking hard?

"I can show you how to fix this," Dada said, looking at Justice.

Justice glared under a heating face. Not like she cared. Okay. She did.

Sandesh pulled his hand away. "No. It's perfect. Thanks."

Aw. Love for him, sharp and steady, fired another neuron, stored another cherished memory.

Dada looked like she was about to argue the fact, but Justice interrupted with, "Just saw your baby daddy in the gym, surrounded by munchkins playing soccer. You might want to rescue him," then turned and led Sandesh down the hall to the open doorway on their left.

His warm hand loosely held in her own, she slipped into the drawing room. The drawing room. Momma's idea of a joke. It was literally a room for drawing—more accurately, painting—not the traditional drawing room for greeting guests. Hardy. Har. Har.

Easels, stools, blue and red cabinets splotched with every shade of paint, along with shelves lined with art supplies. The astringent smell of paint cleaner and the dull smell of paint enveloped her. She rubbed her hand back and forth against her nose. Ew. Artists might have acute sight but their olfactory sense had to be diminished.

Two artists sat on stools and painted at easels. Momma and a teenager. The kid was all skin and bones and stiff shoulders. Someone from the school?

Maybe. But whatever Momma saw in this frail girl made her special indeed. Momma had taken off her niqab. Revealed her scars. Mostly she didn't, not even with her daughters.

She only showed her scars to girls so broken that they found comfort with people as wounded as themselves. Just one more way Momma made herself vulnerable to strengthen another.

That was Momma. The woman who'd rescued her. She wasn't perfect, but she did want to do good in the world. "Momma, Sandesh and I are here to speak with you."

She'd expected Momma to put on her niqab before turning around. She didn't. She turned from where she painted a colorful landscape dotted with wildflowers. The slight spasm of Sandesh's hand was all he gave away at the sight of her mother's horrible scars. The vibrant beauty Momma painted only seemed to highlight the peaks and valleys of her puckered, damaged skin. "Come in, Justice. Sandesh."

Technically, they were inside. Momma meant for her and Sandesh to stop lurking in the doorway. Justice let go of Sandesh's hand, walked over, and kissed Momma's scarred cheek. The skin was hard against her lips.

Her mother grasped her hand, looked at the band woven with the garnet on her wrist. Momma's eyes traveled to Sandesh's wrist and the matching band there. "I see it worked."

He winked at her. He winked at Momma? Conspirators. How many of her family had been in on this whole get-Justice-to-marry-Sandesh thing?

"Thanks for the advice. Short and sweet."

Huh. Guy had had a freakin' army. "Nice to see you approve of the whole wedding thing, because I'm here about a wedding present."

Momma raised one damaged eyebrow, or where the eyebrow should have been. "Okay. But first—"

"Nope. No. I need—"

Momma put up a hand, silenced her. "If it is in my power to give, it will be yours."

Oh man. She'd probably regret that. Still, that promise worked for Justice. She grinned at Sandesh as if to say, *Told you*.

He winked back at her.

"I stopped you because you're being rude. You haven't said hello to your newest sister. I believe you have met."

Huh? Justice took a closer look and sucked in a breath so sudden the girl turned.

It was Cee. Cee whom she'd saved. Cee who, in turn, had saved her life.

Cee pushed her stool back with a scrape and stood. Same bony body. Same half-challenging, half-wary tiger, red-brown eyes.

Justice licked lips gone dry, moved toward her. Cee wasn't like Hope. Not physically. Hope was blond. And yet, she reminded her of Hope. In the tension of her shoulders. In the take-me-on-and-you'll-get-more-than-you-bargained-for gleam in her fierce eyes.

That's how Hope had protected her. Stood in front of her when they'd come to take Justice. She held out her hand. "It's so good to see you, Cee."

Cee's fire-burned brown eyes looked at the out-stretched hand. She shook her head. "I know it was you."

Justice dropped her hand. She looked over at Sandesh, who'd moved closer.

Cee stepped forward and tucked her arms around

Justice's waist. "You were the one. You didn't give up on me."

Oh. A moment of warm surprise and, with her throat growing tight, Justice wrapped her arms around the girl's thin body. They stood that way. Holding each other.

From behind, Sandesh placed his warm, strong hand on Justice's shoulder. And something in her heart, a very small piece, but one she'd desperately missed and needed, repaired itself. She felt a spark of something that had been missing for a long time: Hope.

*Now for a sneak peek at the next installment
in the Band of Sisters series*

I Am Grace

Gracie Parish had learned three valuable things in the last two excruciating hours driving around Mexico: The fetal position was only comfortable in the womb. Her deodorant wasn't trapped-inside-a-hidden-compartment strength. And blood circulation could be lost in your forehead.

There had to be an easier way to break into a sex-slaver's home than smooshed inside this malodorous secret compartment, while her brother and his frenemy, Victor, drove into the compound, posing as mano-a-mano live "entertainers."

Sweat salted her eyes, slicked her skin. The good news? If she did die, the house of Hades would feel like an oasis. A spacious oasis.

This was it. This was the absolute last time she took part in her family's insane vigilante schemes. Ugh. Sometimes she wished she'd never been adopted into this mess. She needed a vacation on an island. A Canadian island. Someplace cold.

With a flick of her jaw, she clicked her mic. "How much longer, Justice? I'm roasting."

"Please, you've been in there for two hours. People smuggled out of Mexico stay in that compartment for days."

Days? Days pretending to be the back seat of a car,

while your legs were tucked, foam padding stuck to your skin, your right arm went numb, your right hip screamed, and you could taste exhaust. "Yeah, well, not me. If my cyber skills weren't needed to rescue your boyfriend, nothing could get me into this *Dante's Inferno*. Nothing."

"Chill your white privilege. You're almost inside the compound."

Her sister scored zero on the empathy meter. Zero. "Easy for you. You're on a hilltop, stretched out, over-looking this whole scene through a scope."

"Just playing to my strength. I'm the best shot."

She was a good shot. Hey. No. "You know, this bull-poop has been going on since childhood. 'Gracie's the smallest, she can fit in that pipe.'" She mimicked a child's high-pitched voice. "'Gracie's the smallest, let her squeeze through the vent system. Gracie's the smallest—put her in the smuggling compartment so she can break out Trojan horse-style inside the compound.'"

"Bull-poop? If you cursed, you'd realize bullshit is way more satisfying." She could hear the humor in Justice's voice. "And it's not my fault you're a shrimp."

"Being petite isn't a talent."

"You also have great red hair and hot underwear."

Oh. God. She'd never live that down. "Good thing. Otherwise I'd have no excuse if they find me. Assuming they don't shoot before I explain that Tony and Victor hid me here as a surprise bonus to their sex show."

"Trust me, no red-blooded male is going to shoot you when he gets a look at that thong."

Humiliating. Circles of heat singed her already too-warm cheeks.

Should've just nodded when Justice had said, "Sure, Gracie, pretending to be a stowaway entertainer is better than nothing, but we don't have a costume for you." She'd looked around the desolate plane hangar, thrown up her hands, and teased, "We're shit out of eight-hundred-dollar bras, and there's no Agent Provocateur in sight."

What happened after that was probably one of the top five most embarrassing moments of her life. She'd dropped her pants. She'd lifted off her shirt.

Justice had burst into laughter. Tony had sputtered. Victor had whistled. "Damn, Red, if I'd known you were hiding that, I would've been nicer to you."

Yeah. Top five. Definitely. And this, being in this car, was definitely in the top ten most uncomfortable places she'd ever been.

Well, maybe top fifteen.

"Our boys are pulling up to the compound gate." Justice's voice was low in her ear. "So stay quiet."

The car turned. The crunch of gravel vibrated under the wheels and through her bones. The car jerked to a stop. Her forehead thunked against metal.

Her headset clicked. She heard Justice's breathing and then, "There's a big American Ninja Warrior-like security guard. He seems to be in charge. He's gesturing Tony and Victor out."

Gracie caught the sound of a deep voice, a guy with an American Southern accent. *Southern?*

The car doors opened and shut as Tony and Victor got out.

Come on, come on. It's the home of a human trafficker, not the White House. Just let us inside.

Justice snorted through the headset. "Victor just

pirouetted to show he had nothing to hide. Hysterical. Man has balls."

And then some. She pictured that fine Latino pirouetting in his Magic Mike costume. Victor could fill out a G-string.

"Heads up. They're coming to check the car."

The front car doors opened with a squeak of hinges. Her heart rate jumped to please-God-don't-let-them-find-me pace.

Sweat rolled down her face, perched on her lips. She held her breath.

They'd find her. They'd hear her hyper heartbeat like in Poe's "The Telltale Heart," *ba-boom, ba-boom, ba-boom*. And then they'd shoot her. *Boom.*

Someone climbed into the back seat. Blood *whoosh, whoosh, whoosh*ed in her ears. Her hearing focused in tight. Did he have his knee on her left butt cheek? Not a featherweight.

Oh Lord, please. If she survived, she'd go back to running her bar. Maybe keep her cyber-warrior stuff going on the side, but she'd stay far away from the field. And danger. And death.

His weight shifted. The padding and the springs pressed tight against her hip. Ouch.

No big deal. No big deal.

If they caught her, well she'd heard that Mexicans love redheads.

Is that racist?

Gracie, stop overthinking.

He didn't register her beneath him. Phew. Then again, if this had been a shoddy place to hide, she never would've gotten into it. Petite body didn't mean petite mind.

The door shut with a slam. She exhaled. Thank the universe, Allah, Dr. Phil, and baby Jesus.

Someone got into the front, started the car, backed it up, drove it a short distance, and parked. The car door creaked open and slammed closed.

"Justice—" she whispered.

"Fuck. They parked the car outside the compound. You're like twenty feet from the fucking guard tower."

Fudge. She needed to be inside the gate to turn off the security. Ok. Stay calm. "Don't worry, J. I've got this. I'll find a way in and turn off the electric fence for you."

Honestly. The very last time I do this.

—⁓—

Guarding the front gate of a ten-thousand-acre cattle ranch turned bad guy's hideout, Leif "Dusty" McAllister couldn't help but wonder if he had the luck of an '80s action-adventure star. John McClane's brand of bad luck.

That Die-Harder could be scarfing down burgers at a Shake-n-Steak and still run into a shit show.

Not that he was currently anywhere near that fabulous testament to American culinary prowess. And if he went—God's honest—he'd have to admit he'd been asking for it. Going undercover in Mexico to catch a family of American vigilantes wasn't exactly staying out of the line of fire.

Sure had raised a few eyebrows at the bureau. Uptight, shoe-polish divas. If you couldn't stomach a little cow patty on your boots, you shouldn't stomp around with the bulls. He'd spent months cultivating his relationship with Tony Parish, so when he'd offered Dusty a part in this operation, he'd gone all in. Tony was the reason he was in Mexico, pretending to work for that psycho sex-trafficker Walid.

Dusty motioned the Latino guy with the sparkly G-string and Tony, who wore a similar getup and a belt weighted with BDSM tools—leather hand- and ankle-cuffs, leash, gag, nipple clamps—to stand still while he frisked them.

Tony was tense and clearly less comfortable in his G-string than his partner. Dusty frisked him. Tony shifted from foot to foot. "Dusty."

Even though it was barely a whisper, Dusty froze. Guy was gonna call him by name? Here? Pretty stupid. Or desperate.

Dusty leaned down as he checked Tony's tools of the trade. Those and his steel-toed boots had set off the metal detector wand. Dusty got to a knee. "Take off your boots."

Tony bent down, took off his shoes, leaned next to Dusty's ear. "Gracie in back of car. Can you get her to security?"

Tony's sister was in the back of that car?

This wasn't the original plan. How the hell was he going to get her inside without his men starting to suspect Tony and his pal?

Dusty stood and nodded. "Put your boots back on."

He moved to frisk Victor. The guy winked at him. "Take your time, big guy."

Was he serious? Walid was probably watching this whole exchange. Dusty pointed at his shoes. "Take 'em off."

Dusty checked the guy's shoes, ducked his head, hid his mouth, and murmured, "Justice?"

Inches from him, the guy retied his shoes. "Hillside. Scope."

Definitely not the original plan. His heart started to pick up its pace. She had a scope on them?

This last-minute bullshit must've been sparked when Walid captured Sandesh, Justice's boyfriend. Damn. Could've, would've, should've were lining up at the pasture gate in his mind.

He ran through the possibilities. Tony was going after Walid, so Gracie and Justice must be after Sandesh.

He motioned to the golf cart waiting nearby. "Good to go."

Without another word, Tony and his pal walked toward the cart that would take them to the villa. Just as well. Couldn't afford to keep talking with his men looking on. Sure they trusted him, hard not to after months here, but they weren't total idiots. Poorly trained. Yes. Go-lucky. Yes. Total idiots. No.

Now he had to get Gracie Parish inside the compound without raising suspicion, keep that hothead Justice from shooting anyone, and sacrifice one sadistic sex-slaver to the cause. Hopefully then he'd gain an invite into the Parish family.

An invite he sorely needed to get the evidence to take down the Parish matriarch and vigilante extraordinaire, Mukta Parish.

He cast his eyes to the sky and whatever heavenly power broker might happen to own stock in this shit show. Please. No more surprises.

In answer, the alarm blared from the speakers perched on posts throughout the compound.

Thanks a lot.

The two-way on Dusty's belt sparked to life, security telling him the alarm had started in the dungeon—the old mine where they took prisoners. Looked like Sandesh had gotten restless.

Dusty motioned his men back from Tony and his pal, who had climbed into the golf cart. He did not want to set Justice off. The alarm had to be playing as much havoc with her nerves as his.

He absolutely had to do something, because Walid—a raging loon since his brother's murder—was surely watching.

Adrenaline brushed its chemical magic across his blood, and the entire scene slowed, snapped into bright, glaring focus.

He ordered Tony and Victor out of the golf cart and onto their knees. Best to make it look good.

One of his guards, a recent hire, misunderstood. Deciding the alarm and these two arriving weren't coincidence, he got in Tony's face.

Newbie.

With a calm voice, Dusty spoke to the guy in Spanish. But the newbie bent down, grabbed Tony, hoisted him to standing.

And then the idiot reached for his gun. Dusty put up a hand. "No. Para—"

Pop. Blood splattered from a bullet hole in newbie's head. Tony wrestled out of his dead grasp and ran toward Walid's villa, with Victor a hot step behind.

Bullets started flying. Dusty ducked and ran for cover in the other direction, toward the car and the woman hidden there.

Yep. John McClane's luck. They were gonna die so friggin' hard today. All of them.

Chapter 2

There was no way Gracie could stay trapped inside this sweaty can of a space for one more fudgin' minute.

Justice's voice came through her headset again. "Gracie. They're in. They're—"

An alarm sounded. Her heart sped up—way up. She needed out of this hidey-hole *now*.

Her sweaty, numb fingers flip-flapped against the metal escape lever like a fish on the deck of a ship.

The *pop*, *pop*, *pop* of Justice's gun came through her headset before it clicked off. Why was Justice shooting?

Crud.

This never would've happened if she'd still been with John. She'd probably be a soccer mom, have a garden and soft moments.

Okay, stop, Gracie. Focus on squeezing that metal between your fingers. Not regret. Not the man you lost thanks to Momma and the League.

Easier said—thought, and repeated again and again—than done.

Stay calm. Her fingers cramped, her wrist angled back, she grasped at the latch, pulled. The spring gave with a dull click.

Breathing heavily, she pushed against the padding. The seat cracked open then stopped dead. Fudge buckets.

More shots. Close. Someone fired from behind the car. Someone used the car for cover. Someone fired at her sister. At Justice. Whoever was shooting at her sister was *so* dead.

She angled her knee to aid her pushing hand. The seat began to give way.

Let's hope whoever was firing was too interested in shooting Justice to peer through the heavily tinted windows at the car's interior.

The car door opened. "Let me help you there, Gracie."

She flinched, banged her head. Ouch. Southern accent? Southern accent knew her name? What the hell was going on?

She felt the car shift. Guy must be big. There was a creak, and the seat was yanked open.

Air. She sucked it in, turned and pulled her shoulders loose. Freed. She sat up and blinked at fresh air and man.

Uhm. Oh. She stared straight into the startled face of way-too-handsome. Sunset-brown hair topped by a USA ball cap, a big, easy grin defined by the persistent crease of overused dimples, labor-tan skin, and the sexiest nose she'd ever seen. A roughly carved block, his nose added challenge and strength to a sun-rugged portrait.

Her heartbeat skittered between the dread of tense alarm and the uncertainty of unexpected arousal. Her skin heated to a temperature rarely seen outside a volcano. Of course.

The sensitivity in her body painted every emotion upon her skin in hues of red. From pleased pink to rust-colored anger to chili-red lust. Didn't matter if it was an insult, compliment, or an unexpected sexual attraction that hit her like a bomb, the result was clear on her face.

Topmost embarrassing moment, please take a step down.

His eyes bounced along her body. The red-velvet bra. The matching thong. The ruby piercing snuggled in her belly button. The tattoo along her right side—a woman's long, elegant hand curved with vicious scarlet nails, clutching an enchanted apple, holding it out, as if implicitly offering it to the person now consuming her body.

Consuming her body with eyes of thickest amber, eyes drunk on sun, sex, sand, and champagne.

The heat from his eyes reached out and licked her. Every inch of her grew hotter. Her face. Her hands. Between her breasts. Lower.

The man reached down blindly, groped, and found his two-way. He lifted it to his mouth but spoke to her before he spoke into it. "Darlin', don't be upset by this. I'm on your side. Trust me."

He clicked the radio on. In Spanish, he gave instructions for his men to go out and hunt Justice. He clicked off.

Don't be upset? Did the man have no experience with sisters? Teeth clenched, she reached down and extracted her gun from the hidden compartment. She aimed at him.

A muscle along his thumb twitched, but he kept his Glock 19 down, smiled.

He smiled? Was he trying not to laugh? Oh, buddy, let's see how quickly I can wipe that smile off your face.

"No. No," he said, clearly reading her intent from her furious face. "Don't shoot. I'm working with Tony. I had to send those men so Walid wouldn't suspect us."

Tony? "My brother never mentioned you. And you just sacrificed my sister so Walid, a sex-trafficking supervillain, won't suspect you?"

Her finger tensed around the trigger.

He shook his head. Smile gone. His gun hand remained down. Smart. "I did that so Tony still has a chance. And your sister is good. Honest. Those guys can't shoot. No fooling. One of them shot himself in the foot trying to take his gun out two months ago."

"Gracie?" Justice's strained voice came through her headset.

Gracie clicked her mic on with a flick of her jaw. "Go. I've got American Ninja Warrior."

He did smile at that. "I'm Agent Leif McAllister. FBI."

FBI? Nuts and bolts. The email. The email she'd sent via a secure site to the FBI. The stupid email that proved her a traitor to the family. She swallowed a wave of panic. "FBI? In Mexico?"

"Yeah, well, I'm sort of off duty right now. No need for the agent part, actually. Just thought that would make you more comfortable. My friends call me Dusty."

"Dusty?"

"I've been told I could talk a stone to dust." He reached out with his free hand. "I'm going to help you out of here. Okay?"

"You touch me and I will shoot."

His hand dropped. Good. Nothing like getting the boundaries set from the get-go.

—◦◦◦—

Dusty was pretty sure Tony would have an issue or two with what he wanted to do with his sister. Give him the ruby. Give him the nails. Give him the apple. Yep. He wanted to lick his way down the whole damn tattoo and across that too-pink skin.

But first things first. Getting her not to shoot him. Which meant being honest with her.

Well, no. Not honest.

Telling her that the FBI had gotten an anonymous tip about Parish vigilante activities and he was investigating her family and using her brother Tony as a means to an end would make this whole thing messy. Would cost him his job. And the person he wanted to bust most, Mukta Parish.

He'd give her his cover.

"Your brother recruited me to help take out Walid. I've been working here for months, replacing every decent shot with a lousy one, and learning this place and its quirks like the back of my hand."

She squinted, obviously weighing whether or not to shoot him. She blinked. "Give me your gun."

"That's a no-go." And a hell no. She opened her mouth. Probably to argue. Because after only two minutes of knowing her, Dusty also knew this was Gracie's strong suit. "If my men or Walid see you with a gun on me, things are going to get real complicated."

Her brows drew together, considering. "Give me your gun. I'll give it back when I'm safely out of the car."

"Look"—he glanced around to make sure no one had started to pay attention—"if I wanted you dead, I'd have shot you by now. There's no time. The longer we argue, the more suspicious this looks. You need me, so risk trusting me."

She narrowed her eyes, sizing him up.

Damn. She was going to get them both killed.

He swallowed a big helping of *yes ma'am* that nearly choked him, and placed his gun on the seat.

He straightened, stepping back from the car. The SUV full of men he'd sent after Justice had pulled to a stop high on the ridge and the men had gotten out.

At the other end of the compound, past the barn, main house, and old mine shaft, another vehicle tore out the back gate. Road grit flew into the air as the car screamed away.

Some of his men were already abandoning ship. He took out his two-way and yelled that he had it under control and for them to stop. They went faster.

Perfect.

With his Glock in one of her hands, her small Beretta Tomcat in the other, red-velvet bra, colorful tattoo, belly piercing…Gracie was hot as bourbon whiskey. With a stone-serious expression, she motioned him to the rear of the car. He took two steps back. "We don't have—"

She turned to survey the area, revealing a thong splitting an ass as round and juicy as the apple tattooed across her abs.

"Tiiii…" His voice went up like a hay bale doused in gasoline and torched with a flamethrower. His blood turned to liquid lava, steamed his body, and ironed out the wrinkles in the front of his cargo pants.

He should look away.

She turned, caught him looking. He grinned. Like an idiot.

A bullet thunked into the steel of the car. He dropped a hairbreadth slower than her.

Crouched by the car, adrenaline slapping him upside the head for his stupidity, he raised his two-way and told his men not to shoot.

He returned his attention to her, crouched beside him,

and tried to get things under control. "You need to give me my gun. I can get them—"

Gracie ignored him, raised her Tomcat, and shot over his head. Someone cried out. He leaned in. "Don't shoot. Honestly, these guys—"

She jumped to her feet and ran up the dirt road and through the now unmanned gate. What the hell? He was tempted to let the idiot get herself killed.

Aw, hell. Anxiety putting spurs to his legs, he sprinted after her. A woman with a gun in each hand. *He* must be the idiot.

COMING SEPTEMBER 2018

Acknowledgments

I am sincerely grateful to have had the help of so many talented and giving people in the creation of this novel. A huge thank-you goes to my agent, Michelle Grajkowski, for her encouragement, creativity, hard work, and contagious optimism. Thank you to my amazing editor, Cat Clyne—for her invaluable focus, insight, and wisdom, along with your steady support and gentle encouragements. I'd also like to thank Rachel Gilmer, my production editor, for her keen eye, tireless dedication, and all-around awesomeness. To my publisher, Sourcebooks; Dom; and all the wonderful people on my publishing team, thank you. I count myself beyond lucky to have had the benefit of your hard work, creativity, and guidance.

Thanks to all the magnificent writers and writing groups that have nourished and sustained me, including my fabulous Dollbabies, whose laughter, acceptance, and friendship have allowed me to become more fully myself. My Stonecoast family, David Hewitt, Andrea Fischer, Hannah Strom-Martin, and Allison Hartman Adams—you have given me more than I can possibly repay.

I also want to express my gratitude to all those who read early drafts of this novel, those who gave encouragement and criticism. You helped make this novel better and also helped me become a better writer.

About the Author

Diana Muñoz Stewart is the award-winning romantic suspense author of the Band of Sisters series, which includes *I Am Justice* and *I Am Grace* (Sourcebooks, Inc.). She lives in eastern Pennsylvania in an often chaotic and always welcoming home that—depending on the day—can include a husband, kids, extended family, friends, and a canine or two.

When not writing, Diana can be found kayaking, doing sprints up her long driveway—harder than it sounds—practicing yoga on her deck, or hiking with the man who's had her heart since they were teens.

Learn more or connect with Diana at:
dianamunozstewart.com.
facebook.com/DMSwrites/
@dmunozstewart
purplebeings.com

RUNNING THE RISK

Love is put to the test in the Endgame
Ops series from Lea Griffith

Survival is crucial. Trust is optional. Love is unstoppable.

Jude's life as he knew it ended a year ago. On a mission gone
wrong, he was forced to watch as Ella, the only woman he
ever loved, was killed. Or so he thought…

*"A larger-than-life plot… The pace
is deliciously unrelenting."*

—*The Romance Reviews* for *Flash of Fury*, 4 Stars

For more Lea Griffith, visit:
sourcebooks.com

BLACK KNIGHTS INC.

These elite ex-military operatives are as unique and tough as their custom-made Harleys.

By Julie Ann Walker, *New York Times* and *USA Today* Bestselling Author

Too Hard to Handle

Dan "The Man" Currington is hot on the trail of a rogue CIA agent when he runs into old flame and former Secret Service Agent Penni DePaul. Now Dan's number one priority is keeping her safe—at all costs.

Wild Ride

Former Navy SEAL Ethan "Ozzie" Sykes is the hero everyone's been waiting for. When he's stuck distracting reporter Samantha Tate, he quickly loses his desire to keep her at bay...

Fuel for Fire

Spitfire CIA agent Chelsea Duvall has always had a thing for bossy, brooding covert operative Dagan Zoelner. It's just as well that he's never given her a second look, since she carries a combustible secret about his past that threatens to torch their lives...

Hot Pursuit

Former SAS officer and BKI operator Christian Watson has fought for his life before. Doing it with the beautiful, bossy former CIA operative Emily Scott in tow is another matter entirely.

"Her best yet... This razor-sharp, sensual, and intriguing tale will get hearts pounding."

—Publishers Weekly, Starred Review for *Wild Ride*

For more Julie Ann Walker, visit:

sourcebooks.com